DAUGHTER OF THE MIST

MERLIN'S LEGACY

Other Five Star titles by Quinn Taylor Evans:

Daughter of Fire

DAUGHTER
OF THE MIST

MERLIN'S LEGACY

Quinn Taylor Evans

Five Star
Unity, Maine

Five Star Romance.
Published in conjunction with Zebra Books, an
imprint of Kensington Publishing Corporation.

Cover photograph © Alan J. La Vallee

April 1999
Standard Print Hardcover Edition.

Five Star Standard Print Romance Series.

The text of this edition is unabridged.

Set in 11 pt. Plantin by Al Chase.

Printed in the United States on permanent paper.

Library of Congress Cataloging in Publication Data

Evans, Quinn Taylor.
    Merlin's legacy, book 2 : Daughter of the mist / Quinn
Taylor Evans.
        p.   cm.
    ISBN 0-7862-1768-5 (hc : alk. paper)
    1. Arthurian romances — Adaptations. 2. Merlin
(Legendary character) — Fiction. I. Title. II. Title:
Daughter of the mist.
PS3555.V258M46 1999
 813'.54—dc21   98-32198

DAUGHTER
OF THE MIST

MERLIN'S LEGACY

Prologue

Mist swirled through the cold night air like silken strands of thread at a weaver's loom. It spun a silver web about the moon, curled around the flames of torches, and glistened at the mantle wrapped about the slender young woman who stood at the battlement walls.

"He will come to you, in a time that is not a time and a place that is not a place," the Voice whispered.

Light from the torches framed her. Her hair was like spun gold. Her skin was bloodless across high cheekbones, pale lips softly parted. Her green eyes were like forest shadows, dark with the hunger of unknown passions.

She seemed no longer mortal but like some otherworldly creature of silver and gold like the mist at dawn as the words whispered to her again. Then, as she leaned far over the battlement walls, she saw the creature.

It came to her through the mist, dark as night sky, sleek and powerful, all muscle and sinew beneath glossy dark fur that glistened as it leapt down onto the battlements. That sleek, dark head angled toward her. Eyes gleamed as it slowly stalked her. There was no escape.

The beast's breath plumed in the cold mist. Sleek muscles rippled and coiled beneath the black satin coat with a deadly power that was both terrifying and beautiful. Then the creature was upon her, dragging her down beneath that powerful strength and deadly beauty.

The creature could easily have killed her. But instead of fangs sinking into her flesh, the creature's breath brushed against her skin with a sensual heat. Instead of claws tearing her apart, the beast's strength closed gently around her, and heat like a lover's caress stroked her beneath the mantle.

He will come to you.

Again, the words whispered through the mist as the creature raised its head and revealed, not the terrifying beast, but the lean features of a warrior with hair as dark as night, eyes the color of summer sky, and a powerful body that gleamed golden like the dawn.

Like the dawn he came to her, and like the mist at dawn she surrendered, until he burned inside her with a fierce, golden passion.

One

Inverness

Brianna was awakened by a hand suddenly clamped over her mouth. She clawed at the broad, gnarled hand, trying to pry loose blunt-tipped fingers.

The acrid stench of a torch clutched at her throat as she dragged panic-filled gulps of air into her lungs. Light from a torch trembled across the walls of the chamber, illuminating the scarred, bearded features of the fierce giant who stood over her.

Then, soft green eyes widened in recognition, and the giant's hand loosened and fell away. Slender brows drew together as she heard shouting and the distant but unmistakable sounds of battle beyond the door to her chamber.

"What is it?" she demanded. "What's happened?"

Without answering, Thomas pulled her from the bed. The bedside candle fluttered wildly as he stripped the largest of the thick fleece skins from the bed and hastily flung it about her shoulders.

His mouth was set in a hard line wreathed by coarse, russet beard. The patchwork of scars that webbed his face was all the more gruesome in the grim expression that etched them more deeply in the ruddy skin.

Beyond the door, barred from the inside, the sounds of battle grew louder and more distinct.

Hours earlier her kinsmen had gathered and lingered long over their ale. She had gone to bed amid good-natured shouts

9

and challenges of physical strength among the younger men while older warriors dozed beside the fire and pondered the uneasy future of the highlands.

But this was no contest of strength. These were the sounds of a full-pitched battle that came from within the fortress!

"You must tell me what has happened!" she demanded as she grabbed the sleeve of his tunic. But no explanation moved through the gentle giant's thoughts to connect with her own in that special way that bonded them.

Instead she sensed his urgency and a bleak stubbornness of will that spoke of danger — words the giant could not speak because his tongue had been cut out long ago.

Brianna's own thoughts raced. The chieftains of the north had gathered at Inverness to discuss the news from the south beyond the borderlands with England, and the growing threat from the Viking raider, Mardigan.

For more than twenty years Mardigan and his men had sailed into coastal ports and raided the northern shores of Scotland. But he had become increasingly bold, sweeping inland and across the moors to attack villages and farms.

Other raiders plundered for food, crops, and livestock, and quickly moved on. But Mardigan plundered for far more than the bounty of foodstuffs and animals. His men raped and brutalized the women, murdered the men and boys, and burned the villages of the northern clans.

He made no secret of his ambitions — Inverness. The stronghold that protected all of northern Scotland.

He sought a landhold through marriage, in the north country — a tie that could not be broken, and blood ties to the northern clans through sons that would come of that union.

But now another danger threatened the autonomy of the

northern highlands. William of Normandy had proclaimed himself king of England. For weeks, the well-armed Norman army had been marching north.

This was not the first time Duke William had sent his army north. Months earlier, before the winter snows, a small army of knights and soldiers had encamped in the rocky hills. Brianna remembered well her first encounter with the Norman soldiers who had surprised a Norse raiding party and driven them off.

Several Normans died that day and the chieftains feared Scotland might next be laid waste beneath the Conqueror's sword in retaliation. The atrocities suffered by the English at the hands of the Norman invaders was well known. But there had been no retaliation.

The Norman army had retreated without further incident, and it was widely speculated that Duke William's ambitions to secure the north country against outside claimants to his own throne might work in favor of the northern clans.

The English to the south were always regarded with suspicion, but rumor had it that William had no further ambitions for conquest in Britain. The highlands were regarded as a poor relation whose fortress door must be well fortified against those who might try to take the throne of Britain by way of the back gate.

Brianna's adopted father, Cullum, laird of Inverness, had spoken long and convincingly to the chieftains. He argued that they could not hold their lands against two enemies — Duke William with his vast Norman army, and Mardigan's raiders.

According to rumor the Norman army was now little more than two days' ride from Inverness. Perhaps an alliance could be made, he persuaded as the chieftains sat about the council table in the hall two days earlier. Such an alliance might well be their only hope against the Norse butchers who repeatedly plundered and burned the villages, and murdered their kinsmen.

"They rape our women," Cullum had spoken bluntly. "They plant their seeds deep and mingle their blood with ours so that we will never be rid of them."

Once that happened, he warned, the Norse barbarians would grow even more powerful and the clans would have no hope of extricating Mardigan.

He and his men must be driven from the shores of Scotland once and for all before it was too late. But they could not do it alone. An alliance with William of England would give them the strength they needed.

Only days before, highland warriors had tracked down one of Mardigan's raiding parties. Though they fought fiercely, the raiders were outnumbered. Many had died.

Their bodies were thrown into a fishing boat and piled over with pine boughs. The boat and its cargo were set aflame according to Norse traditions, and then cut adrift on the outgoing tide. Flames and smoke were seen for miles along the coastline — a vivid example to Mardigan and the rest of his men.

Then, before it had burned completely, the boat suddenly began to sink, taking the dead to a watery grave rather than the glorious Viking ending that would have scattered their ashes to the heavens as they believed they must be.

But highland defiance had come at great cost.

Four more villages had been burned, the nearest very close to Glenross, the landhold of her mother's family. The kinsmen had struck back fiercely. Several raiders had died. This time their bodies were left to rot where they fell. But many highlanders had also died.

Afterward, the chieftains argued long and fiercely at Inverness, as Cullum pointed out that this warring could not continue.

Many opposed any alliance, arguing that no English king could be trusted. Most outspoken was her childhood friend, Malcolm. He and his father, Ian, were at Inverness when word came from Mardigan that he wished to be allowed to speak before the chieftains about terms of peace.

Though highly suspicious of his intentions, the council agreed and set the terms for the meeting. The fortress hall was like an armed encampment ready for battle when Mardigan entered the fortress three days later with two score of his men.

He spoke of peace, a peace which could only be obtained through an unbreakable alliance. The alliance he sought was marriage to Brianna.

"You will not refuse, old man," Mardigan had warned, teeth flashing amid handsome, arrogant features, and leaving no doubt in anyone's mind that his demands might be negotiable.

"A hundred more of my men await my signal. Yield and lives will be spared. Refuse," he gestured at the chieftains who sat about the council table, "and all will die. This is a small thing to ask, and it will end the bloodshed."

Though Cullum had forbidden her presence, Brianna listened from the corridor that adjoined the kitchen.

She heard Mardigan's boastful threats, and the outraged exclamations of the chieftains. Cullum's face contorted with a fierce rage beneath the white of his beard. His fingers clenched around the handle of the blade at his belt at the insult of the demands that were made.

From her hiding place, Brianna was enraged. Many highlanders had died. Several were her own kinsmen. Now Mardigan came to Inverness under the guise of peace and made demands that were little more than more plundering and pillaging. It was easy for any to see his true ambitions.

Before Cullum and the chieftains could give their answer, she stepped from the shadows and strode proudly, defiantly into their midst.

"He does not refuse you," she replied, in a clear voice for all to hear as she crossed the hall through his assembled men, and drew the attention of all.

"*I* refuse you."

Mardigan spun around sharply. His head lowered like that of a wolf as it suddenly catches the scent of its prey. His gaze narrowed, Nordic blue and as cold and hard as arctic winter. She stood before him, armed only with highland pride and stubborn defiance.

He towered over her. Muscles flexed along the length of his bare arms. In the V-cut of the fur vest he wore, she saw the ridges and angles of battle-hardened muscles beneath whorls of golden hair that covered his chest.

Hammered gold war bracelets gleamed in the light of a dozen quivering torches, and she wondered how many of her kinsmen had fallen before the blows of a Norse war ax wielded by those powerful arms.

He was powerfully built with thickly muscled legs wrapped in leather leggings, feet spread in a wide stance as if he already wielded the power at Inverness. Burnished gold hair was worn long to his shoulders with a thick plaited braid at each side of his face. Lines etched the bronze leather of his face. He was in the fullness of his manhood, but he was not a young man. Nor was he a fool.

Within him, she sensed something dark and evil beneath the powerful strength, the gleam of gold bracelets, and those cold blue eyes that impaled her with undisguised lust. He raised a clenched fist as though he intended to strike her.

There was a sudden stirring of movement as the hand of every kinsman reached for their weapons. But Mardigan did not strike her. Instead, his large hand coiled like a serpent around the thickness of her hair where it lay at one shoulder.

Gathering it in his fist, he held it to the light, eyes gleaming at the rich, gold satin that spilled through his hand as if it were a treasure he'd already claimed. Then he twisted it about his hand like a rope he slowly coiled tighter and tighter, forcing her closer until he held her imprisoned by her hair, his hot breath burning against her cheek.

"I will have you, Brianna of Inverness and heiress of Lochonnen," he vowed. His hooded gaze darkened. "And we will have fine lusty sons." And then the threat, "Or the land will run red with the blood of your kinsmen."

Concealed within the length of her sleeve, she felt the reassuring coolness of the slender blade she always carried. It had belonged to Cullum, handed down from father to son for generations, and by right should have gone to Cullum's son.

But he and his wife Mirren were childless before Brianna came to them. They had showered her with love, and named her Cullum's heir with the ceremonial passing of the dirk at Samhuin two seasons past. It was a blade with which the Lochonnen heir would defend her home and clan.

When Mardigan pulled her closer as if to claim a kiss to seal his promise, she eased the blade from its sheath, nimbly brought it up, and thrust the tip into the vulnerable bearded flesh under his chin.

"You will never see the deed done for your blood will be the first to flow!" she vowed, and then watched with satisfaction as those cold eyes widened with surprise. Then his mouth twisted with a cruel smile.

"I do not need to see it, Brianna. The feel of my flesh

15

inside you will be enough to know that it is done."

He laughed confidently as heat flamed her cheeks at his crude words. Ignoring the blade, he reached out unexpectedly and pinched her breast. He grinned cruelly as she winced with pain, but did not cry out.

"You will like it," he assured her, his voice gone low so that only she heard. "I can see it in your eyes. Soon you will be begging to have me between your legs."

She refused to cry out, or give in to the tears of anger, humiliation, and loathing. She pressed the blade deeper and watched with satisfaction as his expression changed when blood slid down the blade. His blood.

"What you see is your own death!" Brianna vowed.

Swift and powerful, Mardigan's hand came up and clasped about her wrist. His fingers dug into her flesh and slender tendons, trying to force the blade from her hand.

All about her weapons were seized as highlander and raider alike became eager for blood. Cullum's powerful voice echoed in the great hall as he stepped forward, unarmed.

"You have my daughter's answer, Mardigan. And mine. Leave while you still draw breath."

Mardigan's hand tightened at her wrist. His face was very near hers. She glimpsed something in that cold, ruthless gaze she had not seen before — a darkness of the soul far colder than the color of his eyes.

A deadly, taunting smile curved his cruel mouth. His hand finally loosened about her wrist as he released her. The signal to leave was given to his men. But before he left, he leaned close.

"It is only just begun, Brianna. You will be mine."

Then he and his men left, disappearing through the gates and into the hills and forest surrounding Inverness as easily as they had appeared. Afterward, the gates of the fortress were always closed and barred.

Now, the sounds of battle came from within the fortress, a tragic reminder that the gates had not been enough to hold back Mardigan and his warriors.

Thomas stood as immovable as an oak that had suddenly taken root at her chamber floor. When Brianna would have gone to the door, he stopped her.

"I must go to Mirren. She will need me," she protested, but it was as if she argued with that oak.

Stubbornness and resolve set the giant's scarred features as the sounds of battle reached the hall outside her chamber. His thoughts were urgent as they connected with hers. Going to the window, he threw open the shutters. Through the opening, the sky was just beginning to lighten. Below sheer walls were the rocky cliffs.

"You must leave before it is too late! They must not find you here."

She understood, but shook her head adamantly. She would not leave without him.

"We leave together, or not at all."

"I cannot fly, mistress. There is no time! Do not argue! You must go now!"

"I am not the one arguing," she pointed out. "I will not leave you." Blows fell against the stout door. It could not hold for long.

Seeing that she would not be persuaded, Thomas nodded and pulled her across the chamber to the wall at the back of the chamber. He thrust the torch into her hand, then swept aside the heavy woven tartan that spread across the wall.

He pressed the heel of his hand against the base of a triangular stone, as he leaned his shoulder into the wall. The stone moved beneath his hand. Then, with a grating sound a section of the wall opened, revealing the looming darkness of the passage beyond. Icy air from the passage sucked at the flame of the torch.

Cullum had the wall built when Brianna was a child, creating two chambers on the second floor where there had previously been only one. New stone steps had been laid at the far end of the hallway connecting the second floor chambers to the main hall below.

The old steps, which had been built over a hundred years earlier with the original fortress, had been sealed into the wall between the two chambers. Cullum then had a secret opening cut into the back of each chamber to be used if there was ever a need to escape the second floor. Brianna stepped into the icy darkness of the passage.

She felt along the opposite wall for the handle that released the section of stone wall that opened into the laird's chamber. Surely Mirren would be there, waiting for them. But Thomas pushed her past and down the steps of the passage.

"We cannot leave her," she protested. But with his insistence she sensed something troubling. Thomas would never leave Mirren or Cullum.

Behind her, stone grated against stone as the panel closed back into place, sealing them off from the sounds of the attack. Ahead, flame from the torch pooled on steps glistening with moisture that seeped from the walls.

She shivered in spite of the thick fleece about her shoulders. No words were spoken. Brianna followed silently, an ache of foreboding closing around her heart.

Where were Cullum and their kinsmen? Was Mirren safe?

Where were the other chieftains who had not yet returned to their holdings but had remained a few days longer at Inverness?

What of Malcolm and his father?

18

They reached the bottom of the passage, a niche in the narrow hall that connected the kitchen and scullery to the main hall. Thomas laid a firm hand at her shoulder in restraint as he opened the hidden door.

Brianna heard the sounds of fighting — the clash and scrape of blade against blade, shouts and screams amid the painful cries of the wounded, and the pitiful moans of the dying. She pushed past him and stepped into the connecting corridor. The destruction in the main hall stunned her.

Long tables, where the chieftains had sat across from each other in counsel only hours earlier, had been overturned, platters and flagons scattered to the floor. Benches had been smashed.

Fires smoldered in the pungent grasses that covered the floor of the hall. But the most devastating were the bloodied bodies of the maimed and dying.

Amid the death and destruction she recognized the bodies of two chieftains. All about them were the scattered dead of their kinsmen. But Malcolm and his father were not among them.

She stepped over the bodies of several of her own kinsmen, searching for Cullum. Then she saw him.

He and a half dozen kinsmen whom she knew well had met the attack at the bottom of the steps to the second-floor chambers. Leaving the safety of her own chamber, Mirren had joined him there.

Cullum's men had died at his feet, hacked to pieces as the attackers slashed through them to get up the stairs. Cullum was slumped against the stair wall. When Thomas tried to pull her back, Brianna wrenched out of his grasp. In her thoughts, she heard his urgent warning that they must flee. But she could not.

The attackers had abandoned the main hall for the

second-floor chambers. With the dirk in her hand and clad only in her night shift she made her way to the stairs.

Her heart constricted as she stepped over bodies, the hem of her gown soon bloodied. The war vests and helms of Mardigan's dead warriors lay among the muted colors of woven wool tartans of several northern families. Eventually she reached Cullum.

He had been the last to fall, his blade still clutched in his fist even though his sword arm was all but severed from his stout body. The second blow had killed him instantly, opening a wound from his shoulder down through his chest, his lifeblood pumping onto his clan wool.

His expression was neither peaceful nor serene, but one of fierce outrage that could not be eased even by death. It was as though he still defied the butchers who had attacked Inverness.

She laid a hand lovingly against his bristled cheek. Grief welled inside her for the gruff but gentle laird of Inverness who had taken in an orphaned child and claimed her for his own. For all that he had done for her, she could now do nothing but mourn him. Then she saw the slender hand that lay over Cullum's shoulder as though to protect him.

Mirren lay against the wall behind him, a slender dirk clasped in one hand, the other across her husband's shoulder as if defending him.

Her rich, dark hair, only just beginning to streak with gray, spilled loose about her shoulders except where it matted against the side of her head. A powerful blow had smashed her skull. Her sightless eyes stared blankly back at Brianna.

Sounds came from the top of the stairs. The murderers were there now, ransacking her chamber and beating down the door to the laird's chamber.

Her fingers, wet with Mirren's blood, closed around her

own dirk as she came suddenly to her feet. She would have charged up the stairs if Thomas hadn't stopped her. His arm clamped about her waist as he dragged her from the foot of the stairs.

When she struggled, his arm hitched tighter beneath her ribs, pressing against her lungs and cutting off any protest. His fierce thoughts sliced through her anguish and struck like a physical blow.

"They died protecting you, lass! Will you make a mockery of their deaths now by giving these butchers the very prize they seek? We must leave now! Or their deaths will have been in vain."

She slumped in his arms as the fight went out of her. She nodded and Thomas' grasp loosened about her. As he lowered her to the floor, she drew a ragged, shuddering breath. Tears stung at her eyes as she glanced one last time at Cullum's and Mirren's mutilated bodies.

She thought of her cousin Gillie and prayed she was safe. Gillie had left just the night before to return to Glenross to the north.

She was the daughter of Mirren's older sister, Anne. Unhappy in her marriage, Gillie arrived at Inverness a fortnight ago as she did often, and asking that she be allowed to visit for a while.

Cullum had been furious, for it was no secret that Gillie was unhappy in her marriage, and had fled rumors that she had taken a lover. Mirren, loving and gentle, had persuaded him to allow Gillie to remain.

Mirren was the second born daughter. By right her sister should have been the first to wed, but the laird of Inverness had fallen in love and would have no other.

Upon their marriage, Mirren's father had given the landhold of Glenross to the laird as his daughter's marriage property. Anne had been settled with another landhold nearby.

All was suddenly silent at the upstairs chambers. Then there were shouts, and though Brianna could not understand the words, she understood the sound of anger. Mardigan had not found the prize he sought. Then light from torches suddenly appeared at the top of the steps and pooled into the shadows of the hall below.

"We must leave now, mistress!" Thomas warned urgently.

His large hand clamped around her upper arm. They fled the main hall by way of the corridor adjoining the kitchen. The yard beyond was chaos as the inhabitants of Inverness fled for their lives.

Thomas pulled her behind the dovecote where the pale gray birds Mirren raised cooed softly, adjacent to the pens that contained Cullum's hunting birds. He pushed her inside one of the pens.

Wings fluttered wildly at the sudden intrusion. Then the doves calmed once more. In the pens, two young falcons moved restlessly on their perches. Thomas pushed her to the floor of the pen and covered her with straw as they heard warriors approach.

She did not need to see them to know that Mardigan was with them. She would always remember his voice — the lustful pride and arrogance, the coldness with which he'd vowed to return to Inverness after her refusal to accept his offer of marriage. Pain squeezed around her heart for those she had lost. Mardigan had kept his promise.

"Search every building, every pen, and every cart," Mardigan ordered his men. "Lady Brianna must be found. She is the key to all I seek. Before this day is gone, we will be wed. Before the night is gone, she will be breeding with my first son."

As his men set off to carry out his orders, another joined them.

"You have found Lady Brianna?" Mardigan asked, eagerness low at his throat.

"Nay," the warrior replied hesitantly. Through the slats in the dovecote, Brianna saw the blow that felled him as Mardigan stood over him, those brutal fists that she remembered so well clenched with rage. When he would have struck the warrior again, another intervened.

"There is news," the second warrior explained. "Many of the highlanders were seen fleeing. She may be among them." The news stayed another blow at least for the time being.

"Aye," Mardigan replied with narrow-eyed speculation as a thought occurred. The lady Mirren's landhold lay to the north, across the moors at Glenross. Her daughter might seek safety there. A slow grin spread across his beard-wreathed face.

"Search every building," he repeated to his men, already fairly certain they would find nothing. His hope had been to catch everyone at Inverness unaware, surprise them, and claim his prize. But when Brianna was not found in the upstairs chamber, he realized that she had no doubt found some means of escaping the main hall.

He turned sharply. "When you have searched the yard, give word to the men to be ready to take up the search beyond Inverness." His thoughts had already turned toward Glenross. Surely a maid and a dim-witted mute could not travel fast.

His eyes gleamed. Soon Inverness would be his and none could deny his claim with the daughter of the old laird as his wife. The lust of battle became another sharper lust as he thought of her beneath him. Aye, she would give him fine, lusty sons.

The three warriors split up, each setting off in a different direction. Brianna held her breath as one warrior slowly approached the dovecote, walking the length of one side then the other, his shadow knifing through the slats of the pen, his footsteps growing faint and then returning.

She had witnessed Mardigan's brutality. This warrior was not likely to shirk his duties. She heard the scrape of his boots in the dirt very near, then abruptly there was silence. When she poked her head out of the straw, Thomas pushed her back down with a fierce expression that warned her to silence.

The pens were small and narrow, lined with perches and niches for nests on both sides. The ceiling was built low so that the birds couldn't build their nests in places impossible to reach.

The narrow space was far better suited to the young boy who usually cared for the birds than a man of Thomas' height and size. He was forced to stand hump-shouldered with his head bent low to keep from hitting it.

Suddenly the blade of a sword was thrust between the slats of one wall. Then it was thrust through again and again, at intervals all along the length of the pen.

Thomas' fingers dug into her shoulder in silent warning as the sword was then thrust between the wood slats along the other side of the pen. Startled birds flung themselves from their perches amid cries of alarm. Feathers, dust, and straw filled the air.

The sword was thrust through several times more, this time drawing blood. The warrior grinned with satisfaction as he slowly pushed open the door of the pen.

Sunlight filtered through the walls. Dust rose from the humped mounds of straw that lined the floor of the pen. Startled from their perches, several birds flew past him in a flurry of straw and feathers.

Then as the dust settled and the remaining birds quieted at their perches, he saw what must have startled them. A grotesque, misshapen creature rose from the corner of the pen.

The poor wretch's body was twisted and gnarled. A large hump rounded one shoulder. The creature stared back with the blank, lackluster expression of the simpleminded. In his hands, the creature cradled a silver falcon.

The warrior glanced warily at the vile, ugly wretch with a scraggly beard and with the expression of a half-wit. Blood stained the creature's vest. No doubt he had wounded it.

The creature made disgusting grunting sounds like that of an animal as it lunged toward him. The warrior jumped back warily. Perhaps it was not human after all, but a troll!

He believed in such wretched creatures. His old grandmother told stories of them around the cook fire when he was a child. It certainly looked like a troll.

They were foul, ugly beasts of the underworld with the stench of the dung-heap about them, sent into this world to bring misfortune and disaster to all whose path they crossed.

The warrior kicked at the creature. It was a glancing blow and the creature tumbled out of the pen, sprawling into the dirt of the yard.

As the creature fell, the falcon escaped, wings unfurling as she flew high overhead against the leaden sky until she disappeared.

The warrior kicked at the creature again. It rolled a short distance away and then sprang to its feet. It grunted and slobbered through a lopsided grin, its eyes rolling about.

Then, it suddenly seemed to grow larger. The bent and twisted body transformed as the creature stood to its full height.

The warrior slowly backed away, his grandmother's warnings vivid in his memory of such creatures who could change themselves at will, and the spells they cast that transformed mortal men into stone and piles of dung. When the creature lunged at him, he turned and fled.

Thomas' sharp gaze lifted to the sky. He squinted against the rising sun as he marked the flight of the falcon overhead. With a grunt of satisfaction he turned and left the fortress by way of the crawl space in the wall behind Lady Mirren's gardens.

As he fled into the woods, smoke rose from the stout timbers of Inverness. It spiraled upward until it connected with the sky, and became as dark as the coming storm that blanketed the horizon.

He found Brianna by the shore of the lake where she had often played as a child. She knelt in the shelter of the ancient rowan tree. Her head was bent. Thick pale gold hair shielded her features. But the trembling of her shoulders betrayed the tears she cried, and the slender hands clenched into white-knuckled fists revealed her unspoken pain and rage.

Even though he moved like one of the creatures of the forest, she sensed his presence. Then, she felt his hand at her shoulder, and his gentle, comforting thoughts connected with hers. She felt the love and strength that had always protected and guided her.

"Mardigan and his men will not give up their search."

She nodded, the pale silk of her hair swinging loosely about her bent head.

"We must go quickly, to a place that is safe where he cannot find you."

Her head came up, the veil of her hair sweeping back from taut features and the haunted expression in her green eyes.

"Nay, Thomas," she said fiercely, the last images of Cullum and Mirren etched painfully in her memory.

"I will not go. Nor will I hide."

"But you cannot stay," he protested. " 'Tis not safe, lass. If

26

Mardigan and his men were to find this place, I could not protect you."

"I will not run!" she repeated adamantly. "Nor will I offer myself up like a lamb to the slaughter."

"What will you do then, lass?"

"I will fight him."

"How, mistress?"

Staring over the dark, still water of Lochness she remembered the creature of her dream — a warrior who bore the darkness in his color, yet carried the color of the sky in his eyes. A fierce, powerful warrior who feared nothing.

Was there such a warrior among those who had been loyal to Cullum?

"We must persuade the other chieftains to return to the council. Together we will find a way to stop Mardigan. If we flee to the hills and hide, then he has already beaten us."

"What of Inverness?"

Her soft green gaze darkened with resolve. "I am now the laird of Inverness."

Two

"Sweet Jesu!" Stephen of Valois exclaimed as he blew into his cupped hands to warm them.

"The cold has turned the sweat beneath my armor to ice. And the wind has been blowing up my backside since morning camp. Is there no warmth in this cursed land?"

It was midday beneath a leaden sky and the Norman army had stopped at the edge of a heavily wooded forest no more than two days ride south of Inverness to rest the horses.

Tarek al Sharif, commander of the army by order of King William of England, listened to the young knight's good-natured grumbling as his gaze scanned the forest clearing.

"This northern clime might cool even your Persian blood," Stephen remarked, a smile creasing his handsome features, so like that of his father, the king.

"Is there any hope there may be at least two tolerable highland wenches to ease our discomfort?" he asked as he swung down from his warhorse and loosened the cinch.

"By what we have seen on the ride north I hold little hope for it." He snorted with feigned disgust. "We may all be forced to warm ourselves as that fool DuLonge. I swear not a sheep has been left untouched since the borderlands. The man is a cretin, of course, but a warm and well-satisfied one while the rest of us take our ease in our gloves, and try to warm ourselves in our bedrolls."

Tarek did not immediately reply, but continued to watch the perimeter of trees with an uneasiness that had increased with each passing day.

Sharply angled brows, dark as a raven's wing, drew together in a frown over startling blue eyes — the legacy of his Persian mother and the fierce Norse warrior who had made him a bastard.

It was a bond he shared with Stephen of Valois, for William of Normandy, the Conqueror and newly crowned king of England, could never acknowledge his son born to a young Bretton woman when William was barely fifteen.

Yet, unlike the father Tarek had never known, William had kept Stephen near him since he was old enough to walk. Stephen had been well educated. When he had gained his knighthood, he fought at William's side in countless campaigns. But the relationship between father and son was an uneasy one.

Stephen was often reckless. He constantly took risks William's other knights did not, determined to prove himself worthy of his father's love and recognition.

Yet along with his need for his father's love was a deep and bitter resentment that his mother had been set aside when Stephen was an infant so that William could marry Mathilda of Flanders.

The alliance with the Flemish royal house had brought wealth and a sizable army to Normandy, a marriage of power and ambition.

In London as William consolidated his power, plans were made for Stephen to wed a Saxon noblewoman. The marriage would have given Stephen a certain acceptance at court that the circumstances of his birth denied him. As proud and headstrong as his sire, he adamantly refused the match, choosing instead to return to the north country with Tarek al Sharif.

Now, the young knight remarked cynically, "Perhaps I

should have accepted the Saxon bride my father chose for me. But God's truth, that dame's frozen thighs could be no colder than this place."

"It is not the cold I feel," Tarek said with that uneasiness he had felt ever since leaving the borderlands, unable to rid himself of the feeling they were constantly watched.

Months earlier William had sent his army north amid reports of murderous raid by foreigners hoping to claim the English throne.

At a place called Brecon, south of Inverness, they had encountered a band of fierce raiders. Many lives were lost in the battle. But many more would have died if Tarek had not been warned of it beforehand by a beautiful creature who seemed to appear out of the mist.

He had ridden ahead of Rorke FitzWarren and his men, searching for signs of the raiders. Stopping to water his horse at a highland pool, a young woman had suddenly appeared to warn him that raiders were nearby.

Her hair was like spun gold, her eyes as green as a highland glade. Yet she seemed not a creature of this world, as if she had stepped through the sunlight and mist from some other place. Then she had reached, taking his hand as she led him to a place that cut through the rocks that rimmed the pool by which he might escape.

The encounter was sharp in his memory, as it had been every day since. Even now, his fingers closed, the memory of the silken softness of her skin burning against his.

As the raiders drew near that day he had glanced back to ask her name, but she was gone. All that remained was the swirling mist that gathered at the edges of the pool, and a sleek graceful swan that glided across its silvery surface.

He had left that secluded highland pool by way of the escape she had shown him and carried his warning of the raiders to Rorke FitzWarren and his men. He had never seen her again.

The raiders were defeated. Those who survived had fled into the hills. Afterward, William's army was urgently summoned back to London to put down a dangerous threat from his own brother, the Count de Bayeau.

The count's plans were defeated and he was sent back to Normandy in disgrace, and imprisoned. William was crowned king of England shortly thereafter in a lavish ceremony on Christmas Day at Westminster Abbey.

His first order of duty was to reward those loyal to him for their service. Among those favors granted was a special bequest to Tarek al Sharif.

As a warrior, Tarek sold his services to the highest bidder. Before the conquest of Britain, the only reward he sought was gold. But his encounter with the beautiful young woman who had saved his life lingered in his memory.

The girl's pale golden beauty haunted him as no other. It burned in his blood like a fever, and whispered to him in that place between sleeping and waking, a memory of sunlight and mist that became an obsession and would not be forgotten.

When asked by the king what reward he claimed for his loyalty, he had named Inverness in the far north country.

William readily agreed to this most unusual request. There was much for him to gain in having a well-armed ally to the north, who guaranteed protection of the northern shores against the ambitions of foreign usurpers like Canute of Denmark.

Tarek had been much teased over his unlikely choice over a rich Saxon holding in England. Only Lady Vivian, Saxon by birth and now William's trusted advisor, understood his choice for she possessed the powers of a sorceress and had seen the true reason within his thoughts.

But she had also feared for him and had drawn him aside with an urgent warning, for they shared a bond of friendship.

"I have foreseen your return to the north country in a vision," she confided. "There is great danger. I fear for your life."

He had thanked her for her concern and then smiled at her grave expression. "I shall carry the warmth of your friendship with me, and perhaps a protective spell," he suggested.

"You have what little protection I may offer," she said sadly. "I fear it may not be enough. Be careful who you trust."

He had felt the weight of her words the entire journey, in the inhospitable cold that gripped the land and slipped beneath the heaviest tunic to settle in the bones, unseen eyes that seemed to constantly watch, and now this place that seemed to close about them with unseen dangers.

The horses sensed it too. They moved nervously at their tethers, gazes alert, ears twitching back and forth. The Arabian mare suddenly tossed her head in alarm.

Tarek whirled around and came face to face with a band of fierce warriors who stood at the edge of the forest and surrounded them.

Beside him, Stephen lunged for his battle sword. Tarek stopped him.

"You would be dead before you drew it from leather," Tarek warned in a low voice. To his other men who suddenly became aware of the warriors and also reached for their battle swords, he shouted, "Hold! Do not draw your weapons."

The warriors were a rugged lot. They wore coarse woolen shirts and leggings, and lengths of woven wool in shades of brown, black, and green that blended with the colors of the forest, flung over their shoulders and gathered about their waists front and back with a wide belt.

Shaggy manes of hair fell wildly to their shoulders. Their

faces were smudged with soot, mud, and something that might have been animal dung, and disguised their features.

They were well-armed with short, blunt swords or battle-axes. A second weapon — a short-bladed knife — was thrust into their belts or the tops of their boots.

By the looks of them, they were highlanders, fierce Scots warriors whose clans were distinguished by those pieces of wool cloth with distinctly different markings that denoted family kinship. Much like tribes in the deserts of the eastern empires.

For several moments no one moved or spoke. Finally one of the highlanders nodded to the younger warrior beside him. They slowly strode forward, hands at their weapons.

One was lean and tall with fiery red hair that hung to his shoulders, and sharp blue eyes. He was young, with a handsomeness that suggested he enjoyed favor with women.

The other warrior was stout of build though not as tall, and older. His reddish hair was streaked with gray, and he moved stiffly as though troubled by some infirmity. But there was no betrayal of weakness in his gaze, as fierce, defiant, and unyielding as the younger warrior who bore a resemblance to him.

Perhaps they were father and son, for the likeness was as strong between them as the one between Stephen and the king.

The older warrior met his gaze directly, apparently unconcerned with the number of Norman soldiers and knights he confronted.

"Who leads these men?" he demanded.

Tarek stepped forward. "I lead them."

That fierce, scrutinizing gaze swept over him, then fixed on the curved Persian blade secured at his saddle.

"Ye are far north of the borderlands," the Scot observed.

"We have been sent by King William of England," Tarek replied, careful to say nothing that might offend.

"Ye trespass on lands of the northern clans!" the younger warrior said bluntly.

"We come in peace," Tarek said calmly, aware that every word, each movement was carefully watched. "With an offer of protection for the northern clans."

The younger warrior snorted. "Protection? Is that the Norman word for butchery and murder, as we've heard about in London?"

"Silence, lad!" the older warrior ordered, flashing him a warning look. He turned to Tarek.

"The northern clans have no need of Duke William's *protection*. We protect what is ours — our families, and *our* land. Without interference from others." His mouth snapped closed in a defiant, implacable expression set amid the hard ridges and deep lines of his face.

"We have seen many burned-out villages and freshly turned graves."

The old warrior shrugged. "There are always disagreements between the clans."

"These villages are on lands held by the laird of Inverness," Tarek pointed out. "Lands of his kinsmen."

The warrior's gaze narrowed even further at discovering Tarek had some knowledge of the clan system of kinship.

"And the weapons we found on the bodies of others who were left to rot, were not the weapons of the highlands. They bore the markings of foreign raiders."

"And your king thinks to offer protection against these raiders?" the young warrior demanded. "The Conqueror is a benevolent man." His voice dripped with sarcasm.

"Cease lad!" the older warrior spoke sharply.

Tarek's gaze met that of the one who spoke with authority.

"The king is concerned about the threat of invasion in the north country. He sends his army to protect against this. It is a matter I wish to discuss with the laird of Inverness. Are you the laird?"

"I speak for him in such matters," the older man replied. His gaze shifted past Tarek to the Norman knights and warriors.

"You have brought a sizable army with you," he observed. "Our kinsmen spoke of it." His eyes glinted. "They said they could smell you comin'."

"No doubt they spoke of our horses."

"Aye, perhaps," the older warrior agreed, sharp eyes watching him intently. "Foul beasties they be."

"True," Tarek admitted, watching the cunning old badger carefully as he pointed out, "but they can cross four times the distance of a man in half the time, while carrying him astride. It would seem a fair exchange."

The old Scot grunted. "Aye," he agreed. "Then perhaps ye should hand over the beasties as a gesture of kindness from King William."

Stephen of Valois almost choked with laughter, except the old warrior made no joke.

Tarek seemed to give the matter some consideration, mindful of that gleaming war ax and the other weapons drawn about them.

"If I were to give you our horses, then we would be afoot," he replied thoughtfully.

The old warrior's eyes gleamed. "Aye, that is the truth of it."

"The king might have no objection," Tarek said with a shrug. When Stephen would have burst out in outrage at such a suggestion, he gave him a warning look as he slipped a hand beneath the Arabian mare's muzzle and lifted it to stroke her finely chiseled head. In the dark gleam of her eyes he saw the reflection of the highlanders and watched for any sudden movement.

"But I am especially fond of this one, and," he added, repeating what the old warrior had said only moments earlier as he continued stroking the mare, *"I protect what is mine."*

"You are a fool to set such store by the beast," the old warrior said bluntly, his hand closing over the handle of his sword.

"And you are outnumbered." The sword was eased back into the leather sheath at the warrior's belt.

The highlander shrugged, a hint of a smile twitching at his bearded mouth.

"Aye lad, but you'll be the first to fall."

Tarek smiled. "Not before you've tasted the steel of *my* blade."

His hand rested on the handle of the gleaming Persian sword. He saw the glint of curiosity that mixed with challenge in the highlander's eyes as he again glanced at the unusual sword.

"Well then," the old warrior replied. "We'll never know the outcome if our blood is the first spilt."

"Then, perhaps we should exchange words rather than blood," Tarek suggested.

"Perhaps," the old warrior agreed. "I am called Ian. And this brash lad who speaks his mind before he thinks it, is my son, Malcolm."

"I am Tarek al Sharif. I come in peace," he replied and prayed it would be so. For if just one of his men became impatient and drew steel, there would be no hope of peace, only more war. Now the uneasy game of diplomacy began.

"I would like to meet with the laird of Inverness," he insisted.

Ian nodded. "Aye."

"Nay, father!" Malcolm blurted out angrily. "Ye canna bring them to Inverness."

"I speak for the laird!" his father reminded. "Dinna speak out so agin me!"

With a furious glare at his father, Malcolm spun about and disappeared into the thick tree cover. Ian sighed as he turned back to Tarek.

"The council of chieftains will meet in three days." Then he laid down his conditions. "You will bring no more than a dozen of your men."

Beside him, Tarek sensed Stephen's outrage that he would even consider such terms. Tarek warned him to silence.

"Agreed."

Ian nodded. "In three days then."

Then, as suddenly and silently as they had appeared, Ian and his kinsmen disappeared once more into the forest, the trees and thick undergrowth closing around them as if they had never been there at all.

"I will take some of the men and follow!" Stephen said vehemently as he turned to his horse. Tarek stopped him.

"Do not."

Stephen was incredulous. "And leave them hiding in the forest to cut us down one by one at their pleasure? I do not trust the one called Malcolm. He has the look of blood in his eyes."

Tarek smiled. "I recognize it well." Then he became serious once more. "If they wanted us dead, it would already be done."

"They would be dead as well," Stephen argued defiantly. "We outnumber them ten to one."

"Some perhaps," Tarek agreed. "But many more of our men would be dead, and that is a price I am not willing to pay. Did you notice their armament and weapons?"

Stephen scoffed. "They wore no armor, and their weapons are crudely made."

Tarek nodded. "No armor to weigh them down or hinder them in the thick tree cover," he pointed out.

"They appear and disappear like the scirocco — the desert wind. Here one moment, gone the next, and just as impossible to see where it will appear next. And their weapons, while not as finely made as ours, are easier to wield. They strike, they kill, and then they disappear.

"I have heard these highlanders are formidable warriors. They have kept the English beyond their borders for more than five hundred years." There was admiration in his voice as he released the reins of Stephen's horse.

"A man who chooses not to understand his adversary, is soon defeated. William taught me that." Then his gaze narrowed as he stared through the trees where the highlanders had disappeared.

"We cannot secure a landhold and fight both the Scots and the raiders. We must divide and conquer. We will meet with the chieftains."

"Will you tell them that you have come to lay claim to Inverness?" Stephen asked. "I do not think they will yield because the king orders it. A dozen men will not be enough to fight our way out of a well-fortified fortress when they learn our true purpose."

"I have no intention of fighting my way out."

"Then how will you convince them to hand over Inverness?" Stephen asked.

Tarek flexed his fingers and stroked the flat, curved blade of the Persian sword. The coolness of sharp steel was real and deadly beneath his hand.

"They have a weakness. I will find it." He swung into the saddle and gathered the reins. "But I see no reason to delay this meeting for three days," he added with a sly smile as he whirled the Arabian mare about.

At dusk the following day, as the sinking sun became a blood-red ball on the misty horizon, Tarek al Sharif and his men surrounded the fortress at Inverness.

Three

The gates of the fortress slowly opened.

Several Scots warriors walked out to meet them. A full two score more could be seen within the fortress at the entrance. Their weapons were drawn, expressions fierce.

Stephen of Valois reined his warhorse in beside Tarek. "And this Scot bids you bring no more than a dozen men?" he spat out contemptuously. "There are no doubt twice more this number inside that cannot be seen waiting to cut us down."

Tarek angled him a glance. "Perhaps." Then his gaze scanned the battlement. "Yet, only a handful guard the walls."

"Let us see how the laird of Inverness greets us," he suggested as he urged the Arabian mare slowly forward, through the line of warriors who stood with weapons drawn.

Alert to every possible danger, his gaze scanned every building, the expressions of those who silently watched as they passed by, the scarce number of people and animals inside the fortress, and walls where repairs had been recently made.

A good many men were inside the walls, but not nearly so many as he expected for a gathering of chieftains and their kinsmen.

"All is not what it seems," Stephen commented as they rode side by side across the yard followed by the ten men he had chosen to ride with them.

They were battle-hardened warriors who had fought in

many campaigns across the Byzantine empire and pledged their loyalty unto death to Tarek al Sharif. Among them was Gavin de Marte, a knight of King William. His brother's death in the encounter with raiders months earlier had brought him back to the north country seeking revenge.

Tarek nodded his agreement as he glanced at the burned out ruins of the animal pens, blacksmith, and tanners' shed. He caught the pungence of smoke that still lingered amid the ruins. More than one Scot bore a bandage at a freshly dressed wound.

"There has been trouble here," Stephen speculated as he too smelled the smoke that lingered. "No more than four days past."

Tarek nodded but said nothing in response as they dismounted before the steps of the main hall. The doors opened and several highland warriors came down the steps to meet them.

They wore leather leggings, fleece vests, with woven plaids in varied patterns of brown, green, and blue wrapped about their shoulders and belted at their waists.

They were fierce and rugged, wide of shoulder, with legs like tree stumps, and all carried weapons. For several moments they confronted one another on the steps of the fortress. Then one shouldered his way between them — the Scot, Ian, they'd met in the forest the day before.

The unruly beard framed the frown at his mouth. Disapproval glinted in the old warrior's eyes and etched hard lines in the ruddy leather of his face. His hand was clasped over the handle of his sword, knuckles gleaming white at the battle-scarred hand.

"The agreement was to meet in *three* days," the old Scot reminded him. "And ye have brought more than a dozen men with ye." His gnarled hand flexed over the handle of the sword he wore as he indicated men who remained outside the gates. "Ye took great risk comin' afore the agreed date. Ye might have been cut down at the gates."

"Or your men within," Tarek reminded him of their previous conversation in the forest. "As for the terms of the agreement, I have brought ten men with me *inside* the walls of Inverness. As for the arranged time, those were your words, not mine. I saw no reason to delay when we could easily reach Inverness in one. And the forest seemed a likely place for attack."

Ian grunted. "Ye are a man who chooses his words carefully, and holds another to his with even more care."

"Words can be as dangerous as weapons," Tarek commented. "I have learned to use them carefully."

The Scot nodded. "Aye, I'll remember that of ye next time, Tarek al Sharif."

He was surprised the old warrior remembered his name.

"A strange, foreign name that is. Persian ye say? It's a warm place, I've heard."

Tarek was equally impressed with the man's knowledge. "Much warmer than this cold land of yours," he replied.

"Aye," Ian again acknowledged, his eyes sharp and filled with mistrust. "There's reason we wear the breeks beneath the wool. Most who come to the north country find the land inhospitable and doona stay."

Though they exchanged pleasantries, the old warrior's expression was anything but amicable, and his meaning was not lost. For all the appearance of a barbarian, the old warrior was shrewd and cunning as a fox.

"Except for Mardigan and his raiders," Tarek replied.

The old fox's gaze narrowed. He said nothing but turned and gestured for Tarek and his men to follow. As they walked among the Scots warriors, all were aware of the weapons that remained drawn on them.

The hall was made of stone and wood. Several long tables had been pulled into the center of the hall in preparation for the evening meal. One table was set lengthwise across the ends of the other tables. Underfoot, earth floors were covered with freshly strewn grasses.

A fire smoked heavily at a stone hearth large enough for a man to walk through. Above the hearth hung a length of wool woven in black, blue, green, and white. No doubt the colors of the laird of Inverness. These northern chieftains wore their woven wools proudly, like a king's banners.

Serving girls appeared, carrying platters filled with simple food. Several bore marks across a cheek, chin, or at a swollen eye. Yet, there was nothing subservient or abused in their manner. Their expressions were sullen and defiant as they set out the evening meal.

More than once Tarek caught the glance of a highland girl watching with an expression as fierce as any warrior. Had they weapons instead of platters, he was certain they would have used them on him and his men.

The Scots were all dressed much as those they had met in the forest, with woolen leggings and shirts, fleece tunics, and lengths of wool in slightly different patterns worn over.

They were bound by blood and called themselves clans, each led by a chieftain who was their leader by right of birth. It was an ancient bond, much like the desert tribes of the Byzantine empire, large extended families bound by blood with a loyalty no amount of gold could buy.

Yet, for all the orderliness of the hall and the fierceness of those within who guarded it, Tarek once again sensed something was very wrong. For among the warriors he also noticed several recent wounds that spoke of more than a simple skirmish.

"There has been trouble here," Stephen whispered.

Tarek nodded his agreement, "The floor is freshly strewn with grasses and the walls scrubbed with lye, even in the midst of such fierce cold weather."

"They are trying to hide something," Stephen concluded, matching his strides as they crossed the great room of the central hall. Again Tarek nodded his agreement.

The sweet fragrance of the grasses reminded him of exotic Persian gardens, only far more subtle. The sweetness permeated the air and mingled with the acrid stench of smoke from the torches at the walls and the hearth, the aroma of meat simmering over the fire, and something else equally well known.

Every warrior recognized it, for it was something never forgotten once he fought his first battle. No amount of scrubbing or sweet fragrances could disguise the foulness of death.

"Many men died here," Tarek said. "The stench of it still clings to the air as over a battlefield."

With narrowed gaze, he scanned the warriors gathered in the hall, then returned to the length of wool displayed over the hearth.

He frowned. No more than a dozen of the highlanders wore that same distinctive wool. Surely a man as powerful as the laird of Inverness had more kinsmen, when no less than a full score of warriors stood beside each chieftain.

Had the men of Inverness been called away? Were they perhaps elsewhere within the fortress, waiting even now to strike at him and his men? Or, had some other fate befallen them?

The chieftains sat at the head table. Ian sat in the middle with his son, Malcolm, at his right-hand side. The young highlander glared at them with contempt and undisguised resentment.

The other warriors sat at the other tables, their gazes wary and mistrustful. Perhaps they had been discussing the presence of the Norman army in the highlands even as Tarek and his men rode up to the gates.

"Ye are either a brave man, or a fool, takin' it upon yerself to abuse the laird's generosity. Yer actions might be seen as treachery."

"I have been called both," Tarek admitted with a glint of self-deprecating humor in fierce blue eyes. "But I see no less than four score of your warriors within the walls of Inverness, while I have but a handful to protect my back. If there is treachery, it will not be by my command."

All about them, the Scot's kinsmen and other warriors shifted warily at the implied insult. Beside him, Stephen's hand closed over the handle of his sword. Malcolm reacted instinctively, coming out of his chair with blade drawn. Ian stopped him, his hand closing over his son's arm, forcing his hand back down onto the top of the table, and pinned it there.

"Aye," Ian said thoughtfully. "Ye've a way with words. Let us speak then. But we will eat and drink first."

"I thank you for your hospitality, but my men hunted in the forest," Tarek explained. He watched the slow rise of color in the Scot's face at the knowledge they had helped themselves to the bounty of the laird's forest. The old warrior's hand again closed in warning over his son's arm.

"Then you will drink with us," Ian insisted. "It would be an insult to refuse."

Metal tankards were filled by the serving girls as they passed round the table. A tankard was handed to Tarek.

He had no taste for bitter English ales, but this was a different brew. And he wondered what else might have been added to the tankard. Yet he understood the inherent challenge that was made with the offering of it. A wise man might refuse to drink with the highlanders. A wiser man would not. He accepted the tankard.

"We do not have Lady Vivian's healing powders to aid us," Stephen warned, with the same thoughts. "If the drink has been poisoned, you are a dead man."

"Perhaps you would drink it for me," Tarek suggested.

"I would rather skewer that old fox through his gizzard, and the young pup along with him."

"If I die, you have my permission to do so."

Meeting the Scot's challenging gaze, Tarek lifted the tankard and drained it.

Unlike the bitter English ales, the amber liquid went down smooth and sweet. Then turned to fire. It burned at his throat, all the way down, and then exploded into an inferno at his belly that robbed him of air and watered his eyes.

The old Scot grinned, sly as a fox. All about him, other warriors watched with sly smiles.

"Ye like it then?" Ian asked, with gleaming eyes. "It warms the belly, does it not?"

"It does," Tarek replied with husky voice, the only two words he could manage between numbed lips. But if it was poison, it had a far different effect than any he knew.

The fire soon burned to a radiant glow that spiraled from his belly down into his legs and the length of his arms. His lips felt numb, his throat tight, and everything about the hall took on a soft haze. He carefully set the tankard down aware that all the highlanders watched him.

"It's a fine brew," he declared. His gaze locked with Ian's. In the old warrior's eyes he saw reluctant admiration.

"There are few who drink as ye have and remain standing." Ian remarked, watching him with those shrewd eyes.

"Ye are a trusting man and perhaps more fool than you know."

"No," Tarek croaked. He cleared his throat and began again. "I simply gave orders to my men to kill you and your son if I did not survive."

"By God!" Malcolm exploded angrily. "I'll not stand for this! He accepts our hospitality, and then insults us!"

"In that," Tarek replied as he gathered his vaguely confused thoughts, "we are even."

Across the table, Ian's shrewd gaze narrowed. "Aye," he acknowledged. Then without looking at his son, he ordered, "Sit and stay yer weapon, lad! Or leave the hall!"

Malcolm did not leave, nor did he sit. Instead, he left to stand behind his father in defiant stance, arms folded over his chest, his intense gaze boring into Tarek al Sharif.

Brianna watched the confrontation from the shadows where she had stood weeks earlier and listened to Mardigan's demands. Thomas stood protectively beside her.

She had sent Ian and his men to find the location of the Norman army and determine their purpose in the north country. But when he returned he warned her the man who led the Norman army might not be easily dealt with.

When the guards sounded the alarm, she had watched the line of torches in the gathering darkness from the battlements as the Norman army approached — two days before the appointed time — a reminder of Ian's warning.

Now Tarek al Sharif and his men were surrounded by Ian's warriors, outnumbered, yet bold and unafraid.

This barbarian with the strange sounding name had the bearing of a warrior, but he wasn't dressed like the Norman knights with their cumbersome chain mail armor worn over padded tunics, with chain mail hose.

He wore no armor at all. Instead, his tunic was soft leather, belted at the waist, and worn over a linen shirt of unusual cut with wide flowing sleeves, leather breeches, and high boots. Instead of the cumbersome Norman broadsword, the sword he carried was narrow at the base, wide at the tip, and curved in a chilling smile of death in the light from the torches.

His hair was dark and fell to his shoulders in thick silken waves. Several days' growth of beard darkened his cheek and the angle of a strong jaw. She could see no more than that as he stood facing the council.

"Now, we will speak of what brings the Norman army *uninvited* to the north country," Ian said before the council.

"You are not the laird of Inverness," Tarek reminded him. He saw the flicker of response in the Scot's eyes, the unguarded resentment. Then the warrior's lids lowered to hide his thoughts, and Tarek knew he'd guessed correctly. The old warrior was hiding something.

"The council makes decision concerning the clans," Ian replied bluntly. "Anything you would say to the laird you may say here, and it will be taken under advisement by the entire council."

"The king's words are for the laird of Inverness. I will give them to no other," Tarek replied bluntly.

Tension filled the hall as the two warriors confronted each other. Brianna saw the mistrust and suspicion all about her as both Scots and Norman warriors seized their weapons. If she did not stop them, then blood would again stain the walls of Inverness.

Thomas tried to restrain her as his thoughts urgently joined with hers in silent warning. She gently loosened his fingers over her arm as she stepped from her hiding place in the shadows and slowly made her way through her kinsmen to the center of the hall. One by one they reluctantly stepped aside to let her pass until she stood very near the council table.

"Then you must speak with *me,*" she announced in a clear, firm voice.

Every gaze in the hall fastened on her. But in the shifting light from the torches she saw only one, startling blue beneath the slash of jet black brows drawn together over the fierce expression of Tarek al Sharif as he turned at the sound of her voice.

Her throat suddenly went dry. The air became trapped in her frozen lungs. His gaze was intense as it fastened on her.

He was tall, and powerfully built, and he moved with the agile grace and restrained power of a sleek animal. Like a creature of the night, a creature that leapt battlement walls, its fur glistening in the mist — a creature of dreams.

But Tarek al Sharif was not a creature of the night or dreams. He was a man, who had been sent by the English king. And she knew him.

Months before she had come upon a man beside a remote highland pool, fleeing a band of raiders. They would surely have killed him if she hadn't helped him escape. Now, he had returned, with demands from the English king. Demands for the laird of Inverness.

Tarek slowly walked toward her.

Her lips parted on a startled breath. Her eyes were dark as forest shadows in the pale oval of her face, bones gleaming stark white beneath skin at hands clasped tightly before her as though clasped about some invisible weapon.

She was slender as a water reed in a gown of soft gray wool that pooled about her feet at the floor. Her hair was plaited in a gold satin braid that spilled over one shoulder and fell to her waist. Silver and gold. Like sunlight and mist. More than a memory, more than a whisper that haunted his dreams.

He saw the confusion that creased delicate skin above slender golden brows, the tension that quivered through her like a tightly drawn bowstring, her quickly averted gaze, and knew that she too remembered that first encounter.

"Are you the laird of Inverness?" he asked when he stood close enough that he could have touched her. Her gaze snapped back to his.

"The laird is dead. I am his daughter," she explained, in that soft, cool-as-mist voice that had haunted his dreams. Her chin lifted proudly and her back straightened like that of a warrior defending sacred ground.

"I now make decisions in all matters that concern Inverness."

Eyes like morning mist stared coolly back at him, betraying nothing of her inner thoughts, nor even a hint of the recognition he had seen a moment before. A shadow moved behind her as a large man stood protectively near with sword in hand.

"Why has the English king sent armed knights and warriors to the north country?" she demanded with all the defiance and pride of a chieftain.

He glanced about the hall at Inverness, seeing with warrior's eyes what they did not want him to see — the gleaming, fresh-cut lumber at a recently repaired table, warriors who had been recently wounded, and the sweet, pungent grasses hastily strewn about the floor to cover the stench of death. Then his gaze came back to rest speculatively on the slender young woman who stood before him.

"There have been more attacks by raiders in the north country," Tarek explained, choosing his words carefully for in spite of the memory that bound them, he sensed her mistrust.

"The king is aware the northern clans have suffered great loss, and offers his protection against these foreign enemies."

He saw the surprise that leapt into her eyes, immediately

followed by doubt and mistrust.

"Protection?" Malcolm interrupted angrily. "Or is it that your king is concerned another might try to claim the English throne?"

He rounded the table where the chieftains sat and confronted Tarek. "There are those with equal claim."

Tarek denied nothing. "Inverness is far from London, and difficult to defend. The king offers protection through an alliance."

"An alliance?" Malcolm replied incredulously. " 'Tis well known Duke William of Normandy makes no alliances, but takes what he wants," he reminded his kinsmen.

"He is called the *Conqueror,* and for good reason. Perhaps he intends to conquer the north country as well," Malcolm suggested.

"The king offers an alliance," Tarek repeated calmly amid angry outbursts from the Scots. "Of mutual benefit to both."

"Or the blood of both?" Malcolm suggested.

"What mutual benefit does the king propose?" Brianna asked.

"The strength of the Norman army joined with the northern clans to drive out the raiders," Tarek replied.

"And Norman soldiers entrenched on northern soil," Malcolm pointed out. "With an army already here in the north country, what is there to stop the Conqueror from taking the whole of Scotland?"

"If William wished to take Scotland, it would be already be done," Tarek told him, repeating something similar he had once told Ian. "But he has no ambitions for Scotland," he assured them. "Only the protection of the northern shores against others who would threaten his claim to the throne of England."

"What assurances do we have of the truth of this proposed

alliance?" Malcolm demanded.

"You have my word, and the king's seal on documents that I carry."

"The word of a barbarian, and worthless parchment! No English king may be trusted," Malcolm argued, and found support in the nodded agreement from several kinsmen.

"There is nothing to be gained but oppression and the heel of the English boot at our necks."

Tarek did not argue but instead turned to Brianna, for he sensed her willingness to listen. A willingness that he would use against her to gain what he wanted. When he spoke, he spoke directly to her, for beneath the pride and defiance, he sensed the tenderness of a beautiful young woman who could not bear to see him killed by raiders.

"Your villages will be safe and your farms will prosper. Your families will no longer be butchered and murdered. Mardigan will be driven from your shores, and the north country will be secure once more. But without the alliance, Mardigan will return."

Her eyes had gone dark. She winced as if she'd been struck. He'd guessed correctly. Mardigan had been here, no doubt responsible for the old laird's death and the deaths of many more.

"We'll have nothin' to do with the English," another Scot added his argument to Malcolm's. "Five hundred years we've no' needed the English. We've no need of 'em now, especially the one who calls himself the Conqueror. To my way of thinkin' he's no better than Mardigan."

The words of her kinsmen weighed heavily. Yet, he saw doubt in her eyes, and conflict in drawn, delicate features.

"Nothin' is given freely," Ian pointed out. "What does yer king ask in return for his protection of the north country?"

Arguments momentarily ceased. Shouts of outrage and

angry bickering were replaced by a barely concealed hostility as the Scots waited for his answer. Tension, like that before a storm, filled the hall.

The old Scot crossed the hall and stood before Tarek in a defiant, wide-legged stance, his hand resting over the handle of the sword secured at his belt.

"The one who calls himself William the Conqueror is not one to give something for nothing. What are the terms for such an alliance?"

Tarek turned to Brianna. When he reached out, he heard the sound of several blades being drawn, then the deadly answering sigh as his warriors drew their own swords.

There were only twelve of them, but nearly two hundred more waited beyond the gates. It was for that reason he had wanted them clearly seen through the gates and from the battlements, rather than hiding in the surrounding woods.

His eyes narrowed. His expression was confident. He had found the weakness he sought in the pain of truth in Brianna's eyes. There was no longer any doubt how it would be done.

He reached out and gently lifted the thick gold braid from her shoulder. It was heavy, like fine satin as he stroked the rich gold between his fingers, imagining it unbound as it was that day long ago. Then, coldly, ruthlessly as if he held a blade to her throat, he named his terms.

"You."

The hall erupted with violent protest from the Scots. Stephen stepped to his side and blocked Malcolm as he advanced with drawn sword.

"You are mad!" she whispered.

Tarek sensed the shock and outrage that quivered through her. He saw the anger and defiance that glittered at her eyes.

"I am most serious," he assured her. Then he closed in, like a hunter stalking its prey.

"How many have already died, Brianna?" he asked with brutal frankness. "Your father? And all of his men?"

Her breasts rose and fell in shallow gasps of remembered pain beneath the soft gray wool of her gown as he guessed the truth they had tried to hide from him so that he would not see their weakness.

Pressing his advantage, he said coldly, "The air still reeks with their deaths. How will your people defend themselves when Mardigan strikes again? How many more must die?"

Mardigan would return. Tarek saw the certainty of it in the haunted look at her eyes, like a wound that would not heal but lay open and exposed with the pain of losing those she loved.

When Brianna closed her eyes, she again saw the blood that had stained the walls, Cullum and Mirren brutally struck down defending each other, and her. And with it the memory of Mardigan's vow.

He would return and her people would die. Unless he was stopped. There was no hope of that unless an alliance was made with the English king. Cullum had believed it. She was caught as surely as a rabbit in a snare.

"What you ask is impossible," she told him. "The chieftains would never accept marriage as a condition for an alliance. You and your men will be killed."

"Perhaps," he conceded. "But two hundred more of my men await my return. If I do not return, Inverness will be put to the torch."

Tears of outrage glistened at her lashes. "You are no different from Mardigan."

"Do you prefer an alliance with the raiders, with the blood of your father still staining the earth beneath your feet?" he asked, and saw the answer in the anguished expression at her face.

Hope slipped through her fingers. The chieftains argued fiercely while their kinsmen pushed an armed confrontation to the point of certainty. If she did not agree to his terms the chieftains and their kinsmen and all who remained within Inverness would be slaughtered. He offered an alliance, but held her people hostage unless she agreed.

Months ago she had saved his life. Now, she wished she had let him die.

"I will have your answer now, Brianna," he insisted.

Thomas' fierce anguished thoughts connected with hers, trying to persuade her against it.

She glanced at Tarek al Sharif. If she refused, her kinsmen and the other chieftains would fight to the death to defend her decision. More blood and death.

"I must have time to think," she said.

"I will have your answer now," Tarek insisted.

She closed her eyes as though seeking inner strength, or uttering some last desperate prayer. But in the darkness behind her eyes she saw only blood and death. Whether for those who had already died or those whose deaths might come from the decision she must now make, she could not know.

When she opened her eyes, the bleak ghostly images remained to haunt at the edges of her vision. She made the only choice she could.

In a hollow voice that ached at her throat, she said, "I accept your terms."

"Nay!" Malcolm shouted in outrage. He lunged at Tarek with his sword. It was deflected by Ian's own blade. At his orders, Malcolm was restrained by his kinsmen and dragged off. Grim-faced, he turned to Brianna.

"Is that yer true answer, lass?" Ian demanded. "I must know."

She nodded bleakly. "It is."

"Then summon your priest," Tarek told him. "For we will be wed tomorrow."

Ian's furious gaze met his. " 'Tis impossible. There is much to be done before vows can be spoken. Surely you would not dishonor the lass in such a way before her own people."

"I will marry her," Tarek replied, his mouth set in a thin hard line. "In that I honor her above all others. Summon your priest," he repeated. "The vows will be spoken, or she will go to my bed without them."

Then turning to Brianna as his men gathered around him, he warned, "Do not think to escape. I will find you. And then I will lay waste to what remains of Inverness."

Four

Brianna sensed Thomas' presence even before she heard the sound of stone grating back across stone as the wall panel shifted open and she felt the sudden gust of bitter cold air that swept into the chamber.

As he stepped into the chamber, she glanced anxiously to the door opening. The door had been destroyed, hacked to pieces by Mardigan's men. A heavy woolen tapestry had been secured across the opening to give her privacy. A Norman guard had stood on the other side of that tapestry all night.

No one was allowed to enter her chamber, nor was she allowed to leave, so great was Tarek al Sharif's suspicion of treachery among the Scots. She was a prisoner in her own home.

Thomas had been forced to use the secret passage, for all of Inverness was overrun with Norman soldiers. They filled the chambers and corridors, and camped within the fortress walls.

"You must try to escape!" his urgent thoughts connected with hers. *"The way is clear."*

She glanced uneasily at the heavy wool hung across the opening, terrified the guard may have heard the grating stone. But no one entered the chamber.

Her fearful thoughts connected with his. *"What have you done?"*

"The guard in the passage below will not bother us," he replied.

She became very pale. *"Have you killed him?"*

Thomas grinned, the expression making his surly, uneven features seem all the more frightening. *"He sleeps with a special potion the cook provided."* He frowned and shrugged. *"She did not have enough for the entire Norman army."*

She laid a gentle hand at his strong arm that had protected her as a child. *"I cannot,"* she replied sadly. With all her heart she wished she could. *"I will not run away from the promise I have made, and endanger my kinsmen."*

"This is not your destiny!" Thomas' thoughts reasoned. *"You are not bound to keep this promise. Your father would never allow it."*

"My father is dead," she whispered softly, speaking aloud and with the heartrending sadness she had felt for days, but could not allow herself to feel.

"Even he spoke of the need for an alliance. Thomas, dear friend and guardian, Inverness will fall to Mardigan if this alliance is not made. And it will fall to the Normans if I escape." She shook her head sadly. "I have no choice."

She felt his despair as his great eyes filled with sadness at this trouble he could not save her from. *"I will kill the one called Tarek al Sharif!"* his thoughts answered fiercely. *"The Norman soldiers will leave if their leader is slain."*

"And they will return a hundredfold to slay every man, woman, and child of Inverness, along with all their kinsmen. No," she shook her head sadly. "I have tried to find another answer to all of this but there is none. It must be done. There is no other way."

Sounds came from the other side of the thick wool that hung across the door opening. Several guards approached her chamber. They had come for her.

She glanced to the window at the east wall. Sunlight pierced heavy clouds at the horizon. It was morning. First light.

Thomas' gaze followed hers. *"There is still time. Please, mistress. Do not give in to his demands,"* he pleaded.

"No," she said gently, but adamantly. "I will not risk the lives of my kinsmen." She remembered Tarek al Sharif's promise if she attempted to escape, and shivered violently.

"He is not a man to be betrayed, or taken lightly. Of that I am certain.

"Go now," she whispered urgently. "They must not find you here."

His expression was fierce as he glanced past her to the tapestry. Any moment one of the Norman guards, perhaps even Tarek al Sharif himself would enter her chamber.

Realizing that she could not be persuaded, Thomas finally nodded his agreement. The stone slipped back into place as Gavin de Marte pushed aside the tapestry and stepped into her chamber.

He glanced about as though he expected to find someone there. Brianna held her breath. Her heart pounded violently. Had he heard her speaking with Thomas?

"Has your maid attended you, mistress?" he asked, his features fixed with an expression of concern rather than suspicion. She slowly let out a sigh of relief. If he had heard voices from within, he gave no indication.

She felt the weight of his gaze as he glanced at her gown, the same one she had worn the evening before. A much finer gown was folded in a trunk, but she refused to wear it. She saw no reason to change into something finer. After all she was to be led a prisoner to her own wedding.

Her hair was still pulled back into a long braid from the previous evening. Though she usually unwound the braid at night before going to bed, there had been no sleep for her last night. Nor would she bind it with fine ribbons or strands of amber stones. There was no reason for finery or celebration.

Her one concession was the length of wool that lay over her shoulder, bound by a sprig of dried heather. It was finely made, of black, blue, and green wool, with a white thread woven through. Her family colors, that Cullum had once worn.

She might be a prisoner, forced to wed, but she would not shame her kinsmen or the other chieftains by looking like a prisoner. She had agreed to the alliance. She would see it through for the sake of her people, and with the pride of her people.

"You are to wear this," Gavin said, laying a folded square of black velvet on the table. He unfolded it, revealing a large gleaming emerald suspended from a length of gold chain.

Brianna was stunned. It was a remarkable stone, exotic, gleaming with hidden golden light as he held it before her, and unlike anything she had ever seen. What manner of man forced a woman to marriage, then gave her such a priceless gift?

"You may return it," she said icily.

"Milord has asked that you wear it," Gavin explained. "It holds great meaning for him."

"It holds no meaning for me," she answered sharply, and immediately regretted the harshness of her words. This man had done her no harm. He was merely the messenger and gift-bearer.

"Such a gift should be given and accepted with heartfelt sincerity and affection," she explained.

"Your master bears no affection for me, nor I for him. This is an alliance to guarantee the safety of my people. Nothing more. I will not accept it."

He frowned as he folded the emerald in the velvet cloth. "My brother died in the north country, murdered by raiders. I have returned to avenge his death. I have pledged my loyalty and my sword to milord al Sharif, and I now pledge it to his lady."

She was stunned by his unexpected sincerity and words of devotion. With that keen inner sense she possessed, she sensed a noble, trustworthy friend in Gavin de Marte.

"Thank you for your kindness," she said, unprepared for such unquestioning loyalty.

Gavin admired her courage and felt a deep pang of regret at the unhappiness he saw in her eyes.

"It is time, milady."

Suddenly it seemed unbearably cold in the chamber, even though she had kept the fire built high at the brazier all night. The long sleepless hours of the previous night had taken their toll. She was exhausted, nerves drawn to the breaking point, fearful there might yet be bloodshed. And now there was no more time.

Features drawn, hands clasped so tight before her that the bones shone through pale flesh, she nodded and followed him from her chamber.

Cullum had the small chapel at Inverness built for his wife Mirren when they were first wed. It was small, built only to accommodate the laird and his family. Brianna had been christened there as a baby. Now, it was filled with so many armed soldiers and Norman knights that they crowded out through the doorway and lined the connecting passage outside all the way to the main hall.

She drew up at the sight of their battle armor glinting dully in the light of the torches at the walls, candlelight at the entrance of the chapel gleaming off the blades of their weapons. A stark reminder that this was not a joyous occasion as it should have been, but as she had pointed out to Gavin de Marte, an alliance of armies.

Father in heaven, she thought, uncertainty becoming a

fear that tightened her throat and clutched an icy hand about her heart. Have I made the right decision?

But as she had told Thomas, it was the only decision she could make that at least gave the hope of preventing the death of more kinsmen.

As they approached the entrance of the chapel, Gavin de Marte spoke sharply to his men. They parted to let her pass. Her kinsmen reluctantly stepped aside as well, their expressions fierce and disapproving. They said nothing but all watched her intently for some betrayal of emotion, some indication that she had changed her mind.

She knew it would take only a single word to end all of this madness. Just one word spoken in defiance of the Norman warriors and knights, and the ultimatum that she'd been given, and all would fight to the death to defend her decision.

Instead, she met their questioning gazes stoically, betraying nothing of her inner turmoil and uncertainty, nothing that would bring more bloodshed to Inverness.

All was in readiness as she entered the chapel. The chieftains and their kinsmen stood at the center of the small chamber. Standing behind them and lining the walls of the chapel were more Norman knights and soldiers.

These fierce warriors stood with feet planted wide, gazes cold and impassive. The light from the torches at the walls glinted off the links of their mail tunics. Light from the candles at the altar reflected with a cruel, macabre beauty from the gleaming blades of their battle swords propped before them as if prepared for battle within those sacred walls.

Her kinsmen were equally fierce, dressed in leather padded tunics, breeches, and boots, the leather gauntlets at their hand and arms covered with row upon row of lethal iron spikes that would flay open a man's flesh to the bone with a single blow.

Their tartans carried the colored patterns of their family clans. Their wild manes of hair and unruly beards gave them the look of wild creatures. And the battle-axes, swords, and slender blades they carried gleamed of death.

Malcolm, reckless and headstrong, stood near the altar, his hand clamped white-knuckled over the handle of his war ax, and a murderous rage in his eyes.

The air was stifling inside the small chapel from the press of so many bodies, yet her hands, clenched tightly at her sides, were cold as ice. She faltered slightly as she remembered the last time she had been in this chamber, Sunday past with Mirren.

Had it only been five days ago? And now Cullum and Mirren, and so many others, were dead.

There had been no time to grieve. Father Cadmon had quickly spoken words over their graves. Then the dead were hastily buried against the threat of disease and the greater fear that Mardigan would return.

Pain twisted deep inside at the sight of those fierce weapons gleaming in the torches. They were a stark reminder of the brutality of her parents' deaths and the fate that awaited her.

As they watched the small procession led by Gavin de Marte enter the chapel, Stephen of Valois tried once more to make Tarek see reason.

"This is madness!" he hissed bluntly. "Have you lost all reason? 'Tis not necessary to wed the wench in order to secure the alliance of the Scots."

When there was no response, he whispered in growing frustration, "The girl is comely enough. Bed her if you must, but there is no need for this hasty marriage. The Scots will be forced to accept the alliance when you lay claim to Inverness. 'Tis no different from a dozen different campaigns we have made across the whole of Europe, taking what we want with no need of such as this marriage. If the Conqueror had allowed his knights to wed every woman they bedded across the empires, he would have no army left."

Tarek's sharp gaze scanned the highlanders gathered in the hall. The Scots were outnumbered almost five to one, yet defiant in their show of strength against the greater numbers of his warriors.

Fierce defiance in the face of overwhelming odds. He admired such courage and loyalty. He was certain that to a man they would fight and die if Brianna of Inverness suddenly declared that she would not honor the alliance as he had laid down the terms.

He understood Stephen's misgivings, but in the alliance he saw the means to have what he wanted, and so much more. He shook his head adamantly. He had not taken complete leave of his senses.

"It is precisely for that reason that I will marry the girl. These people will not be broken by the sword. But marriage vows spoken before their Christian god are not so easily broken. The girl has given her consent," he added with a grim smile. "They will abide her decision." Then his mouth thinned to a flat, hard line.

"You are right that I want the girl. I want her as no other. But this is different, my friend. She is highborn, not some camp follower or whore who plies her wares to any man with coin in his purse." His thoughts returned briefly to that memory of their first encounter.

"She is a prize to be valued and protected for in the vows lie a bond of promise and blood. I will not bed her and leave the chance of a child to despise me for making him a bastard." His intense blue gaze angled sharply toward his young friend. For both understood all too well the fate that lay therein.

" 'Tis wiser to take with cunning that which only *might* be taken by force, and then lost," he explained to Stephen. "Your father taught me that at the battle at Hastings."

A muscle at Stephen's cheek spasmed. "Aye," he spat out contemptuously. "But this decision may well cost your life. I do not trust these highlanders, and this marriage will bed you in the thick of them."

Tarek smiled. "That is why I have you to guard my back."

"Does that include guarding your back in the marriage chamber?" Stephen asked, a sable brow lifting over his amber gaze, his handsome mouth curving in a sardonic smile. "You may need assistance with your husbandly obligations since these Scots are so fierce."

"Only if you wish to find my blade at your throat," Tarek warned, equally sardonic. Then he saw Brianna as she stepped through the quivering shadows at the doorway of the chapel escorted by Gavin de Marte.

His gaze sharpened. She wore the same gown she had worn the previous evening, and completely unadorned. He suspected the choice was deliberate. A reflection, no doubt, of her emotions clear for all to see in the drawn expression of her lovely face. She could not know it achieved the exact opposite effect she had no doubt intended.

The subtle, muted gray of the gown emphasized her pale, ethereal beauty, and contrasted with the warm gold of her hair. Her eyes were a brilliant, fiery green in the delicate oval of her face as if the flames of the torches all gathered there in feverish reflection.

Her hair was swept back from her face as it had been the night before, and woven into a thick braid that gleamed like the richest treasure over her shoulder. She was as she had been that day months ago when he first encountered her, a memory of cool mist and radiant sunlight, and she could not have guessed that it pleased him far more than any adornment he suspected she would have worn on the occasion of her marriage had it been under different circumstances.

The one exception was that she was not wearing the emerald of Anshala, a rare jewel handed down through his mother's family. It was the only possession he had of Asmari, and it would have pleased him greatly if Brianna had worn it. But it did not surprise him that she hadn't. For though her manner was calm, even outwardly resigned to the decision she had made, he sensed far different emotions beneath the calm facade.

The previous evening he had glimpsed those emotions in her eyes — pain at the loss of her parents and so many kinsmen, anger at the choice he gave her which was no choice at all, but most of all her bravery and defiance.

He saw it again as Gavin escorted her to his side. As Gavin handed him the piece of folded velvet with the emerald of Anshala still wrapped inside, her green gaze defiantly met his.

In answer, he said curtly, "Bring the priest."

Brianna turned as a small door beside the simple altar opened. Father Cadmon was escorted in from an adjacent prayer chamber by one of Tarek al Sharif's men.

The good priest was a slender wisp of a man, his shoulders bent as though weighted down with the cares of the world. After the attack, he had worked tirelessly, consecrating the graves of the dead at Inverness, giving what comfort and solace he could to the survivors, including Brianna when her grief over the loss of her adopted parents almost overwhelmed her.

He had buoyed her with gentle words of calming strength, a constant presence who tried to ease the ache of loss and the rage of anger that burned inside her.

In a private moment within that very chapel, she had

found him only the day before, beseeching his god in Latin words for the means through this horrible darkness of death that had befallen Inverness. Tears had streamed down his cheeks and briefly their roles had reversed and it was she who had offered comfort, suddenly aware that though he was a godly man, he was still a man with human frailties that he wore in the heavy lines at his face.

Yet now, as he stepped into the crowded chapel, he squared his shoulders, drew himself up, and defiantly met the gazes of the Norman knights and warriors who stood guard. Though his features were haggard and solemn, his mouth thinned and his gaze was steady and stern at the sight of armed warriors in the chapel.

"How dare you bring armed warriors into this place of worship!" he said defiantly. "You will send them all away."

"If I send them away, the Scots leave as well," Tarek replied.

"Then so be it. But I will not have weapons of war in this sacred place."

Brianna watched as Stephen of Valois moved silently to stand very near Father Cadmon. His gaze traveled warily over the priest, head to foot, even though he stood head and shoulders above the cleric and could easily have crushed him with a single blow.

"What objection have you, priest?" he demanded. "When godly enough men have blessed whole armies before battle."

" 'Tis unseemly. This is not a battlefield, but a place of worship," Father Cadmon explained. "I will not have weapons within these walls."

"No weapons, you say?" Stephen asked, his voice suddenly low and speculative, eyes narrowing even further. Then, like the lunge of a hound suddenly upon its prey, he seized the priest, bent him over his arm, and hoisted the hem of the priest's cassock.

Amid shouts of outrage, Father Cadmon's cries of protest, and the sudden singing of steel of drawn swords all around, Stephen exposed the priest's spindly, pale legs, and a third gleaming *leg* that dangled between — a short, blunt-bladed sword hidden beneath the priest's robes.

"And which particular blessing did you think to bestow with this, priest!" Stephen demanded as he unceremoniously relieved the good father of his sword and dropped him to the stone floor of the chapel.

Brianna suddenly went cold at the risk Father Cadmon had taken, for there was no doubt in her mind what he had intended. As if in answer, she heard it in his frantic thoughts as he scrambled to his feet and defiantly faced down the armed warriors who towered over him while her kinsmen formed an armed ring of death about the perimeter of the chapel.

Father in heaven! Blood would run over the very stones of the chapel if she did not stop them.

"Do not!" she cried out fiercely. "There will be no more bloodshed within these walls!" One by one she faced down her own kinsmen. All the while her knees felt as if they would go out from under her and her heart hammered frantically.

Then she looked to Father Cadmon. She reached out, laying a hand at his arm. "I have given my word, I will not break it."

"Dear child . . ." his voice trembled with the equal fierceness of his emotions, for though he was a man of God, he was also a Scot.

"Nay!" she shook her head adamantly. "I am now laird of Inverness," she said vehemently. "As you would honor Cullum with your loyalty and support, you must now give me the same and not interfere." Beside her, she felt Tarek al Sharif's watchful presence.

He could have sent all her kinsmen from the chapel with his own men to remain at guard, for the treachery that Father Cadmon had dared. But he did not. Unlike her own kinsmen, he made no attempt to interfere, but allowed her the authority of the decision, and in that she realized once again, this man was no fool.

"Support me in this," she beseeched the priest. "As you would my father."

Tension thickened the air in the small chapel and smothered over them. Finally, Father Cadmon nodded.

"Aye, lass. I will honor you in this."

All about them, it seemed a collective sigh was released that bloodshed had been averted.

"Begin the ceremony," Tarek al Sharif told Father Cadmon. And then as if announcing it to all those assembled in the chapel, "There will be no further interruptions."

Her hand rested atop Tarek's as the vows were spoken in Latin. Smoke from the torches and the heat of so many bodies pressed together made the air oppressive in the small chapel.

She swayed slightly and her slender fingers tightened. In spite of her defiance and unyielding strength, she suddenly clutched at his hand, as though holding on. Her gaze met his briefly over their joined hands. They were great dark green pools of haunted shadows.

Then he felt her stiffen as though drawing on some inner well of strength, and the sudden, tight curl of her fingers as she defiantly balled her hand into a tight fist within the curl of his hand. She tried to free her hand, but he refused to let her go even when it was no longer necessary for the joining vows.

The Christian vows were finished. Father Cadmon offered his reluctant blessings, the words echoing in the tense silence of the chapel. The priest hesitated and frowned.

"Will you finish it in the old way with the giving of the cloth, lass?" he asked Brianna.

Her startled gaze met Father Cadmon's. With every word, each gesture, she was being bound to this fierce, dark warrior. It was an alliance of warriors and armies against a common foe, not a true marriage. The question hung suspended between them in the still, smothering air, smoky from dozens of candles.

She had wanted only to be done with it, and had not considered this ritual that was part of every such ceremony in the highlands. A gesture of joining far older, and somehow even more binding than the Latin words which had been spoken.

Her hand suddenly trembled as she fingered the edges of the wool that draped her shoulder. This above all, and even more important than the vows she had just spoken, symbolized among her kinsmen, her union with this man.

Her gaze met Malcolm's briefly and in his fierce expression she saw all the emotions that raged within his heart, not the least of which was his love for her. For he had hoped to stand where this fierce barbarian with the strange sounding name and equally strange manner now stood. *He* had hoped to partake of the giving and receiving of the Inverness tartan as a symbol of the union of their families.

Forgive me, dear Malcolm, she willed her thoughts to find his for there had been no opportunity for them to speak of these things. Nor, she sensed, would he have listened. What he would have refused to hear, even if she could have explained it to him, was that even if the Normans had not come to Inverness, she could never wed with him.

She slowly removed the wool from her shoulder and felt another unwavering gaze upon her. That of the fierce warrior who was now her husband.

Could he possibly understand what the giving of it meant?

That among the highlanders, it was more binding than any words that could be spoken between them. Her fingers were icy cold as she removed the length of wool from her shoulder.

The look in her eyes was the same look as the night before when she had stood with her kinsmen — proud, defiant, regal as any queen. Now, just as proud and defiant, almost as if she dared him to take it, she held the length of wool out to him.

He was familiar with such customs, steeped in honor and tradition. This one, he knew, symbolized placing herself in his care and protection. And through her, the people of Inverness.

He had demanded no less and even held the safety of her people hostage to force her acceptance of this marriage. But he sensed that no amount of threats could have forced her to offer the wool and what it symbolized.

He could take it by force, but he could never force her to give it. It had to be given freely of her own will, and with it the unspoken challenge that dared him to be the true laird of Inverness.

He saw the conflict of emotions in her eyes. He wanted to tell her there was no need for this part of the ceremony. Yet, he sensed that his refusal, even to spare her feelings, would dishonor her more and the alliance he had forced her to accept. His fingers closed gently, yet possessively over the soft yet strong fabric.

"I will honor my vows to you and your people," he replied solemnly, his hand closing possessively over the fine, soft wool.

As her kinsmen listened, she gave the only answer that was possible.

"I have spoken my vows before God. Insofar as I am capable, I will honor them."

What did he sense behind her carefully chosen words?

Sadness? Defiance? Treachery?

A tension of silence expanded in the small chapel. Candle flames quivered at the altar. Father Cadmon shifted uncomfortably.

"Now we will be joined according to the laws of Islam," Tarek said as he took her other hand in his and gently pulled her down to her knees as he also knelt so that they faced one another, rather than the altar where Father Cadmon had given his reluctant blessing to their marriage.

When he unsheathed a small dagger from his belt, Malcolm and a half dozen more Scots warriors suddenly closed in, hands at their swords. Thomas silently appeared to stand behind Brianna.

He did not hesitate even with a dozen Norman warriors surrounding him, but immediately drew his sword and leveled the tip of the blade at Tarek al Sharif's chest. All about them, warriors — Scot and Norman alike — were prepared to draw blood.

"No!" Brianna laid a hand over Thomas' larger one, clasped about the handle of his sword.

"Do not, my friend," she implored Thomas, and with a sideways glance at her husband, she assured the faithful giant, "I think he will not harm me."

Ian stepped between his son and the Norman warriors, laying a restraining hand on Malcolm's sword arm as well.

"Nay, lad," he whispered fiercely. "She is the laird's daughter. She has made her decision. No matter yer feelins' in the matter, ye must honor her decision. Or I will cut ye down meself."

Her stricken gaze fastened on Malcolm, silently pleading.

"Would ye have more bloodshed? Including hers?" Ian tried to reason with his son. "Think, mon!"

Eventually, the tension eased from Malcolm's stance.

72

Thin-lipped, pain and anger glinting in his eyes, he nodded.

"But if he harms her, then I will kill him."

"If he harms her, lad, I will help you kill him." Then he cut a glance to Tarek al Sharif.

"Begin your barbaric ceremony and be done with it."

As tempers eased once more, Tarek began the ancient ritual, far older than Christianity.

There was no holy man to say the ancient words of Islam, so he spoke them himself as he reached over her shoulder and gently seized the thick bold braid of her hair.

In spite of her brave words, when he raised the blade he saw her sudden indrawn breath and the alarm that sprang to her vivid green eyes.

She said nothing, yet he sensed her inner struggle and courage as she forced herself not to flinch from the blade so near her face, but stared back at him, the great drowned pools of her eyes dark and wary.

As he raised the blade, Thomas' blade pressed deeper into the soft leather tunic at his chest. He paid no heed, but with a quick flick of his wrist, sliced at the thick coil of braid that lay like molten silver in his hand.

She flinched visibly but made not a sound. The pulse at her throat beat like that of a startled doe that suddenly confronts the hunter. Then he saw the look of stunned surprise that leapt into her eyes when she darted a quick glance and discovered that it was not the severed braid that lay in his hand, but the simple leather cord that had bound it.

Freed of that restraint, her hair fanned across her shoulders like golden mist. He took her right hand in his.

The contact stunned her. Unlike before when she had clung to his fierce strength, his touch was now gentle, cradling her hand as if she were made of rare glass, his warmth wrapping around her cold, frozen fingers, stunning her with unexpected tenderness.

When he spoke, it was almost intimate, as if only they two were in the chapel and not surrounded by nearly a hundred armed warriors ready to draw blood.

"Among my mother's people when a man and woman wish to be joined, their union is symbolized by a golden chain wrapped about their joined hands."

Confusion knit her delicate brows. She watched with wariness and fascination as he twined the leather cord about their joined hands in a precise, specific pattern as he continued to explain.

"The cord is first crossed in this direction as a symbol of their joined lives," he drew the cord across the back of his hand through the thumb and forefinger, drawing it under and across her hand.

Then he crossed the other end of the cord over the first, twining it between his third and fourth finger, and wrapping it then about her hand and drawing both back over their clasped hands. "This symbolizes their joined hearts."

Next, he brought both ends back over the top of his hand, so that one end was then twined about her wrist, the other about his, once more laying the ends over their clasped hands in a never-ending pattern that always wove back into itself.

"This symbolizes their joined souls. In all ways, Brianna, we shall be as one. One life, one heart, one soul, for all eternity." Then he spoke the words in a language unfamiliar to her.

It was very different from Latin, yet filled with subtle nuances and inflections as his voice caressed each word, like a precious gift he offered her. Then his gaze met hers across their joined hands, bound only by the loosely woven cord, but symbolically binding her to him in ways she could not imagine.

"I do not know the words," she said hesitantly.

"In time, I will teach them to you," he replied, the deep timbre of his voice like the gentle caress around each of the solemn words. "In many ways they are very like the words we have just spoken, binding in any language."

"In all ways, we shall be as one," she haltingly repeated the vows he had spoken in English, sensing with each word that something irrevocable had been set in motion. As though they were being drawn into some great unknown from which they could not now turn back.

As the last words slipped away, he still held her hand in his, bound by that simple leather cord. When she tried to pull her hand from his, she found she could not. He held her hand tightly in his.

"In all ways, Brianna."

Her gaze lifted to his. She felt as if he saw inside her. Then he slowly opened his hand, releasing her with such gentleness and tenderness that she immediately felt the loss of it.

Then a loud commotion was heard from the passage beyond the chapel. The doors which had been closed for the ceremony against any other intrusions were suddenly thrown open.

Robert of Mortain, whom Tarek had left in command of the Norman army encamped outside the gates of Inverness swiftly strode into the chapel.

He carried no weapon, but a wrapped bundle in his arms. Behind him followed young John de Lacey and Sir Guy, Gavin de Marte's brother. They were all loyal knights who had accompanied him to the north country.

Oblivious to the threat from all sides, Mortain approached with ceremony. His expression was fierce, his mouth thinned. As he reached the altar he carefully shifted his burden. As he did so, his stained mantle fell open, exposing the bloodied face of a child.

"Duncan Ross!" Brianna cried out, as she recognized the young boy who lay in the knight's arms, hair matted from a wound that had bled profusely, the side of his face almost unrecognizable for the brutal bruise that spread from jaw to temple and had closed one eye.

"Lay him down," she said urgently, bending over the injured boy as the Norman knight did her bidding.

"Bring warm water and clean cloth," she ordered. Tarek nodded when Stephen glanced over at him and the order was given to his own men. He knelt beside her.

"Do you know this boy?"

"Aye," she answered, cradling the boy's head in the bend of her arm. "He is from the village of Glenross, the landhold of my mother's family."

"Is he your kinsman then?"

She glanced up, and for a moment their gazes met. "Aye."

"How did you find the boy?" Tarek demanded.

"The villagers brought him to the encampment just before dawn," Mortain explained. "He had wandered into the village in the night. He said he must speak with the laird of Inverness."

Young Duncan stirred at the touch of her cool hand at his forehead. His eyes were glassy with the fever that raged through his thin body.

"Mistress Brianna?" he croaked from between painfully parched lips. "I must speak with the laird. Raiders . . . at Glenross." Over the lad's fevered body, her stricken gaze met Malcolm's as he knelt beside the lad.

It seemed the boy did not know what had happened at Inverness. Nor of Cullum's death. But how was that possible? Gillie had returned days ago after the attack. Surely she would have told the villagers, for many were Mirren's own kinsmen.

Malcolm swore fiercely. But it was the new laird of Inverness, by the marriage ceremony only just spoken, who rose swiftly to his feet and moved with the authority of command.

"Tell the men to make ready," Tarek ordered Stephen of Valois.

Brianna looked up as young Duncan slumped into feverish exhaustion. He had spoken very little more. But it was enough.

"It was Mardigan," she said, the words tight in her throat. She thought of Mirren's sister, her cousin Gillie and her family, and so many others of clan Ross who lived in the village.

After the attack at Inverness, Gillie had pleaded with Brianna to return with her. Gillie had never shown her any particular fondness and she had been pleasantly surprised at the woman's concern for her.

The small, remote village was of no strategic importance. Nor was it rich in commerce as were other towns situated closer to frequently traveled byways through the highlands. The villagers were simple people who lived off the land.

Because it was so remote, Brianna was certain it would be safe and so had insisted that Gillie return. But in spite of all Gillie's protestations, she remained behind at Inverness unable to turn her back on the responsibilities to the chieftains and kinsmen at Inverness that now fell to her with Cullum's death.

Fear welled inside her. She felt responsible for what had happened and prayed others had escaped.

"How many warriors were there?" Tarek demanded.

She shook her head, having gleaned little more from Duncan before he slipped into unconsciousness. "At least two score, perhaps more. He could not be certain."

"Were there other survivors?"

She looked at him with great sad eyes that for the first time in spite of everything she'd been through the past twenty-four hours suddenly welled with tears.

"He spoke of no others."

"His wounds do not seem so grievous, Brianna. More exhaustion than anything. He will live."

There was a gentleness of compassion in his voice she had not expected. She frowned slightly as she nodded.

"I will send to the village for the healer."

"I pray she is a good healer. More than this lad will have need of her." Tarek seized his battle sword from one of his knights. It gleamed deadly in the flickering light from the candles at the altar.

"How far is Glenross?" he demanded.

"Two days to the north, across the highland moors," Malcolm replied, for the most part past differences at least temporarily set aside.

"Afoot?"

"Aye," Malcolm responded sharply.

"Then, we will reach it in little more than a day astride," Tarek informed him as he belted the Persian sword at his waist. Then he turned and gave orders to Mortain.

"Half the men are to be ready to ride north immediately. The other half are to remain here."

Mortain frowned. "Do you think it wise to split our strength?"

His response was for Mortain, but his gaze fastened on Brianna. "I think it unwise to leave unguarded the very prize Mardigan seeks."

Then he turned to Malcolm. He did not hesitate, but with the confidence of authority informed him, "My men will need food for the ride north."

For several moments there was only silence as the two men

confronted one another. Then, with taut expression, Malcolm nodded. "As will my own. I will see to it."

"Afoot, you will slow us down," Tarek pointed out bluntly. "If these raiders are to be caught it must be done quickly before they disappear again. Your strength is of better use defending Inverness."

It was a logic that could not be argued. "Then my men will remain at Inverness. But I and a handful of my men will ride with you." Equally logically, Malcolm informed him, "You will need someone to show you the way across the moors or it will not matter whether you are afoot or astride. You will never reach Glenross."

Tarek's gaze narrowed appreciatively. "Make ready to ride immediately."

"I'm going with you," Brianna informed them, coming swiftly to her feet.

"It is too dangerous," Tarek answered with a finality that allowed no further discussion. "You will remain at Inverness."

In this at least Malcolm readily agreed.

"I will not!" she responded fiercely, color returning to blaze across her pale cheeks.

"Glenross was my mother's landhold," she informed him tightly. "The people of the village looked to her for protection. Now that responsibility falls to me. I will not sit idly by, awaiting word when there are those who need my help."

Above all, Tarek understood loyalty. And with pride he realized that hers was a fierce loyalty. He wondered if one day she might feel that same loyalty to him. But he also knew loyalty was something that was earned not taken. And he had yet to earn hers.

Fearing another trap like the one he and his men had ridden into months before, he told Brianna with finality,

"You will stay at Inverness." Then he turned to Ian.

"Sir Guy and a portion of my men shall remain to strengthen your defenses. I leave the protection of Inverness in your hands."

Brianna felt as if she'd suddenly been reduced to the status of chattel, a property owned for the value or advantage it brought, and without a consideration for her feelings in the matter.

She sensed that further argument was pointless. The new laird of Inverness would only refuse as he already had, and Malcolm would back him. At least in this, they were in agreement.

"At least allow Thomas to go with you," she implored, laying a hand at Tarek al Sharif's arm and sending her thoughts to wrap around his so that he might be persuaded.

His head came up, his gaze meeting hers with a sudden connection of thought and emotion so fierce and intense it sliced through the protective shield around her own thoughts like a gleaming blade, then raced along each nerve ending like the white-hot brilliance of lightning across a bleak, winter sky.

As if she'd been burned, Brianna reacted instinctively and tried to jerk her hand away. His hand trapped hers at his arm.

When she tried to free her hand, those long fingers curled over hers, then laced between possessively. When she attempted once more to manipulate his thoughts and force him to release her, she again experienced that sudden, powerful intensity of emotion that burned through her senses.

"Thomas is a strong warrior," she hastily explained, trying to gather her scattered wits and tumbling emotions. "The people of Glenross know and trust him. He can be of help to you."

It seemed she heard someone else's voice, the sound of it

low, breathless, and unfamiliar to her, as if someone else answered. Yet she felt her lips moving and knew the scattered thoughts that guided them were her own.

Surprise turned to speculation in those intense blue eyes. The hard, flat line of his mouth softened. He stared down at their joined hands. Once again, she felt the invasion of *his* thoughts, powerful and intense, and sensed his refusal before he spoke it.

"He will be of more help to me here at Inverness," he explained. "In that way, I may be certain of your safety."

"I will be quite safe, milord," she hastily assured him, again attempting to extricate her hand, and her thoughts. "The people of Glenross will have a greater need of him."

"My decision is final," he replied. "Thomas will remain at Inverness." Then he turned as Stephen of Valois once more appeared at his side.

"All is in readiness," Stephen announced.

Tarek nodded, finally releasing her hand. "Give the order. We leave immediately for Glenross."

Beneath a bleak, churning sky, Brianna stood at the battlement wall as the long column of heavily armed knights and warriors slowly rode out through the gates of Inverness.

Even now as their horses slowly made their way down the muddied cart path toward the village below and the mist shrouded moors to the north, Thomas set out astride Father Cadmon's palfrey.

He knew the highlands better than any man. With God's speed and fair weather, and without the cumbersome armor worn by the Norman knights and warriors to weight him down and tire the palfrey, he would easily reach Glenross hours ahead of the slower moving column. And time was precious.

"What will you do, mistress?" Thomas' thoughts had connected with hers as she handed him medicinals she had obtained from the healer.

"I must help my people," she replied somberly. His large, rough hand closed over hers.

"Be careful, mistress. If Mardigan should find you —"

"He will not!" she answered adamantly, her voice quivering with remembered pain and anger for Cullum and Mirren and all who had died beneath Mardigan's blade.

She sensed Thomas' reluctance to leave, sensed too the objections that moved through his thoughts as clear as spoken words. She closed them out.

"There may still be snow in the northern passes. The way may be difficult." She tied the cloth sack of precious powders and dried herbs across the saddle before him. She laid her hand over his.

"Take no chances," she said softly.

In the connection of her hand at his was the unspoken, that she could not bear his loss too.

"And you, mistress," his thoughts connected with hers.

She nodded and stepped back from the palfrey. "We waste precious time. The people of Glenross need you. Go now."

Thomas was out there too now, though she could not see him. As the column of riders became a dark ribbon in the distance, she knew he traveled a more northerly course that would take him into the high country before nightfall.

Malcolm and the others were forced to follow the highland road that cut through the moors because of their great number of horses. The way was known to all who lived in the highlands but it was long and the way difficult, and would cost precious time. They would be forced to stop and make camp as darkness fell.

But Thomas would continue on through the night, afoot

and leading the palfrey when the beast grew too tired to carry him, and guided by his uncanny way of such things that had also guided him to Inverness all those years ago with an apple-cheeked, golden-haired child in search of a family.

And she would be waiting for him.

Mist purled over the battlement wall. It rolled across the smooth timbers underfoot in a silken, silver wave, swirled softly about her feet and then slowly rose upward.

She felt its cool breath as strange, ancient words, the first she had spoken as a child, whispered deep within her from that place of lost memory and dreams.

Her eyes closed, those strange, ancient words turning her thoughts inward, leading her back through half formed memories and old dreams. She heard the words in her soul, and felt them in her blood. The mist wrapped a silken cocoon about her, closing her deeper within herself until it seemed she had ceased to exist.

Was it only moments, or longer? Time did not exist. Still she heard the keening sound of the wind as it howled across the battlements. Her blood burned through her veins. She was leaving that place of memories and dreams spun within a chrysalis of mist, moving toward that distant point of light.

She was drawn to the light, struggling to reach it. Past the pain that tore through her, past those invisible hands that seemed to clutch at her, trying to hold her back. All of her thoughts focused on the light and the image that formed at the center of that growing, shimmering pool.

Slowly it took form. Sleek, silver body, sharply angled beak, lethal talons, gleaming golden eyes, and powerful wings that unfurled and spread on a powerful breath of wind.

Brianna felt as if she were being torn from her own flesh, the air torn from her lungs. It was as if the moment of her death and birth had become one. Her life was ending and beginning.

The pain was intense. She cried out, fighting to free herself from those invisible, grasping hands of what had been as she reached out to the vision within the light.

Then suddenly she was free. She burst into the light. The mist receded over the wall of the battlements as she felt the rush of the wind.

Transformed, the sleek falcon launched herself from the battlement walls, the wind lifting beneath the spread of her powerful wings. She swept north over craggy peaks of snowbound mountains, while far below, the column of Norman knights and Scot warriors rode for Glenross.

Thick smoke spiraled up from the cook fire where a pig broiled at the spit, fat dripping into the hissing fire. Raiders gathered about the fire, their conversation punctuated by lewd comments, bickering, and snorts of crude laughter.

They made their camp in a forest clearing, surrounded by tall stones. The stones were etched with strange carvings, and the faces of some strange god of the trees, earth, and sky.

About the camp other warriors gathered amid the bounty of their raid — rich thick fleece, clothing, food including pickled eggs, squawking chickens, the roast pig's surviving brother that a warrior chased to the shouts of laughter and encouragement from his companions, precious metal stolen from a smithy's forge, trinkets of pale, shimmering amber, and anything else that could be carried off.

The stolen bounty was all piled high in the center of the camp. Occasionally another warrior wandered through and added to the growing pile, while at the far side of the encampment one warrior sat apart, piercing blue eyes narrowed with anger.

"What news?" he demanded of the warrior who had just returned and now stood before him. "Was Lady Brianna found among those in the village?"

With grave expression, the raider shook his head. "The laird's daughter was not at Glenross," he replied hesitantly.

He was struck, the blow slicing his cheek open to the bone. Blood spilled down his cheek and stained his tunic. He yelped with pain, glaring fiercely at the man who stood over him as he pressed grubby fingers into the wound to stanch the flow of blood.

"I was told she would be there. You will find her!" Mardigan informed the warrior as he paced toward the fire, his stride taut and barely controlled, fists clenched at his sides. Blood gleamed at the cuff of a gold war bracelet that encircled one wrist.

"It grows dark," the raider protested. "My men have not eaten . . ."

As Mardigan suddenly whirled back toward him, the raider retreated to sullen, watchful silence.

"She escaped Inverness. She will not escape again. You will search the countryside until she is found," Mardigan repeated. Then he warned, "Do not return without her!"

As the raider rose and hastily returned to his men, Mardigan wiped blood from the edge of the bracelet. The wild mane of long golden hair framed fierce features. A fierce, cruel expression twisted his lips, framed by an unkempt beard several shades darker. Above the ridge of high cheekbones, eyes as blue as a summer sky glittered with a cold brutality, and uneasiness.

He did not like the forest with its unusual standing stones etched with strange images, and the ghostly faces carved in the trunks of trees with eyes that always seemed to be watching them. He wanted to be gone from this place, to lay his plans for Inverness.

Soon, he thought. Soon he would have what he wanted. Brianna of Inverness could not hide forever. She was proud and high spirited. She would attempt to rally her people to fight him. But he knew the Scots as well, and they would not so easily follow the orders of a woman. With the old laird dead, they would soon fall to fighting among themselves, and that was when he would strike.

A sudden shout was heard across the encampment. One of his men returned, dragging a woman behind him. She struggled and fought in spite of the ropes that bound her hands, vivid curses filling the air as she stumbled, fell, and was hauled back to her feet. She was thrown to the dirt at Mardigan's feet.

She had well-rounded breasts that swelled above the torn neckline of her bodice, a slender waist, and full-curved hips. A comely wench with clear skin and features, she was pleasing to look upon.

But instead of clouds of pale, shimmering gold hair spilling to her waist as he had hoped for, this woman's hair was the color of dark mahogany, and the eyes that looked back at him filled with anger were not brilliant green, but brown.

Her captor seized her by the shoulder and dragged her to her feet. She swore at him as she jerked on the rope that bound her wrists like that of a dog being led to its master.

"Take your hands off me, you filthy pig!" she screamed, spitting at her captor. She was immediately struck with a fisted blow at the side of the head.

Momentarily dazed, Gillie soon recovered and launched herself at her captor, her bound hands clawing wildly as she hurled more curses at him.

"Cease!" Mardigan roared.

The encampment was suddenly silent. Mardigan's furious gaze angled from the woman to the warrior.

"Where did you find her?" he demanded.

"Not far from here," the warrior informed him.

Mardigan's gaze narrowed as it came back to rest on the woman. He nodded thoughtfully, then told the warrior, "Leave us!"

When they were alone, Mardigan slowly circled the captive woman. Her hair was matted with twigs and leaves, an ugly bruise swelled across one cheek. The sleeve of her gown was torn as well as the bodice, revealing pale smooth flesh underneath and exposing the pale ridge of collarbone above those ample breasts that rose and fell rapidly with each sharply inhaled breath. He jerked on the rope that bound her wrists, loosening the knot and freeing her.

"Where is Lady Brianna?"

Indignation mixed with rage in Gillie's dark eyes as she gently rubbed the bruised skin at her wrists. "I told the fool," she said, with a look in the direction of her captor. "She's not at Glenross!"

"She was not found at Inverness. The village is her landhold. She would go there," he replied, certain the woman was lying.

When she did not reply, he seized a handful of her hair. Twisting it about his fist, he brutally jerked her head back at a painful angle.

Gillie cried out, clutching at the thick knot of his fist twisted in her hair. "I have not seen her these past days since the raid at Inverness!" She cried out again as his hand twisted tighter. " 'Tis the truth. I swear it!"

Abruptly he let her go. As he circled round to stand before her once more, Gillie glared at him through the tangle of her disheveled hair as she rubbed the painful place at her scalp where several strands of hair had been yanked out.

He stood wide-legged, a dangerous expression in his sharply angled features. The gold war bracelets at his wrists gleamed in the light from the fire as he reached out and seized the torn fabric of her bodice.

"If you lie . . ." the threat went unspoken but was felt in the air that quivered between them.

" 'Tis no lie!" Gillie replied. "I speak the truth!"

She gasped as he tore open her bodice. A hard, callused hand closed over her bare breast, pinching and bruising the tender flesh. When she shrieked furiously, she was grabbed and dragged up against one of those tall stones like a sacrifice offered up to the ancient gods.

Mardigan pinned her against the stone, his weight smothering her screams and protests. Then he yanked up the hem of her gown. Gillie felt the sudden rush of cold air at her bare thighs, then the sudden, crude thrust of his hand between.

She choked with humiliation and rage. Color blazed vividly across her cheeks as his men gathered round to watch, grunting with laughter and making lewd sounds.

She beat at his head and shoulders, which only brought renewed rounds of laughter and more shouts of encouragement. She bucked and spit at him. If she'd had a blade in her hand she would have cut him. Then he thrust his fingers inside her.

Her body spasmed and clenched at the sudden crude invasion. The air squeezed out of her startled lungs. His shoulders pinned hers as he crudely thrust his fingers into her again, while he yanked at the strings of his breeches with his other hand.

Even though she knew it was futile to fight him, she beat at his back and shoulders as his hard flesh sprang thick and hot against her belly. Then as he thrust inside her, Gillie squeezed her eyes tightly shut. She was no fool.

She blocked out the crude laughter and lewd shouts of his men as she endured what must be endured. When he was finished, he lingered against her for a moment, his breath hot against her neck.

When he recovered, he slowly pushed away from her and adjusted the front of his breeches. With hands that shook slightly, Gillie dragged her skirts down. She could feel him watching her. Did he still think she had lied? But when she looked up, she saw a different expression in his eyes. Crude as it was, taken like an animal in front of his men, she realized that she had pleased him.

One of his men came forward. The expression on his face was unmistakable. Oh God, Gillie thought with a sickening lurch. Was she now to be passed among them?

"Leave off!" Mardigan grunted fiercely to the warrior as he seized her by the arm and dragged her with him. Relief welled inside Gillie as she realized that at least for the time being she was safe from the rest of his men. Then a new thought glimmered and her eyes narrowed thoughtfully.

Horrible as it had been — even now her stomach clenched and convulsed at the stickiness of him between her thighs — she might yet turn this to her advantage.

Five

The village of Glenross was situated at the northern border of Cullum's landhold in a small remote valley.

The surrounding hills sheltered the valley from harsh winter winds and provided grazing for herds of sheep. Timber from the forest that covered the eastern slopes of the valley provided wood. The river provided abundant salmon. To the south, toward Inverness, lay the highland moors.

She knew all of the villagers. Most were kinsmen to Mirren and part of Brianna's adopted family. She had spent many summers here as a child. And it was here she had insisted Gillie return after the attack at Inverness, certain the remote village would be safe.

Shrouded by early morning mist, it looked much as it had each time she had gone there with Mirren. But unlike those other times, no village sounds could be heard in the cold morning air. An ominous silence hung over the once-thriving village, and the bitter cold morning air was filled with the stench of death.

Behind the village, the bloated carcasses of black-faced sheep dotted the gently sloping hillside. They had been cruelly slaughtered as they grazed and left to rot where they fell. The small herd of shaggy highland cattle had suffered the same fate. It was a grotesque sight.

Brianna wrapped her shawl more tightly about her shoulders against the fear that became a cold knot that settled deep inside her as she entered the village.

There were no sounds of mothers calling to their children,

no rhythmic ringing of the smithy's hammer striking iron, no calls of greeting. No smoke from cook fires spiraled above the thatched roofs of huts and cottages.

Yet the smell of smoke was everywhere, along with the stench of death. Crows lined the eaves of the cottages and carrion circled overhead. She covered her face with the hem of her shawl against the sickening smell that choked at her throat as she walked through the village.

The attack had come at night as the villagers sat about the evening meal. That was how she found them. Crudely made doors had been kicked in and torn from leather fastenings. Men had been cut down as they reached for something to defend themselves with. Women had been cut down as they tried to protect their children.

The children had been slaughtered with equal brutality, including babies in their baskets and small toddlers barely able to walk. Young boys had suffered the same fate as the men. Conspicuously absent were the older girls of the village. No doubt they had been carried off and brutalized in ways far worse than death.

Was no one left alive? she thought with aching heart as she went from cottage to hut and found only more death. Was Duncan Ross the only one who had escaped?

She found the body of a young man outside the next cottage. He had met the attackers at the door and briefly fought them back. His head was smashed open, his sightless eyes staring blankly. She recognized him, John Simm, the smithy. Clutched in his hand was a smithy's hammer. It had been of little use against the raiders' war axes.

The smithy's wife, Anne, had been with child the last time she and Mirren had been to Glenross. She should have had the child by now. With images of the dead she had found in the other cottages, Brianna stepped over John's body and

91

pushed open the door of the cottage.

It hung precariously from torn hinges. They gave way and the door, made of leather stretched over a wood frame, made a loud noise as it fell amid debris in the cottage.

An iron cook pot sat over a metal grate at the hearth and finely made metal utensils, including bowls and tankards, were scattered across the floor.

Her heart constricted as she found a baby's basket amid the debris on the floor. But there was no sign of either Anne or the baby. Had she suffered the same fate as the other young women of the village?

Rage mixed with grief as she threw down the tiny basket and turned to leave. A sound stopped her. She slowly turned around. It had come from inside the cottage.

She heard it again. It seemed to come from beneath the floor of the cottage. She dropped to her knees and began clearing away debris. When she'd cleared a place on the wood floor she sat back.

"Fool!" she berated herself with tears in her throat. " 'Tis only your wishful thinking."

Then she heard it again and began furiously scraping back the layers of straw. It was matted in soggy clumps where food and water had spilled. She clawed at it until her nails scraped wood flooring.

Pieces of dried grass filtered down through the openings between uneven hand-hewn boards. She heard the scratching sound again. Then she heard a desperate voice that came from under the wood flooring.

"Help me. Please!"

Looking about, she found a long garden tool with a metal blade. John had made many such tools for the villagers. She wedged the metal blade down through the opening between two boards. Several shifted at once, like a movable panel.

She threw her weight against the handle, leveraging the panel up several inches. Instead of dirt, the darkness of an underground chamber gaped beyond the opening. Then a slender hand appeared and wrapped around the edge of the panel, pushing at it. The meager light in the cottage fell across the terrified features of a young woman.

"Mistress Brianna?" Anne Simm said incredulously.

"Aye," she replied through joyous laughter mixed with tears. "Give me your hand."

But instead, she handed Brianna a small wrapped bundle. Then Anne crawled weakly out of the dark chamber beneath the floor. She blinked against the light that filtered in through the shattered doorway.

Her gown was smudged with filth. Dirt streaked her cheek. She was pale and weak from two days without food or water. But she and her baby were alive.

Brianna held the bundle carefully. It moved, the tiny body stretching and squirming against the layers of heavy wool blanket bound tightly about it. She lifted the edge of the blanket and peered into the blue eyes of John Simm's baby.

It made soft squeaking sounds as its tiny mouth opened and closed like that of a small bird. Blue eyes stared at the sudden light.

"He was born five days ago," Anne said weakly. Then she stared past Brianna, for the first time seeing the destruction she had no doubt heard from below. A small sound, very much like that of her baby, broke from her throat.

Brianna went to her, gently returning the baby to her arms.

"They came after dark," Anne explained as she hugged her baby fiercely against her. "There was no warning." Her gaze wandered about the cottage.

"They struck first at the other end of the village," she recalled. "I could hear the screams of the dying when John reached our cottage. He made me take the baby down there." Her glance angled toward the opening of the chamber. "He built it for storing food through the winter." She picked at the edge of the baby's blanket as her eyes filled with tears.

"Then he dropped that panel into place so they wouldn't find us. I heard them. I listened to all of it from down there. And there was nothing I could do." She lifted stricken eyes to Brianna.

"Do you ken, mistress?" she asked, desperation and tears in her voice. "I had no other choice. I had to protect my baby."

Brianna took Anne and the baby into her arms and hugged them both. "Aye," she said fiercely as tears warmed her cheeks. Then she helped Anne to her feet.

"You can't stay here," she said as she reached for a fleece blanket and wrapped it about Anne's shoulders. A bleak sky thick with clouds was visible through the burned thatch of the roof. It would rain before the day was through, and Malcolm and the others would not reach Glenross until tomorrow at the earliest.

She put an arm around Anne's waist. As they left the cottage, they were forced to step over John's body. Anne knelt beside her husband. She smoothed blood-caked hair back from his shattered forehead and gazed lovingly down at the sightless eyes.

"Ye gave yer life for our son, John Simm," she said with equal measures of pain, grief, and pride. "I'll do right by him. He will carry yer name proudly."

Then she pulled the torn and burned pieces of his fleece vest closed over the broad chest as though to keep out the cold.

"Ye were a fine man, and I'll see you buried proper." Then

she rose and nodded. "We can go now."

Safely hidden the past two days beneath the floor of her cottage, Anne was uncertain if anyone else had survived the attack. But she had heard occasional sounds as she lay there, huddled in the darkness, praying the raiders had not returned.

Amid the ruins of another cottage, they found Duncan's family. His mother, father, and two brothers were dead. An older sister was missing. But beneath the rubble they found one survivor, Duncan's grandfather, Bruce Ross.

He had been struck a terrible blow to the head and then left for dead with the others. He'd lain pinned beneath a caved-in portion of the burned out roof unable to move for two days. He smiled feebly as she and Anne dragged the heavy thatch off his frail body.

"Can you stand?" Brianna asked as she put her arm about his thin waist.

"Aye," he answered fiercely, though his body seemed of a lesser mind as he slumped weakly. "And swing an ax too if them murderin' bastards come back!" Then his old eyes filled with tears and frail old shoulders sagged as he saw the bodies of his son and family. His mouth worked but no words came out. He looked at her helplessly.

"Duncan is safe at Inverness," she told him, uncertain whether he knew the boy had escaped. He blinked and his eyes brightened a bit.

"He's alive?"

"Aye, and brought word of the attack. He's a brave, strong boy."

He nodded. "Like his father." Then he glanced back at his son's body. "Will it never end, mistress?"

"Aye," she answered fiercely. "It will end."

He nodded with that same stoic strength that all highlanders seemed to possess, the same as she had seen in Anne Simm.

"Come along," she told him. "We must find shelter until help arrives from Inverness."

She salvaged what she could from the cottage — warm wools and several loaves of thick-crusted bread. The old man's eyes brightened when he saw Anne and the baby.

"John Simm?" he asked. Anne's tearful silence was his answer.

"Are there any others alive?"

"Some may have escaped to the woods," Brianna answered. "There are still these few cottages." She gestured to the far end of the village. It had suffered the least amount of damage as the raiders seemed to lose their appetite for looting and destruction.

He nodded and put a thin arm about Anne's shoulders. It was difficult to tell who leaned upon whom. "Come along gel," he told her, "I'll take care of ye and yer baby."

Their search revealed only more bodies in the few remaining cottages. But Duncan's grandfather and Anne agreed, many were missing. It helped make their grim task a little easier as they laid blankets over the dead, to know some had no doubt fled to the woods and had not yet returned out of fear of another attack.

As they made their way to the last cottage that had escaped remarkably unscathed, old Bruce drew her attention.

"There!" he motioned with his walking stick beyond the village to the edge of the wood. "Someone is comin'."

Anne instinctively held the baby tighter, her other hand clutching at the old man's arm. Brianna looked toward the trees. Two people slowly made their way down the hill toward the village.

Her heart pounded violently as she pushed Anne and

Duncan's grandfather behind the crumbled wall of a burned out cottage. She was not afraid for herself, but it would be impossible to protect them if the raiders returned.

She pressed the blade Cullum had given her into Anne's hand with simple instructions, "Use it if you have to."

"What about you?"

"If it's raiders, I'll try to draw them away. Flee to the moors. There are a hundred places to hide and likely the raiders won't follow. Then you can make your way to Inverness."

Then she fled to a nearby cottage, giving Anne no further opportunity to protest. As she waited, gaze fastened on the slope of the hill, she reached for a stout piece of wood and clutched it tightly in both hands like a club.

Finally, two women could be seen. One smaller and more slender than the other, no more than a girl. As they drew closer, Brianna recognized them. The young girl was called Nel. Her family had lived in the village. The other was her cousin, Gillie. Brianna put the wood down as she went out to greet them.

At sight of her, Nel cried out and ran to her. She flung her arms about Brianna's waist and began to sob uncontrollably.

"Hush lass," Brianna cooed softly, stroking the girl's hair, her gaze going past to her cousin.

"Thank God you are safe, cousin," she said with heartfelt sincerity.

Gillie looked at her with more than a little surprise. A bruise colored one cheek, but otherwise she seemed to have escaped unscathed.

"What are ye doin' here?" Gillie asked.

Brianna smiled. Gillie hardly seemed glad to see her, but then there was very little that pleased Gillie.

"Duncan Ross brought word of the attack," she explained.

She carefully omitted any mention that it had only been that morning he had arrived at Inverness. It would have been difficult to explain how she had covered the distance between, that usually took others at least two days afoot to cross the moor, in less than an hour.

"Are you the only one then from Inverness?" Gillie asked.

"There will be others here shortly."

Gillie saw Anne and Duncan's grandfather as they emerged from their hiding place. "Did others survive?"

"Many are missing. I'm hoping they escaped to the woods as the two of you did."

"I didna escape," Nel stuttered through her tears. "There was no time."

There was no need for the girl to say more. The look in her eyes was like that of a wounded animal. Her face and arms were covered with bruises. Brianna had little doubt what else the girl had suffered.

"How did you get away, lass?" she asked gently.

"They gave me some time to meself near a stream . . ." she hiccuped loudly. "To clean meself after they finished with me." She shuddered in Brianna's arms, laying her head against her shoulder like a child that has skinned her knee. But it was not a skinned knee that caused her tears. Young Nel had suffered far more.

"When they weren't looking, I ran. I kept runnin' til I couldna run no more." She shivered again. "Gillie escaped as well."

Brianna looked at her cousin. "Oh, Gillie . . ."

"None of this would have happened if you hadn't made me come back to Glenross," Gillie protested.

"I thought it was the safest place for you," Brianna replied more than a little stunned.

"No place is safe with them about." Then she glanced

across the village in the direction of her own cottage.

"Have you seen Rabbie," she asked with casual disinterest.

Cullum had arranged the match for the daughter of Mirren's sister. Rabbie McNair was a good deal older than Gillie and a man of some means. He provided well for Gillie. A good number of the sheep she had seen slaughtered had been his.

Gillie had been unhappy from the beginning. It was hoped that a child might change her feelings toward her husband and marriage. But there had been no children.

"He's dead," Brianna said as gently as possible for she had found Gillie's husband inside their cottage.

"Och, well I suppose that's no surprise," Gillie said with a shrug. "He was not a verra brave man."

Brianna felt a ripple of anger at Gillie's lack of compassion for her dead husband. No matter their difficulties, Rabbie had been a good man. It was not his fault that he was not the laird of some rich landhold or that he couldn't fight off two score fiercely armed raiders single-handed.

Brianna wrapped her arm around Nel's shoulders. "Come along, we must find shelter for the night. Anne is exhausted and the baby needs warmth and food."

"Yer not goin' there?" Gillie protested as she saw the direction they took, toward the thatch and wattle hut set apart from the village.

"It has solid walls and a roof," Brianna pointed out. "We can't spend the night in the open."

"But the hag lives there. She's a conjuror. I don't trust her."

"My John repaired her roof the summer past," Anne said with surprising strength in her voice. "I don't care if she's turned herself into a troll if it's warm inside and there's a stout door that can be barred across."

Gillie glared at the young woman, but Anne and Duncan's grandfather already made their way to the isolated cottage with strange figures carved into the wood framing the doorway.

"I don't want to go," Nel said softly.

"There's nothing to fear, lass," Brianna assured her. "You have my word on it."

"Ye will need far more than yer word to protect ye if the old crone conjures a spell on the lot of ye," Gillie warned.

Brianna glared at her, unable to understand her peevish mood when she should be glad to be alive. But then Mirren always said that Gillie had been born ill-tempered about almost everything.

"You are free to go where you will, Gillie, but welcome to come with us."

The other cottages were either burned to ruins or littered with the bodies of the dead villagers. The sky was ominous overhead with the storm that had threatened all morning, and more than anything Gillie hated discomfort. Brianna could not imagine how she had escaped and made her way back through the woods.

Just as she knew she would, Gillie followed them to old Drusilla's cottage, grumbling dire imprecations all the way.

At the door Duncan's grandfather called out, "Open up, old woman, if yer there. Otherwise, we'll appreciate the warmth of yer hearth and thank ye for it when we see ye."

It was a common highland greeting usually given when one came upon an isolated farm or shepherd's hut and sought shelter for the night. No one was ever turned away, and those seeking shelter always left something of value in exchange for the hospitality they received.

At first there was no response. Then, finally, the door

opened a narrow wedge and round dark eyes looked out from a wrinkled old face.

"Away with ye!" the old woman told them.

"We cannot," Brianna told her. "It is cold and we need shelter or the baby will not survive."

"Baby?" The door opened a notch further.

"Aye, John Simm's baby and his wife as well," Brianna informed her, ready to break the door down if the old woman resisted.

"John Simm mended my roof summer last."

"His wife and child need shelter, and the rest as well."

The door opened wider. "A decent man, John Simm," the old woman said. "Come in."

As they stepped inside the old woman exclaimed pointing at Brianna, "Yer the laird's daughter." She glanced past them through the doorway. "Are there no others with ye?"

"They will follow in the morning from Inverness."

As her guests entered the cottage, Drusilla snorted. "Now they need me for more than their boils and fevers!"

"Cease, old woman," Bruce Ross ordered, waving his walking stick at her. "The baby needs dry cloths and Anne is in bad need of food or there will be no milk for the child."

"Jes wait till ye've a boil on yer arse!" she grumbled as she went about preparing something for them to eat.

They ate a meager broth with the bread Brianna had found. The baby soon suckled contentedly at Anne's breast oblivious that so many had died including his own father.

Young Nel tried to eat but her lips were badly swollen and bruised. Brianna cradled the girl in her lap as she fell into exhausted sleep.

Tears streamed Brianna's cheeks as she held her in her arms and gently rocked her, connecting with the girl's anguished thoughts as they became a nightmare of dreams.

She stole the memories of what had happened during the attack, and then afterward when the raiders carried Nel away. She took away the girl's anguish and pain, leaving behind a void where the girl would remember nothing.

But when Brianna took Nel's memories of that night and everything that followed, they became part of her own thoughts, a separate memory that would live inside her forever. And within those horrible terrifying images was a face she recognized and would never forget — Mardigan.

As the girl slept, Brianna bandaged the wound at old Bruce's head. In spite of his stubbornness, he was frail and weak. It was a miracle he had survived.

Late in the day, with watchful glances toward the woods, she gathered firewood from nearby cottages certain the former inhabitants wouldn't begrudge them the warmth. She asked Gillie to bring fresh water from the river.

"Ye don't know who might be there," Gillie protested.

Her patience thin, Brianna replied sharply, "In that cottage is an old woman, a weak old man, a half-starved woman and her baby, and a terrified child. And not a weapon among us. Do you really think it would matter if there was?"

Gillie glared at her. "I've suffered too. Me gown is torn, I've bruises everywhere, and a worthless, dead husband."

"You might have a care for your dead husband, Gillie," Brianna pointed out. "By the looks, he died trying to defend you. Yet, you somehow managed to escape."

"And you would rather I died?"

"I didna say that!"

"There's no need of it. I know how ye have always felt toward me. The mistress of Inverness ye be now. And ye aren't even Cullum's true daughter! He who couldn't even see fit to provide for my mother's family after he wed her younger sister."

Brianna was too weary to argue with her. She seized the bucket herself and trudged off toward the river. When she returned to the cottage Gillie was not there. She might have been worried about her if she didn't know her so well. Gillie would return when she got cold or hungry.

She returned late and with a vaguely grumbled excuse that she had gone to look for some of her things among the ruins of her burned out cottage. She seized a hunk of bread, soaked it in the broth and then curled up sullenly in a corner, wrapping herself in a fine woolen mantle.

The next morning, Brianna and old Bruce went about the gruesome task of tending the dead as best they could while Drusilla watched over Anne and the baby, and Nel. She sent Gillie to the other cottages to look for food rather than listen to her continual grumbling.

She and Bruce worked silently together, the old man determined to help care for his kinsmen and friends. They covered the dead with remnants of fleece blankets and fur hides that had not burned.

Nel joined them at midday. Without the memories of her ordeal to plague her, color had returned to the girl's cheeks. She was confused, but Brianna reassured her that it was perfectly normal after everything that had happened.

"The girl's gone simple-minded," Gillie remarked.

"She'll be fine when the bruises heal," Brianna replied after she sent the girl to the river to wash pieces of cloth needed for the baby.

"And what will you tell her when her belly swells with a child?"

"There is no certainty that will happen, but if it should then both she and the baby will be cared for at Inverness. If she has forgotten what she suffered, then all the better."

"She would be better off if she remembered," Gillie said

sulkily. "Then she would be well warned about men."

"There is no need for her to remember. In time, when she is ready she will wed a good man."

"And will the mistress of Inverness wed a good man?" Gillie asked, her mood no better than the previous evening. "Malcolm perhaps? 'Tis well known how he feels about you. Now, there is a fine, brawny man," she added appreciatively.

Brianna shook her head but offered no explanations. She preferred not to think about the events of the past two days. Soon enough she would have to face them.

"He willna wait forever, ye ken?" Gillie commented. "Perhaps he's already found himself a willin' maid. What do ye say to that?"

"Take yerself off, woman!" old Bruce told her. " 'Tis bad enough we have the crows pickin' at the dead."

Gillie glared at him, then turned toward the cottage. Brianna pitied Anne, but she felt certain old Drusilla could protect them both against Gillie's foul temper.

"Aye," Duncan's grandfather said as he watched her stalk away. "Poor old Rabbie is a happier man dead than alive."

His ruminations about Gillie were cut short as they heard a terrified scream that came from the river.

"Nel!" She ran for the river.

The girl ran toward her, eyes wide with fear. "Someone's comin'."

Brianna followed the girl's terrified gaze across the river. A large man crossed the water upstream, his long legs carrying him easily through shallow pools that had not yet filled with the runoff of winter snow.

He was a giant of a man, wrapped in heavy furs, his great shaggy head covered with a fur cap, hair and animal fur blending and giving the appearance of some great hairy lumbering beast. In one hand he carried a deadly spear the size of a tree limb with a fierce spike at the end. In the other, he carried a seax.

"It's all right," Brianna assured the girl, laughing with relief. "He's a friend." She went to meet Thomas.

He folded her into his strong arms and hugged her fiercely. Then he held her apart, his gaze going every part of her. She saw relief, concern, and traces of anger in his dark eyes as her thoughts joined with his and she assured him that she was well and safe.

"There were only a few survivors," she said, emotion quivering in her voice as they walked together toward the village. "There may be more in the forest. They spared no one — women, children, babies."

"Aye, lass." he acknowledged. Then he asked, *"What of Malcolm, and the Norman warriors?"*

"They have not arrived yet."

"How will you explain to your husband that you reached the village first?"

"I will tell him that I came through the mountains by way of a little known pass."

"And what will you tell him of this marriage?"

There had been no time to speak of it in the confusion after Duncan Ross arrived at Inverness.

"I can never be wife to him," she said. " 'Tis impossible and you know it. I will honor the alliance, and pray that he is a fair man." Then she turned and walked ahead, back to their grim task and away from his questions for which there were no easy answers.

They worked through the afternoon. Thomas' great physical strength and endurance made the grim task go more quickly.

Gillie was conspicuous by her absence while they worked, and then equally conspicuous by her complaining when she returned. Finally late in the afternoon and weary of her complaints, Thomas abruptly threw down his spade and seized Gillie by the arm.

He lifted her clear of the ground, her toes brushing the sod as she swung her legs frantically for a foothold. Ignoring her screeches and the wild flailing of her arms as she beat at him, Thomas strode down to the edge of the river and tossed her in.

A smile spread across old Bruce's face. "Wish I'd thought of that."

The afternoon light had begun to fade as they returned to Drusilla's cottage. Gillie had returned earlier and wrapped herself in a blanket while her clothes dried. She gave Thomas a sullen look and stomped back into the cottage.

Thomas secured the seax at his belt and shouldered a bow found in the village. He set off to the woods to hunt. What little food she had found in the village was quickly gone, and apparently Drusilla had survived on the kindness of those like Anne who saw to it that she had an occasional fowl for her stewing pot.

"Take care, my friend," she frowned with concern as she laid a hand at his arm. He nodded and set off for the woods at a brisk run.

Their water was almost gone. Brianna seized a bucket and set off for the river.

In the growing darkness, she stumbled over the carcass of a dead ewe at the water's edge. Mindful of fouled water, she moved upstream with a thought to remind Thomas of the dead animal in the morning.

She walked out on rocks rimmed with traces of snow. At the edge of the rocks where the water ran more swiftly, she dipped the bucket.

She sensed them before she saw them. A dangerous presence that brought her head up with alarm. Then, in the gathering darkness as the sun set at the edge of the frozen sky, she saw the fiery glow of torches that swarmed through the village.

Panic set in. Malcolm and the Norman soldiers couldn't possibly reach Glenross until tomorrow. That could only mean one thing — Mardigan and his men had returned.

The bucket fell from her fingers and swirled away in the water. She slipped on the slick rocks as she quickly retreated back to the shore. At the water's edge the slushy mud caught at her slipper. She pulled free and lunged up the embankment.

She skirted the village, running from one burned out cottage to the next, panic throbbing through her veins as she thought of Anne and the baby, Nel, Gillie, and old Drusilla, helpless with only Duncan's grandfather to protect them.

She sent her thoughts to Thomas, but there was no response. Had he too seen those torches? Had something happened to him? Why didn't he answer?

The dirk Cullum had given her was clenched tight in her fist as she ran to the end of the village. Then she left the protection of Anne Simm's cottage and ran toward the small cottage nestled in the trees at the edge of the village.

She sensed the warrior's presence in those brief, fleeting moments before he grabbed her. Powerful arms closed around her, pinning her arms at her sides. She lashed out with her feet and tried to twist free as she was swung clear of the ground.

Then that strong arm suddenly shifted higher beneath her ribs, pressing brutally against her lungs, squeezing until she couldn't breathe. She heard vague, foreign-sounding words as the light of those torches wavered and swam in her blurred vision.

She went limp in her captor's arms. She immediately felt his grasp about her loosen. Slick as an eel, she slipped from his grasp and dropped to hands and knees at the ground. As a hand closed over her shoulder, she drove her elbow back hard. She connected somewhere near her attacker's midsection. His breath went out in a loud, painful sound followed by a harsh, guttural curse.

Dragging lungfuls of crisp, cold air into her smothered lungs, Brianna launched herself back to her feet and would have escaped if not for the hand that closed around her hair.

Swearing profusely, her captor hauled her up under one arm like a goose trussed for market. Her hair fell over her face in a thick tangle that blinded and smothered her. She struggled and fought as the warrior rose unsteadily to his feet. Then she was carried back through the village, back through that blur of torches.

Then he halted and Brianna was suddenly released. She fell to the ground in a tangle of skirts, twisted shawl, and disheveled hair.

Light from the torches gleamed at the slender, deadly blade clutched in her hand, and the tangled torrent of shimmering gold hair that spilled around her shoulders.

Her breasts rose and fell rapidly beneath the soft wool gown. Patches of color burned across her cheeks, and her eyes were the color of brilliant emeralds.

Tarek al Sharif stared with growing anger at his fierce, beautiful wife.

Six

"What are you doing here?" Tarek demanded.

Stephen of Valois grimaced as he doubled over with pain from the blow Brianna had landed with amazing and crippling accuracy.

"What King Harold could not at the battle of Hastings," he struggled to stand upright, an expression of torture on his pale face, as he spoke through clenched teeth, "laying waste to the Norman army."

Norman warriors gathered all about them. The light from their torches played across Tarek al Sharif's cold features.

Brianna was stunned as she recognized the Norman warriors. One thought tumbled over another along with a tumult of emotions — sudden, enormous relief that it was not Mardigan and his raiders that had returned to Glenross, then uncertainty followed by growing apprehension as she confronted the man who was now her husband.

He grabbed her by the wrist, fingers clamping over slender bones. Her fingers went numb. The blade fell to the ground at her feet. All about them Norman knights and warriors stared with surprise and the same unspoken question.

She had no doubt that he could have easily snapped the bones in her wrist. She felt it in the bruising tension of that powerful hand, saw it in the narrowing of his eyes. She had made a grave miscalculation in thinking that he would be easily persuaded that she had merely taken another route to reach the village.

"Or perhaps," he suggested, "a better question might be *how* you got here?"

His warriors and knights surrounded her with expectant silence as they too waited for her answer, their battle swords gleaming in the light of the torches. Their expressions were fierce and filled with suspicion. They trusted her no more than she trusted them. She had made an alliance, but she had perhaps also made a pact with the devil.

"Brianna?"

Her gaze snapped around at the sound of a familiar voice.

"What are ye doin' here, lass?"

Malcolm pushed his way through the Norman warriors who had gathered about her. Relief poured through her at the sight of a friendly face.

"I had to help my kinsmen," she hurriedly explained, with a pleading look in her eyes as she turned to her friend.

"But how, lass . . . ?"

"That is something I would also like to know."

She ignored Tarek al Sharif as she explained to Malcolm, her thoughts reaching out to his in silent plea.

"I came by way of the old shepherd's pass through the mountains," she replied, willing him not to give her away.

"I was not at all certain I could find it again, but I had to try. You do understand?" She saw the confusion in Malcolm's eyes. Then it was gone.

"Aye," he slowly answered, then added, "But you should not have come alone."

"I did not," she replied, still not meeting Tarek al Sharif's gaze, afraid that he would see the lie. "Thomas is here as well."

Then, a terrified scream shattered the silence. It came from the edge of the village. Tarek al Sharif and his men drew their weapons.

"Nel!" Brianna replied.

"There are others?" Tarek demanded.

She nodded. "A handful who survived. They've taken refuge in a cottage at the edge of the village."

"Stay here," he told her, as he turned to give orders to his men.

"I will not!"

Before he could stop her, Brianna pushed her way through his men and was running back through the village.

When she reached the cottage, she discovered the door shattered and a half dozen Norman warriors standing in the doorway. Nel was screaming hysterically. Startled awake, the baby had begun to wail. Brianna clawed her way through the heavily armed warriors to reach those inside.

"Do not harm them!"

Old Bruce defiantly confronted the warriors with an ax clutched in frail hands. Anne stood just behind him, arms trembling as she raised a heavy sword. Drusilla huddled in the far corner, protectively clutching the baby against her while Nel burrowed at her shoulder like a frightened animal. Gillie crouched in the shadows by the hearth.

"All is well!" she told old Bruce, trying to restrain him. "They are from Inverness!" But he refused to lower the battle-ax.

"They are not Scots warriors!" he replied with surprising ferocity.

"No," she admitted. "But allies with a common cause." She was more insistent this time as she tugged at his arm.

"They come to give help, and protection against Mardigan."

He looked warily at the fierce warriors, some wearing chain mail armor. A new light filled his old eyes, along with growing bewilderment.

"They are Norman warriors!"

"Aye, they join our fight against Mardigan. Please, put down your weapons."

Near the hearth, Gillie slowly emerged from the shadows. "Put down that ax, you old fool," she snapped. "That rusty blade would be of little use against their battle swords."

He finally lowered the ax. But his narrowed gaze remained fastened on the warriors.

Tarek finally reached the cottage and his men stepped aside as he entered. In a sweeping glance Tarek took in the survivors of Glenross. Malcolm entered just behind. His gaze immediately found Brianna.

The survivors were a pathetic lot; the defiant old man, the gaunt young woman with dark circles beneath her eyes, a shriveled old crone, a baby, a weeping girl, and the young woman with calculating eyes who stared back at him and his men with undisguised curiosity rather than fear.

"Are there others?" Tarek asked.

"Those you see are the only ones found alive," Brianna answered solemnly.

For a moment their gazes connected, his startlingly blue amid strong, sharp features, hers filled with shadows of the death and atrocities she'd found in the village.

Lowering her own weapon, Anne went to Nel, cradling the girl and crooning to her, trying to ease her fears.

"Please leave," Brianna implored him. "The girl has been through a great deal. Your men frighten her."

Her slender hands were balled into tight fists. She wanted to throw them all out and bar the door. But she could not. For she had made an alliance, and this man was now her husband. She shivered at the thought and wondered again if she had made a worse bargain than the one Mardigan offered.

She did not know. She knew only that the man who now

112

stood in the cottage with his men surrounding the village was no fool, nor was he a man to be bargained with lightly. He had already proven that in the marriage he had insisted upon to bind the alliance.

She sent her thoughts to him, uncertain if he heard them for this man was not like others. She sensed no response, no whisperings that might have revealed his thoughts. Yet, eventually he nodded and quietly ordered his men from the cottage.

"See that these people have whatever they need," he told Sir Gavin. "And have the healer we brought from Inverness sent to the cottage. She may have something to calm the girl."

Brianna let out a sigh of relief as his men turned to leave. But when she tried to move past him to help Drusilla with the baby, he stopped her.

"You will please come with me."

"They are my kinsmen. I will not leave them."

"I have need of you in the village."

"The girl will need a woman's kindness to ease her fears," she protested and then explained what should have been obvious for him to see. "There is more harm than the bruises you see, and Anne has more than she can handle with the baby to care for."

He glanced across at Gillie, and told her, "You will tend to the girl. If there is anything else you need, inform my men."

When Brianna would have protested further, he told her softly, "There are worse things to endure. The girl is alive and if she possesses even half the courage and strength I have seen in your other kinsmen she will recover and be strong again."

She had not expected his kindness. It caught her off guard. "They know and trust me," she argued. "Surely you can understand that having armed warriors about will only frighten the girl."

"I would not have any of them unnecessarily frightened any more than they already have been," he told her. He glanced past her to the survivors of Glenross, crowded into the small cottage with only a feeble old man and a sickly woman recently from her birthing bed to protect them. Then he turned to Malcolm, who stood protectively at Brianna's side.

"They know and trust you," Tarek told him. "I place their safety and care in your hands. See that they have whatever they need and give whatever orders you deem necessary for their protection." Then he turned to Brianna.

"Surely you have no objection."

She stared at him in amazement. There was none she could give and well he knew it. She replied stiffly, "Of course not."

It was Malcolm who started to protest, but she cut him off for she sensed that to protest further would only cause more strain in an already difficult situation. And she needed time to consider this unexpected side to the man with whom she had made such a dangerous and precarious alliance.

"Please take care of them until I return," she implored Malcolm. She saw anger immediately leap to his eyes. The muscle at his jaw quivered beneath the beard-roughened skin, his lips drawn into a hard, taut line. She sensed what he wanted to say. But finally, with a cold glance at Tarek al Sharif, he nodded his reluctant agreement.

"Aye, Brianna. I will do as you ask. But only because *you* ask it."

Then she felt Tarek's hand at her elbow. She was anchored to his side by his hand closed tightly over her arm as he led her from the cottage.

Light from dozens of torches glowed throughout the village as his men surrounded and swarmed through it. It spread

114

across the broken walls of cottages and huts, mingling with eerie shadows as if hundreds of fiery creatures stole through the village.

A bonfire had been built in front of Anne Simm's cottage. Flames spiraled up through the rubble of debris that had been piled high, and played across Tarek al Sharif's features.

They were strong, hard features that could be stunningly handsome as when they had stood together in the chapel at Inverness and spoken the marriage vows. But now, fleetingly, she again glimpsed the terrifying creature of her dreams. Lean, powerful, sharply angled features were made sharper still by the play of light and shadow, and the intense expression in startling blue eyes.

As in her dreams, she had the sensation of being stalked and a sudden wildness of fear entwined with other emotions she'd never experienced before.

Her throat was tight and her mouth dry. She tasted the fear at the back of her throat along with those other emotions as clearly as if she now stood on the battlements. She closed her thoughts to other images from those dreams — the painful ache of some unknown longing, and the fierce physical joining as the creature had leapt upon her.

She pulled up sharply and demanded, "What do you want of me when you have an army of knights and warriors to do your bidding? Surely there is little that I can do."

"There is a great deal that only you can do," he replied, as his hand loosened about her arm. But he did not free her. Instead, his fingers slipped down her arm to her wrist, closing around it with a warm possessive strength, the same as when they had stood before the priest in the chapel at Inverness and he had claimed her as his wife.

"Glenross is the village of your kinsmen," he explained, his fingers lightly stroking her wrist. "By your own words you know it well. Well enough," he reminded her, "to arrive by way of a little known mountain pass."

His blue eyes glittered with something that she might almost have believed was humor. And she had the growing suspicion she had not fooled him at all with her lie.

"Aye," she answered carefully.

"You have considerable knowledge of the village, and the surrounding countryside," he went on, holding her wrist gently imprisoned in one hand, while he traced the patchwork of veins beneath her skin with the fingers of his other hand.

"I have need of that knowledge if we are to protect the village against another attack."

It was a logic she could not argue. Her wariness eased gradually, although she was aware Malcolm could just as easily have given him the information he needed.

"I will help in whatever way I can."

He stepped to one side, and drew her closer to the fire. "It grows colder." His expression changed as she saw a faint glimmer of humor in those unusual blue eyes. "Your highlanders are indeed hearty warriors if they can survive such cold with only their wools wrapped about them."

She had no intention delaying long enough to warm herself by the fire. But she could see that in this too, she had little choice.

"You would do well to remember that," she replied. "Highlanders are not weak, mewling maids. They will hold their own beside your knights and warriors."

Several of his men joined them about the bonfire, including Stephen of Valois. He looked at her warily after their previous encounter and moved several paces away.

"I hope you will not suffer any lingering injury," Brianna offered as apology, fully aware of the vulnerable place she had struck him. " 'Tis only that your men surprised me. I thought Mardigan had returned."

He snorted. "I hope the same." Then he added with wry appreciation, "I think you misjudge your ability to handle Mardigan and his men. If that blow is any indication, I think you could reduce them all to mewling maids. Upon my return to London I will have my battle armor improved to cover certain vulnerable areas."

Her cheeks warmed with embarrassment. "Do not misjudge Mardigan. He is ruthless and without mercy." Then she turned and listened intently as Tarek spoke with his men.

All about them warriors swarmed through the village. Other bonfires were lit before the remains of other cottages and in a perimeter about the village, like flame colored jewels of a necklace. At a glance it seemed as if William the Conqueror's entire army protected Glenross.

Then, from across the village there were suddenly shouts that drew everyone's attention. Several warriors approached, dragging a man. He fought and struggled fiercely. It was Thomas.

She did not need to connect her thoughts to his to know what had happened. No doubt he had seen the torches from the forest and, fearing as she had that Mardigan might have attacked again, he had quickly returned.

Brianna saw the flash of a blade in one warrior's hand, a club raised by another. As others closed in, she connected her thoughts to theirs, replacing their thoughts with numbing confusion as she ran to Thomas.

He looked up as she reached him, his bloodied gaze meeting hers in silent communication.

"Cease!" Tarek ordered as he recognized the man they held prisoner. He pushed his way through them, gently pulling Brianna away.

"Can you stand?" he asked Thomas, who had been thrown to the ground by his captors. Thomas looked back at him blankly.

"Do not play simple-minded," Tarek warned. "I know you understand far more than you let on. Can you stand?"

Thomas glanced at Brianna, then nodded.

"Release him," Tarek ordered. "He is friend to the old laird of Inverness."

When Thomas once more stood on his own feet he then asked, "Are you injured?" Thomas slowly shook his head in answer.

"Good, I have need of every able-bodied man." When the mute giant looked at him with a mixture of wariness and suspicion he explained, "My men will need your help in setting up defenses for the village."

Thomas' gaze connected with hers, his silent question then connecting with her thoughts. She nodded as she assured him, *"Do as he asks."*

Satisfied by her silent words, Thomas nodded his agreement. He joined Tarek and his men about the bonfire as plans for the protection of the village were made. With a stick, Brianna sketched the village in the mud. She outlined the perimeter of the village, then sketched the village itself recalling every cottage, hut, and distinctive landmark.

"Mardigan and his men attacked from the forest," she explained what Anne had told her. "Because Duncan's family lives at the opposite end of the village not far from Drusilla's he was able to escape across the moors toward Inverness."

"Which direction did Mardigan and his men flee afterward?" Tarek asked.

"Gillie and Nel were abducted as they fled into the forest. They escaped and made their way back to the village."

"Then they did not leave by way of a little-known mountain pass?" Tarek suggested, his blue gaze taunting as it met hers, a cunning smile lifting one corner of his mouth.

"No," she calmly replied, even though her blood pounded wildly through her veins. He did not believe her for a minute.

For several moments his gaze remained fastened on hers. Eventually he looked back down at the crude map she had made in the thick mud and studied it, a frown replacing that brief smile.

He nodded and gave his orders to his men to set up fortifications about the village in all directions. Though reluctantly, Thomas went with them.

When they had gone, Tarek turned to her. "What lies across the river?"

"A small valley. The villagers graze their herds there in the summer."

"Might Mardigan and his men have gone there?"

She was startled that he would ask her. She shook her head. "There is no way out of the valley except across the eastern rim of the mountains. And with winter still hard upon the high country he would be a fool to attempt to cross them."

"What of the moors?"

Again, she shook her head. "Mardigan and his men are very superstitious. They believe the moors are haunted. They would not go there."

He looked over at her, that amused expression returning. "The moors are haunted?"

"Aye," she answered quite seriously. " 'Tis said they are haunted by the spirits of dead warriors, that their voices can be heard on the wind."

A jet black brow angled sharply over one eye. "Do you believe they are haunted?"

"It does not matter whether I believe it," she replied. "The highlands can be a forbidding place. Many have lost their way and told stories of voices that guided them to safety. But a man might never find his way across or back, unless he knows them with the blood of a highlander."

"The blood of a highlander?" he asked doubtfully, the smile reaching those blue eyes.

"Aye," she replied, certain that he mocked her. " 'Tis said that every mountain, rock, river, and valley is known to all Scots even if they've never set foot upon them. So deeply are we bound to the land by the blood of those who have gone before. Do ye ken what I say?"

Her words thickened with the odd sounds of the highland dialect. The sound of her voice was like warm, golden honey.

"Ken?" he repeated the strange sounding word.

"Do you *know* what I speak of?" she repeated with growing exasperation. "It's something you feel in your bones. An instinct of the way of things."

"Ah," he said with understanding, trying to suppress his own smile for he enjoyed the sound of her voice and laughter far too much to divulge he had known what she meant all along.

"I know well what you mean for I carry the memory of my home in my blood as well."

She frowned slightly for she had not considered that a warrior who fought beside William the Conqueror across several empires called any place home outside of the conquered battlefield he fought on.

"Is your home far from here?" she asked with undisguised curiosity for she had heard stories of the middle empires from distant kinsmen of Cullum's who had traveled there.

"Very far," Tarek replied with a betrayal of longing he had not intended. "It is a land of pale pink sand, sultry night wind, golden temples, and a brilliant blue ocean," his voice warmed as he thought of it, a place of memory and dreams that burned through his blood.

The words created images in her mind that she could only compare to that which she knew, and fell far short. For the winds that blew across the highlands chilled to the bone even in summer. The North Sea was cold, gray, and forbidding, a place of fierce storms, and even fiercer enemies beyond in distant lands. There were no golden stone temples in the highlands, only wood and rock fortresses, and thatched and wattle cottages. And she had no comparison for pink sand.

"It is difficult to imagine such a place," she said, gathering her shawl more tightly about her shoulders against the cold that set in as the fire burned low.

He stirred the fire with a stick, adding more pieces of wood as he spoke. "The sea is the color of sapphires and emeralds, in shades of blue and green."

Having placed several pieces of wood on the fire, he rose and slowly walked toward her.

"The stone in the temples and the walls that surround Antioch are as white and smooth as polished marble. So bright they are almost painful to look at."

She forced down the natural instinct to retreat as he slowly drew closer, refusing to reveal any outward sign of fear even as her heart pounded wildly.

He halted no more than inches away. Though he blocked the warmth of the fire, he seemed to radiate heat. His voice was low and silken with a warmth of memory wrapped around each word.

"The sand is the color of the sky just before the sun has slipped below the horizon and its light bathes the faces of the clouds."

He reached out and smoothed back stray tendrils of golden hair that had come loose from the braid and framed her face. His fingers lightly brushed her cheek.

"And the wind is like the caress of a lover's hand. Once felt, it is never forgotten."

Her eyes were soft drowned pools of liquid green, her lips parted on a sudden, startled breath.

Then, somewhere across the encampment, came the loud, fierce sound of a warrior's cry. Other shouts were heard as warriors poured out of ruined cottages and awakened those about other bonfires. Through the din and confusion, she heard a harsh guttural curse, and an explosive threat.

"Take your hands off her, ye bloody barbarian!"

Brianna's dulled senses slowly cleared as she recognized Malcolm's voice.

He and the other warriors had returned from Drusilla's cottage. His expression was furious as he charged across the village with drawn sword.

"Malcolm! No!" she gasped as she sensed his thoughts and deadly intentions. Ignoring the danger to herself, she ran to him. Behind her, she heard the sound of another blade being drawn. The sound of that deadly steel made the blood go cold in her veins.

Malcolm swore savagely as he pushed past her toward the man who waited with deadly calm beside that bonfire.

"Aye," he hissed. "Draw your blade, barbarian. Let us be done with this! For I will not let you touch her again!"

Brianna ran after him. She grabbed at his sword arm and pulled him around.

"Leave us, Brianna!" he told her. "This is between him and me."

"Nay!" she said fiercely. " 'Tis between you and me, and I say you will not do this. I forbid it!"

"I will kill him for touching you."

"It is naught for you to say, Malcolm. 'Tis my choice. And

if you would kill him and risk bringing war down on my kinsmen, then you must kill me first!" she blocked his way though he was easily twice her size.

"You do not know what you say, lass."

"I know exactly what I say!" she answered fiercely. "I am the laird of Inverness. I have given my word before the council of chieftains! And there is naught you can say about it, Malcolm of Drummond, that will change it!"

"Ye were forced to it!" he replied, his gaze fastened on the man who stood behind her. "There is no man in the highlands that would hold ye to it."

"Aye!" she readily agreed, her fingers digging into his arm, refusing to let go. "Forced by Mardigan! And by the blood of our kinsmen! If you kill him, Mardigan will have what he wants! And the highlands will run with Scots blood until none is left! Do ye no' see, mon? Look around ye! See what's left of Glenross!

"Did ye see the bodies as ye rode in?" she asked furiously, desperate to make him understand. "No laird would sacrifice his kinsmen for himself! Nor will I! This alliance must stand!"

He did look around then, his expression tortured at sight of the destruction around them. Then his gaze came back to hers.

"But ye belong to me!" he said softly.

"I belong only to myself, Malcolm. Those were childish games that can never be!" Brianna told him. "That is what you dinna understand." Then hurtful as she knew it was, she told him with blunt but gentle honesty, "My feelin's never went beyond friendship. I would never have wed with ye."

He looked at her with tortured eyes. "I would give my life for ye, Brianna. Ye have only to ask it."

"I do not want your life, Malcolm. I want your friendship and loyalty."

"Ye have that, lass," he vowed. "Always."

She nodded. "Then, please go, and speak no more of this. Find Thomas and help in whatever way you can to see the village well protected for Mardigan may yet come again to finish what was left undone. We must stand together against him. It is our only hope."

His shoulders sagged as though with defeat. But his gaze was hard and cold as he looked past her to the warrior who stood with drawn sword.

"If you harm her," he warned Tarek al Sharif. "Your head will be the first to fall."

"Malcolm! Please!" she implored him.

"You have my word, that she will be safe."

Brianna felt the tension ease out of Malcolm's arm. He slowly lowered the sword. There was such pain in his eyes.

"Ye place yer hopes with that barbarian?" he whispered fiercely. "What if ye are wrong?"

"What other choice is there?"

He stared at her, searching for doubt, any sign that she wavered in the least. But he saw none. He sighed heavily and dropped the tip of his sword to the ground.

"I will do as ye ask, but do not ask me to change what is in my heart."

It was all she could ask for. She glanced back at Tarek al Sharif. He slowly lowered his sword as well. Several of his men had also drawn their swords and stood ready to cut Malcolm down if he had attacked.

"There is much that must yet be done tonight," Tarek reminded them all. Then he turned to Gavin.

"Go with him. Our men are to be paired off with the Scots." He glanced speculatively at Malcolm, his expression thoughtful.

"I leave the choice to you, Malcolm of Drummond, as to

which of your men should be paired off for you know best the temperament of your own men."

Malcolm was stunned. "After what has happened, you ask me to share in giving orders to your own men?"

Tarek nodded. "And share the responsibility of command as well."

Malcolm glared at him. "You are a fool."

"Only a fool seeks to bind an ally with force. You are a warrior. Your people have suffered. You will not jeopardize your fellow kinsmen for your own pride."

"Nor are ye a fool," Malcolm said with grudging respect. "Aye, I will do as ye ask, for now, and for my kinsmen. But there will come a day when this must be settled between us."

"I will be waiting."

Brianna turned back toward the fire as Malcolm left, his own kinsmen flanking him on one side, Sir Gavin and several Norman warriors flanking the other.

Tarek stood before the bonfire in wide-legged stance with that curved sword held loosely in his lowered hand. He was framed by the light of the fire, his features hidden in shadows. Yet she could feel those blue eyes watching her.

"He cares deeply for you," he said, returning the sword to its leather sheath. "As a man might care for a lover."

"We were never lovers," she informed him, trying to understand the sort of man who would allow a man who had just sworn to kill him to keep his sword, not to mention offering a position of authority.

"Though for a long time it was his hope that we might be wed."

"But not yours?" Tarek speculated.

"The bond is strong between us," she admitted, "as friends who have known each other since childhood."

He was unconvinced as his gaze was drawn across the village where Malcolm stood with his men. The Scot turned and for a moment his gaze fastened on Brianna. His expression was intense, filled with myriad emotions he made no attempt to hide, the least of which was longing.

Tarek might have claimed her for wife, but the Scot had the advantage of time — time to form deep bonds of affection and trust, and time for love to grow in spite of her denial. Whereas she knew him only from a chance meeting.

There was no basis for trust or even the most meager affection between them. She had accepted his terms for the marriage only because she had no other choice. Under any other circumstances they might've been enemies as much as Mardigan was her enemy.

But he wanted more than words spoken before the council of chieftains and sanctified before a priest of her faith. He wanted more than an alliance of armies united in a common cause.

He wanted the way she had looked at him that day by a highland pool, that had haunted his dreams every night since. He wanted the sweet, breathless sound of her voice as it had been that day when she warned him of danger. And he wanted her cool touch on his skin as it was when she had taken his hand and led him to safety.

He must go slowly with her. He must earn her trust, perhaps some trace of affection, and then they would discover the pleasures to be found with one another.

Brianna too watched, but for a far different reason. Malcolm was her friend, but she felt his anger and resentment in spite of his words and feared she could not entirely trust him. Then she frowned as her gaze scanned the perimeter of the village that she had outlined in the crudely made map she had drawn.

Warriors, both Norman and Scot alike, once more moved noisily about the village carrying out orders. They called out greetings to those they knew almost as if they wished to be heard. Others sat about other bonfires while still more had already bedded down for the night. There seemed to be far more warriors and knights than she had watched ride from Inverness.

Tarek joined her as she mentally counted the rounded shapes of sleeping warriors about the fires, those who moved through the village, and still more seen inside the well-lit ruins of cottages and huts, together with those who guarded the perimeter. She counted a full four score and ten, not including those who remained to guard Drusilla's cottage. Almost twice the number that had left Inverness!

Her gaze swept back to those warriors sleeping about campfires. Only moments before others had awakened at the sudden confrontation and drawn their swords. But an equal number had not, but slept on.

She looked at him aghast as she realized the truth. "Those warriors are not real!" she exclaimed.

She wasn't certain which was the more startling — the truth she saw as his gaze met hers, or the wicked, handsome smile that transformed his lean, sharp features.

"A necessary deception," he replied, making no attempt to deny it. "Never let the enemy know your true strength. If you have a dozen men, let him believe you have three times that number."

Her astonished gaze swept the village again — now the armed encampment of Glenross — then returned to his. For a moment her guard was down, her clear green eyes sparkling with laughter.

"You are a conjuror, milord," she said with undisguised admiration. "Drusilla would be envious." At his questioning look, she explained, "The villagers believe the old woman to be a witch."

"I am no conjuror," he admitted, his mouth curving down at one corner in a crooked half smile even more handsome than the one before with a sort of self-deprecating charm.

"Would that I were," he thought briefly of the beautiful young sorceress, Vivian of Amesbury, daughter of the old one Merlin. "I would conjure an army ten times the number of my men and drive Mardigan into the sea before the next dawn."

"Would that you were, milord," she replied. "For then there would be no need of this alliance you have forced me to."

He was trapped by his own words. He could argue with her, he could tell her that he had no intention of setting aside the alliance, that Mardigan had merely provided the key to it. He could reveal that Inverness was his before he ever left London. But he did not.

Instead, he said, "Tell me what you know of Mardigan."

She shivered, for to tell him of Mardigan it was necessary to tell him of the death and destruction Mardigan had brought to the highlands. She stared into the flames of the fire and shivered again as images of the death and destruction at Inverness filled her thoughts.

It was as if night had stolen the sun. The smile vanished from her lips and her eyes, replaced by a profound sadness. Her arms were wrapped tightly about her, as if against a sudden coldness, or perhaps trying to hold something in. He saw the trembling of her shoulders, the physical gathering of strength even as exhaustion seemed to overwhelm her, and that indomitable highland pride.

"Mardigan has learned the ways of the highland warriors by living among them," she said quietly, hating even the sound of his name, recalling the way he had boldly stood

128

before the chieftains and demanded her hand in marriage.

"He hides in the forests and valleys, disguising himself and his men. Then he attacks. Only a few have escaped and lived to tell of it. No family in all of Cullum's landhold has escaped death at his hands." She shuddered as she recalled the carnage at Inverness, and her own narrow escape.

"He is treacherous and cunning, completely without mercy for man, woman, or child."

She was so lost in the pain of those memories that she was not aware he stood very close, until she felt a sudden weight about her shoulders. She looked up as he wrapped a warm fleece about her. His hand brushed the curve of her chin as he tied the leather lacings at her neck.

It was a simple thing, something Cullum had performed countless times when she was a child. But there was nothing simple in the sudden pleasure of his touch that seemed somehow intimate and possessive.

Her gaze met his, like that of a startled doe suddenly caught in the light of a hunter's torch, terrified yet lured by the flame and unable to flee.

She still felt his heat when he no longer touched her, but in a far different way. It was like the memory of something deep and primal felt in her soul. She took an instinctive step back, closer to the fire as if seeking its warmth, when in truth she was already far too warm.

"Inverness is all important to him," she went on to explain, struggling for every word, trying to bring some order to her scattered thoughts. "He will do anything to claim it for it holds the key to power in the highlands."

"And claim the daughter of Inverness for his wife," Tarek added, for he had heard whisperings of Mardigan's visit to Inverness weeks earlier.

"Aye."

"But Cullum refused him?"

Her chin angled a notch higher. "I refused."

"You might have accepted his offer of marriage and sought an alliance with the Norse raiders."

Her thoughts gathered and calmed once more. "And made an enemy of King William? I think not." She shook her head. "Better to drive an invader back into the sea than to fight another across common borders of land."

"You accepted the lesser of two evils?" he suggested.

Her clear green gaze met his. With blunt honesty, she reminded him, "I accepted nothing, milord. You gave me no choice."

The truth of her words stung, reminding him of the alliance he'd forced upon her. And the deception she had not yet discovered. He felt little satisfaction in the reasons why she'd chosen him over Mardigan.

The village had grown quiet with only the intermittent hiss or pop of heated sap at the bonfires, a distant conversation that murmured low, the occasional movement among the guards nearby as they warmed themselves against the cold, the restless movement of the horses nearby at their tethers.

It might have seemed peaceful if not for the charred remains of the cottages, a stark reminder of the brutality and death suffered there and the weapons both Norman and Scot warriors kept near at all times.

"It is late," she said, as Sir Gavin and several of his men returned. Some went inside the cottage where they laid out their pallets. Sir Gavin warmed his hands at the far edge of the fire.

"I must return to Drusilla's cottage."

"You will be safer here."

There was a finality in his voice that brought anger quickly to the surface. "Surely her cottage is safe with so many of your men guarding it."

He shook his head adamantly. "You will remain here."

She glanced about the crude encampment made before Anne's cottage. "Aye, I can see that I would be much safer here," she replied sarcastically.

"You will not sleep by the fire," he replied calmly. "I prefer to sleep with something solid at my back. Then I know from which direction the enemy will come."

His emphasis of where they would both sleep turned anger to panic. He picked up a rolled bundle of furs and walked toward the opening of the cottage. She stared at him, her face suddenly pale. He stood beside the broken entrance, so that she could enter before him.

"I do not mind sleeping by the fire."

"I do."

She gathered the fleece more tightly about her as she slowly walked toward the cottage.

"You will sleep next to the back wall," he informed her. "It is safer." He entered behind her, stepping over several sleeping men as he sought the far corner. There, he made a thick pallet of the warm furs.

To argue was pointless. She crawled across the layers of furs, flattening herself as far against the wall as possible. Surely she was safe with so many of his men lying head to foot in the cottage. But as a precaution she wrapped several layers of fur about her like a protective shield.

She watched him warily from her warm cocoon. To her surprise he left the cottage. With the fire at his back, she watched as he spoke with Sir Gavin. Though she could not hear their conversation, she sensed there had been no further difficulties. She prayed the truce between their warriors would continue for all their sakes.

Then, beyond the fire she saw the shadow of a large man

who moved silently through the encampment to linger close by. She smiled to herself as she sensed Thomas' comforting presence. If she needed him, he would be as close as her thoughts.

She fought to remain awake, but it was a battle she could not win. Exhaustion overcame her, warmth closed around her, and she dreamed old dreams . . .

Seven

"Brianna? Wake up, Brianna. You are such a sleepyhead."

Brianna turned deeper into the warmth of the furs, but that gentle, sweet voice followed her there.

"It's late. The sky is already light. The sun will be up soon. Come little one, get out of bed." The voice pulled at her, drawing her from her dreams, pulling her out of the gauzy cocoon of sleep and into the light.

She turned, peeking out from under the arm thrown over her forehead, and watched the shadow of the slender woman as she moved about the cottage.

She was young, the silken blue of her gown and the cloud of brilliant red hair that fell to her waist glistening in the light of the candle that burned nearby. The woman turned and smiled at her. She was beautiful, with fragile features and clear green eyes.

"Come quickly, Brianna. It's time to meet the others."

As if she watched herself from outside her body, Brianna pushed back the thick furs and slipped out of bed as the woman again beckoned to her. But she was startled and confused, for the one she saw was not herself as a woman grown, but a child.

"I'm coming," the child called out. *"Wait!"*

"Don't worry, little one," the woman assured her. *"I won't ever leave you alone."*

"Are they here, yet?" the child asked excitedly.

"Yes, Brianna, they're all here. Just as I promised you they would be. It's a very special time." There were tears in the

133

woman's voice. *"Now, we'll all be together again, even if it's only for a little while. But you must hurry. Before the sun is full up."*

Brianna watched in stunned fascination as the slender child with bare feet beneath her gown, and a radiant tangle of white gold hair tumbling to her waist hurried from her bed, driven by some unknown urgency. *They* were all here.

But who were they?

Then, at the doorway of the cottage, the little girl stopped for a moment and turned to look back over her shoulder toward the bed. Her eyes were a clear, bright green, the color of a highland glade, her features fragile but with a fierce strength and an impish humor. Her eyes danced with excitement.

"You must come with me," she beckoned.

"Where are you going?" Brianna asked.

"To the hollow hill. They're waiting for us. Just as mother said they would be."

Still struggling to understand this dream-vision as she seemed to watch her much younger self, Brianna hesitated.

"Who is waiting for us?"

"They're waiting for us. Don't you remember?"

She didn't remember. She couldn't understand any of this. The little girl grew impatient with her, glancing back through the doorway of the cottage.

"It's almost dawn. We have to go now," she said insistently.

"I can't. I don't understand."

The little girl gave her an odd look. *"What do you mean?"*

"I don't understand any of this."

"Yes, you do," the little girl admonished her with a smile. *"All you have to do is remember. Then you'll understand all of it."*

Tears choked Brianna's throat as she struggled to remember but could not. "I don't know what it is that I'm supposed to remember!"

"*Brianna!*" the woman's voice called again, more distant now. The little girl grew more impatient to join her.

"*You have to remember! You're part of it. You have to come with me through the mist.*"

"*Brianna! Hurry!*" the woman called again.

"*You have to come,*" the little girl insisted. "*We all have to be there.*"

"Where?"

But the little girl had turned back to the doorway without answering. Then as her name was called again, she ran out of the cottage. Brianna threw back the warm furs and ran after her.

The little girl had already reached the end of the cottage path that ran through a lush garden rich with vegetables, herbs, and summer berries. Brianna called after her.

She didn't look back but instead kept running along the path past an orchard with trees weighed down with ripe glistening fruit and nuts, and then along ancient hedgerows as the sky grew light and mist lay along the ground.

"Wait!" she called out.

"*Brianna!*"

"Wait for me. Please." The hem of her gown tangled around her ankles and she fell.

"Wait," she called after them. "Please wait." Tears stung at her eyes.

"Mother? Please don't leave me."

Her senses cleared as she became aware of her surroundings: the cottage steeped in darkness; the still twilight at the gaping doorway as those in the encampment slept the last hour before dawn; the rattling sounds of warriors who slept head to foot sprawled across the floor of the cottage; the unfamiliar warmth of the man who slept beside her with a sword under his hand — her husband.

The deep wrenching pain of the dream receded, but not the images. Strange images of people and places she did not know but seemed familiar somehow.

She slowed her breathing and the fierce, rapid beating of her heart. Senses sharpened with an animal awareness of her surroundings. Tarek al Sharif slept undisturbed on the pallet of soft furs beside her, as did the other warriors. She rose silently, and gathering her shawl about her shoulders, slipped from the warm furs. At the gaping doorway of the cottage, she paused, staring out into the gathering gray of the coming dawn.

Her gaze was drawn to the dark outline of trees of the forest that lay just beyond the village, aware of something that beckoned to her.

It wasn't so much something she heard or saw, but something she felt in the subtle shift of the wind, a sense of something beckoning to her, waiting for her there.

She hesitated at some vague, instinctive warning. She'd never been afraid of the dark before, but now she hesitated at something she should remember but could not. It was as if it was there at the edge of her memory, hovering, teasing at her from its hiding place beyond her consciousness and refusing to come out. And so she was left only with her instincts to guide and protect her, as she pulled the shawl more tightly about her and set off toward the forest.

Tarek wasn't certain what it was that awakened him. It might have been a noise, although as he listened for it again, he heard nothing. It might have been a movement, although nothing moved within the gray dimness of the cottage. Or it might have been the cold that seeped through at the edge of the pallet and warned him. Brianna was gone. But not long, for the fur still held her warmth.

He immediately rolled to his feet, the sword slipping to his hand with the practiced ease of one whose life had depended upon it many times in the past. Sleep vanished instantly from his senses as he stepped cautiously over sleeping warriors and through the shattered doorway into the gray predawn morning.

The last of the embers glowed at the fire from the night before. As his gaze swept the village, he saw both Norman and Scots guards at their posts revealed by the occasional plume of their breath on the chill morning air, or the occasional stamping of feet to warm themselves.

He was not surprised to find Thomas sleeping beside a nearby fire. For he was like Brianna's constant shadow, always at her side. He frowned at the thought that she was now gone and her protector slept on unaware.

Tarek moved along the outside wall of the cottage, keeping to the shadows as he went to the horses. The Arabian mare snorted in greeting as she stirred at her tether. Other horses nearby still dozed undisturbed, weight shifted onto three legs, heads hanging low over their tethers. No one had passed this way.

He circled round the other direction and found traces of imprints in the newly fallen snow that blanketed the village. They were small and barely visible. No soldier had made those tracks, but someone light of weight and moving carefully at the edge of the shadows so as not to be seen by the guards.

He followed the tracks across the village to the old woman's cottage. Here they stopped briefly, as she had no doubt checked upon those inside. For the prints disappeared at the threshold of the cottage.

Stephen immediately awakened at the fire that had been built near the cottage. He came to his feet with the instinctive reflex of a warrior alert to danger.

"What is it?" he asked, the short, narrow blade the Scots preferred already in one hand, his broadsword in the other.

"Where is she?" Tarek asked curtly.

Confusion shadowed the young knight's eyes. "I know not of whom you speak." Then understanding dawned, and a roguish smile began at the corner of his mouth.

"Your bride has fled already?" he quipped, laughter replacing the sleep at his amber eyes. "Perhaps the prowess I have heard so much about is overrated, my friend. Or perhaps you would have been better served by the woman, Gillie." He grinned knowingly. "But your loss was my gain."

Tarek was not in a pleasant mood. But he kept his temper in check. "I must find her."

Stephen sobered as he realized that this was more than merely a nervous, inexperienced bride having flown her husband's side.

"She is not here. Perhaps she sought privacy for womanly needs."

Tarek shook his head. "There would be no need to venture this far. Are you certain she is not inside?"

"You may see for yourself." Stephen stepped to the door of the cottage and opened it. All inside still slept soundly, the baby making soft gurgling sounds. Brianna was not among them.

"When did you last see her?" Stephen asked with growing uneasiness.

"Not since yester eve." His friend's apprehension communicated itself in the taut line of his mouth and the hard mask of his features.

"I'll alert the guard."

"No," Tarek stopped him. "To alert our guard will also alert the Scots that she is gone. The alliance is too fragile. It could cause trouble if they believe she has fled or come to some harm. Especially Malcolm of Drummond."

"What about the mute, Thomas? He is never far from her side."

"He still sleeps near the cottage. She left without him." Tarek frowned with growing uneasiness. "Say nothing to anyone. I will find her."

"And if you cannot?" Stephen asked bluntly. "She knows the land like no other. There are a hundred places she could hide and never be found. She might even have returned to Inverness."

Tarek shook his head. "She would not leave her kinsmen. Yester eve her thoughts were only of them. No," he shook his head adamantly, uneasiness growing. "She has not returned to Inverness. It is something else. And I must learn what it is."

"I will go with you," Stephen said, sheathing the smaller blade at his belt.

"If I am not quickly returned, it will be for you to see the survivors safely returned to Inverness."

Anger and frustration hardened Stephen's handsome features, and in that moment he looked very much like his father. "You cannot go alone! 'Tis foolishness!"

Tarek flashed a smile. "You forget, my young friend, who has taught you how to move as silent as the air and just as invisibly." He laid a hand on the young warrior's shoulder.

"If I have not found her by the time the sun is full above the horizon, I will return to camp and continue the search with a full, armed guard. By then her own people will have discovered that she is gone."

Stephen nodded reluctantly. "But only until the sun is just

above the horizon. If you have not returned at midday, I will lead the guard to find you."

Tarek found her tracks beyond the cottage. They led to the wood that bordered the village. His frown deepened as he set off after her, wondering what could have sent her into the forest, alone and unprotected.

Brianna's footsteps were silent in the newly fallen snow as she entered the forest. There was only the sound of her own frantic heartbeat, and soft clouds as her warm breath plumed in the frigid still air.

She was used to the stillness of a forest in those moments before dawn when the inhabitants still slept in their burrows and in their nests. Even owls ceased their night hunting in the predawn to sit like bearded old monks in wool cassocks on low-hanging branches, their feathers ruffled against the cold. Occasionally an eye popped open to survey the surrounding forest, and then slowly closed, as they dozed with the coming dawn.

But now, before first light streaked the sky, the owls still hunted as rodents sought their burrows after their own night hunting. Yet there was no sound. Not a screech, the stir of a wing, or the squeak of a woodmouse. Not even the breath of the wind could be heard or felt. It was completely still. Strangely so, as in those waiting moments before a storm even though the storm that threatened the previous afternoon and evening had passed, and the last of the stars glittered in a clear sky now streaked with dawn.

But as she went deeper into the forest, it grew steadily darker as less and less light filtered through the branches of the trees.

It was an ancient place of old oaks, alder, and dense pine. The forest was haunted by faces that leered with grotesque expressions at the gnarl of a severed tree branch, or the hollowed out burl in a trunk that looked like the surprised "O" of some goblin's mouth framed by chunks of bark that formed a bulbous nose and bulging, leering eyes if one looked close enough.

She ignored those silent guardians as she walked deeper into the forest, drawn by something she couldn't define and had never experienced before.

Snow blanketed the ground, piling into drifts beneath barren trees. But in other places where the midday sun normally found its way to the floor of the forest, old snow had melted and puddled into shallow pools. She knelt beside one, cupping her hand for a drink of water.

Frowning, she drew back abruptly. There had been no need to taste it to know that the water was fouled, for she could smell its stench. Yet, even though she had not touched the surface, it rippled as though the surface had been stroked by some unseen hand.

She extended her hand over the surface, stunned when it flattened and went completely still. Leaning closer, she noticed for the first time that there was no reflection on the surface of the water. Instead it was like looking through a dark glass onto another place with a faint, golden light glowing at the center that seemed to grow steadily larger until she realized that it was not a light at all, but a golden object.

Then, as it grew closer still, as though rising from the depths, she saw it clearly. The Grail — the ancient, mystical cup that according to legend had not been seen for over five hundred years.

It was suspended in a growing darkness that closed around it. Then, as clearly as the Grail had revealed itself to her, it was gone. The surface of the pool was completely dark, dull, and lifeless.

She suddenly felt cold, a deep, aching coldness of the soul that had nothing to do with the predawn of the forest. As she started to move away from the pool, the surface bubbled and churned as though by some tumultuous force. Something dark and sinister broke the surface, rising out of the depths of the pool, reaching for her.

She fell back, crawling beyond its reach as it spilled over the edges of the pool, spreading along the ground toward her, and enveloped the trunks of the nearby trees with a power of evil so strong it smothered the air and pressed down on her without even touching her.

Overhead the birds were startled from their perches and took flight. The shrill screech of a woodland creature added its terrified warning to theirs. It seemed those imaginary faces carved in tree limbs and trunks came alive and also cried their warning to her. Brianna scrambled to her feet and fled the edge of the pool.

As she ran, it seemed the forest grew darker instead of lighter as it should with the coming dawn, and she knew the evil of darkness followed. It ran through the hollows, slipped through the trees, and along every path, closing in.

Branches tore at her clothes, whipped at her hair, and stung at her cheeks. She plunged across a stream, the landmarks no longer familiar. Like a startled doe she headed for high ground. Someone else's thoughts collided with hers and she was certain they must be Thomas'. Surely he had followed her. But where was he? What was happening?

Thick gorse scratched at her legs. Tree limbs snagged at her clothes and hair. She tore free and lunged down a steep incline. She glanced back, all her senses turned toward that evil, unaware of the one who waited for her.

Hands grabbed her arms. Then she was flattened against the rough bark of a massive oak at the edge of a clearing. A powerful arm clamped around her as a hand smothered over her mouth and prevented her crying out. When she tried to kick out, her legs were pinned by powerful thighs that molded hers as she was pinned by her captor. Through the tangle of her hair that blinded her and the terror that claimed the rest of her senses, she heard a harsh warning.

"Do not cry out!"

There was a familiarity in the accent and the harsh tone, and she realized where she had heard it before. Her eyes widened above the smothering pressure of that strong hand clamped over her mouth as she stared into the fierce blue gaze of Tarek al Sharif.

She quit struggling and willed herself to relax. His hand immediately loosened over her mouth. When she did not cry out he removed his hand from her mouth. His arm loosened about her.

He pushed back the heavy tangle of her hair. "You are not harmed?"

The rough tenderness in his voice stunned her, almost as much as the faint stinging warmth where his fingers grazed a scratch at her cheek. She shook her head.

" 'Tis not safe," she warned. "There is danger . . ." No sooner had she spoken than she heard the sound of someone moving through the forest nearby.

There was much crashing and tearing of limbs as something or someone approached, moving then stopping, as if uncertain of the direction she had taken and searching for some indication in the brush and undergrowth. Then they heard voices and the distinctive sound of steel as several pursuers hacked their way through the heavy undergrowth.

The darkness in the forest lifted as the sky lightened overhead, making it easier to see, and be seen. He swore softly.

Then as the voices grew louder, Tarek pulled her behind the massive oak.

The trunk of the oak was easily a sword's width across and gaped open like a savage wound. The bark surrounding the wound was blackened and burned away where it had been struck by lightning. He motioned her to say nothing as he pulled her inside the crevice of the splintered trunk.

The burned out hollow was dark and narrow. He drew her tight against him, her legs scissored between his. If they were discovered it would be impossible to draw his sword. He eased the sword down beside him, and slipped a deadly looking, slender bladed knife from his boot.

The voices drew closer, some as near as only a few yards away. Overhead, the morning sun angled down through the top of the trees, glistening off the white gold of her hair like a shining beacon.

The warmth of his breath brushed her cheek as his other hand slipped behind her neck, pressing her head into the curve of his shoulder, the bright gleam of her hair hidden from view.

He had worn no armor when he left the village, not even the thick-padded leather tunic. Instead he wore only leather breeches, boots, and a woolen shirt that offered no protection against an enemy sword, and even less protection against the stunning heat of his body as it pressed against hers from shoulder to knee.

Her hands were trapped, flattened between them at his chest. There was no room to move or escape. The warmth of his breath brushed her forehead, while beneath her cheek she felt the fierce strong beating of his heart.

Her senses filled with the feel and scent of him, the tang of male sweat that blended with the pine scent of the forest, and the deep woodsy smell of the oak hollow. As the footsteps sounded very near in the breaking of twigs and crunching of leaves underfoot, the warmth of his breath whispered across her senses in strange-sounding, foreign words that she understood in her soul, in the gentle tenderness of his hand at her hair, and the comforting beat of his heart.

She squeezed her eyes tightly shut, uncertain if they would live or die, certain only of his strength that spoke to her in ways she had never experienced before. She answered in the frantic uncertain beating of her own heart.

There was no warning. In one moment, the sun shone brightly through the trees and he was certain they had no hope of escaping discovery. All that was needed was for one of these men to pass by the tree and then turn around, and they would be found. There would be but one outcome.

Tarek did not fear death. He had faced it countless times before. He would meet it bravely and accept his fate. He had always believed there would be no regret. Until now.

Then, as brightly as the sun had shone, it was obliterated behind a cloud of mist. It swirled through the trees, blanketed the ground, and enveloped everything in a thick vaporous cloud, making it impossible to see one's hand in front of one's face.

It was not cold, but warm, like being wrapped in warm spring rain of his native Antioch. It stroked the skin like a whisper, shrouding the senses, until the only reality was the slender young woman he held in his arms, and they were safely hidden in the mist.

The voices around them became frantic as their pursuers became disoriented and lost their way. Shouts turned to curses. There was the sound nearby of a sword being drawn.

"You fool! Do you want to cut off your own arm?"

"I can't see in this damn mist. It came out of nowhere. I

tell you, the forest is haunted," another replied, his voice rising with fear.

"There!" another shouted. "It's clear over there. Follow me!"

Others responded and followed, some passing by so close to their hiding place Brianna heard the scrape of a steel blade and smelled the pungent stench of the animal skins their pursuers wore. She shuddered. With eyes closed she concentrated on the tangy warmth of Tarek's skin beneath her cheek at the opening of his shirt and the comforting strength of powerful muscles beneath her hands at his chest.

There was a fierceness in the lean strength of his body pressed against hers, an intense protectiveness that stirred a strange feeling very much like hunger, but far deeper as if it might never be satisfied. And his hand at her hair was like being touched by the warmth of the sun.

Gradually, as the voices faded and all that remained was the silence of the forest around them, his hand loosened in her hair.

"They have gone," he whispered against her forehead. "Do you know who they were?"

Her head came up. Her face was pale. She nodded. "It was Mardigan."

Her gaze fastened on his mouth, the curve of his strong chin, the texture of his skin in shades of dark gold made darker still by the shadow of beard that sharpened the lean angles and emphasized the smoothness of his lips. Her own lips parted on some response that went unspoken. Beneath her hands she felt the fierce beating of his heart, and then felt her own equally as fierce in her blood.

Confusion filled her eyes, making it seem as if the mist had become a part of her, muting the clear green of her eyes to dark gray. Delicate golden brows drew together as her gaze met his. Her startled breath mingled with his.

Desire clenched at him, pulsing through his erect flesh as his hips rode hers. She didn't struggle or fight him. Instead, she stared back at him, her breathing rapid and shallow as though terrified. But there was no fear in her eyes. It was gone, replaced by a stunned fascination.

"It is very dangerous here," he said, stroking his thumb along the curve of her bottom lip.

"Aye," she whispered, her eyes widening at his touch, felt along every nerve ending, as if his hand had stroked every part of her body.

All about them the mist had lifted. The sun once more shone through the trees as new voices sounded in a mixture of highland and Norman accent.

Tarek swore softly as the mist seemed to clear from her gaze as well, and she once more looked back at him with clear green eyes filled with wariness and defiance.

"Milord, please," she said with growing alarm. "Your men will be upon us soon."

He slowly released her.

Thomas found them, the giant moving with unerring certainty through the forest until he located the charred oak as though guided to her by some invisible bond. Stephen of Valois was not far behind.

Seeing that Brianna was unharmed, he asked, "What happened? We heard others in the forest."

"It was Mardigan."

Instead of clearing, the mist swirled thicker until it was a thick cloud that blinded the hand in front of one's face.

Mardigan whirled in one direction then the other, unable to discern which direction he had come or the direction of his men. He cursed the damned mist, waving his sword arm as if he could wave it aside. But it only thickened, a heavy damp cloud that closed in as it closed out the sun that had only moments before been visible.

Cursing again, he stood perfectly still, trying to locate his men by a telltale sound in the forest — the snap of a twig, the rustling of leaves, voices. But just as he could see nothing, he heard nothing as well. And then the mist grew darker with every passing moment, until it seemed as if the dawn had once more become night.

"By the gods!" he swore, the leonine mane of shoulder length gold hair matting damply against his skull, mist beading across fierce features. "What trickery is this!"

Earlier he had followed the sounds through the forest as birds left their nests and woodland creatures stirred from their burrows. His men had brought word of someone in the forest. No doubt another damned peasant that had escaped Glenross, he thought at first.

He had roused his men with more than one well-placed kick. With thick tongues and aching skulls from indulging in mead taken from the village, they had complained bitterly. But word of warriors seen at Glenross had filled Mardigan with rage and contempt. Highland warriors, his men reported. And many more they did not recognize.

Now a woman, alone, had left the village and entered the forest. Mardigan and his men fanned out in an arc, sweeping toward the edge of the forest just beyond the village, for one of his men said the woman possessed unusual golden hair and green eyes. Mardigan had grunted with satisfaction.

His strategy had worked, for he was certain the woman his men had seen was none other than the daughter of the old laird of Inverness. And she had almost been within his grasp, if not for the cursed mist that seemed always to cling to the land. As quickly as he had found her, she was gone, escaping in the mist.

Then the mist slowly began to clear, although it grew no lighter. It was dark as night, an oppressiveness clinging to the trees and rocks. And there were none of the sounds that should have been heard in the forest any time of day or night — the rustling of birds in the trees, the call or shriek of an animal or bird at the hunt, not even the stirring of the wind. Those gnarled faces carved in tree trunks seemed to leap out at him with their leering expressions. Pagan spirits that ruled the forest according to the ancient Celts.

"Barbarians!" he spat out, his throat suddenly tight and dry. "Meet my sword," he challenged the silence, "and we will see who is the more powerful."

"Be careful what you wish for, Mardigan," a sultry, voice replied.

Mardigan whirled around. The voice seemed to come from the trees, the rocks, the very darkness that surrounded him. It was a woman's voice, silken and low. It seemed to cling to the very air. He whirled back around.

Like curling wisps of smoke, the last of the mist seemed to retreat from the forest floor, and through the darkness that enveloped the forest he thought he saw someone approaching.

"Who are you?" he demanded, squinting at the figure that slowly walked toward him. Gradually the figure took form and shape, that of a slender woman with a long flowing mantle that blended with the darkness that surrounded her.

Her hood was drawn forward. Only part of her face was visible as she drew closer, and revealed nothing at all except the silhouette of a slender throat and chin.

She might have been seventeen or three score and seventeen years, for her features were completely shrouded by the hood, her body enveloped in the heavy, thick folds that swirled about her ankles as she walked.

"You know who I am," she replied, stopping only a few feet away. Slender hands emerged from the folds of the mantle and pushed back the edge of the hood, revealing fragile delicate features, full curved mouth, and a mane of glorious white gold hair that spilled past her shoulders to her waist.

Mardigan seized her wrist in a powerful grasp, dragging her against him. She did not cry out or struggle, nor did she fight him. Instead, her hands slid up the front of his tunic, fingers curling over the edge of his leather tunic.

"Everything you desire will be yours," she promised. His other hand closed over the thick silk of her hair. Desire spiraled through him and clenched at his flesh, straining the front of his breeches.

With unnatural strength she tore open the front of his tunic. Lust glazed his eyes as he felt her woman's softness and a surprising rare strength as her head angled forward, then searing pain as she sunk her teeth into the skin at his chest.

"Bitch!" he swore, yanking her head back by the silken tangle of her hair.

Her laughter echoed in the oppressive darkness that surrounded them, a dark feral sound like that of some half-crazed beast. And the eyes that looked back at him were not vivid green but dark as death. He swore again as he tried to push her away. But he could not. She was stronger than any man.

"Who are you?" he demanded.

She pulled him to her, dark, vacant eyes staring back at him above the curve of her mouth. She pulled him with her to the ground, the folds of her mantle falling open to reveal that she wore nothing underneath.

150

Equal amounts of desire and a raw, naked fear twisted inside him, feeding each other as her slender hands loosened the front of his breeches. He couldn't have fled had he wanted to. Her strength was unnatural, like that of six men, preventing escape.

"Who are you?" he repeated as she freed his flesh and opened her pale, gleaming thighs. With that unnatural strength that he couldn't resist or break, she pulled him to her, guiding him inside her.

"Damn you!" he cursed as sweat beaded his body in spite of the dark coldness that closed around them — a cold sweat of something unknown and dangerous, even as his flesh joined with hers.

The coldness spread to his hands and arms like death as she moved beneath him. He heard his heart beating faster and faster, until it seemed it would burst. His thoughts became numb until he could hardly remember where he was or what was happening. He felt as if his very soul was being pulled from his body in an agony of pain unlike any he had ever experienced in battle.

He screamed at the moment of climax. It felt as if his body was being torn apart, shattering into a million pieces, lost in the darkness.

Eight

"It has been a fortnight since the attack on Glenross," Malcolm told his kinsmen gathered about the council table at Inverness. "Now four more villages have been burned, flocks slaughtered, innocent families murdered. And we're still no closer to stopping these raids than we were before."

He slammed a fist down on the long table. Metal tankards rattled with the force of the blow. All gazes turned toward Tarek al Sharif.

"We must protect the villages," Malcolm said angrily. "Or all the north country will be laid to waste."

"Only a fool would divide his strength," Stephen of Valois argued, making no attempt to disguise his intense dislike as he stood suddenly, his chair scraping back across the earthen floor.

"And thereby find his army hacked apart, piece by piece." They were like two caged lions, ready for battle.

"Who are you calling a fool?" Malcolm demanded, the anger and frustration of the several days since returning from Glenross pushing the discussion closer to the breaking point as tempers on both sides of the table flared dangerously.

"Any man who exposes his strength to an unknown enemy is a fool!" Stephen spat back at him.

"Perhaps!" Malcolm retorted, face colored with rage. "But at least he dies with a blade in his hand instead of carpenter's tools!"

There was no argument from the Scots who sat about the table, their voices added to his by their nodded agreement.

Their disdain for the work everyone had been given since returning from Glenross was no secret. To a man, they had complained long and hard about the extensive repairs and renovations Tarek immediately ordered upon their return to Inverness.

Though well-armed patrols of Normans and Scots rode the nearby countryside, most of the men — Scot and Norman alike — had been pressed into service rebuilding the main fortress, including a taller outer wall now being built of stone and in the manner of the Norman siege fortifications.

As they argued among themselves, Tarek watched and listened from where he sat at the long table, one hand resting casually on the arm of his chair, the other wrapped loosely about a tankard still full to the brim with ale.

He now occupied the laird's position at the table, a position Ian had yielded stoically in the name of the newly formed alliance. His mouth curved in a thoughtful frown as he considered what each man had to say.

As Brianna entered the hall, her gaze was immediately drawn to him. Amid angry shouts and argument, she stepped back into the shadows at the wall, not yet wishing to be seen. From her hiding place, she could watch all that went on without being seen. And she could watch Tarek al Sharif.

He sat with deceptive calm, his lean body relaxed in the large chair Cullum had once occupied while those about him argued and complained bitterly. The calm at the center of the storm.

While others drank their fill and thumped their empty tankards for more, he silently watched them all, his expression revealing nothing of his inner thoughts. While they argued, he said nothing but instead listened, his strong features caressed by the light of the fire and set with a thoughtful concentration.

Increasingly foul of temper, Malcolm turned on him as tension in the hall became explosive.

"What say you?" he demanded, leaning across the table toward Tarek. "How many more Scots must die before Mardigan is stopped?"

The hall suddenly grew silent. Malcolm's disdain was like the edge of a drawn sword — dangerous, deadly, eager for blood.

"What say you?" Malcolm repeated, eager for a fight. "Or are Norman words filled with false promises rather than deeds?"

Tarek slowly looked up. His gaze sharp as he contemplated the assembled Scots.

Unlike the highlanders who prided themselves on their physical strength and prowess in competition, he moved with a Spartan efficiency. A containment of power so intense and completely controlled that it drew the eye, for one could never anticipate what his next move might be.

Brianna shivered as she remembered that restraint of power as they hid together in the forest of Glenross, the contact of his lean body against hers and the strange longings she'd never experienced before — intensely pleasurable feelings that confused her.

Since then she had avoided him as much as possible. It was not difficult with the fortress overflowing with kinsmen, soldiers, and Scots left homeless after their villages were burned. As the daughter of the old laird, it was her responsibility to see to the countless details of housing and feeding so many who had sought refuge within the fortress walls.

Warriors, soldiers, and knights slept head to foot in the main hall and spilling out into the yard. She had given Anne Simm and her baby her own chamber. Young Nel slept there as well. Brianna slept on a small cot near the hearth. She had

Thomas place her husband's battle gear and few clothes in the adjacent laird's chamber.

They were crowded. There was only the small amount of privacy that a drawn curtain could offer. It had made avoiding him easy, and reinforced that she had no intention of being his true wife.

During the day she was busy with the chores and endless details of the household. By night she sat late with the chieftains and Tarek's knights, listening to strategies and arguments.

For her nightly escape to her own crowded chamber, she could always count on some matter of grave importance needing his attention. On more than one occasion, he had begun a conversation with her and been called away on some matter of importance. When he returned, she was always gone.

Given time, she must convince him that theirs was a marriage in name only, for the sake of the alliance. Once he accepted it, he would no doubt seek his pleasure elsewhere. Perhaps with Gillie, for her cousin had made known her willingness from the very beginning.

Perhaps he already had. For Brianna noticed on several occasions that whenever he was within the hall, Gillie was never far away.

Her cousin was always close by. She allowed none of the serving girls near. Instead she began serving his meals herself. She constantly hovered at his elbow, refilling his tankard, removing his muddied boots, taking care of whatever need might arise.

As Gillie took on those duties which normally would have fallen to a wife, Brianna experienced an inexplicable tightening sensation that made it difficult to breathe at the thought that there were no doubt other needs Gillie attended too. Many times she saw her waiting for him in the passage outside the laird's chamber, greeting him with a smile and an intimate expression that suggested some secret they shared. She had overheard Anne berating her for her boldness.

"Do not lecture me, Anne Simm," Gillie snapped at her. " 'Tis her own fault if another warms his bed. Besides she has no interest in such things.

"You have heard yourself she agreed to the marriage only for the alliance between our warriors and the Norman knights. But I say she's a fool, for he's a strong warrior and knows well how to please a woman."

Then with sharp eyes and a hard smile, she informed Anne, "I've heard it said that those in the eastern empires know thousands of ways to please their women. After the clod I was wed to, anything more than one would be a novelty.

"So I'll take my pleasure where I can find it and to the devil with them that says anything agin it. Besides, I hear he tried to give her a rare, fine jewel when they were wed and she refused it. If all she cares for is the alliance, then so be it."

" 'Tis not all he cares about," Anne replied. "I've seen the way he looks at her."

Gillie snorted. " 'Tis only the look of a man who needs a woman to warm his bed. And I've plenty of warmth to give. So shut your mouth and tend to your squalling brat."

As she listened to their conversation, Brianna felt that painful tightness as if she could not breathe. It should not have mattered to her if he took another woman to his bed.

Now she watched and listened as he sat at the laird's table while those about him shouted and argued. Malcolm was determined to force a confrontation. His anger was like a wound that festered with poison. Only days before he had confronted her near the kitchen.

He had pulled her into the scullery, slamming the door on

the wide-eyed young serving girl. He had turned on her with pain-filled eyes.

"Why do you defend him when you know our people are being slaughtered by Mardigan's men, and he has not been able to find the murderin' bastard? Have you whored yourself to that dark-skinned barbarian?"

She was both stunned and hurt by his words. "You dinna understand, Malcolm. You don't see it clearly. We are doomed without the help of the English king even if he is William the Conqueror." But he was in no mood to hear a logical argument.

"I've seen the way he looks at you, Brianna. He does not consider it just an alliance of words. He wants more from you Brianna, and he'll no' be put off forever," he warned.

"You're wrong. He has no feelings for me beyond this alliance for his king."

"I am not wrong. I've seen it in his eyes, the way he looks at you when you do not realize it. It is only a matter of time, Brianna. He'll no' be satisfied to sleep in the laird's chamber with you in yours and walls between. What will you do then? What will you tell him?" His fingers hurt as they dug into her arms as if to punish her.

"Do you think the vows you've spoken with that barbarian matter to me?" he asked. "I would have you to wife, with God's blessing or without it. It matters not to me. I love you, Brianna."

Pain clenched at her heart at the thought that jealousy had driven him to be so hurtful.

"It matters to me. I have made vows before God, and the council of chieftains. I will honor those vows in so far as I am capable, and so must you. When the time comes, I will make him understand that I can never be wife to him in that way."

"Tell him now," he insisted. "And be done with it."

She pried his fingers loose. "I cannot."

"Cannot or will not?" The look in his eyes was furious and dangerous. He refused to understand that there could never be anything between them. At least not in the way he hoped for.

"I cannot!" she replied. "I will not jeopardize the alliance."

"And if he should die? What then?"

She grew cold at his words. "If he dies, King William will send the whole of his army north to avenge his death. God help us all if that happens, for no one will be left alive."

"Brianna . . ."

"There is nothing you can say that will make me change my mind. I have given my word and I will keep it."

He had left her then, too hurt and angry to speak of things she refused to hear. But she sensed it was not ended. She realized also they had not been alone, as she saw someone move in the shadows just outside the kitchens. But when she looked no one was there. Whoever had been listening had disappeared.

"You argue among yourselves like old women haggling at market," Tarek now told the assembled Scots and Norman warriors. "We waste time. There are other matters of greater concern."

"Aye," Malcolm snorted with contempt. "The construction of another Norman fortress as a monument to King William while more Scots die. By what right do you now make decisions for Scots warriors on Scots land?"

Tarek's gaze slowly met his, and even though she stood in shadows several feet away, Brianna saw the dangerous, predatory look in that unusual blue gaze. His manner was much like that of a cat, with a dangerous, carefully controlled energy that reminded her of a lean, deadly panther, capable of scaling battlement walls.

"Any man who refuses to learn from the past is doomed to repeat it," he calmly replied. "I do not intend to repeat what has already taken place, including the attack on Inverness because of poor fortifications — fortifications," he added, "which Mardigan is well aware of."

A memory stirred, as though it had lain sleeping. As if someone else had spoken those same words, but she could not remember where or when.

She listened with growing fascination as he refused to be provoked to anger. Like a cat he was careful and cunning. He met Malcolm's accusation with unnerving calm. But the calmness was deceptive, for she sensed the coldness of anger that lay beneath it.

"Wot sort of gibberish is this?" Malcolm exploded angrily. "Ye come here with yer strange words that have no meaning for us. The devil take ye, ye thievin' barbarian!"

The sound of steel rang throughout the hall as Tarek's men drew their swords at the insult. If there was a moment when all might be lost, she realized it was now. And Malcolm would be the cause of it.

As dear as he was to her, she could not allow him to do this. She stepped from the shadows at the entrance of the hall and into the deadly silence that promised bloodshed.

The attention of Norman and Scot alike turned to her. It was as if they all waited for her, the daughter of the old laird, to speak and take sides. And by the expression on Malcolm's face, there was only one acceptable choice she could make.

Her thoughts reached out to his, weaving through them, slipping beneath the wall of anger, desperate to make him understand what he had refused to accept. But she could not be certain she reached him.

159

Then, she crossed the hall, rounding the end of the laird's table to where Tarek al Sharif sat across the embattled table from her own kinsmen.

She stood beside his chair, her hand resting on the high back. Every gaze in the hall remained fastened on her. Countless times she had stood in that same place beside Cullum's chair and listened to his arguments with the chieftains. Where anger failed she knew that a firm decisive hand might prevail.

"The clans failed to stop Mardigan before," she said in a clear, strong voice. "What has failed in the past must be done differently, or we have no hope of stopping him."

"What know you of these things?" Malcolm flung back at her across the table. "These are matters of war. Not woman's matters."

She felt as if she'd been physically struck. No one had ever spoken to her like that before. Not Cullum, nor any of the chieftains. Nor Malcolm.

They were all suddenly uncomfortable. She saw it in their lowered gazes and the frowns at their faces. Beside her, she saw Tarek's eyes narrow. At the table before him, his hand clenched a fist. She sensed his anger, then saw it as his other hand quickly shifted to the arm of the chair less than a hand's width from the slender blade he wore as his belt.

The air in the main hall was charged with tension. Although not in so many words, Malcolm challenged not only the alliance, but her authority as the daughter of the old laird. If she did not act quickly, blood would flow at Inverness. Tarek shifted forward in his chair, a lean, predatory movement startling familiar from her dreams. With an instinct as natural as breathing, she laid a hand upon his shoulder.

It was a simple gesture. But there was nothing simple in the physical contact, nor his warmth felt through the soft linen of his tunic. It radiated through her fingertips then slipped deep inside, warming all the cold places deep within her. It was like touching the sun and for a moment she was too stunned to speak.

Then, he laid his hand over hers. His hand was much larger, closing over hers with deceptive gentleness, for beneath that callused hand more accustomed to a battle sword, she sensed strength and great restraint.

Her hand trembled beneath his. He did not release her hand. Instead, he laced his fingers through hers. His strength flowed through her, as she faced her kinsmen and the other chieftains.

"My family and many more kinsmen are dead. Glenross and a score other villages are destroyed. Graves fill the hills and valleys. The earth runs red with Scots blood." Her voice grew steadily stronger with her own anger at memories of Mardigan's vicious attack at Inverness that had left so many dead.

"This rebuilding of Inverness will cost more Scots lives in time wasted," Malcolm argued.

"Perhaps. But when it is done, then many Scots will be protected within these walls. Can ye no' see?" she spoke to them all. "Too many have already died because Inverness could *not* be properly defended. Including many of clan Drummond!"

Silence filled the háll. There was no argument that any who had been at Inverness during that bloody battle could give to what she said. Not even Malcolm.

"You may well doom us all by this alliance with the English king," Malcolm said furiously, a much deeper pain twisting his features with hatred.

"Perhaps, only time will tell of it. But one thing is certain, we are already doomed without it."

"Silence!" Ian, Malcolm's father, slammed a gnarled, battle-scarred hand down on the council table. "We will argue the matter no more! We will give the alliance a chance. For without it we have none." He turned, his gaze scanning the faces of his fellow chieftains.

"Those who are in agreement with the alliance say so." There was a grumbling of acceptance among the Scots.

"And those who be agin it?" he then asked. There was an awkward silence in the hall. Malcolm glared at the younger clan members who had decided not to challenge their elders.

"The devil take ye!" he swore, hurling a tankard against the hearth. He withdrew to the hearth where he sat sulkily in the shadows.

As weapons were once more set aside and resheathed, Ian roared boisterously to the serving girls. "Bring the ale and keep it flowing. All this argument has given me a fierce thirst." Taking a fresh tankard from one of the girls, he took a healthy draught then slammed the tankard down on the table.

"Blade! Stick! Shield!" he roared. "Let the games begin! And we'll see who is the best warrior." Across the hall tankards were raised and others answered his challenge.

Serving girls with tankards clutched in their fists darted down the length of one table and then the next, distributing the ale, coloring at lewd comments from both Scots and Norman warriors, sidestepping a groping hand or a hasty kiss. Raucous laughter erupted as new challenges were hurled from table to table. Weapons that had only moments before been raised in anger were laid out across tables as a large wooden board was brought out and laid across the table of the chieftains.

Brianna sighed with relief. A bloody confrontation had been avoided for now. Whatever resentments and hostilities remained would be taken out in games and contests of physical competition. At the worst, there would be a few bruises and scrapes, sore muscles, and possibly a few cracked heads.

When she tried to pull her hand from his, Tarek stopped her. "Do not leave. Please stay." He drew her down beside him, her hand still clasped in his.

"But there are things I must attend to," she protested, uneasy with his hand closed around hers with a pleasurable warmth and strength that seemed somehow intimate as though they were lovers and not merely partners in a military alliance.

"Someone else can attend to them. I would rather have you here." As her hand stiffened within his, he added, "So that you may explain the intricacies of the game to me." He inclined his head toward the large board that lay across the laird's table.

It was carved with a pattern of squares — six across and six down, each carved with a strange looking symbol. The symbols were patterns of one, two, or three waving lines, some marked with a perpendicular straight line, others marked with a combination of wavy lines, small circles, a picture of a bird, fish, star, sun, or crescent moon. No two symbols were alike.

Games of sport and chance were much favored in the middle empires and so he was not unfamiliar with the concept. Some were played for gold or jewels or some prized possession. The stakes were determined by the players. Some games had even decided the outcomes of wars. He had known others where a daughter, favorite wife, or concubine was the prize, still others where the players wagered their own lives.

"What do the symbols represent?" he asked, determined to distract her from her excuses. She always had excuses, some responsibility or duty that kept her occupied elsewhere when he would have preferred the pleasure of her company.

They had been wed three weeks, and he still knew little more than when he had first seen her beside that highland pool months earlier.

"They are ancient rune symbols," she explained hesitantly. "They represent the elements of the known world, earth, fire, and sky."

"How is the game played?" he asked, as four of her kinsmen each chose a side of the board to stand at. Straws were drawn to determine the order in which each warrior would take his turn while tankards of ale were refilled and wagers were placed.

"It is a game of skill, memory, and physical challenge," she explained. "In order for the game to begin, the scorekeeper selects three squares on the board at random."

She indicated a small, pinch-faced highlander, whom he recognized as the old laird's seneschal. He already had some dealings with the man for he kept the written accounts of all matters at Inverness.

He was a judicious man with an amazing grasp of numbers pertaining to crops, herds of sheep, landholds, and the precise number of warriors who owed clan loyalty to the laird of Inverness.

Tarek had consulted with the man regarding the holdings of Inverness, for it was necessary to determine just how long the fortress might withstand a siege with the ever-increasing numbers of people who sought refuge. The man had been astounded that he had such an uncanny concept of numbers for such things. It was a skill that had given him a particularly uncanny grasp of military strategies as well.

"And once those three squares are chosen?"

"The first player must repeat that same exact order, adding another square to the sequence. Each player in turn, adds a square to the sequence. He must repeat the pattern exactly. The scorekeeper makes note of each selection and marks it on parchment for all to see. In that way all who watch judge the game."

"What happens when a player chooses incorrectly?"

"He must forfeit one of his weapons — *knife, blade, shield*. Hence the name of the game."

She indicated the symbolic blade that each man lay on the table before him. The slender knife, called a dirk, carried a man's clan symbol on the blade handle. At his side was his battle sword. The small round metal shield was held by one of his kinsmen. All part of a highlander's battle gear.

"And if a man loses all his weapons?" he asked as the game began and the first three squares were chosen.

"He must face the man who next loses his weapons in physical competition."

"Without any weapons or protection," he surmised the obvious, his gaze resting on her rather than the intricacies of the game, which seemed simple, almost trivial at first, but on closer look soon revealed itself to be a game of cunning and strategy as intricate patterns of squares were chosen, making the sequence increasingly difficult.

"Aye, until only one remains. Then he faces the champion with the weapons he has left," she further explained.

"To the death?" Tarek asked.

She shook her head. "We need our warriors. One warrior may not take another's life." A frown curved her lovely mouth. She clearly did not care for the game.

"But you still disapprove of the game," he surmised, watching the myriad expressions that moved across her face.

"I cannot see the reason in beating each other senseless, all in the name of competition over a foolish game."

"Yet, according to your own words, it is a game of skill, memory, and cunning. Hardly a game of fools."

"The one who risks life and limb in a game is the fool."

"Not if the prize is worth winning."

She snorted. "They wager over casks of ale and weapons. What good are more weapons if they lose an arm?"

"I do not see any one-armed highlanders," he observed with a smile curving one corner of his mouth.

"Cullum would not allow any competition to go so far."

"And now you hold that position of authority."

"It is not necessary for me to sit and watch. All know my feelings in these matters. They are the same as Cullum's."

"And what of Malcolm of Drummond?" he asked, his gaze fastening with thoughtful concentration on the young highlander who sat at an adjacent table, holding his empty tankard aloft to be refilled as he watched the game intently. Occasionally he glanced across the hall to the laird's table, his hungry gaze lingering on Brianna.

"Malcolm has never been bested," she replied.

As the game continued she explained certain strategies. At first she continued to try to free her hand from his, but when she could not, she seemed to accept the sensual bonds that kept her at his side. She even laughed when one of the players, a man popular with the other highlanders for his good humor, played, making lewd and comical comments about what each of the symbols represented.

He wove it all into a bawdy story, rhyming the crude, colorful words while his fellow kinsmen roared with laughter and encouraged his antics. Though he lost early in the game, forced to surrender all his weapons, he winked to a nearby serving girl as he assured her he had not surrendered the most important weapon of all.

To make certain she did not mistake his meaning, he cupped his ample manhood that bulged the front of his breeks and with much rolling of eyes promised he would prove it to her later. The girl fled the hall with blazing cheeks yet grinning behind her apron.

As he watched the highlanders as they played with their guard down, Tarek gained yet another insight. There was more to be learned from men at their leisure than in the past weeks of living among them. With ample draughts of ale and the challenge of the favored game, they were relaxed, unguarded, the stoic, fierce demeanor stripped away.

The man who seemed the most fierce in confrontation often was like a playful child. Those who were most quiet, were the ones who studied the game intently.

Several hours later, most had already played one game. New challenges were called out promising the game would last far into the night. Malcolm of Drummond sat across the hall among his kinsmen, downing good portions of ale, his temperament becoming more and more quiet and sullen with each round of play until he stood abruptly as the last round ended, slammed his tankard down on the table and called out a new challenge.

"We will not play for weapons," he announced. "We will sweeten the pot and play for higher stakes." He swung around so that he was facing the laird's table. "Surely you have no objection," he asked of Brianna.

"No," she answered warily. "I have no objection."

"Then who will take up the challenge?" he asked, turning back to the tables of Norman and Scots warriors, kinsmen, and chieftains.

"Conal?"

"Och, no!" the good-natured Scot replied with woebegone expression and hand over his heart. "I've lost too much already this night, and if I lose any more sweet Meggie wilna be so sweet." Men around him broke out into laughter, for the maid Meggie of the blushing cheeks was also known to have a fierce temper.

"James?"

"You beat me soundly the last time we played, Malcolm. All I have left is me short-blade and I canna have you takin' that from me."

"You've always had a short blade, Jamie," another warrior called out to more rounds of laughter.

"I'll play with ye," a highlander called out. His name was McDrury and he was kinsman to Malcolm. He was also the winner of the evening. His eyes glinted with anticipation of taking on the renowned champion of Inverness.

"I'll play as well," Stephen of Valois announced to the sudden silence of the hall. For no Norman had played that evening. All kinsmen watched Malcolm in anticipation.

"Aye," Malcolm said, eyes narrowed with satisfaction. "I accept. Now, we must have one more to fill the board." He swung around, his gaze measuring every man there, then finally resting on Tarek al Sharif.

"What say you, barbarian?" he challenged. "You and your man against me and mine. Norman against highlander. And for much higher stakes."

Beneath his hand, Tarek felt hers stiffen with sudden tension.

"What is the wager?" he asked.

Malcolm's eyes glinted with cold satisfaction. "The wager is Brianna."

Nine

All about the hall was the sound of uncomfortable movement among knights and warriors. The relaxed atmosphere in the hall was suddenly charged with expectation.

"I will not be wagered, Malcolm of Drummond!" Brianna sprang out of her chair. "I make the decisions for Inverness, not you."

"Are you afraid he might lose?" Malcolm challenged.

"I am afraid of nothing and well you know it. But this is foolishness."

Tarek stopped her and pulled her back down into the chair beside him.

"I will not allow it," she said vehemently, her words low between them. "You need not accept his challenge, and no man will say naught against you. For all know the anger that rules his heart."

"You're wrong," Tarek replied, "I must accept." Then his gaze fastened on Malcolm where he stood in the center of the hall, awaiting his answer. He nodded, accepting Malcolm's challenge. "Let the game begin."

"You must stop this," Brianna implored Sir Gavin as preparations were made for the game. The laird's table was carried to the center of the hall where all could gather around and watch. The scorekeeper was given a place at the head of the table so that he could clearly see the sequences made by each warrior, with no chance of mistake in the tally.

Since that day when he had escorted her to the chapel, a bond of friendship had formed with the gallant knight.

He tried to ease her fears.

" 'Tis only a game, and he has played such games before."

But it was of little comfort to her. If Malcolm won he would press his claim. What then of the alliance? She had visions of battle breaking out within the walls of Inverness.

"Are you of so little faith, Brianna?" Tarek asked as he drank some of the strange, dark bracing brew he favored.

Unlike ale it did not dull the senses but instead sharpened them. She had tasted it once. Kaffe it was called, made from dark ground beans, the powder tied in a linen pouch, and then steeped in a pot of steaming water.

He preferred it laced with honey and an exotic spice called cinnamon. It had an unusual and not unpleasant taste when sweetened and flavored with the spice. While the other warriors had been drinking ale all evening, he had been drinking the strong, dark kaffe. It might be his only advantage.

"No," she answered truthfully, for in other things he had shown himself to be a more than worthy opponent. But this was different. The game was not known to him and Malcolm was known not to always play fairly, especially if the stakes were very high. "But if you should lose . . ."

"If I should lose and stand by the wager, then the alliance and the marriage is forfeit," he explained what was abundantly clear. "Which would you regret the loss of the most?"

The moment he asked the question he regretted it. She had been desperate for the alliance to save her people, whereas there was nothing between them but the words of ancient ceremonies.

He rose from his chair and took the short-bladed knife from his belt. He laid it on the table at his place at one side of the board.

"Please," she implored, laying a hand over his, though she did not know what she asked for — Please do not accept the challenge . . . ? Please do not lose . . . ? Please do not die.

Her fingers were cool where they lay over his, pale and slender against his scarred hand. Like fine pale satin that whispered across his senses. She looked at him as she had that day beside a highland pool when a breathtakingly beautiful girl had appeared out of the sunlight and mist and saved his life.

"You must learn to have faith in me, Brianna," he said, a devilish smile curving his mouth as he winked at her. Her hand tightened over his.

"You must not take Malcolm, lightly," she warned. "He has bested every man he has challenged."

"I take no opponent lightly," he assured her. "Particularly when the stakes are so high."

She looked down at the dirks and short-bladed knifes that had been laid at the table, each symbolic of the warrior who carried it. Malcolm's was embossed with his clan sign — that of a stag. McDrury's clan emblem was that of crossed swords. Stephen of Valois carried the symbol of his father's house of Normandy while no emblem adorned the handle of the blade Tarek al Sharif carried.

She seized the blade from the table, and with a glance across the playing board at Malcolm, unbound the green ribbon from her braid. She wound it about the handle and tied it off, then replaced the blade. Tarek's hand closed warmly over hers at the handle of the blade. For a moment their gazes met.

"Malcolm is a shrewd player, but there is a key to his choices," she whispered. "He makes his own choice of a new square to be added to the sequence in a particular order, left to right. That way he cuts down the likelihood of forgetting one of his own moves and has only to concentrate on those made by the others."

His hand tightened. "Why do you tell me this when it could mean his defeat?" Gone was his humor of a moment before. Sensual heat burned where there had been laughter, like that day she had reached out to a stranger.

"It is for the alliance," she insisted. "I will not see it set aside because of his anger and jealousy."

He smiled faintly. "I thank you for telling me, but I have no intention of losing."

"Let the game begin!" one of the highlanders shouted.

Stephen began the first round, selecting the first three squares. Then it was McDrury's turn, increasing the sequence by one additional square. And so it continued for several rounds until the third round when the challenge returned to Stephen of Valois.

"You realize," he announced to those at the table with a mischievous grin, "that if I win, then the lady Brianna is mine."

Malcolm, of course, had given that possibility no serious consideration. He snarled at Stephen, "Play Norman and see the error of your thinking."

Brianna watched with growing anxiety. All four men showed a remarkable capacity for the lengthy pattern of moves. Finally, McDrury faltered. Distracted by his kinsmen, who chanted colorful words, he was uncertain of the next square in the complicated sequence and chose wrongly. The hall grew silent as all gazes fixed on the scorekeeper.

"Fault," he announced.

"Your blade is forfeit, McDrury," several kinsmen called out, slapping him on the back good-naturedly for he had succeeded to the sixth level, much farther than ever before.

He had already surrendered his shield and knife in two previous mistakes. Now he raised his hands as he yielded his blade. "But I'll get you yet, Malcolm of Drummond," he challenged. But Malcolm was not listening. His narrowed gaze was fastened on Stephen of Valois.

"It is your move."

Another round continued, taking up where the last had left off. Stephen had already lost the symbolic sword he played with. Now, as the game became more complicated, he lost his shield.

Then it was Tarek's turn. He still had all three weapons as did Malcolm. Brianna stood close by, watching every move intently. Malcolm's kinsmen flanked him. It was against the rules to call out a move if a contestant was uncertain. Instead, they gave their support in comments meant to distract the others.

Tarek seized his short-bladed knife with Brianna's green ribbon tied about it. With the tip he pointed out each succeeding square in the sequence. The number was now up to twenty-four.

"Fault," the scorekeeper called out. Brianna's stunned gaze fastened on him. She had seen the wrong move but could say nothing to warn him. His sword was forfeit. It was laid with the others, to be reclaimed by their owners afterward, for a man's sword was like his name and though it might be taken in battle, games such as this were just that, games. Except for Malcolm. Then it was his turn.

Two more rounds followed. Then Stephen of Valois chose an incorrect square and was defaulted. It was deliberate. Brianna's stunned gaze fastened on the young knight.

"It would seem," he told the remaining two players, "that the contest is now yours." His gaze met Tarek's as he made a slight bow, then he moved away from the table. It was Tarek's turn.

Two more rounds followed, then Malcolm defaulted and lost his shield. Just as she had said, he played the same pattern, concentrating on remembering his opponent's moves while his moves were a matter of board sequence. But he grew uneasy as the difficulty of the sequences continued. Then he lost his blade. Angered at the loss, he threw the battle sword against the wall where the other swords lay. It embedded in the wall.

"The next loss is yours, barbarian," he vowed, for each man now had only the slender blades remaining. Another round was played. Brianna's nerves grew taut.

All about the hall her kinsmen and Tarek's knights had grown quiet. They no longer shouted encouragement or made ribald comments, but watched intently as it took more and more time for each man to complete the painstaking sequence which now numbered thirty-six squares. It was now Tarek's turn.

He chose slowly, deliberately, his concentration fastened not on the board but on Malcolm. Each move was agonizing. Even Brianna was uncertain of the next move. What if he lost?

This was no game for Malcolm. He would never surrender the prize he had fought for even if it meant war in the highlands. Her only hope would lay with Ian as laird of clan Drummond. He might prevail over his son but at what cost among the clans and kinsmen.

Her palms were sweaty. Suddenly it seemed too warm in the hall as if a dozen fires had been set. Then Tarek made his final three moves in rapid succession, adding one additional. His intense gaze fastened on Malcolm across the board, a smile of challenge curving his mouth. He knew he had chosen correctly even before the scorekeeper shouted out for all to hear.

"Correct sequence. It is the Drummond's turn." The attention of all turned to Malcolm. Brianna held her breath. No game had ever advanced this far. Could Malcolm remember the exact sequence with his own system to aid him?

Tension drew out in the hall. All about her it seemed that Tarek's men moved quietly to stand among her kinsmen and Malcolm's. Her gaze came back to Malcolm as he began the sequence. Thirty-eight squares must be chosen in exactly the right sequence.

He chose quickly and confidently through the first twenty moves. Then he became more cautious. Brianna sensed his thoughts working furiously, going through the sequence again and again. She sensed too the first signs of his uncertainty. He could not remember the sequence precisely.

She looked at Tarek. He too watched Malcolm, and by the look in his eyes she realized that he had sensed Malcolm's hesitance in another way — the way of the hunter that stalks its prey.

Everyone waited expectantly. Then as if suddenly certain of the pattern, Malcolm designated the last three blocks in the sequence and added a fourth. He looked across at Tarek with a triumphant expression as all listened for the scorekeeper's verdict.

"Fault," the seneschal announced in a clear but regretful voice. Malcolm exploded with rage.

"You fool! Check it again!"

"I have checked it twice," the poor man declared with a frightened expression as if he expected the hall to be brought down around his ears. "It is as I have said. You have one fault, Malcolm of Drummond. You reversed the third and last symbols in the sequence."

Brianna stared at Malcolm in amazement, for those were his own choices. Anger had gotten the better of him and he couldn't even remember the symbols he had chosen himself.

He drove the tip of his blade down into the surface of the board, glaring furiously at Tarek al Sharif. "If you wish to take the blade you must claim it with your own hand for I'll no' yield it to you."

Tarek picked up his own short-bladed knife with Brianna's ribbon bound around the handle. He shrugged. "As you can see, I already have a fine knife. I have no need of yours." He drove the blade down, embedding the tip not in the game board, but in the top of the laird's table as though staking his claim once and for all.

"I have already claimed the only prize I seek." His hand closed over Brianna's. Malcolm turned and strode furiously from the hall. His father, Ian, approached the laird's table as the game board was carried away with several new notches cut into it.

"Ye played well. My son has been outspoken," he said by way of apology. "He does not accept loss well."

Tarek nodded. "Inverness needs all of her warriors, Ian. Especially those who will not accept loss. But what took place here tonight was a game. Nothing more."

Ian measured the man and slowly nodded and assured him, "Aye, nothing more."

When he had gone to join the others in toasts of ale, Brianna turned to Tarek, confusion in her eyes. "How did you do it?"

He retrieved the short-bladed knife from the table, his strong fingers lightly playing along that deadly sharp blade as though caressing it and causing Brianna to shiver.

"In order to win, you must know three things."

"What are they?" she asked with undisguised curiosity, for it was clear that although she had tried to help him, he was clearly capable of figuring out Malcolm's method of winning.

Tarek became very serious. "First, you must study your opponent. You must be able to anticipate every move before he makes it. Second, you must watch for that moment that

176

comes only once in every battle, when everything may be won or lost. That is when you strike hardest with everything you possess."

"And third?"

His clear blue gaze met hers. "You must have absolutely no fear of dying. Dying is loss, and if you fear losing, then you have lost before you have begun."

She shivered violently in spite of the heat of the fire at the hearth at her back. He had been prepared to die to prevent Malcolm claiming her as the game prize.

"You are cold," he said gently.

"No," she stammered, trying to find her voice. All along she had feared that Malcolm might kill him and jeopardize the alliance. She realized now how foolish those fears were.

"What is it then? Do you regret that I did not lose."

"Nay!" her gaze came up sharply and met his. "It is not that. It is just that . . ."

"What, Brianna?"

"I must go," she said hastily. "I have stayed too long. There is much to be done." She turned and quickly crossed the hall, eager to leave and to escape uncertain feelings she did not understand. He caught her at the doorway to the main hall, pulling her into the shadows outside the hallway.

"You didn't have to tell me his system for winning the game."

"You did not need it."

"Still, you did not need to tell me."

"Yes I did."

"Why?"

"I had to be certain you would win." She tried to twist out of his grasp but he would not allow it. He gently held her prisoner, his fingers clasped over her wrists.

"Thank you, Brianna."

The sound of his voice brought her head up. It was different from before, low, tender, like a caress.

"Thank you," he said again, the words whispering across her lips as his mouth closed over hers. There was no time to think or react. Or escape.

His mouth was like warm satin as he kissed her lips apart. His breath mingled with hers, the taste of sweet fire filling her senses. Her startled gaze met his as strong hands glided up over her shoulders, fingertips brushing across each cheek, then stroking back through her hair as he angled her mouth beneath his and kissed her again.

"Be my wife, Brianna," he whispered as he again coaxed her lips apart, the tip of his tongue stroking at the center of her upper lip, lingering to tease at the sensitive whorl of flesh.

She gasped, startled by the intense pleasure of the simple contact, her own tongue flicking instinctively over the place he'd touched. As she drew another breath, he kissed her again.

"In all ways," he whispered, his voice harsh in his throat.

This kiss was different, powerful and possessive. Gone was the tenderness, replaced by a bruising passion. Her lips parted willingly at the intense pleasure of his tongue slipping between in a physical claiming that was as intimate as lovers joining.

She suddenly pulled back, abruptly ending the kiss. Her eyes were filled with dark shadows of emotions. Confusion drew her golden brows together as her next breath shuddered out of her startled lungs.

"Brianna . . ." he said with an urgency that made no attempt to disguise his need for her.

"I can't," she replied, desperate to make him understand what she herself no longer understood. "It's not possible."

"It is more than possible, Brianna. And I vow it will

happen, but only when you ask it."

Suddenly he felt her stiffen. There was a movement in the shadows at the doorway as someone approached. She quickly stepped back from him as one of his knights stepped through the doorway. It was Gavin de Marte.

"Milord? There are matters of strategy you wanted to discuss." He looked from one to the other and turned to leave. "It will wait."

"No!" Brianna told him. "Do not leave. I am needed elsewhere. Good morn to you, Sir Gavin."

Tarek cursed as she seized her opportunity and escaped up the stairs, no doubt to the chambers above. Or perhaps to the battlements where he knew she often fled. Her own chamber offered no privacy with the woman from Glenross, her baby, and young Nel who now slept there at night.

"What is so important?" Tarek asked. "Stephen knows my plans." His anger was barely controlled as his gaze remained fastened on the top of the stairs where she had disappeared.

"Aye," Gavin acknowledged. "And our men do not argue his authority, but the Scots are reluctant to follow his direction."

Realizing there was no escape from the weighty matters of duty, Tarek spun about on his heel. He swore again. "Why is it always so cold in this place? Will spring never come to this land."

Gavin suppressed a grin. "Perhaps I should see about those fur-lined breeches you spoke of. They will ease the cold that plagues you." Tarek threw him a murderous glare as they returned to the hall.

"I've no need of fur-lined breeches."

"Not by what I have heard." The smirk on Gavin's face was unmistakable.

"Be careful, my friend."

"A warning?" Gavin feigned surprise.

"A promise," Tarek assured him. Gavin's grin deepened as he accompanied him back to the laird's table.

It was late afternoon when Tarek strode from the hall with the intention of seeking that second-floor chamber where Brianna had no doubt fled. But he stopped at the sight of young Duncan, the boy, who had lost his entire family at Glenross except for his grandfather.

The boy sat dozing against the wall outside the main hall. With the wariness of one who has lived with the constant threat of death, he immediately awakened. Firelight from the torches at the walls flickered across his youthful features and hesitant expression. He looked like a terrified waif as he came to his feet and approached Tarek.

"You said I should see you, milord," Duncan reminded him. "About taking care of the mare."

Since arriving at Inverness the boy had been like a shadow following him everywhere.

There was a sound in the boy's voice that was not lost on Tarek. It was a hesitance of knowing one is not wanted, of waiting to be ordered away, of knowing he had no place in this world except the one he made for himself.

Once, he had been such a boy, in spite of his adopted parents who tried their best to assuage the pain of his royal, bastard birth. But always there was an uncertainty that dominated his life. As it did the boy's.

"I have not forgotten," Tarek replied.

He thought of the stables, newly built at Inverness for the Scots had few horses and no stables. It was the first structure he had built to protect the Norman warhorses during the next winter.

With a lingering thought to the plans he had hoped for, he realized the stables offered more privacy than the main hall at

180

Inverness. He wondered, with a slow smile, if he might lure Brianna there, for it seemed the only place where they were not likely to encounter the entire population of Inverness.

His temper mollified, if not the raging ache below his belt, he told young Duncan. "Come, I will introduce you to the mare."

"Introduce?" he said aghast. "Does she talk?"

Tarek smiled. "There are times when I am certain of it. But she does not speak in words, she speaks in her own way. And you must learn her language so you may gain her trust, for she trusts very few."

"She is a fine, rare beast, milord. I have never seen such beauty in an animal." Duncan's young voice echoed along the high walls. As the large doors were opened and a Norman guard appeared briefly visible beyond, a shadow separated from the others as someone watched them leave the main hall.

The light from the torch flickered across Gillie's disappointed expression. A curse whispered in the chill of the late afternoon air as opportunity was thwarted once again.

After the game she had waited outside the main hall hoping to draw the attention of Tarek al Sharif for she had ambitions of her own.

The formality of the marriage itself mattered little to her, for she had discovered in the few weeks since returning to Inverness that her cousin's marriage was not a true marriage, but made for the sake of the alliance.

Now as she watched him leave the hall with the boy, she again experienced that ache of desire that she had felt for few men, the center of her body moist and hot for him.

Anger sharpened her features as she turned back toward the main hall in frustration. She was only slightly mollified by the certainty that it was only a matter of time before he came to her willingly. For he was hot-blooded and would not suffer a cold marriage for long.

Malcolm reached for Gillie as she passed by. She protested angrily, then relaxed as the light from the torches fell across his features.

"Not now," she grumbled, still angry that her plans for Tarek al Sharif had been thwarted. But equally angry, the warrior was not of a mind to listen to her protests.

He dragged her into the shadows beneath the angle of the stairs. There he pushed her up against the wall, his hands rough at her breasts.

"I told ye!" Gillie spat out angrily. "Not now." Her protest was smothered under the bruising power of his mouth as his hands pulled the hem of her gown up over her hips.

She beat at his shoulders and back, but without success. Instead, he pinned her to the wall, his hips grinding against hers as he loosened the laces at the front of his breeches.

"I said *no!*" Gillie cried out angrily. But he ignored her as he wedged her thighs apart and thrust inside her.

"Ye bloody, ruttin' bastard! I've no protection!" But her protests ended suddenly on a gasp of startled pleasure. Instead of struggling, Gillie clung to him, her eyes gleaming with a new plan.

Ten

When Tarek left the stables he climbed the stone stairs to the battlements. Though it was late, surely Brianna would be calmer now, and they might speak of things between them.

In the weeks since he'd forced her to the marriage he had come to understand just how much more he wanted from her than the advantageous alliance with the Scots that the marriage provided. He wanted it all.

He wanted her at his side at night as well as in the hall by day. He wanted her cries of passion as well as her words of counsel. He wanted her to be part of his life in all ways, and he wanted to give her sons. Not fatherless bastard sons whose hearts might one day be filled with hatred against him, to match his own for his father, but strong fine sons and daughters born of a true marriage that aligned their people against the threats of foreign invaders. Sons and daughters whose blood would bind them to the land for generations. He wanted a place that was truly his that he could call home. He wanted her.

But when he got to the battlements, she was not there. He frowned, for he had spoken with the girl Nel and knew she was not in her chamber.

His gaze scanned the darkness that lay over the fortress. Once before she had left safety to go into the woods surrounding Glenross. It had almost ended in disaster.

Only by good fortune had they escaped when the mist filled the forest and hid them, for he could never have protected her against the raiders. Afterward she had refused to speak of it any more than to offer the excuse of herb gathering to acquire certain medicinal leaves for the injured at Glenross.

He knew of such matters for Lady Vivian was skilled in the healing ways, and he had not pressed her further about her reasons for going alone into the forest. But he sensed there was far more she had not told him.

He did not question her loyalty. Too many kinsmen and her own family had been murdered by raiders. Her loyalty to the Scots was unquestionable. And she had accepted the alliance of their marriage, if reluctantly. Still, he knew so little about this girl whose beauty and fire of spirit burned through his blood as no other. He had claimed her to wife, and he had promised her she would be wife in all ways. But he must find a way to make that her choice as well.

The battlements were cold and dark except for the light of the moon that spilled across the stones, and empty in this particular corner he knew she favored. It looked out over the village below, the forest, and the ocean cliffs beyond.

His men guarded the walls both day and night. But this corner was unapproachable from beyond the walls and the guards did not venture here. It was also for that reason that he knew she came here. But she was not there.

He swore as he turned from the wall, determined to find her. In the ghostly gray light of the moon, a silvery flash on the stones drew his attention.

It was a glossy feather, pale and shimmering, the white-gold threads gleaming in the light of the moon. He stroked the feather between thumb and forefinger. It was soft as satin and warm to the touch, as if it still held the heat of the creature who had lost it.

He frowned as his gaze once more searched the night sky and he listened for the sound of wings, recalling a small,

184

well-trained falcon that once belonged to Lady Vivian of Amesbury. But he had seen no such hunting creatures about Inverness, only the ruined dovecote in the yard that had since been repaired. And this was not the feather of a dove.

He tucked it away inside his tunic. He would ask young Duncan about the sort of bird it might belong to, for the boy seemed to know everything that went on at Inverness. He would know if the dovecote at Inverness housed such a bird.

It had been so long since she had last been to the ancient place Brianna wasn't at all certain she could find it. But as though some inner instinct guided her, she found the glistening lake of water in the swirling clouds of mist at the edge of the forest.

Here, years before, she had come as a child, lured by instinct. It was that same instinct of all creatures — birds who return to the same nesting grounds each year, or animals that return to the same hunting grounds — the lure of some place known only in the soul.

Here she had played beside the lake, drawn as children are to the crystal clear depths that revealed stones covered in shades of green with moss and underwater shadows of hidden places beneath the rocks where she imagined creatures lived. The lake glistened as the silvery light of a lopsided moon penetrated the forest so that she could see her own image reflected on the surface.

The face that looked back at her was no longer the face of a child waiting expectantly for a glimpse of some imaginary water creature in its depths. Her reflection startled her, drawn features framed by white gold hair that hung past her shoulders in wind-blown disarray. And eyes that looked back at her, haunted by half-remembered dreams, visions of things she could not understand, and a childhood prophecy that tor-

185

mented her. They were not her eyes, but the eyes of someone else.

She had seen those eyes before in dreams. They were the eyes of a beautiful flame-haired woman, calling to her, telling her it was time to get up.

"Mother?" she whispered.

The surface of the water rippled as though in answer. Then once more it lay still as glass, reflecting the pale light of the moon that glowed behind her, framing her with a silvery nimbus, her features shrouded in shadows. Except for her eyes, which glowed brilliant green, as green as the leaves of the rowan tree, its branches hanging over the edge of the lake.

"One leaf, two leaf, three leaf . . . " She remembered ancient words, all but forgotten until now.

She picked three leaves from the rowan and pressed them between her flattened palms. Then, kneeling beside the lake, she extended her hands, palms pressed together, over the still, gleaming surface, at the same time she turned her thoughts inward, seeking that inner place of ancient dreams and visions deep within her soul.

As the door to the past opened, she opened her hands and allowed one leaf to fall to the surface of the lake. As it floated on the surface, she repeated the ancient words.

"Leaf afloat, leaf so green, help me see what is unseen."

As the first leaf glided away, she released another, repeating the words. And then released the third, repeating the incantation again.

Each leaf traveled the same direction as the one before it, as though guided by some unseen current, creating ripples across the surface like concentric circles rippling out from the dark center until one overlapped another.

She stared incredulously at the perfect pattern, for she immediately recognized it even though it was barely visible in the water. The two circles expanded until they touched the edges of the lake, the overlapped center like an opening at the heart of the joined circles. Drawn by unknown powers, Brianna extended her hand over the rippling surface, and repeated, "Reveal to me what is unseen . . ."

Light splintered up from the depths of the lake, piercing the center of the joined circles, revealing images of the past, present, and future — a gentle, kind man, handsome of face, with extraordinary blue eyes and loving smile. Then it was replaced by another image of a dark haired warrior who carried the sword of Islam. Tarek al Sharif.

And finally, another warrior with golden hair, eyes as cold as death, powerful hands wrapped about the handle of a giant war ax. Blood soaked the warrior's tunic. He slowly lifted his head and looked at her. Mardigan. And through the unusual vision unlike any dream, she sensed that he was very near.

A sudden coldness seized her, wrapping around her heart. The surface of the lake darkened. The opening at the center of the overlapping circles closed as the vision disappeared. Whatever else might have revealed itself to her was now gone. But her certainty of Mardigan's nearness remained, and intensified.

She lifted her head trying to catch a change in the scent and sound of the surrounding forest. Her senses sharpened, her head coming around as a subtle shift of an air current brought a smell that hadn't been there before — the smell of man, redolent with sweat, grime, the stale leavings of a meal recently eaten, and the stench of blood.

Pale, downy hairs raised along her arms and at the back of her neck. Her heart pounded violently. Mardigan's men were nearby and well hidden where they might never be found. Unlike the Norman soldiers with their bright tunics and gleaming armor, they lived off the land and blended with their surroundings. And continuously eluded capture.

She pushed to her feet and followed the rim of the lake to the edge of the forest beyond. Her senses warned her of the danger, yet she could not leave until she knew exactly where Mardigan and his men were.

The forest was heavily wooded and dark where no moonlight penetrated. Her senses guided her, eyes keen, hearing sharpened to the slightest sound. Finally, angling through the dense tree cover, she found them.

They had made their camp at the base of a rock outcropping, well-protected against any surprise attack. A score of men gathered around a campfire, the skeletal remains of a carcass smoldering at the crude spit. Occasionally the blade of a weapon gleamed in the dying firelight. Their unwashed stench filled the night air, redolent with the scent of the game they'd killed, unwashed male sweat thick with the scent of recent battle, and a raw, animal smell of sex.

Their laughter was raucous, their language lewd as one of them rejoined his companions. Behind him, he dragged a young woman. An angry red mark spread across one cheek and the expression on her face was dazed as she stumbled along behind him.

The bodice of her gown gaped open. She was dazed and made no attempt to cover her breasts. The skirt of her gown was stained and her hair was matted with leaves and twigs.

"Eh," one of the others grumbled. "It's my turn at her."

Mardigan sat across the camp from his men, his shoulder-length hair burnished golden in the light of the fire, his face taut with hard angles as he carved a strip of meat from a haunch of venison.

"Perhaps you would like a taste of her first," the raider suggested to his companion. Then his tone grew mocking. "It is rumored the daughter of the laird of Inverness has been bedded by the Norman lord sent by the Conqueror."

"It is my turn," another argued. "And I don't much care for your leavings."

As tempers flared and weapons were drawn, Mardigan came to his feet.

"Cease!" With blade in hand, he separated them, throwing one man to the ground dangerously close to the fire.

"We cannot attack the Scots if we fight among ourselves!" he shouted at his men. "The next man who speaks out will feel the love of my blade!"

Swords were lowered. As the argument ended, Mardigan cast aside his own blade and grabbed the woman. Instead of taking her from the camp as the others before him had, he threw her down on the pallet of furs beside the fire. When she protested feebly, he struck her. She stared mutely past his shoulders as he pinned her to the ground with every intention of taking her in front of his men.

Then, as he dragged the woman's skirts up over her hips, a piercing shriek shattered the night, silencing the raiders' laughter and crude comments amid a frenzy of powerful wings and slashing talons. As Mardigan turned, those talons slashed at his face, opening flesh to the bone. He flung himself away from the woman.

"Run!" Brianna's thoughts connected with the woman's, slashing through her pain and stupor as surely as those slashing talons. *"Escape while you can!"*

Slow to react, her body bruised, and in much pain, the woman struggled to her feet. With dazed eyes she glanced about the encampment, searching for the one who had spoken to her.

"Run! Into the forest. I will find you!" Brianna assured her. *"But you must go now!"*

Again the falcon swept the camp, providing the only

chance the woman might have. His face streaming with blood, Mardigan cursed at his men.

"Kill the creature!"

A skilled huntress, the falcon made one more pass at the encampment, her aim unerring as she slashed the side of another man's head, severing his ear. He shrieked with pain as he fell to the ground, clutching the side of his head.

"The woman!" another shouted. "She's fled into the forest."

Enraged curses were heard among wails of pain as the falcon also fled into the forest. She followed the sound of the woman's thrashing through the brush and low-hanging branches, swooping near once, the woman frantically altering her course in another direction.

Twice more the falcon swooped down on her, near enough for her to feel the brush of wings against her shoulder, but never harming her. And each time she turned in a new direction, terrified of those deadly talons.

The woman reached the ridge, the sounds of her captors not far behind her. She stumbled down the small slope toward a gleaming lake of water.

Brianna saw the woman as she reached the edge of the lake. She grabbed her by the arm with one hand, the other clamped over the woman's mouth. Terrified eyes shown wide above the edge of Brianna's hand. Her own breath came in strangled, dragging gasps as the woman struggled frantically to free herself.

"Do not scream!" Brianna warned. "I will not harm you."

The woman gasped in surprise as Brianna slowly lowered her hand. "You're the one I heard," she said with confusion. "But I saw no one. Where were you hiding?"

"Nearby, in the forest. We must leave this place." There was no time for lengthy explanations. Even now, Brianna heard Mardigan and his men approaching. Any moment they would be upon them. Brianna motioned her to silence.

"We must hide or they will find us." She pulled the woman with her behind a fallen tree that lay beside the lake, drawing her mantle about the woman's shoulders.

"They will surely find us here," the woman protested. "We must find another place."

"There is no time. We will be safe," Brianna promised her. "You must trust me."

As Brianna wrapped her arm protectively about her shoulders the woman exclaimed, "You've been injured!"

Brianna wiped the blood from her fingers.

" 'Tis nothing," she insisted, then motioned the woman to be silent.

They huddled together beside the fallen tree, while the sounds of Mardigan and his men came more clearly through the forest. As they broke through the trees into the clearing that surrounded the lake of water, mist began to rise from its gleaming surface. It thickened and grew dense, blanketing everything, making it impossible to see.

Thomas was waiting for her on the battlements when she returned just as dawn appeared on the horizon, his thoughts connecting with hers with an urgency of concern.

"You have been to the ancient place."

She was cold and exhausted, and leaned heavily against his broad shoulder as she told him of Mardigan's encampment in the forest and the woman she'd brought back to Inverness, who had survived a raid on her village but watched as her entire family was murdered. Because she dare not leave the woman alone she had been overlong in returning.

Now the woman, Enya, waited outside the gate at the gardens where Brianna had left her. She could not bring her to

Inverness through the main gate for then everyone would know that she had been outside the gates and returned with the woman. It would raise questions impossible to answer.

"He has been looking for you."

There was no need for Thomas to explain whom he meant. Tarek al Sharif. Somehow she must convince him that she had merely been seeing to the needs of others at Inverness, and the woman had just arrived asking for her. Her head ached, pain throbbing behind her eyes.

The transformation had been much more difficult this time, the aftereffects lasting much longer than usual. She had lingered too long in the other world. Even now, she felt a coldness of not being quite herself.

"It must seem that she has brought me word of the raiders," she explained to Thomas.

At his skeptical expression, she explained, "She is grateful to be alive, she will not betray me by revealing that *I* was the one who found her in the encampment. She will tell everyone that she escaped." And in truth, she had. With a little assistance from a friend.

"Now, I must reach my chamber before the others awaken. Though she is my kinswoman I do not trust Gillie."

Thomas nodded his agreement. *"Aye, the woman is ambitious. She would not hesitate to discredit you to milord al Sharif."*

She glanced at Thomas, surprised by the unmistakable respect in his voice, for there were few other than Cullum who received it. He had never respected Malcolm.

He thought the Scots warrior too impulsive and hasty in his decisions — the kind of decisions that sent most of the other chieftains and warriors from Inverness after the council meeting, and left Inverness vulnerable to attack.

They kept to the early morning shadows of the outlying buildings as they quickly crossed the yard to the door that

192

opened off the kitchens and pantry. Once inside the main hall, Thomas led the way down the darkened hallway to the door that opened onto the hidden passage.

Brianna hesitated as she too remembered the last time she had used the passage, and the death and destruction that had awaited them when they reached the main hall.

Her emotions were still fragile. It was always so after her journey into the other world, as if she existed precariously between both worlds, part of both and not wholly of one or the other. Tears — that very human expression of emotion — pooled in her eyes at the memory. She hastily wiped them away.

"You must be very careful," Thomas warned, his thoughts connecting to hers with new urgency as she stepped past him to the opening of the passage.

She nodded, laying a comforting hand on his arm, drawing strength and comfort from his human warmth. "Thank you, my friend."

When he made to follow, she stopped him. "I will be safe now. You must go to Enya and care for her. I fear for her, if she remains outside the walls any longer. And it must seem that *she* has brought word of the raiders.

"Bring her to me. It must seem as though I have heard of it first, and then I will send word to milord."

Thomas nodded his agreement as he closed the stone panel behind her.

There had been no time to take a torch from the wall, so she made her way through the narrow darkened passage, up the flight of stone steps, guided by her heightened senses. At the top of the passage, her hand unerringly found the lever that opened the panel. As she placed her hand upon it, she immediately sensed a physical presence in the room on the other side.

She did not sense danger, it was merely a physical awareness along each nerve ending that alerted her in ways others were not.

She chided herself for her foolishness. Of course she sensed the presence of others, since her chamber was now occupied by survivors from Glenross. As she released the mechanism and the panel shifted away from the opening, she sensed it even stronger.

The hiss from the fire at the brazier was the only sound as she stepped from the passage. The tapestry billowed gently on a current of icy air that followed her from the passage, then settled back against the wall as she closed the panel behind her. No other sounds came from inside the room. Confident she had not disturbed Anne and the others, she stepped out from behind the tapestry.

The fire at the brazier provided the only light, a soft glow that steeped the edges of the chamber in deep shadows. She hesitated, making certain she hadn't awakened anyone, then stepped into the room and pushed back the hood of her mantle.

"Good morning, Brianna."

Eleven

Brianna whirled around. The flames at the brazier framed a glorious nimbus about hair that fell past her shoulders in a tumbled disarray of shimmering white gold, flickered across fragile features that suddenly seemed all the more fragile beneath pale, taut skin, and reflected in the startled green of her eyes.

"Welcome back, wife," he said, in a way that was far from welcoming as he came out of the chair where he had been waiting for her.

He moved with stealthy grace, a shadow separating itself from other shadows, lean, agile as a cat as he stood and slowly crossed the chamber toward her. His glance followed hers to the empty bed and pallet of furs beside it, as if he knew her thoughts as easily as she knew those of others.

"They have been made comfortable elsewhere," he assured her, at the same time assuring her that they were completely alone. Then he asked, "Where does the passage lead?"

She watched him warily. She knew the temperament of men like Malcolm, who were hasty, volatile, too outspoken, and too quick to anger. But she did not know the temperament of this man who watched her with an animal keenness like a cat stalking its prey. She would have much preferred his anger.

"It leads to a hallway near the kitchens," she answered hesitantly.

"A means of escape without being seen." His gaze fastened on her as if daring her to deny it.

She denied nothing. "Thomas and I used the passage the

night Inverness was attacked."

"And tonight?" he demanded. "Did you leave the fortress?"

She sensed he already knew the truth, or in the very least would know if she lied.

"Yes."

"Why?"

"To get away from you."

She had gone in search of answers to the only place that had ever offered her any, the strange waters of the ancient lake to which she was strangely connected. She had hoped she might find some greater truth there, some vision in the deep, blue green depths that might help her understand what was happening to her. But it was his face she had seen in the depths of the lake, a portent of something in the future that had not revealed itself to her.

He winced, as though he had been physically struck. She expected anger, for Malcolm had reacted in just that manner when she had tried to make him understand that they could not be wed, that she did not return his feelings. He had been furious, violently so, and was angry still. But this strange, dark warrior from another land, who had bound her to him against her will for the sake of her people, said nothing. And in the silence, she sensed she had hurt him far more deeply with the truth than any lie she could have spoken.

The heavy tapestry panel over the door opening was suddenly thrown back. Stephen of Valois rapidly strode into the chamber. His expression was tense.

"A woman has asked to see Lady Brianna. She survived a raid and has brought word of Mardigan and his men." The words were edged with eagerness. "They are in the forest less than a day's ride south of Inverness!"

Tarek's own gaze was speculative, cool as arctic ice, and fastened on hers. She saw the questions that went unasked, heard them as easily as if the words had been spoken as he struggled with the truth she had told him.

"The men await your orders," Stephen added. "And the Scots have assembled as well."

Tarek nodded, frowning as he gave his orders. "Every third man will ride with us. The rest will remain to defend Inverness." When they turned to leave, he felt her hand on his sleeve.

"They have the advantage in that they travel light and fast, unencumbered by the weight of heavy armor. The clothes they wear blend with the forest. They will be upon you and you will never see them until it is too late."

Dark brows angled sharply over intense blue eyes. "How do you know this?" he asked.

"You forget, I know much of Mardigan."

That blue gaze bore into hers, as if he was trying to see what more lay behind the words and the touch at his sleeve.

He did not reach out to her, but still she felt his touch in the same way she had felt it long after that chance encounter beside a highland pool months ago. And the same way she had felt his touch every time since.

He nodded, and said to Stephen, "The men will wear only breeches and tunics that blend with the colors of the forest. They will only carry weapons which can be easily concealed. If the raiders blend with the forest, then so shall we."

He did not immediately follow as Stephen left to carry out his orders, but hesitated as though to say something more.

"We will speak of this again, Brianna." Then he was gone.

Tarek swore under his breath. "By the Prophet, I hate this cursed forest!" Beside him, Stephen of Valois grinned.

"The forest, or the cold?"

"Both! 'Tis unnatural for one to endure such coldness.

Will spring never come to this cursed land?"

"By what Malcolm has told me, this is spring. And a bonnie warm one at that." Stephen made a poor attempt to smother his humor. "Perhaps you are in need of those fur-lined breeches to warm your thin, Persian blood," he suggested.

"Or perhaps a fur-lined wench!" Sir Guy suggested, rolling his eyes as he joined in the banter. "It might help ease the ride on that mare in these cold climes."

"To be sure, the mare is the only thing he has ridden," Stephen chided. "The Scots maid seems ill-tempered toward her wifely duties. However, she seems particularly skilled at flying the nest at every available opportunity."

"Why not shout to the tree tops?" Tarek responded, his keen-eyed expression murderous, "And announce our presence in this damnable forest for all to hear, especially Mardigan. Then it is certain that the only thing any of us shall ride is the edge of a raider's sword."

"He is most foul of temper," Sir Guy commented as Tarek al Sharif rode on ahead to check with his point guard.

"Aye," Stephen noted with a wounded grin. "Upon our return to Inverness, for all our sakes, we will make certain the woman Gillie is available to him, for she has made no secret she would gladly warm his bed. And 'tis certain his wife has not."

"If we live long enough to return to Inverness," Sir Guy added his voice in agreement. "I am not certain which is the more dangerous — Mardigan or milord's temper. And I swear Gillie is a spirited woman." His brows waggled with good humor. "She has a taste for pleasure."

"Aye," Stephen agreed, remembering the woman's eagerness at Glenross. "But especially with a fat purse of Norman gold."

"What else might we spend our gold on in this cursed land?"

There was no time for further conversation as Sir Gavin rode hard back along the line of Norman soldiers, dressed in tunics and breeches that blended with the colors of the forest. The raider encampment had been found.

It was empty, but not by many hours. Malcolm grunted as he rose to his feet beside the still warm remnants of the fire. He shoved past Tarek al Sharif, making no attempt to disguise his contempt.

"An hour ahead. No more," he said, as he seized blade and war ax and secured both at his belt. With a sharp nod to his own men, he set off afoot into the forest.

"The bastard will get us all killed," Stephen swore, his gaze narrowed as he watched the Scots disappear through the heavily wooded trees. He glanced to Tarek al Sharif.

"Leave the horses," Tarek ordered. "The forest is too dense to follow astride, they will only slow us down." He glanced warily about, his gaze hard as he glanced at a score of hiding places. As Stephen made to secure his horse and follow the path the Scots had taken, Tarek stopped him.

"We will flank the Scots," he told Stephen.

"And outflank any attack that may strike at them," Stephen grinned as he saw the cunning of the plan.

Tarek nodded. "I learned that from your father. Never attack straight on."

"He always favored his men over his son," Stephen acknowledged.

At mid-morning on the sixth day, they heard the sounds of battle. With the certainty that they were very near the raiders, Malcolm and his Scots had moved far ahead just before daybreak. Tarek's men had paralleled their movement, at a flanking position. Also certain that they were very close,

Tarek had sent word for the Scots to hold back so that they might coordinate the attack. They had not waited.

Tarek quickly gave orders and split his numbers, sending half his men under Stephen's command in a circular movement to the northwest, and taking the rest of his men in a northeasterly direction. Once they were in position, they would join the battle from two sides.

The Scots were outnumbered, the battle bloody. Fought in the depths of the forest, trees and brush were hacked to pieces in the fierce frenzy. Tarek cursed the dense foliage and the foolhardiness of the Scots as he and his men came upon the battle.

An arrow with a crimson streamer attached was shot aloft to signal their position to Stephen and his men. Another arrow was seen in answer, a signal that all was in readiness. Tarek let out a battle cry as they plunged into the battle.

Already the bodies of the wounded and dying littered the floor of the forest. Soon the foliage about them ran crimson with blood. Outnumbered, the Scots had lost many good men. But still the survivors fought on, rallying as the Norman knights and warriors joined the battle.

"These Scots are blood-thirsty fools to attack against such odds!" Gavin grunted as he cut down one raider and wounded another.

Tarek countered a raider's blow, then spun about, slicing across the man's belly with his curved sword. When the man's body hung impaled on the tip of the blade, he kicked him away with a measure of disgust for such foolishness. He had wanted to surprise the raiders with the hope of taking Mardigan alive. Now the best they could hope for was to survive. He plunged on, meeting yet another raider blade.

The battle waned, like some great bloody creature taking a deep breath, and then continued with renewed ferocity. In the thick of battle, their slashing weapons had carved a bloodied clearing in the dense foliage.

Sharp in memory was the battle of Hastings, fought months before, and the bodies of the dead that had littered the English plain. By the Prophet! he hated the damnable forest where the enemy might be hiding behind the next tree.

Across the clearing he saw the Scots fight fiercely, waver, then rally in spite of the great numbers of their dead. Tarek fought his way toward Malcolm's men, closing the pincer of the attack while Stephen closed it from the western flank.

As one raider fell beneath his blade, he spun around and saw another with a short, blunted blade sink it into Malcolm's shoulder. The Scots warrior screamed in agony as he went down on his knees. The raider raised his blade for the death blow.

The gleaming Persian blade caught him low at the belly, opening him gullet to breast bone, and staggering his blow off target. The raider's blade halted mid-air as if stopped by an invisible hand, then the warrior crumbled to the ground beside Malcolm. Tarek went down beside him, one arm going round his waist as he pulled him to his feet.

"Leave me . . ." Malcolm snarled fiercely.

"By the Prophet you will walk!" Tarek told him equally fierce, as he took his weight and dragged him to the edge of the clearing. "I'll not give your people more reason to hate me by leaving you for dead."

He eased Malcolm into a place of safety away from the battle. When the Scot resisted and struggled to get to his feet to take up the battle anew, Tarek pushed him back to the ground.

"You'll provide too tempting a target," he spat out at the man who made no attempt to disguise his hatred. "Your sword arm is useless." Taking Malcolm's other hand, he shoved it against the gaping wound at the Scot's shoulder, forcing him to hold the flesh together. Then he demanded, "Did you see Mardigan?"

"Across the clearing," Malcolm grunted in pain. "You'll know him by the size of him. He's a match for you, with wild yellow hair, and eyes cold as a whore's heart."

With a nod, Tarek plunged back into the battle, fighting his way across the clearing where Stephen and his men fought fiercely against the raiders. Gavin rejoined him, guarding his back. As they added their numbers to Stephen's, the raiders no doubt sensed that the battle was now hopeless.

A fierce cry went out among the raiders. They broke off fighting, turned and fled into the forest.

Tarek and his men gave chase, until it became obvious they were chasing the wind through the trees. He gave the orders for all to retreat to the clearing, with a careful watch kept for any raiders who might still be about.

The raiders had lost at least a score of men, but Mardigan was not among them. Tarek's men had escaped with several injuries. But the Scot's had not been so fortunate.

Overeager, hasty, and lacking discipline, they had plunged into the battle heedless of the raiders' greater numbers, and paid a high price. Eight Scots were dead, an equal number gravely injured, including Malcolm.

"Mardigan?" he grunted with pain, his skin gray beneath the spattering of raider blood.

"Fled," Tarek answered. "Into the forest with his men."

"Follow the bastard!" Malcolm ordered.

When his men would have obeyed, Tarek counterordered, "Hold!"

"You bloody barbarian!" Malcolm screamed. "They are my men. They follow my orders."

"Outnumbered and like sheep to the slaughter if they

follow!" Tarek informed him. "It is done for today. You have already lost eight men, with an equal number crippled and maimed. Mardigan and his men have scattered into the forest. You will never find them. We will see to the wounded and take what victory we can from this day, for Mardigan has sorely felt the sting of our blades."

All about them, Scots warriors looked from one to another. Malcolm's expression faltered, the argument more than he had strength for. He nodded, aware that Tarek could have berated him before his men for foolishly sending them into battle. But he had not. He slumped back against the tree trunk where Tarek had dragged him to safety.

"You saved my life, barbarian."

"Yes."

"Why?"

Tarek crouched down beside him, lifting away the front side of his tunic. The wound was deep and he had lost a great deal of blood, but he would live — if they got back to Inverness without delay.

He shrugged. "I will not say that I did not consider letting the raider's blade fall where he intended."

Malcolm watched him through narrowed eyes. "Yer bloody honest, barbarian." He grimaced as Tarek placed a thick wad of cloth against the wound to stanch the flow of blood and pressed it firmly, eyes glinting as Malcolm winced with pain.

"Yes, but in truth I could not see the reason to waste the life of a skilled warrior. I've seen too many good warriors die on battlefields, and Inverness needs all her warriors."

"I am indebted to you."

"I ask nothing in return." At Malcolm's look of surprise, his eyes sharpened. "Except for one thing."

"Aye," Malcolm grimly acknowledged. "What is yer price?"

"You will heed this warning. That which is mine, I will hold unto death." And if Malcolm did not completely understand, he explained, "Brianna is my wife with vows spoken before your God and mine. What passed between you before means nothing. But you have my oath that if you transgress in this, Scot, I will use this blade to finish what the raider intended."

"I think there must be Scots blood in your veins, barbarian, for you fight as fiercely as a Scot," Malcolm said in response. Then he nodded, "I will not transgress the vows that have been made, unless she so chooses."

"She will not," Tarek assured him.

As the other wounded were tended he made his way across the clearing to his own men. Stephen of Valois joined him.

"They have fled as if they were never here," he reported after sending several men into the forest for some sign of the direction the raiders had fled. His voice was filled with contempt.

"They left three of their wounded behind."

Tarek nodded. "We will take them back to Inverness. Perhaps they can be persuaded to give us information. What of Mardigan?" he asked.

"Fled as well."

A metal object caught the light of the sun as it filtered through the tops of the trees. Tarek knelt in the blood soaked foliage, retrieving the object. It was a medallion that fit the palm of his hand.

It was made of hammered gold and embossed with the image of a dragon's head framed in a circle of flames. His fingers clenched over the medallion, the edges cutting into his hand, as he reached inside his own tunic and retrieved the medallion that hung about his neck.

He had worn it for over a score of years, and for just as

many years he had searched for the man who had worn it before him. The man who had raped and disgraced his mother. His father.

The medallions were identical. His fingers closed once more over the medallion found in the bloodied forest. No body had been found near where he discovered the medallion. It must have been dropped by one of Mardigan's warriors. With a longing, fed by a lifetime of hatred, he stared in the direction the raiders had fled and knew that the man he sought was among them.

"By the Prophet," he swore, "I vow I will find you. And then I will kill you."

Twelve

Brianna dreamed that she went to the lake. The air was sharp, the forest steeped with dark shadows, the grass wet beneath her feet and brushing her ankles as she was drawn deeper and deeper into the ancient stillness of rocks and earth and trees.

She was drawn to it by that unerring sense that always led her, as if she were guided by some greater power that commanded her — a turn this way, through the large rocks, and beneath the low hanging bough of a particular tree, identical to scores of trees around her.

The wind guided her, brushing against her face, bringing a particular scent, whispering through her senses, leading her through the darkness that seemed to seep through the forest, consuming pale beams of silvery moonlight, spreading a smothering mantle over the trees, and blocking the glitter of stars above, following her with a coldness of foreboding.

More than once, she stopped and turned, certain that someone or something followed. But there was nothing there. Nothing but the darkness that in her dream seemed to reach out for her. Quickly, she turned, unable to name the fear that filled her soul as she followed the ancient voice that spoke in her blood as she sought the ancient place of visions.

She found it, shrouded in mist, the surface shimmering with an inner light that seemed to reach out of the depths. In her dream, she extended her hand over the surface, fingers opened as if she might seize the light from the depths of the lake. As before, a pattern appeared on the surface, two circles entwined in a never-ending pattern with the power of the light strongest where they overlapped.

As darkness enveloped the forest about her, she concentrated on the light, feeling its heat pour through her, its golden rays glowing about her hand then up the length of her arm into her body. Her head went back as the power filled her, burning through her blood, filling her soul.

The sky overhead exploded with the light of a billion stars that coalesced into a single point of light so powerful that it pierced the darkness of night, throwing it back like a heavy curtain thrown over the world.

Like a sword that carved the darkness of the forest, the light plunged back to earth, slicing through the veil of mist that surrounded the lake, cleaving open the gleaming surface of the joined circles to reveal a portal in the shimmering water.

Instinctively, she was drawn to the portal of light. Deep within her a familiar voice whispered, and with each word came a memory that drew her closer and closer. This, she sensed, was what she had been searching for. Beyond the portal, she would find the answers.

The light trembled. Then it seemed to fade, the portal a shadowy image that too seemed to fade as a growing darkness surrounded the lake and seemed to reach for the light, drowning it as the surface of the lake also darkened. It bubbled and boiled, distorting the circles until they too faded.

"No!" Brianna cried out, reaching out to the fading light as if she could hold it back and prevent it disappearing. Her visions and dreams always brought her to this place. She was connected to it, but for reasons she didn't understand. The only thing she did understand was that the answers she sought lay beyond that portal.

"Wait!" she pleaded. "Don't go! I must know. Who am I?" Tears filled her eyes and spilled down her cheeks. Her hands clenched into fists of frustration and helplessness.

"Why is all of this happening?"

It was only another dream. That single thought tumbled over and over in her head, churning through the mist that slowly lifted from about her numbed senses. Then a voice, gently called to her. The voice moved through her thoughts, dear and familiar, like a lifeline to the real world. She seized it, focused on that voice as she slowly emerged from the mist.

"Be at ease, lass. Yer safe now. No harm will come to ye. I'm here now."

She awakened slowly, shuddering as her body struggled to throw off the bone-aching weariness and lethargy that dragged at her like invisible hands holding on, refusing to let her return to the conscious world. She blinked against the painful light of dawn, and then shivered anew as she realized she was not in her bed. Nor was she inside the fortress.

"Thomas?" It was his voice she had heard, calling to her thoughts, bringing her back. It was his strength that supported and warmed her as he cradled her close, like a father cradling a child.

"Aye, lass?"

"Where am I?" But even as she asked, the last of sleep left her dulled senses. She clearly saw the notched wall of the battlements and felt the cold stone of the walkway beneath her. And she knew.

She had not merely dreamed of the lake at the edge of the forest this time with its overlapping circles in the water, or the light that opened a portal into another time and place. Nor was it a dream when she saw the darkness that destroyed the light, forcing it back, closing the portal.

It had all been real, and it happened with increasing frequency since Tarek and Malcolm had followed the raiders.

Last night she had locked herself in her chamber behind the newly replaced door.

But always it was the same. The restlessness in the hours before sleeping. Then finally sleep troubled by dreams. Always the same dreams. She was looking for something. Her search took her far beyond the fortress, deep into the forest to the same place.

The dreams always ended the same way. The portal was closed, the light smothered by the darkness, with only silence in answer to her questions.

Tears slipped down her cheeks, icy from the return journey just before dawn.

"What is happening to me?" she wept. "What does it all mean?"

Thomas held her close, trying to comfort her as he had when she was a child. But the child was a woman now, tormented by thoughts, feelings, and memories she didn't understand.

"*Hush, child,*" his thoughts reached out, attempting to soothe her fears and uncertainty. "*Be at peace. You will sleep now, peaceful, undisturbed by these things.*"

But as he cradled her, Thomas' brow furrowed, for he knew his thoughts brought her no lasting peace. The dreams would come again, and again. He could not stop them. There was only one who could.

He gathered the mantle warmly about her, frowning at the mark at the back of her left shoulder where the neck of her gown dipped low. The mark of two perfect circles, overlapping one another in an ancient symbol.

He drew the mantle over her shoulder as well and lifted her, weighing barely more than a child, and carried her down from the battlements, across the yard as dawn filled the sky, and then up the hidden passage to her chamber. This entrance too had been barred from the outside. Still she had escaped.

He laid her on her bed. Already she was in a deep sleep where no dreams might reach her for a time. It was always so afterward.

A soft rapping at the door drew his attention. With a ferocious expression he opened it, expecting her cousin, Gillie. For she had become like a shadow to his mistress the past weeks since the warriors had left. Never missing the opportunity to make known her intention to be mistress to Tarek al Sharif. But it was not Gillie. Instead, it was the woman, Enya, whom his mistress had rescued in the forest.

She asked no questions, just as she had not asked the times before. She merely accepted what she could not understand as she moved past him to the bed, drawing the furs more tightly about his mistress.

"I will stay with her," she told him, just as she had before. Then she looked at him and smiled, revealing that she was not an unpleasant looking woman. The lines eased about her mouth, and the ever-present shadows beneath her haunted eyes faded as she looked upon him with gentleness.

"I'll wager ye've not had a wink of sleep, waiting up on the battlements." She did not expect an answer for she had quickly become used to his silent ways.

"Go then," she told him. "Get some rest." Her voice took on a steeliness. "I owe her my life. No harm will come to her while I draw breath."

Thomas glanced to the door.

Enya understood his silent meaning as she saw the direction of his gaze. "Aye, I'll set the latch after ye've gone. That whore's stench will not enter this room."

Satisfied that his mistress was indeed safe for now, Thomas nodded and turned to leave. Enya followed him to the door, laying a gentle hand at his arm.

"Yer a kind and loyal man, Thomas. Ye serve yer mistress well."

Unaccustomed to affection from anyone save his mistress, Thomas jerked his arm back. He immediately saw the pain in Enya's soft brown gaze.

"Aye," she said sadly. "Like the others, ye think I'm no better than Gillie after what the raiders did to me."

Sadness, almost as painful as the brutality she'd suffered, ached in her voice. He felt it as surely as a knife wound thrust deep beneath his ribs.

"I suppose I canna blame you," she said softly. "But my promise stands. I would defend mistress Brianna with me life." She turned back to the bed. Thomas stopped her, his great paw of a hand gentle at her shoulder.

He had soothed his mistress' childhood fears, uncertainties, and pain. He tried to soothe Enya's anguish as best he knew how. But nothing prepared him for the pain and anguish he felt in her.

He reached out to her with his thoughts, but found they tripped over themselves and he couldn't express any of them so that she might understand. And he was afraid his thoughts might frighten her. It had to be done carefully so that she understood his meaning without thinking that he had invaded her mind.

But at the moment, he could not sort them all out. Nothing in his experience prepared him for Enya's indomitable spirit, her fierce loyalty to his mistress, or the gentleness of her touch at his arm. And so, he responded the only way he could, as she had by laying his coarse, callused palm tenderly against her cheek.

Her eyes lit up with surprise at the rough tenderness of his hand. She placed her own hand over his. "Ye are a fine man,

Thomas. As fine as any laird or king."

His face grew warm at her words, for no one had ever said that about him. Or at least in such a way. With even more confused thoughts, he hastily left the chamber, hesitating outside the door only long enough to make certain she dropped the crossbar into place.

"Drink it all," Enya said firmly as she held the metal goblet to Brianna's lips.

Brianna winced and gritted her teeth, the sound of the pungent, bracing liquid sloshing inside the goblet like the roar of the ocean to her sensitive hearing.

Her head pounded, pain pulsing behind her eyes. Each sound — the rasp of the covers being pulled back, the rat-tat-tat of a bird at the shuttered window opening, the hiss of the fire at the hearth — was amplified a hundredfold to her heightened senses. It was always so upon waking after one of her deep sleeps.

But the warm tisane helped, soothing her aching muscles, warming the blood in her veins, easing the pounding at her temples so that she could finally pry her eyes open.

She suspected this must be what a man's head felt like after a night of drinking. The description seemed much the same. She wondered, too, if a man experienced the same melancholia of spirit.

"What hour of the day is it?"

"Mid-morning," Enya answered as she unbolted the shutters and eased them open.

"And Gillie has not been about?" she asked, teeth grating against each other at the thought of the woman.

Since Malcolm and the others had left, Gillie had spent a great deal of time in the laird's chamber. She was constantly scrubbing and cleaning, and it was unusual for Gillie even to lift a hand to tend to her own cleanliness. The past week, she insisted a thick tapestry be laid over the stone floor. Each midday, she carried a pitcher of honied mead and a tray of food in anticipation of their return.

At first, Brianna ignored her. With so many extra people now housed within Inverness, it had been a relief to have the woman out from underfoot. Then Enya had casually mentioned that Gillie had moved her own things from the pantry where she slept with Nel, Anne, and the baby. Brianna wondered if her cousin might have found a lover whose bed she now warmed.

Then only a few days ago, venturing into the laird's chamber for a journal Cullum was always writing in, thinking it might provide answers to some of the questions that plagued her, she discovered where Gillie's pallet, clothes, and few odd trinkets had disappeared to.

A much-mended, freshly laundered gown lay atop the wood trunk decorated with embossed Persian carvings. A crudely made wood hair comb lay beside one made of fine, smoothly polished sandalwood, not quite touching but with an intimacy of proximity that was unmistakable.

Seized by feelings she didn't understand and could barely control, Brianna wanted to hurtle both combs into the brazier. But Gillie's voice had stopped her.

"I hope milord returns soon," she said from the doorway behind Brianna, her voice low and dusky with myriad other hopes that went unspoken but were nonetheless blatant. " 'Tis lonely without him."

Brianna knew the last was spoken for her benefit, for Gillie made it very clear the position she hoped to occupy in Tarek al Sharif's household when he returned — that of mistress. The words were meant to wound and cause doubt, and succeeded magnificently, but for reasons

213

Brianna could not understand.

She reminded herself that their marriage was nothing more than an alliance of armies in the fight against Mardigan. And yet, she experienced an intense, longing ache for something more. Something that was hinted at in the burning warmth of his kiss, in the lean, hard length of his body pressed against hers, and the tenderness of his words when he had said, *"Be my wife in all ways."*

She had fled the laird's chamber, and with the same determination she had avoided Gillie every day since. But she discovered that she too listened for the shouted call of the sentry that riders approached, and continuously sought the battlements that looked out over the entire countryside.

Enya often found her there, bringing bread or cheese from the kitchen, wrapped in a square of cloth when she had no interest in taking her meal in the main hall with the others, including Gillie.

They ate in silence, until Brianna could bear it no longer. "Do not say it!" she told Enya in a fit of pique. "Not one word!" she admonished.

"I have said nothing mistress," Enya replied, giving her an odd look.

"No, but you were thinking it," Brianna insisted, for the woman's thoughts had come as easily to her as if she had spoken.

"I know not of what you speak," Enya said with feigned innocence.

Exhausted by dream-filled nights and days filled with uncertainty over Tarek's return, Brianna whirled on her. "You know perfectly well of what I speak. You have heard the rumors and whispers about Inverness. It is as if every stone in every wall knows."

"Knows what, mistress?" Enya replied with such sweetness of innocence that Brianna wanted to flay her alive.

"That my marriage is a marriage of words only for the sake of the alliance."

"Just as you wished it to be," Enya pointed out what was also well known to every Scot. She shrugged. "I do not see the dilemma."

"There is no dilemma!" She could have sworn the woman smiled.

"Then why are you shouting if everything is exactly as you wish it to be?"

Because everything was not as she wished it to be. In truth, she did not know what she wished for. She did not understand anything of these human emotions. She did not understand why she was more apprehensive each passing day that word still did not come from Malcolm and the Scots. She did not understand why it was so important that Tarek al Sharif was alive and unharmed.

"I do not wish to discuss it," she replied.

That was days ago, and still there was no word from Tarek's men. Nor was there word from the surrounding countryside. Now, after the previous night, her emotions were even more uncertain and close to the surface.

At noon she did not take her meal with the others in the main hall, but sought the solace of the gardens where tentative shoots and leaves from seedlings Mirren had set out in the midst of winter poked through the earth seeking the warmth of the sun.

All about her was the noise of construction, shouts and curses as more stones were set into place at the stout wall that gradually closed around Inverness, and would also close out their enemies.

Among the workers were Norman soldiers and Scots warriors who constantly lined the battlement walls and stood guard. Others ventured out astride, keeping watch about the countryside, for present in everyone's thoughts was the fear of attack with a third of the men gone.

She heard the first cry from the walls. Riders approached Inverness. One word sliced through the instinctive fear that was her first reaction. *Riders.*

She hastily hung the waterskin with which she'd been watering the plants at the gate post. Halfway across the yard to the main gate she realized that half the dirt of the garden was no doubt smeared across her skin and clothes. It caked beneath her nails and smeared the toes of her slippers. She doubled back, breathlessly announcing their arrival to Enya as she ran up the stairs.

"Where is my clean gown?" she demanded, unaware of the anxious tone in her voice as she whipped the yarn tie from her hair.

"It is here," Enya informed her. Brianna whirled around, her fingers fumbling as she tried to unlace the bodice of the stained gown.

"My hair . . ."

"I will comb it for you."

"My slippers . . ." She jerked at the laces of her gown. They knotted hopelessly beneath her nervous fingers. Enya pushed her hands aside, and nimbly unknotted the laces.

"Yer other pair is brushed and clean."

"My hands," Brianna wailed.

"Water works miracles, mistress."

"There is no time!"

"There is time enough."

There was. Barely. The skirt of the dark forest green gown whispered over the toes of her clean slippers. Her hands — with clean nails — nervously twisted at her hair which fell to her waist in a shimmering golden torrent. Enya swatted at her fidgeting fingers.

"You will ruin it."

Then she stepped back with a smile of satisfaction. "Now, you look somewhat better than a goat girl."

Startled, Brianna blinked. Then she burst out in nervous laughter. "Let us hope I smell somewhat better than a goat girl."

Enya smiled reassuringly. "That you do, mistress."

It was then young Duncan burst into the chamber announcing that Tarek and his men had just ridden through the front gates of Inverness. His eyes were bright, but his expression grave with the news he brought.

"Many have been injured."

Brianna seized him by the arm. "Who has been injured?"

"Many of our kinsmen, and the Norman warriors as well." More than that he could not say.

Fear building along every nerve ending, Brianna told him, "Find the healer and send her to me."

When he would have argued about making a trip to the village now, she said fiercely, "Do it now. The wounded will have need of her." He did as she told him, grumbling loudly.

She encountered Thomas in the main hall below. His thoughts assured her that all was in readiness for the wounded. She sensed, too, his silent words of comfort and strength.

"Courage, lass."

But she didn't feel courageous. She was terrified as she ran down the steps from the main hall and across the yard where both Scots and Normans gathered around the returned warriors.

The people of Inverness also filled the yard — Scots wives, lovers, and children hoping for sight of their loved ones, Ian who stood with the gathered chieftains who had remained at

Inverness rather than returning to their own landholds, survivors from other villages who now made Inverness their home, and women who had found lovers among the Norman knights.

As she pushed her way among them, she caught sight of Stephen of Valois. But he sat astride alone, no other rider beside him. Fear clutched at her heart. He was never far from Tarek's side.

Many knights and warriors had already dismounted, assisting the wounded from their horses. Then she caught sight of a long-legged, fine-boned horse. The Arabian mare! And young Duncan's rich brown cap of hair as he jubilantly greeted the rider astride, in spite of her orders to fetch the healer.

At that moment she did not care that he had disobeyed, for the rider's head bent low beside the boy's was dark as a raven's wing, hair long and drawn back with a twist of leather thong. And the hand extended in greeting to the boy was deeply bronzed with the warmth of the sun in his skin.

"Milord!" a cry went out among the others. A woman's voice, filled with excitement and ease of familiarity, like that of one awaiting a lover's return. It was Gillie.

She wove her way among the Scots and Norman warriors. Shoving young Duncan aside, she went up on her toes as her arms went around Tarek's neck. Her eager mouth found his in a kiss that spoke of far more than casual greeting.

An unexpected pain seized below Brianna's heart, and for a moment she could not draw an even breath. Then she abruptly turned back to the main hall, encountering Thomas at the steps.

"There are many wounded, mistress," Thomas' gentle thoughts gave her strength.

"Aye, Thomas. We must do what we can for them. Duncan has been given instructions to bring the healer from the village."

He nodded. *"I will see that he returns quickly."* His expression was grave as he looked out across the yard. *"Many have not returned."*

She turned, focusing on the number of warriors, both Norman and Scots, whose names she had all memorized before they left.

"Malcolm," she said with a worried frown of concern for her friend.

She found him among those who had been gently lifted down from their horses and carried into the main hall. His hand sought hers as he was carried up the steps by his fellow kinsmen, his father at his other side.

"He saved my life."

At her surprised expression, he smiled faintly. "But for a moment I thought he would surely take it." Then he was being carried past her, Enya, Anne, and young Nel efficiently seeing the wounded inside where they would be made comfortable until the healer arrived. She too turned toward the main hall.

"Brianna."

His voice had haunted her dreams, the memory of his touch had haunted her senses. She had thought it was enough to know that he was safe, especially after seeing him with Gillie. But at that moment she knew it was not enough. She wanted to turn around at the same time she wanted to run. But there was no running away from the things he made her feel.

She had cried every day and every night since he left, with no clear understanding of what it was that he made her feel, except that she needed it. As surely as she needed air, as surely as the trees of the forest needed the rain, and night needed the dawn.

Then as others moved past them into the hall, including Stephen of Valois, she felt his hand at her wrist. Gentle restraint, tender persuasion as he slowly turned her to face him.

"You are well, milord?" she asked stiffly, keeping her gaze averted from his, wary of what she would see there. At least Gillie had been needed elsewhere. She did not think she could face them together.

"Well, enough."

The bone-aching weariness in his voice brought her gaze up. In his words, she sensed the fierceness of the battle fought, his grief at lives lost, and something else that slipped away before she could understand it.

"Many died." In those words, she heard his frustration of anger that Mardigan had escaped.

"Aye," she said, her sadness adding to his, "but many more raiders died I have been told." For she had heard of the number of their losses and knew that for the first time Mardigan's men had been defeated in battle.

"It is not ended. Mardigan escaped."

"He will not escape next time."

"No, he will not." Then his gaze angled past hers to the main hall, bright with torches and a warm fire at the hearth in spite of the midday hour.

"Malcolm?" he asked, with a surprising genuineness of concern.

"He is of tough, Scots blood. And too stubborn to die," she assured him.

"Brianna . . ."

Just the sound of her name, low in his throat, stopped her. This time she could not look away. Her gaze met his, fierce, filled with countless emotions from the battle long past, and the battle that still waited between them. Then the sound in his throat was equally fierce as he pulled her to him.

His hands went back through her hair, tangling it, fingers pressing into her scalp as he held her for his kiss. His mouth was equally fierce, forcing hers open, his tongue gliding past her startled lips to thrust between with a fiery heat.

This was what had haunted her dreams and every waking moment, the startling, sweet, sensual pleasure of physical joining that promised so much more.

She tried to cling to the image of Gillie kissing him, for then anger would be her weapon against him, but she discovered that she could not.

The anger slipped away beneath the assault of the seeking heat of his tongue gliding along hers, of his breath mingling with hers, the fierce possessive power of his hands tight in her hair.

"Brianna," he whispered.

There was something dark and needy in the sound of her name. Something that spoke of far more than weariness or the fierceness of the battle past, and sliced through the lethargy of heat that had dulled her senses. It was desire. A man's desire for a woman. His desire for her.

"Milord, please . . ." she whispered frantically, her hands coming up between them to push him away.

She did not look at him. There was no need of it. He knew what he would see in her eyes, for he heard it in the quiver of panic at her voice. It was not him that she feared. It was herself. He tasted it in that kiss — first her surprise, then the fire he tasted at her mouth that quickly leapt between them and threatened to burn out of control, and finally that moment when desire became fear.

Tarek slowly released her. When she turned and would have run up the steps, he reached out and stopped her.

221

"You will be wife to me in all ways, Brianna."

She refused to look at him. Her face was expressionless. She was once more the laird's daughter who had bargained for an alliance to save her people. Yet, he felt the heat that leapt at her skin, and the tremor that passed through her.

"Please, milord. The wounded need me."

He opened his hand and let her go, his gaze following her as she fled up the stairs. "In all ways," he vowed.

Thirteen

"Ye have magical hands, lass," Malcolm sighed, the only outward sign of pain in the grimace that contorted his features.
"Gentler than the healer with her foul-smelling concoctions, or
the old hag Drusilla with her equally foul potions that she keeps
brewing."

Brianna smiled. In the days since Tarek and the Scots had
returned, she had found an amicable truce with Malcolm. He
seemed more accepting of the alliance she'd made.

"Drusilla means well."

"Bah! The woman's a charlatan. Not one man will claim
that she has magical powers. And she keeps sprinkling that
wretched brown powder about." With typical Scots nature he
grumbled, "I tried to get her to tell me what was in it. I don't
trust the old hag."

Brianna's eyes glinted with laughter, the first in many days
for three more kinsmen had died of their wounds. With the
loss of so many others, it had been a sad time at Inverness. Of
late there seemed to be too much sadness, and she discovered
the pleasure of a smile. It felt good to find a little laughter
amid so much gloom.

"You are brave!" she exclaimed. "You might not like what
you hear. From what I've been told, she favors eye of newt
and bat wings." She laughed again at Malcolm's horrified expression, quite gruesome when taken as a whole with the cut
that angled down over his forehead and a nasty bruise from
the butt of a sword handle.

"It's good to see you smile again," his own expression

transformed then, into what might have passably been a smile in response. He added his agreement to her earlier thought.

"There has been too much loss and grief at Inverness."

She finished adjusting his bandage. He lay on a pallet before the hearth in the main hall. The others lay about them, dozing, or taking hearty broth under Enya's careful eye and firm manner. The woman had lost three patients after their return from battle, she refused to lose any more.

"Aye, there has been," Brianna agreed.

"But there would have been far more to grieve, if not for the barbarian," he added by way of grudging acknowledgment, bringing her surprised gaze up to his, for in the days since their return he had not spoken again of what happened during the battle. Only that first brief admission that Tarek al Sharif had saved his life. A debt of honor for any man, but a most serious one for a Scot as proud and stubborn as Malcolm.

His gaze did not quite meet hers, and from their long friendship she knew he wrestled with that pride.

"Ye were right, Brianna," he finally admitted, his mouth snapping shut around the words that seemed most difficult for him to get out.

"The Normans are fierce warriors. But yer husband fought like a true Scot. I would swear he has highland blood, for the man showed no fear or hesitation, and a cunning any Scot would envy. Where we rushed in he wisely chose his own place and time to join the battle. Mardigan and his men had no chance then. There is much we can learn from him. Aye," he repeated, "Ye were right."

His gaze fixed on some distant point across the hall, perhaps an irregular stone that did not scrutinize his confession or grin back at him with satisfied expression. But Brianna was not about to let him off that easily, for he had not been easy with her in these past weeks.

"What do you speak of?" she asked with feigned innocence, for she would not be satisfied until he had said the words.

"Ye know damned well wot I'm talkin' aboot!"

"I have no idea." Her voice simpered with enough sweet innocence to gag a hedgehog. He glanced at her suspiciously, his expression once more fierce in his wounded and swollen face.

"The damned alliance is what I'm talkin' of!" His hand made a fist as he pounded the pallet beside him. She suppressed a smile.

"Ye were right to make the alliance," he went on and she made no attempt to stop him. "For we would have been slaughtered if not for the Normans. They are much skilled in battle. I can well see how the English king lost his throne. But I will never like the terms ye agreed to. And ye canna hold it against me." His voice grew rough with the anger he'd carried the past weeks.

She laid a hand on his good shoulder.

"The terms were not of my making," she reminded him. "I had no choice."

"And does he give ye no choice as well when he takes his pleasure of ye?" His voice quivered with a mixture of rage and sorrow.

"Och! I'd have ye still, Brianna. It is no matter to me. I know your true heart, and yer Scots through and through."

How could he possibly know her true heart, when she did not?

"Malcolm, please," she begged, "do not take up this argument again when we at last have found a measure of peace with one another." Then to ease his mind, because it mattered not whether he knew.

225

"The marriage is a marriage in word only. And that is by my choice." There was a hollow ring to the words and she wondered if he heard it. For in truth she had no choice. Just as she had tried to make Malcolm understand *they* could never be husband and wife.

But just as he had refused to understand her refusal to be wed with him, he would not understand her reasons now. And what could she possibly tell him? That she could not be truly wed to any man.

"And when Mardigan has been driven from Scotland?" he asked. "What then, Brianna? For I do not believe that Tarek al Sharif will leave willingly after it is done. What choice will you have then?"

"You must rest," she told him, avoiding his troubled gaze. She did not have an answer. "If Scotland's sons do not recover from their wounds, then Mardigan will not be driven out."

She gathered her basket of bandages and pushed to her feet. Malcolm stopped her with a hand at her arm.

"I have wronged ye, lass."

She thought he still spoke of his doubt of her decision for the alliance. "It is forgiven."

"Will he live then?" Ian asked as he came to stand beside her.

"Perhaps," she said with much grimness, as if the matter were still in doubt. Then she gave the chieftain a smile. "He is too stubborn to die."

"Och, well, I suppose he comes by it honestly."

"Oh?" Brianna asked with feigned innocence. "I cannot imagine why."

Then she left father and son to discuss the recent battle for it was the first day Malcolm was coherent enough to speak of such things, after the fever that had taken hold because of the wound at his shoulder.

Enya had been invaluable in the past days. Unlike other women who continued to weep about and mourn their losses, Enya had poured her mourning over the loss of her family and the brutality she'd suffered into hard, physical work. She had been a whirlwind of activity since the return of the Scots, taking charge of the main hall like a field commander.

With the already swollen population of Inverness, they were now wall-to-wall with pallets in the main hall. The fire at the hearth burned constantly against the early morning and evening chill that still clung to the countryside, and kettles were constantly simmering with hearty stews and broths.

Outside in the yard was hardly better. More villagers were encamped in makeshift enclosures, and soldiers were constantly coming and going through the gates of Inverness. The walls were now fully closed in.

During the day Norman and Scots warriors practiced battle skills together beyond the gates, with guards constantly at watch on the battlements. By night, Ian and the other chieftains met with Tarek al Sharif and his knights in the corner of the main hall where the tables had been shoved, planning the next strategy against Mardigan.

Strategy was new to the Scots. Always before, they defended their land and homes when attacked, but never striking on the offensive. Now they listened, giving valuable information about the physical aspects of the countryside, other clans and kinsmen who could be relied upon for their loyalty, and those who would throw their lot in with whoever the winds of fortune favored.

After their return, there had been no opportunity for private words between her and Tarek al Sharif. Only that brief, soul-searing encounter on the steps of Inverness. In the days since she had worked alongside the other women, sleeping in the main hall to be near the wounded, seeking out her own chamber only long enough to find a clean gown.

Enya seized the basket of soiled bandages from her and handed her another filled with warm bread, cheese, hard-cooked eggs, and a goatskin of ale.

"You've the look of the walking dead," the woman chided her. "You need fresh air and a bit of the sun in your cheeks. Take this to the men at the stables, for they've been training hard all morning and I will not have them tramping horse droppings into the main hall for midday meal."

"You've not been outside either," Brianna pointed out.

"Oh, I've had a moment or two up on the battlements," Enya confessed. When Brianna's delicate golden brows lifted in surprise, Enya added, "Just to get a bit of wind in me sails. Thomas was kind enough to accompany me."

Brianna's brows lifted all the way to her hairline for it seemed Thomas had been spending a great deal of time with Enya the past few days. Whenever she was in the hall, he was never far away.

"Do not look at me so," Enya scolded her gently. "He's a good man, and with him about . . . well, no other man would dare approach me."

Brianna understood. In the first few days after Enya's arrival it was clear some of the men considered her of the same status as Gillie who made no secret of the company she kept. But Enya was different and in spite of the brutality she'd suffered at the hands of Mardigan and his men, she had a proud spirit. Thomas, with his gentle, protective ways, was just what she needed.

"No," Brianna agreed with a smile. "No one would dare bother you." She tucked the basket under her arm, feeling more strongly than ever over the past days of confinement the need to feel the sun and wind on her face.

The sunlight stunned her. And for several moments, she simply stood on the steps of the hall, her face lifted to its radiant warmth after the past days. A light breeze blew across the yard, bringing with it myriad smells and noises.

There was now an organized order to the overcrowded yard that before had resembled a military encampment, village faire, and noisy market all rolled into one.

No more. Mounted warriors had taken their practice outside the main gates. Villagers who had sought the protection of the fortress had been relocated to the far side of the compound behind the main hall, with access to the kitchens.

A smithy had set up his stall near the newly built stables at the other side of the compound, his hammer ringing in the clear, spring air. Several women had set up their looms in a weaver's stall.

As a woman set up candle making, the smell of tallow mingled in the air amid the acrid stench of lye soap from the laundry. They called a greeting to her as she gaped in amazement at the order with which everything had been organized, like a well-planned village within the protective walls of Inverness.

"How did this happen?" Brianna asked a robust, apple-cheeked Scots woman who shooed her children out of the way of a passing cart laden with timber that would fuel the fires of Inverness.

"The new laird," the woman answered without hesitation. At Brianna's questioning look she cut a glance toward the stables.

"He organized it like a military camp. And we've not had one accident or child run down by a cart since."

As Brianna followed her gaze, she realized who the woman spoke of. With her hand shielding her gaze, she caught sight of Tarek as he emerged from the stables.

She had avoided him since his return, confused by her uncertain emotions. Now, as she watched him with Stephen of Valois, the blade of his Persian sword catching the sun as it carved and sliced the air in mock combat, she felt the ache of that conflict even stronger.

The air had a rare and welcome warmth. Both warriors had set aside protective armor and padding and stripped to their waists beneath the midday sun.

Stephen of Valois was tall but with a leanness of youth still apparent in his well-muscled body, and in the reckless abandon with which he wielded his broadsword.

His dark sable hair framed an intense face and gleaming amber eyes fixed purposefully on his adversary. His shoulders gleamed with runnels of sweat that streamed down his body, plastered dark whorls of masculine hair across his chest, and soaked the waist of his breeches.

He was as finely made as any man she had seen among her father's kinsmen, for they often engaged in bouts of good-natured rivalry at wrestling, dirks, or battle-axes. But his movements were quick, intense, then retreating and striking again, more those of a trained warrior who has met many combatants on the battlefield.

The young knight, who seemed to carry the weight of the world on his shoulders, could pick from any of the young maids, or experienced women of Inverness to warm his bed. The only imperfection to his handsome prowess was the wide seam of pale, recently healed flesh that ran from his shoulder in a curving arc across his chest down across his ribs.

Seeing it now, fully healed, she could not imagine how he had survived it. For it was a gruesome scar, that only enhanced his appeal among the Scots women — and particularly young Nel — for they were used to seeing their men so marked, like a badge of courage.

By contrast, Tarek al Sharif moved with an intense but fluid grace. Like that of a cat. His concentration was unwavering, completely focused on his opponent.

She could feel the intensity of those compelling blue eyes as he seemed to gauge every movement before Stephen made it, his blade anticipating where Stephen's would strike next.

He was wide of shoulder, thick muscles bunching and then stretching with each powerful move beneath the gleam of dark, bronze skin, and then tapering to narrow waist and hips.

Sweat glistened across angles of smooth skin that easily drew the eye to his chest, the ridge of ribs sheathed by yet more layers of muscle, and glistened in the ribbon of jet black hair that seamed his hard flat belly and then disappeared into the waist of his breeches. About his neck he wore a gold medallion.

Beneath the leather breeches, she saw the outline of equally hard thigh muscles that swelled and tensed with relentless power as he drove repeatedly against Stephen of Valois.

He blocked a blow, moving with an efficiency of energy that wasted nothing and made Stephen's attack seem overzealous almost to the point of being out of control. Then he countered, his blade slicing in to nick once, twice, three times as they fought, with an amazing restraint that left no doubt that any one single blow could have ended in death if not for his precise control of the blade.

With that perfect efficiency he wore Stephen down until the younger warrior began to move recklessly, exposing his scarred left side, barely escaping the loss of an eye, while tiny runnels of bloodied sweat appeared at his chest and arm from those tiny nicks.

"Become one with the blade," Tarek explained, not boastfully but in the way of mentor and student. "The blade must already be there before you have thought of the next strike. Every move must be instinctive. Make your circles of motion smaller.

"Do not waste your strength needlessly with overlarge movements when smaller ones will do, for you may have need of that strength to outlast your opponent. And finally," he made a surprise move, swinging the Persian sword opposite his previous strike pattern, so that the tip sliced the air at Stephen's midsection with such deadly accuracy that had it been an inch closer he would have been disemboweled.

"Strike where your opponent least expects it and never take him for granted or break your concentration. Force your opponent to break his."

In what could have been a fatal moment, Stephen had glanced in her direction, then immediately returned his concentration to his opponent. It was just enough that facing an enemy blade, he would have been dead.

"Most enemies do not bring their women into battle with them," Stephen snorted. "Especially ones quite so beautiful."

Still, Tarek did not look in her direction, nor even seem aware of her presence. "No, they do not. That is another rule you must remember. Always expect the unexpected, and you will live to fight another day."

Stephen was breathing heavily but a smile pulled at his handsome mouth amid a tangle of sable hair and sweat that streamed down his face and neck. Then it ran with the blood from those small nicks and made it seem as if he might have been mortally wounded.

Tarek had received only one wound and Brianna wondered if it was entirely by accident, or if he might have allowed it to ease the younger man's sense of defeat, for it was obvious who the winner was this time. But one day she had no doubt Stephen of Valois would be a formidable adversary because of his lessons learned under a Persian blade.

Stephen seemed to have suffered no lasting wounds to his pride. Wiping the blade of his broadsword, he then went to a nearby water barrel used for the horses and doused his head and shoulders until none of the blood remained. Then he good-naturedly issued a challenge to Tarek for later.

"I will best you yet," he said with undisguised certainty, but in a way that gave a glimpse into the deep friendship that existed between the two men. Then Stephen crossed the yard in her direction.

"I have brought food and drink for the midday meal," she lifted the cloth from the edge of the basket.

"Thank you no, mistress. I must find that old bat of a healer for these wounds so that I may live to fight another battle." He winked at her.

"Someone should explain to him that if he slays all his knights, he will have none to fight the raiders." Then as he walked past he winked again. "Be careful of his blade, mistress."

"I have no intention of challenging him to combat."

"Exactly as I said." His expression curved into a devilish smile at his handsome, sweat-streaked face. *"Be careful of his blade."*

When he had gone, she turned back to the stables. Tarek had gone inside. She hesitated until she heard the banter of conversation from within. Secure in the safety of numbers, she crossed the yard and entered the stables.

It smelled of fresh timber hand-hewn by the carpenter at Inverness, fresh grass barely sprouted from the winter soil, dust, and horses.

Open at both ends, it was lined on either side with stalls

that could shelter nearly one hundred horses. Further proof that the Normans did not soon intend to be gone from Inverness.

She had paid little attention to the construction, but was aware that the horses were now taken beyond the walls to graze on shoots of spring grass on the surrounding hillsides where they could be easily guarded. For there was no grain at Inverness save that for the sheep and fowl, and the last of the winter grain needed for making bread.

Her eyes slowly adjusted to the muted shadows of the stables with sunlight streaming narrow fingers of light through gaps in the uneven boards at the side walls. Dust clouded underfoot and glittered in a shaft of sunlight.

The buzz of conversation ceased as two warriors exited the opposite end of the stables. All about was suddenly silent, except for the faint, distant scratching of some opportunistic rat or family of mice that had no doubt already taken up residence. Brianna turned to leave.

"What have you there?"

She turned, backing up against the work table covered with leather harnesses in need of mending. The harness-maker was not about. She shifted the basket nervously from her right to her left arm, like a battle shield she set in place between them, as Tarek approached from where he had been splashing off the sweat and blood of battle.

Beads of water glistened in the midnight black hair that fell to his shoulders and at the tips of thick dark lashes.

She nervously fingered the cloth that covered the basket. "Cook sent the midday meal for your men. But they all seem to be afield." She made to cut past him and leave the stables, but he reached out, seizing the basket.

"What has cook prepared?"

Imprisoned between him and the table, she backed once

more as far as she could against the edge of the table.

"Bread, cheese, eggs. But there is a fine stew at the hearth," she suggested, hoping he would prefer it and she might escape. "A warm meal would suit better."

"This suits me," he replied. "Will you share it with me?"

"I am not hungry." Her stomach growled in loud protest, making a liar of her.

Merriment glinted in those sharp blue eyes that seemed to see far too much. "Your stomach does not seem to be in agreement. Stay," he repeated. "I would ask your opinion of a matter I have given much thought to."

He took the basket from her and set it upon the table in back of her, removing her protective shield.

"What matter is that? Surely you seem to have things well in hand without asking me."

"But this is a matter which affects you as well, and I would not make a decision on it without first asking you."

"Very well, then," she agreed. "What matter is it?"

"I would like to discuss it over a full stomach, and when it is not necessary to shout over the noise of your stomach to make myself heard."

Seeing that she might sooner be able to leave the stables and his company if she laid out the meal and ate with him rather than argue about it, Brianna turned and began removing the contents of the basket. She immediately realized that she had perhaps been very foolish turning her back on him. But instead of closing the distance between them, he remained standing where he was with the empty space previously occupied by the basket between them.

As she set out first the wheel of bread, still warm from the oven, then goat cheese, eggs, and the skin of ale, he casually reached around her, his fingers brushing hers as he plucked an egg from her hand.

The contact was brief, completely innocent, yet it sent a frisson of wild heat the length of each finger, across her dampened palm, and up the length of her arm as she remembered the last time he had touched her. He cracked the egg on the table and peeled it as she set out honey and spiced peaches.

She spread the bread with honey as Tarek skewered a fat golden peach from the small crockery with the blade at his belt. Neatly severing the peach in half with flashing teeth, he offered the other piece to her.

"Please take it, or I shall be forced to feed it to the mare. She is already spoiled by the treats young Duncan brings her."

Because she couldn't bear the thought of a horse eating such a rare morsel, and for other reasons she didn't care to admit, she nibbled the peach from the tip of the blade.

Peach juice dribbled on her chin. She wiped it with her hand, then busied herself spreading honey on another thick slab of bread, oblivious to the way he watched every movement. The efficient way she spread the honey without allowing any to run down the edges and be wasted. The quick precise flashes of the blade as she sliced the cheese. The delicate curve of her throat above the neck of her gown and the pulse that beat beneath fragile, almost translucent skin.

"What matter did you wish to discuss?" she asked when she had completed the task and found her hands suddenly idle, and the silence around them suddenly disquieting. When she turned, she turned into him and discovered he had moved much closer.

He reached around her and seized a piece of honied bread. He frowned slightly. "It is about young Duncan."

It was not what she had expected. She was certain he had only pretended to wish to discuss something with her to keep her in the stables, for he had tried several times the past days to speak with her after that searing kiss upon his return.

"What about him?"

He took a bite of bread and chewed it with a thoughtful expression, still standing so close that she could feel the heat of his body, and see tiny beads of water that glistened across his bronzed shoulders, the darker whorls of flesh of male nipples, and with a quick downward glance, the feathering of midnight black hair that tunneled the waist of his breeches.

"Yes." He had taken several bites, and offered the golden crust gleaming with a residue of honey to her as if they were companions on the best of terms.

"The boy's situation has weighed heavily on me," he went on to explain.

She watched the way his tongue flicked a crumb at the corner of his mouth, and immediately remembered the taste of him hot in her mouth.

"It has?" she replied with some confusion as her thoughts scattered. She could not imagine why Duncan's situation was of concern to him.

"The boy has no family," he commented, taking another piece of bread oozing with honey.

"Many have lost their families in the raids," she pointed out.

He offered her a thick crusty portion of bread, the sharing of it somehow intimate. Still he made no attempt to touch her or come any closer.

"That is true. But Duncan has only his grandfather. The old man is very feeble and will not likely last another winter." It was not said unkindly but with a gentle bluntness that sliced through any pretense.

She knew he was right. Duncan's grandfather had already voiced his own concerns for the lad, for there were no other kinsmen who might take him in.

"The boy is good with horses," he went on to explain. "The mare has taken to him. And there are few she accepts."

She could see the direction of his thoughts. Duncan must have a family to care for him. "Anne might be persuaded to take him," she suggested, yet Anne already had her hands full with a new baby. A prospective husband might be persuaded to accept a suckling babe, but a young boy who could not yet work to help support the family meant an instant family of four mouths to feed.

"Might you be persuaded?" Tarek suggested. Her surprised gaze met his. The solution seemed so simple, yet infinitely complicated.

"I know what it is to be without a family," he continued. "It is an emptiness of the soul that can never be filled." His voice went low and quiet, the words forced from some place deep inside so that she could only imagine the effort and pain it took to say them.

"I would like to foster the boy," he said, finally lifting his gaze to meet hers. "Inverness will be his home — not sleeping in the yard as he has, but in a place of his own. He can learn how to ride and handle a blade, but he will also study. For there is much to know of the world beyond."

What he suggested were ties that bound him to Inverness, and her to him through her people. He spoke of the future, together, as if the vows they had spoken would bind them both to Inverness and each other for always.

It was impossible, yet it was the only chance Duncan might have for a future different from that of a warrior. And impossible as it was, she felt tears sting at her eyes for the kindness of it from this fierce warrior.

"I would like it very much," she gave the only answer she could, one that was filled with countless meanings. "I will speak to his grandfather about it. It will ease his mind."

"I was not certain you would approve of it." He stepped closer, reaching around her for a slice of cheese.

"Why not? I am very fond of Duncan. He is a fine lad."

"He can be very . . ." His expression was thoughtful as he searched for the right word.

"Stubborn?"

"Yes."

"Willful?"

His smile transformed his face from thoughtful to breathtakingly handsome, almost boyish.

"Most certainly."

Brianna shrugged. "Och, well, he is a Scot."

"I suppose I will have to learn how to deal with stubborn Scots." Again there seemed to be far more meaning than just the obvious in what he said.

"I think you already have. You and Malcolm seem to have struck a truce with one another."

He stepped closer, reaching around her to skewer another peach which he offered to her. She accepted it, because it seemed safer to do so than break their amicable mood by refusing.

"Does it please you?" he asked.

"It does. He is a good friend."

He shrugged. "It also seemed the wise thing to do. The Scots are most headstrong and stubborn. Your highlands will soon find themselves without men. I thought I would save his life in spite of his best efforts to lose it."

"Thank you."

He was standing so close now that she could see each individual lash at those unusual blue eyes.

"For saving his life, or the peach?" his voice was low, innocent yet intimate. His breath brushed her lips, tasting both sweet and spicy from the peaches. When had he moved so much closer?

"Yes . . ."

"Which is it, Brianna?" he asked, his breath once more brushing across her lips. This time her own lips parted as if she could taste him as well. "The peaches, or Malcolm's life?"

"Yes . . . I mean both . . . Please, you're confusing me . . ."

"Look at me, Brianna."

Her gaze slowly lifted to his, even as her thoughts willed it otherwise.

"It has been four days since we returned, and yet every time I have tried to speak with you, you have fled. Why?"

"I have been needed elsewhere," she explained, not meeting his gaze. "With so many wounded . . ."

"There are others to see to the wounded. Enya seems well suited to caring for them. I should have such a field general in my army. That is not the reason." He brushed her cheek with the back of his fingers.

"Do not," she said with rising panic as she turned away from his touch, even as she longed to feel it again.

"Do not?" he asked, his voice like rough velvet. His fingers moved beneath her chin, forcing her gaze back to his. He stroked the curve of her lower lip with his thumb. "And yet, your eyes say otherwise."

"No," she insisted, a pleading sound. "I cannot . . . It is impossible."

"Why is it impossible?" he asked as his head angled down beside her, his breath warm across her cheek. "I have pledged my sword to your people. Our people have shed blood together in battle against the same enemy. We have spoken vows before your god and mine." And then, the most impossible words, "Be my wife, Brianna. Lie with me. Let us share our bodies with each other, for I have loved you since first I saw you those long months ago. You are what brought me back to the north country."

Her gaze was filled with torment of the secret she carried. For he could never understand, or accept it.

"It is impossible."

"All things are possible."

The words whispered across her cheek to the corner of her mouth. He blurred in her vision, dark and golden, his touch like warm satin.

"I am not what you think . . ." She protested, even as her mouth instinctively turned toward his. He cradled her face in both hands. Thick dark lashes slowly closed over intense blue eyes.

"You are the sun," his mouth brushed hers, startling the breath from her lungs. And then returned, so that she felt every word at her lips. "You are the mist at dawn."

"I am not like other women . . ."

His lips teased a sigh of pleasure from her. On a faint whimper her lips instinctively parted beneath his.

"I cannot feel . . ."

In a kiss far different from the one days earlier, his hands slowly pushed back through her hair, lingered as if stroking each individual strand, then angled her mouth beneath his and slowly kissed the lie from her lips.

The dull ache she'd experienced for weeks grew like a hunger. As his mouth shifted over hers, she cried out at the sudden loss, then shivered as he lifted her to the table, changed the angle, and kissed her again.

"Can you feel this?"

"Yes." Her lips parted as the sweet hot velvet of his tongue stroked between. Marveling, she whispered, "You taste of honey."

"And this?"

He twisted his hand in her hair, like a rope he coiled about his hand as he drew her head back for a far different kiss as he pressed his mouth against the curve of her throat.

She gasped, part loss part discovery as she experienced warm velvet gliding down her neck, then dipping into the tiny valley at the base where her pulse beat frantically through her veins.

Tarek shuddered. She tasted of cool wind and warm sunshine. Then he discovered the dusky taste of her just beneath the neck of her gown — the sweetness of early morning rain mingled with the fragrance of spring — all of it earthy and primal, as when the sun warms the land, dries the rain from the leaves, and washes the sky as her blood heated through her veins. And promising so much more that lay beneath the gown.

His mouth returned to hers, dipping, tasting, then dipping again as he slowly made love with his mouth. She quivered in his hands like a frightened creature terrified to stay, terrified to run, her mouth clinging to his, her breathing jerky as her slender hands came up between them in helpless confusion.

His hand wrapped around hers, pressing both to his chest so that she might feel the fierceness of his heart at the same time he whispered, "And this."

Slender fists slowly uncurled. Her hands flattened and lightly stroked across chest muscles that quivered and then hardened beneath her touch. Then began a slow, sensual exploration as her hands stroked tentatively over the curve of hard male muscles.

When he kissed her again, slender nails dug, then flexed, then dug in once more. Like that of a cat. And like a cat, he caressed her with the back of his hand down the side of her breast, his thumb stroking slowly across the peak through layers of soft wool.

242

She shivered again, her body giving the answer she tried to deny as the nipple hardened beneath his palm.

"And this." His voice was suddenly harsh in his throat. The laces yielded and his fingers brushed bare, warm flesh.

Her breasts were high and firm, her pale skin almost translucent, the nipple the color of dark sand. His hand tightened in her hair. When he kissed her again, she gasped as his mouth closed over her.

This was what he had longed to taste, the soft woman flesh of her as he laved the taut flesh with his tongue, then suckled it into his mouth as if he could drink passion from her.

"Yes." Her voice was a tangled sound at her throat, then a startled gasp as he tenderly nipped at her with those flashing teeth.

Driven by a desperate longing since the first moment he had seen her, Tarek slowly tempered the fire that burned through his blood. He went slowly, building the fire within her, feeling it burn through her body in the sweet fire beneath his lips at her breast, and beneath his hand as it slowly moved up her leg beneath the wool gown.

His flesh throbbed as he sought the sweet fiery center of her, stroking his hand across her knee, then slowly up her thigh.

Chaos built along every nerve ending with each gentle tug at her breast, a sweet oblivion of sensation experienced all over again low at the center of her.

He had moved between her thighs, drawing her knees open so that he fit against her. Through the haze of that oblivion she felt his warm hand at her knee, then stroking up her thigh.

She ached with feelings she could not understand. It grew more intense with each tug of his lips. And then he touched her.

Tarek groaned as he discovered the sweet hot center of her. She was wet, her heat opening to him as he gently parted downy folds of flesh, and stroked inside her.

"Tarek!"

His name was both a startled gasp and a litany of prayer on her lips as she clasped his shoulders. She had never spoken his name before and the impassioned sound of it filled him with a longing he had never imagined.

He stroked his thumb across the small bud of woman's flesh and she quivered. He stroked deep inside her and she arched as though to take him deeper still.

"And this?"

"Yes," she cried.

"Then touch me, Brianna as I have touched you," he whispered in an agony of desire as his mouth closed once more over hers, and he guided her other hand to the shaft of flesh that strained the front of his breeches. His fingers wrapped about hers, as with a groan of agony he closed them about him.

Stunned and bewildered by the torrent of sensations that poured through her, Brianna no longer tried to understand. She only felt.

She felt the sweet fire of his mouth at hers, the fiery rain he drew forth from her body, and then the warm satin of his blood-engorged flesh filling her hand.

Thick veins wrapped the shaft of flesh that thrust up from the whorl of midnight black hair. He guided her, moving her hand beneath his from the flared tip down the full length, her fingertips brushing against pouches of heavy flesh that held his seed.

His voice was ragged as her hand moved with a will of its own. "Be wife to me in all ways, Brianna."

As he kissed her again in a slow mating of his tongue with

hers, his hand tightened over hers and she felt the blunt tip of thick flesh pressing against her.

Her body ached for something she could not comprehend. Yet, she felt herself opening to him, his flesh pressing between the folds of her flesh, then a faint dull pressure as he gently opened her further.

From beyond the stables, voices were heard very near. That of Norman warriors returning from the practice field outside the walls of Inverness. Their conversation was loud, filled with exhaustion, and jibing comments spoken in Norman French. They were the first to return. Others followed as the day's practice ended.

They spoke in ribald tones of a particular maiden both admired, betting each other which would be the first to bed her. Beneath his hands, Brianna stiffened as she surfaced from the haze of desire that enveloped them. He felt the panic that stiffened in her slender body as she too realized discovery was imminent.

Cursing his misfortune, but cursing his men's poor timing even more, Tarek's first thoughts were for her. She had been so uncertain, doubting of her ability to experience a woman's pleasure. Until a moment before, they had almost found that pleasure together. She made a desperate, strangled sound as she tried to push him away.

"Do not," he said gently. "There is no time. Stay as you are."

"We will be seen," she said frantically.

"They will think nothing of it if we seem but to converse." He closed the front of her bodice, her breasts still wet from his kisses. Then equally efficient, he adjusted the front of his breeches, his flesh still slick with her wetness, and lowered the hem of her gown.

She scrambled off the table. Seizing the basket, she

ducked her head, refusing to meet his gaze as color spread across her cheeks and down her neck.

"Brianna!" he whispered.

Her head came up. Her gaze met his briefly. It was filled with shadows and a feverish brightness at the same time. "Please," she implored him, "Do not follow."

Then she fled past him. If his men noticed and thought anything amiss they gave no indication as they put away their weapons and spoke of the hours after supper when they would test that certain maiden's preferences. Then others joined them, competition still keen between them, even though weapons had been set aside.

Retrieving his sword, Tarek left the stables, and went in search of her. But every effort to find some moment alone with her was thwarted, as if fortune conspired against him. Yet, throughout the evening, during the long meal, and the discussions of battle strategy afterward that always dominated the late evening hours, when he looked for her, she did not avoid his gaze.

More than once, he saw the bright gold of her hair among the shadows of the hall, and his gaze was drawn to her. As if she sensed that he watched her, she turned and met his gaze. Her eyes were still bright as they had been that afternoon in the stables. She looked away only when her attention was drawn elsewhere by someone asking something of her.

His hand clenched over the handle of his tankard as he watched her, his thoughts filled with the memory of that encounter only hours past when he had refused to accept that she was anything less than a woman full of passion and desire, and had then proved it to them both.

Even now, his flesh grew hard as he remembered the yielding softness of her, the sweet rain of her passion as it slicked his way, and the moment when he had pressed at plea-

246

sure's gate and she had clung to him, her woman's flesh opening to him.

The tankards were refilled around the table, except for his which remained untouched. Conversation droned on, of matters which held little interest for him. He responded vaguely to questions asked, or when Stephen of Valois made a comment beside him. Since returning from the encounter with Mardigan's men, meals had become more amicable between the Scots and Normans because of the trust which had been forced in battle.

When he looked for her again, he saw the golden brilliance of her hair in the light of the torches near the main doors to the hall, and knew where she had gone. He rose, determined to discuss this with her, for they could not continue as they had before, and he would accept nothing less than that she was his wife completely. And if she would not . . .

The wind had come up, whipping across the yard as he crossed it in long-legged strides. Instinctively, he glanced to the gate — secured — and the guards along the wall. With the new moon just above the eastern horizon, he saw their silhouettes against a cloud-strewn sky at their positions.

Smokey fires, whipped by the rising wind, dotted the yard at encampments. In the growing dark, dogs snarled and growled at each other nearby, no doubt over a cast-off bone. The horses stirred restlessly in the stables, and birds fluttered wildly at their perches in the dovecote as before a gathering storm. He vaulted up the steps to the battlements.

He found her there, silhouetted against the twilight of night sky, her hair the color of moonlight.

Her mantle whipped about her slender body as she leaned forward, hands braced on top of the battlement wall with her face lifted to the wind. Then, as if sensing she was not alone she turned and their gazes met.

Her skin was like Persian marble, her green eyes enormous and haunted in her pale face, her hair white gold and tossed on the wind like a shimmering nimbus of light that framed her. Then she left the wall and slowly walked toward him.

As she drew closer he saw the feverish light that glowed in her eyes as it had earlier that afternoon in the stables, and the color that flamed her cheeks.

Standing before him, the moonlit satin of her hair streaming about her on the wind of the rising storm, she seemed otherworldly as if she were not truly mortal, and he thought of the Jehara, the mythical, magical creatures of the immortal world.

Then she moved into his arms, slender hands framing his face as she lifted her mouth to his, and answered the silent question in his eyes with a fierce passion.

"Yes."

Fourteen

Her mouth was cool beneath his, then burned with fire. She tasted of wind, cold night air, and desire. As passion exploded between them, the storm unleashed its fury around them.

The first droplets of rain beaded at her lips as they parted beneath his, and his tongue thrust inside, tasting all of her, drinking her in. The wind lashed the battlements and whipped her mantle about both of them as he lifted her against him, the softness of her breasts pressed against his chest as her arms went around his neck.

"Make me feel what a woman feels." Her voice broke softly, part hope and part desperation of some longing she did not understand as she changed the angle and fit her mouth to his, this time her small tongue darting between his lips to taste him as he had tasted her.

A wild restlessness burned through her, then centered low inside her and coiled until it became a dull ache as her hips pressed against his.

She felt his response in the flesh that hardened against her belly and imagined him as he had been in the stables, all gleaming dark flesh, heavily veined, and straining toward her. Then pressing hot against her, and the way her own body had welcomed him. And welcomed him now.

Her face was pale as lightning flashed above them, her features fragile, yet breathtakingly beautiful as her eyes glowed with passion.

Her breasts rose and fell with each frantic breath dragged into her lungs. Her fingers tangled in his hair as her lips parted beneath his and she gently suckled his tongue into the sweet darkness of her mouth.

"Make me your wife in all ways."

His hands pushed impatiently back beneath the thick folds of her mantle, over slender hips, and the curve of her bottom as he lifted her and then guided her legs about his waist so that his erect flesh, straining through layers of clothes, molded the cleft of her body. He rocked her hips against his, his fingers gently bruising as the long-banked fire raged beyond control.

"In all ways," she breathed against his lips.

He pulled the hem of her gown up over her hips and removed the barrier of his own clothing until her warmth molded his. She was already wet, her body slicking over him with her own hot rain, as if she had become the storm.

A startled, breathless sound came from her parted lips as his hands clamped her bare hips. As he lifted her, her slender hand closed around his swollen flesh, guiding him to her.

Her slender legs clasped his waist with a fierce strength that matched his own and the storm that exploded the sky above them as he thrust inside her.

Her back arched and her head went back. Lightning sliced the darkness overhead, bathing her features in light. Her expression was both torment and ecstasy. And like the lightning that burned across the sky, she felt the lightning that tore through her flesh, and burned deep inside her.

"In all ways we shall be as one, Brianna," he whispered, repeating the ancient vows they had spoken when they were wed.

"One life, one heart, one soul for all eternity."

A wild torrent of joy poured through her, banishing the doubt and fear. She clasped his shoulders, the storm that built within her growing apace with the storm that lashed the battlements as she again experienced the dream vision of that night long ago.

Of being high atop the battlements and the fierce, magnificent creature that leapt the walls. As it attacked, she had felt its warmth beneath her hands and clung to that warmth and fierceness, as she now clung to him. Then, the creature had gently sunk its teeth into her flesh in a claiming of passion, as his flesh now thrust inside her.

He was the creature of her vision, a fierce dark cat, an animal of the night who had claimed her dreams as he now claimed her body and soul.

And now, as in her vision, she gave herself to the fierce dark beast in a mating of passion and flesh. And the cry of pleasure she made to the storm, was primal, like that of a creature finally joined with its true mate.

Afterward, she lay against him, the folds of her mantle sheltering them, his flesh still clasped within the tight fist of her body.

She stirred, raising her head. Her eyes were dark, irises like black velvet, completely open, unguarded, fathomless, as if he was looking into the future and the past.

She was fragile and light as goose down in his arms, yet warm as a resting fire that but waits to be rekindled. Her mouth sought his.

"I did not know," she whispered as she moved closer in his arms and felt him grow hard once more within her. Her surprised gaze met his, then darkened even more. Her breath caught on a startled gasp of pleasure and wonder as he slowly rocked her hips against him, and she felt him press against her belly as he had before, only this time inside her.

"Now you do," he said with fierce tenderness.

She made a sound of protest when he gently eased from her body and straightened their clothing. Then, wrapping her mantle about her, he swung her into his arms, and carried her from the battlements.

The guards at the entrance of the main hall were his own Norman guards. If they were surprised to see him carrying the old laird's daughter in his arms, they were wise enough to say nothing.

The doors of the large hall were open as they returned, challenges of physical prowess being called out over yet another round of ale. But both Normans and Scots seemed oblivious to anything else as he carried her past to the stone stairs that led to the second-floor chambers. In the passage at the top he turned toward the laird's chamber.

A fire had been laid at the hearth, no doubt the work of Duncan who had unofficially taken on the position of Tarek's squire. Everything about the chamber was tidy and neat, everything in its place, with a tray with sweetmeats and a bowl of the precious spiced peaches at the table for the pleasure of the new laird of Inverness.

He did not carry her to the bed, but instead to the fire where he removed her wet mantle and laid it over a nearby chair to dry. Then going down on one knee, he removed first one slipper and then the other, in turn rubbing each foot between his hands.

"I am not cold," she said. As he looked up at her, her fingers loosened the ties of her bodice. When he stood she took his hand and pressed it against her bare breast. The brilliant blue of his eyes hardened with desire. His jaw tightened, his voice low and thick.

"No, you are not."

Still, she shivered as he stroked the dusky peak, rolling it beneath his palm until it was taut and hard. Then he bent low over her, his tongue flicking over that distended peak, and repeated gruffly, "You most certainly are not," as he suckled it deep into his mouth.

She gasped at the exquisite pleasure that began at her breast, spiraled down through her belly, and was then felt all over again at her womb, an echo of desire that increased in intensity with each tug of his lips. Her hands went back through his hair, clasping him to her as he then pushed back the other side of her bodice and drew a second aching peak between his teeth.

He pulled the wet fabric back off her shoulders and down the length of each arm.

"Undressing you is like peeling a peach," he whispered thickly as her gown skimmed her hips, thighs, and finally fell to the floor.

"Is that difficult?" she asked breathlessly as both his hands lightly stroked down over the curve of her bare bottom as she remembered how he had held her before, and the exquisite pleasure that had followed.

"Sometimes almost impossible, but well worth the effort." He swung her up into his arms, her wet hair trailing over his shoulder and halfway to the floor.

"You could eat it with the skin left on," she suggested, her own hand moving to the ties of his tunic, then distracted by the hard plane of warm flesh beneath and the distended male nipple that responded to her touch.

"But half the pleasure is in peeling it," he said against her lips as he lowered her to the bed of soft furs.

"And the other half?" she asked as he stepped away from the bed only long enough to remove his wet clothes so that when he turned back to her, he was all gleaming bronze, lean, hard surfaces, and dark, compelling shadows.

He was breathtakingly beautiful, muscles stretching then bunching with a restraint of power as he returned to the bed, then stretching again as he placed a knee on the edge of the bed and moved over her, pinning her into the furs.

"The other half," he said, his voice both harsh and gentle as his head lowered over her and he once more drew her nipple between his lips, "is in the savoring of the fruit."

Her skin seemed afire. Everywhere he touched and tasted, her skin quivered as if that touch was more pleasurable than the last, until she writhed beneath him, her body filled with a growing restlessness of urgency.

"Tarek, please . . . !" She reached for him as she had before, her slender hand closing around his erect flesh, lifting her hips in an urgency to be joined with him again.

"All in time," he whispered, as his hand gently removed hers, his fingers clamping about each wrist as he slowly drew them up over her head and pinned them there. Then he began a tender assault, tasting every inch of her from her lips to the inside curve of her ear, then down her neck to dip between her breasts.

She was taut as a bowstring, her back arching as she ached for the feel of his mouth at her breast. But he had other places in mind as his head dipped lower and his hands pinned her shoulders, and his tongue found the small, satin whorl of her navel.

Her belly spasmed, ancient words whispered in a litany of growing desire as he continued his downward assault, and whispered again, "All in good time."

Then as he released her shoulders, she felt his warm breath stirring the patch of curling hair between her thighs. When his hands stroked down to each knee, gently parting them, she went completely still beneath him.

He tenderly parted the folds of her woman's flesh, swollen from their first joining. She was all pale pink and soft gold like the dawn, the delicate bud of her pleasure distended and aroused, and gleaming with the wetness he had summoned from her body. He blew gently against the downy curls, parting them as he stroked into the dark, hot center of her, and savored her.

She tasted of sun-ripened nectar and a sultry dark essence that he realized with a sudden intense arousal was the blending of her own golden sweetness with the pearl of his seed from their first joining.

His hands spread over her belly, thumbs touching, fingers clasping over her hips as he tasted her again and again. For he realized with a sudden fierce possessiveness that even now a part of him was inside her, joining with her, becoming a part of her. And the taste was all the sweeter with a longing ache of hunger that had lain within him for a lifetime.

She cried out beneath him, the words ancient and unknown to him, but her need clear to see in the flush that colored her skin, each gasp of air that was dragged into her lungs, the wild tangle of her hair as it spread over the furs, and the fever in her eyes. He had taken her to the brink of fulfillment. Now she looked back at him with confusion and blatant sexual arousal as she came up on her knees and reached for him.

Her mouth was eager and hungry beneath his, her tongue slipping between his lips to taste him. She made a soft, dark sound at the back of her throat, part surprise and all pleasure. Then as the kiss slowly ended, her questioning gaze met his.

"You taste of a sweetness I have never known."

"You have always known it," he whispered against her lips. "You have only now tasted it." At the soft frown that drew her lovely brows together, he explained, "It is yourself you have tasted, the sweetest honey joined with my seed inside you."

Her eyes darkened, as her hand went behind his neck and

she drew him down for another kiss, and whispered, "I am still hungry, milord."

She was in awe of the power and strength of him, so finely made, yet with a lean and dangerous grace as when he wielded the sword. She was pale and small against him, yet she felt a wondrous power she could not have guessed at as she felt him grow rigid and hard within her hands, stroking him as he had stroked her, discovering him all over again, each sharp edge and hard plane, every curve of muscle, like the dark creature of her dreams.

He was as warm as the sun and smooth as polished stone beneath her questing hands. What she had discovered with him took her breath away and made her blood burn like fire in her veins, dispelling all the doubts and fears since she was a child. He need never know the secret she kept when they could share this.

He held her as if she was made of glass, hands sculpting her, whispering ancient foreign words across her skin, tasting the rain and wind that seemed so much a part of her as if she was some wind-born creature.

The thought stirred another, and then it was gone in a blaze of desire as her slender hands caressed him, stroking each pulsing vein at his erect flesh, then closing around him as her woman's flesh had closed around him then stroking back in an exploration of wonder to cradle the fleshy pouches beneath. A glistening bead appeared at his heavily veined flesh.

"You see how my body weeps with need for you," he whispered thickly.

With that same wonder of discovery she took the liquid pearl onto her fingertip, then brought it to her lips. Her gaze met his, dark, smokey green, no longer curious but aflame with her own desire.

On a groan he kissed her deeply, his hands stroking back through her hair to hold her as he plundered her mouth, his blood afire at the sight of her tasting him.

In answer, she gave him everything, matching his hunger for her with one of her own, touching, stroking, stunning him with her passion. Her body was taut, straining, shivering with a newly discovered need.

He understood as he gently turned her so that her back was toward him. She made a soft sound of protest, trying to turn in his arms, but he persuaded her as he lowered her onto her belly at the bed and gently sunk his teeth into the skin at the back of her shoulder as he leaned over her.

She gasped, first surprise and then pleasure as the bite became more tender bites across the back of her shoulder to her spine. She found this new position most pleasing with his hand at her breast as the nipple throbbed and ached.

Then his hand lowered over her belly, stroking lower to the thatch of hair between her thighs. On a shudder of desire, she opened to him, making a pleasurable sound as he slipped two fingers inside her. Her hips moved against the gentle thrusts of his fingers until she was arching against him. Then he slowly withdrew, leaving her in a daze of frustrated, unfulfilled desire.

"Please," she whispered. "I must feel you inside me."

"All in good time, Brianna," he whispered, his breath warm at the back of her neck, and in a tone no doubt intended to be soothing, but which heightened her arousal all the more at the memory of other places his breath had warmed her.

"It must be done with care," he said, each word a torment as he stroked through the strands of her long hair that fell over her shoulder. "You are still very new at this." And he felt renewed desire at the knowledge that no man had ever touched her as he had.

She made a small sound of surprise as he gently lifted her hips, pulling her back against him as he knelt at the bed, followed by a sound of pleasure as he tenderly opened her.

"Tarek?" her voice was thick with desire as she reached back to touch him, and ended on a startled gasp of pleasure as he bent low over the curve of her back and slowly pushed inside her.

She had seen animals come together in such a way, and again her thoughts filled with images of that fierce, dark cat claiming her atop the battlements, wild, primitive, in a joining as deep as her soul.

With one arm about her waist, Tarek pulled her back against him so that she felt the warmth of his chest at her back, her bottom cradled by his hips.

He shuddered with an intensity of pleasure he had never known with any woman as his other hand closed over her right hip and he gently rocked her against him, feeling her ease about him, then suddenly clench tighter with her own pleasure, pressing deeper with each thrust until he touched her womb.

He opened his hand, stroking low across her belly where even now beneath pale skin and slender muscles he was firmly sheathed inside her, and experienced a feeling of oneness he had never known before. A feeling that had begun that day long ago beside a pool when she had reached out to him, and now completed with his flesh deep inside her.

"Tarek . . ."

She shivered in his arms, her breath coming in short, choppy sounds. Instinctively, she began to move against him as they had before, desperate to ease the ache of desire that had not lessened with their joining, but only intensified.

He whispered strange foreign words against her cheek as

his head lowered beside hers, holding her gently, slowing her eager movements.

"All in good time. You must trust me, Brianna. Let me take you there. Let me show you the way, so that you will find your pleasure as well." He lowered his hand from her hip to the throbbing cleft of her body, as his other hand closed over her breast.

Her body spasmed and she gasped with pleasure as he wet her with his fingers. She was small and tight, her delicate woman's flesh stretched taut around his shaft, the small bud above hardened with desire.

Her muscles spasmed and clenched around him all the tighter, then the slick heat of her own wetness that he stroked from her eased him deeper as her body answered his tender loving of her.

He slowly began to move inside her, withdrawing, then gently pushing back inside her until he was wet with her arousal and she took him easily. Then she began to move tentatively against him, experimenting, arching her back, then rocking her hips back so that she was completely open to him and the pleasure intense in this new way as she felt his strength and power surging inside her.

As he built the desire and pleasure apace within her, Brianna felt a power she had never known. Eyes closed, head thrown back, her body answering each thrust of his, she experienced once again her dream vision of the magnificent dark creature on the battlement walls, its body joining with hers in a fierce passion.

"Please," she whispered, her eyes bright with the fever of desire, "let me touch you."

He could not imagine how more completely they might *touch* one another than with his flesh firmly held within hers. Then all thoughts fled save one as she touched where he had touched at the joined center of their bodies.

Her slender fingers stroked his flesh at the opening of her own body, then gradually lower to the pouches of soft flesh wrapped in a cocoon of midnight dark hair that nestled warm and full against her.

He swore softly, "Brianna, if you continue, it will all quickly be over," as his body responded to her touch. He gathered her against him, stilling her seeking hands, but he could not still her restless movements, or the sudden tightness as her body quickened around him, her sleek muscles clenching and spasming over his flesh, and the startled sound she made as she climaxed.

It exploded with the power of a thousand suns, a white hot agony of pleasure so intense she feared she would die of it. His hips clenched against hers as he thrust deep inside her at that final moment. She cried out, the contractions of her muscles stroking him like a powerful fist.

Fire burned through him, and then his body was rocked with the powerful spasms of release as his seed burst inside her.

Fifteen

Brianna surfaced slowly through the haze of exhausted sleep. Sounds came from the other side of the heavy tapestry bed hangings.

She moved tentatively within the warm fur-lined cocoon of the bed, trying to discern the sound. That of water being poured and the brief murmur of voices.

"Is there anything else I might bring, milord?"

Then the haze of memory also cleared as she recognized Tarek's voice.

"No, that will be all. Good eventide, Enya."

And as her memory cleared, her body warmed at the thought of the hours past as she clasped a thick fur against her. Then the bed-hangings were thrown back.

"Go away," she protested, burrowing deeper into the soft furs, clinging to the sensual haze of sleep.

"That is not what you asked of me a little while ago," Tarek reminded her as his hand went in search of a slender ankle as it disappeared beneath the edge of a fur pelt. They began a game of hunt and seek through countless layers of furs, until she lay gasping for air as he finally pinned both arms and both thighs in one place, and then expertly extricated her from the bed.

"Noooo!" she groaned softly, burrowing against his chest. "It cannot be morning yet."

"It is not. It is hardly past midnight." His voice at his chest rumbled beneath her cheek, sending faint thrills of pleasure along her nerve endings.

"Then why have you awakened me?"

"I did not. You awakened me. Or to be more accurate, your stomach awakened me. And I cannot tolerate a wife with a snarling stomach."

She lifted her head, green eyes peering at him through a veil of white gold hair that spilled over her forehead. "You interrupted my meal at midday," she reminded him, recalling how the basket of food had, for the most part, gone untouched.

"And you interrupted my evening meal," he shot back at her as he brushed his lips across hers. The kiss ended abruptly as she was swung away from him, furs snatched from her gloriously naked body, and she was deposited in a large wood half-barrel from the laundry.

But instead of heavy shirts, linens, and strong lye soap, it was filled with clean, steaming water. All sounds of protest were smothered by an exclamation of startled pleasure.

"How did you persuade the laundress to part with one of her barrels?"

His unusual blue eyes narrowed with amusement and a certain cunning. "I didn't. I stole it."

"She'll have your head for this," Brianna pointed out, for the woman's reputation was well known. "And a few other body parts as well."

"It is worth whatever price, if it brings you pleasure."

"Oh, it does!" she exclaimed amid a burst of bubbles, as she submerged and then quickly resurfaced, scooping her hair back from her face.

He watched her antics with warm eyes, enjoying her at play as he had enjoyed her far more serious play earlier. She was like a sleek seal that he'd once seen, finding great pleasure in the warm water.

"Many believe that if one bathes too often they will sicken

and die," she pointed out.

"Do you believe it?"

"If I believed it, I would smell like a goat."

"I assure you, you do not smell like a goat. And I am not in the habit of sleeping with goats."

"And yet you thought I needed a bath." She lifted a slender arm and sniffed delicately. "Have I perhaps offended you, milord?"

He lifted a heavy strand of wet hair from her shoulder and smoothed it back. This playful side of her was like discovering a breathtaking young maid by a highland pool for the first time.

"You please me very well," his voice was low and thick at the memory of the passion they had shared. "I was concerned that you might have suffered some discomfort afterward. Hot water can be very soothing."

Her eyes widened, like vivid green pools, with undisguised surprise. "Aye, it can be," she agreed, then her gaze angled away from his as if with sudden embarrassment at the mention of the hours past.

"I assure you, I am quite well. I suffered no discomfort." She paused, and added, "Only at first." Then her gaze lifted once more and met his with that directness of honesty that he had come to value in her.

"And it was not really a discomfort. In truth, milord, you pleased *me* very well."

It was his turn to smile with some inner thought as he stared down at the surface of the water and discovered another pleasure, that of her body glimpsed through the shimmering depths — the curve of her breasts bobbing beneath the surface, her slender arms wrapped around her knees, concealing other places.

It had not occurred to him that it might have been otherwise, for always before with a woman he had been certain of their pleasure even with the most exotic creatures to be found in the Byzantine empire. But he discovered that it pleasured him even more to hear her speak of it, just as she had pleasured him with the sounds she made as they made love, and the inexperienced yet eager movements of her body.

His fingers trailed the water where the loose ends of her hair floated on the surface, draped her shoulders, and curved over the top of a breast. He followed the line of water, his fingers lightly stroking that glistening curve.

He heard the subtle change in her breathing, that told him of her arousal, now familiar to him, and the way the flat moon of her nipple warmed by the water, suddenly puckered and grew taut apace with the hardening of his own flesh. Already, they knew each other with a physical instinct.

Then he stroked lower, along the inward curve of her thigh to the soft, watery center of her, tenderly stroking as he remembered the pleasured hour past when it seemed he could find no greater pleasure than to lose himself in the wet heat of her body.

As if drugged by the sweet intoxication of heat and his touch, her eyes closed and her head went back on the rim of the barrel. Her legs parted as she opened herself to him and waited with a tension of anticipation that quivered through the water.

But the sensation that she experienced next was the sweet, wet heat of his mouth, lightly brushing hers. She made a sound that was a combination of surprise, pleasure, and disappointment.

"It is too soon, Brianna," he told her with a sternness of concern for her, for in truth he ached for her again. "We will wait, and after a while discover other pleasures with each other."

264

"How long?" she insisted, sitting up in the water with an impatience that sent water sloshing over the sides of the barrel.

He laughed, for she was like a willful child who had just been told she could have no more honey cakes.

"Until I say it has been long enough," he told her, reaching for her hand.

"How is it that you will make such a decision, when it is my body?"

"Because I am infinitely more experienced in such matters. Now I will wash you."

Her eyes were liquid green and wide with surprise. "Is that the way between men and women in the Byzantine empire?"

"No, usually the woman washes the man. She washes afterward and never in the same water."

"Why not?"

"Because it would be impure."

"Then why are you going to wash me?"

"Because," he told her, returning with a cake of soap in one hand, and then going down on one knee beside the barrel, "it pleases me."

She looked about her skeptically at the barrel. "I do not think there is room enough for two in here."

"It might be a bit tight," he conceded.

"I do not think that you could keep to your decision about the next time we make love if we were to share this bath."

"You are probably right. Now turn around."

The soap was faintly spicy, exotic, and familiar, for she had smelled it before on him. He lathered it across her shoulders and down her back, and through her hair. Then he lathered it down her neck and across the front of her shoulders, and they both discovered the pleasure of soap gliding across other places.

He squeezed water from her hair. She felt his fingers linger at her shoulder.

"It is a most unusual mark," he commented, his warm fingers tracing over the mark on her skin that was no larger than a small coin. It was rose-colored, and gave the appearance of two small circles one slightly overlapping the other. There were other much tinier marks outside the circles.

"I was born with it," she explained, with a growing tightness in her chest when he still said nothing. She slowly turned in the water beneath his hands, her clear green gaze searching his.

"There are those who believe such markings are a sign of evil," she said slowly, wondering if he believed such things. For in truth she knew so little about this dark warrior who was now her husband and laird of Inverness.

He heard the hesitation in her voice, saw the uncertainty in her gaze, at the same time her shoulders squared and her head lifted proudly as if she defied him to believe it. He smiled tenderly.

"There are also those in the far eastern empires who purposefully make such markings on their bodies for adornment as proof of their status or achievement in their culture. I have seen such adornments covering the entire body. Great elaborate designs . . ." he turned and gestured to the stitched pattern in the bed-hanging, "much like a tapestry." Her eyes grew large with amazement as she listened.

"And," he went on to explain, lightly brushing a wet tendril of hair back from her cheek, "there are those cultures which highly revere those who are born with such marks, for they are the chosen ones."

"Chosen ones?"

He nodded. "They are so marked, it is believed, because they have been chosen by the gods above others to be spiritual leaders, or rulers." Nothing in his manner gave any indication, and she wondered which he believed.

"Do you find the mark offensive?"

There was very nearly defiance in her voice as if she dared him to. He suppressed a smile. She was beautiful, proud, and had a keen intelligence that would bow to no man. By the Prophet! She stirred his blood as no other. An ethereal creature that was as strong as the finest steel blade.

"I would find it offensive only perhaps if it were the mark of a wart hog." He watched her expression with growing amusement as she tried to imagine a creature she had never seen, but which by its very name conjured up unpleasant images. She couldn't seem to decide whether to be amused, outraged, or relieved.

"A wart hog?" She blew out in disgust. "I don't think I would much care for it either."

"Nor I," he assured her, his smile curving more deeply. "I would find it most distracting to be staring down at a wart hog on your shoulder when making love as we just have."

Her cheeks colored and grew warm, as well as other places, as she too remembered the way they had come together, his wide shoulders pressed against hers, his hand moving low across her belly as he opened her and entered her in a most pleasurable and unexpected way.

Even now her belly quivered and clenched at the memory of his body joined with hers, and she wondered how long before he would consider it no longer "too soon." For in truth she felt no discomfort except that of muscles used in ways she was not accustomed to. Not at all unpleasant, but with a delicious fatigue that made her stretch and anticipate the next time with a sensual longing. Even had he not grinned at her, his sensual lips curving back from gleaming teeth, she was convinced he teased her. Wart hog indeed!

She flipped water at him. It sprinkled across the tunic he had donned, belted loosely at his lean waist, and glistened in the midnight black hair that waved past his shoulders. She enjoyed their play, for it took her mind off other matters. At least now she knew she was capable of feeling what a woman feels when she is joined with a man. But beyond that, she could not know.

Her bath had rapidly cooled. He pulled her to her feet and scooped her from the barrel. Water sluiced off her body and puddled at her feet as he set her to the floor, wrapping her in a large linen cloth. As punishment for his dousing, he nipped at a bare shoulder. She gasped, and her head came up. The look in her eyes was not one of outrage, or pain, but a wild, potent desire. It seemed even the most playful gesture had a devastating effect on the senses.

He abruptly turned her toward the fire at the brazier, and commanded, "Sit and warm yourself before you catch your death of cold. I swear I have never known such a cold land. I do not understand how any survive."

"We survive very well, milord. The cold strengthens the body. It is only that your blood is too thin."

"There is nothing wrong with my blood," he assured her, his blood warming as he watched her dry herself. Then he joined her, fanning her wet hair before the fire, drying it between his fingers, the exotic fragrance of the soap experienced again in every strand that was like spun gold.

At a grumbling request from her stomach, they spread out the food Enya had brought from the kitchen and ate before the warmth of the fire.

"Tell me of your home," Brianna said as she nibbled at a piece of bread spread with honey.

"I have no home," he answered, throwing more pieces of wood on the brazier. They caught, spicy heat flaring once more to warm the chamber.

She stopped nibbling. "Everyone has a home. Even though Cullum and Mirren were not my true parents, I found a home here with them as good as any I could hope for." Even as she said it, a memory shifted, of some other place seen in visions and dreams, and other gentle, loving faces. Then just as quickly it was gone.

He frowned as he sat beside her, elbow propped at bent knee as he stirred the fire with an iron poker. "A home is a place filled with love and family who care for one another. It can be seen even among your kinsmen. They are bound by fierce loyalty, and a deep abiding love of this land, and the ties of blood. I have never experienced such a thing."

She shivered in spite of the warmth in the chamber, at the thought that he had never felt that deep bond that meant love, safety, and happiness.

"But you had a mother and father. Everyone has." She saw his hand tighten over the poker, like a sword he thrust savagely into the raging embers.

"Yes," his voice was low and tight in his throat. "Everyone has a mother, and *father*." But the way he spoke the word father, revealed that he felt no love for the one who had sired him. Then he told her of Asmari, the favored daughter of a rich and powerful emir, the bridal caravan that had taken her as a girl of fifteen, accompanied by her old aunt, to Antioch to meet the young man she was to marry, and the attack on the impregnable city by Norse raiders who had then raped and plundered the surrounding countryside, taking the daughter of the emir captive.

"The emir paid the ransom, for he loved Asmari very much, even as much as his first born son. But she had been dishonored."

Brianna said nothing, for there was nothing that could be

said. Instead she listened.

"She was raped by the Norse raider who took her captive. Though she eventually returned to her family, the marriage they had planned for her was no longer possible." He turned to her then, his handsome features taut with a coldness of hatred that reflected in his unusual blue eyes — the mark of the father who had sired him. The pain of Asmari's shame was his own.

Instinctively, she reached out to him, her fingers brushing his.

"It was not her fault. She was innocent," she whispered.

"I have never blamed her," he said. "There were others enough who did."

"How could they blame her?"

"It was said by some in her family that she should have resisted. Even if it meant taking her own life to prevent the shame it brought to her family."

Brianna shivered. She was not naive. Such was often the outcome of war. Many good Scots women had suffered similarly at the hands of Mardigan and his men.

She thought of Enya, who bravely faced down the men at Inverness. At first they treated her no better than Gillie, who gave herself freely to any warrior who wanted her. By contrast, Enya had earned the warriors' grudging respect with her kind ways and healing skills, holding herself apart from them, and making it clear in both word and gesture that she would not be treated like a whore.

She had been forced to make her point with the tip of a blade pressed dangerously against a warrior's groin when he ignored her refusal of his advances. She had confronted him for all to see in the midst of the evening meal in the great hall. Since then no one bothered her, while sadly, Gillie was the subject of their crude jokes and slanders.

Brianna's heart ached for Asmari and what she had suffered. It ached even for the child Asmari had borne who was the most innocent victim of all. His voice was low and filled with wrenching pain as he continued to tell her of his mother.

She wanted to stop him, to tell him it wasn't necessary for her to know it all, but she sensed his greater need to speak it, like a bitter flood that could not be held back.

"Not long after her return to her family," he went on to explain, "she realized that she was going to have a child — a bastard that would bring more shame upon her family." It was said with such coldness and self-loathing that Brianna shivered, but she said nothing, for she sensed there were no words of comfort she could offer.

"Asmari was sent into the hills to live with a family until her child was born," he continued after a while. "Afterward she returned to her family, but she was not allowed to bring the child for it would have been a constant reminder of her shame.

"The child was given to a merchant in Antioch and his wife to raise, for the man owed a debt of honor to the emir. They had no children of their own and it was thought they might accept the child as their own." The way he said it, revealed that they had not.

"The lowliest dog in the streets would find more kindness from a stranger than the boy received from them."

It tore at her heart the way he always spoke of the "boy" as if it was someone he had known once, instead of himself.

"The child was well educated for the emir had made it a condition in placing the child with them. But there were things the emir's wealth and power could not guarantee. Such as the love of family, and acceptance."

"What about Asmari? Surely she must have wanted to keep her child."

271

He nodded, his expression softened. "I am told that she did. She was not given a choice." He threw another piece of wood onto the brazier.

"She came to see the merchant on a visit to Antioch, with the pretense of purchasing silk cloth from his store. I saw her one time. I remember that she was very young with gleaming black hair, and she cried as she handed me a small wrapped package that contained two gifts.

"She told me to keep them always, they were of great importance. I do not remember anything else about her." It was said with a deep pain of regret, and longing.

"What was the gift?"

"One was the stone I gave you the day we were wed. It was given to Asmari by her father, and given by his father before him. He never knew that she had given it to me."

"She must have loved you very much," she whispered past the sudden thickness in her throat.

"Perhaps, though she never spoke of it. I believe it was too painful for her, for though I was the child of her womb, I was also the child of her shame." He turned and stared at the fire in the brazier. "When I was seven, she took her own life, unable to live with the disgrace."

She was so stunned for several moments she could say nothing. Then, finally, she asked, "What was the other gift she gave you?"

He reached inside the front of his tunic for the medallion she had seen earlier that day at the stables. It lay gleaming in the palm of his hand, embossed with the head of a strange-looking creature.

"A bastard spawn, a shame she could not live with, and the medallion, were all that he left her with."

The bitterness of hatred once more filled his voice, and she knew he spoke of the man who had sired him. Then he produced a second, identical medallion.

"I found this in the glen where we encountered Mardigan and his men."

"It is the same," she murmured, staring at the twin medallions.

"Yes, the very same." Pain and hatred hardened the words and the features of his handsome face.

"And you believe it belonged to one of the raiders?"

"Perhaps, or someone who knows of my father. Such a mark is like a tartan cloth worn by the kinsmen of one family."

"And if you find him?"

"*When* I find him, I will kill him."

She could not bear the pain of hatred she heard in his voice. It was cold and frightening, making him a stranger to her after the passion they had shared. Coming up on her knees, the linen wrapped about her, she gently framed his face not knowing if he might push her away.

He did not, but looked at her, with such a coldness of emotions that it seemed he might be incapable of feeling anything else. She could not tell him that what he felt was wrong, for she understood it very well. In many ways they were not vastly different, for the Scots were also proud, and many had killed to avenge the dishonor to their loved ones.

Instead she sought to find what she had discovered with him earlier, a fierce warmth of passion that might somehow assuage the pain of his shame.

"My adopted mother, Mirren, lost four stillborn babies. A fifth child lived only to one year and then died of fever. Once, Mirren told me there are things in life which can be born upon the soul because they must, and others which cannot. She could not bear the loss of her babies, so when I came to them I helped ease that loss."

With a certainty understood in her soul and which she

could only try to make him understand, she told him, "It was not that Asmari could not live with her shame for if that was so she would have taken her life long before. She could not bear to live without her child."

He looked at her then with an intensity of pain so deep and profound that she wanted to weep. But along with the pain was also a glimmer of hope at a possibility he had not considered.

"Only words."

"Or perhaps truth?" she suggested.

"As you see it."

"As I know it," she insisted. "There are things which can be endured, because they must be. But I think the loss of a child could not."

A tumult of emotions could be seen in his face, not the least of which was tenderness.

"You humble me."

She smiled softly. "Nay, milord," she assured him. "Humility is not known to you."

He took one of her hands between his and kissed her opened palm. "I think you shall perhaps teach it to me, for you have the power in your slender hand to humble me to the most obedient servant."

"Obedient?" she asked, her eyes growing round with surprise, and then gleaming with a far different thought. "In all things?"

"In things which are within my power to give you," his tongue flicked over the tender, exposed skin, making her shiver.

Her voice grew husky. "Then I command you to make love to me again, milord. For it has been long enough. And surely it is within your power."

She shifted a slender shoulder, the linen spilling to her

knees so that she was suddenly, gloriously naked. With a sudden fierceness that spoke of the boy's pain and loneliness, and the grown man's strength of power, he gathered her in his arms and quickly bore her to the bed. There with a barely controlled fierceness that constantly battled the more rational need to be gentle with her, they came together like midnight sky and morning sun, dark upon pale gold as she welcomed him with slender arms, and the quickening heat of her body.

"I was right," she sighed as he moved over her, gleaming bronze, male flesh thrusting erect and proud between their entwined bodies. "There is *no* humility in you."

Then a ragged whisper of need as she wrapped her legs about his lean waist, opening herself to him, and finally, a fierce sound of pleasure as he thrust inside her.

"Aye, milord," she whispered on a gasp of mounting desire. " 'Tis indeed within your power."

Brianna was not certain what had awakened her. The chamber was still except for the fire at the brazier that had burned low, the remains of a log shifting in the bed of embers. She wrapped a fur about her as she went to the brazier, placing more logs upon it.

Soon the fire burned, greedily consuming the fresh cut pine. There was no movement from the bed, only the sound of Tarek's deep breathing that stirred a feeling of profound wonder and tenderness within at the memory of the past hours they'd shared.

Pushing back the details of their complicated lives, she hugged herself. For she had discovered in his arms that it was truly possible to be a woman in all ways.

You must never know, she thought silently to herself. For I could not bear to see the look in your eyes if you did, and then for you to turn away from me.

She did not fully understand these new and strange feelings. Love? She did not know. She felt many overwhelming emotions that she had not thought she would ever feel, and had only just begun to sort out. She only knew that having experienced these very human emotions, with so many more rushing at her with each passing moment they were together, that she could not bear to ever lose it.

She wrapped the fur about her more closely, suddenly chilled in spite of the fire. Her fingers brushed her shoulder and she thought of the strange mark she carried and which she had seen at the lake at Lochonnen.

She sensed a stirring and put the memory aside. But Tarek slept on, his breathing unusually deep for a warrior trained to be alert to the shift of the wind. As she turned toward the bed, the light from the fire at the brazier that spread golden patterns across the walls, suddenly seemed to swallow inward on itself.

Shadows grew at the walls as the light grew dimmer. When she turned back to the brazier the fire that had burned steadily and bright only moments before now sputtered as if it were dying.

A foreboding of some malevolent force moved across her senses, as if the darkness had entered her thoughts and slipped beneath her skin. And she knew they were not alone. Someone, or something was there in the chamber.

She sensed it in the way of the forest creatures with a deep, inner instinct of something evil and dangerous. It pressed down on her, smothering, cold, and foul as if something had touched her.

"Brianna?" His voice was muffled and distant as if from very far away. And then much closer, as she focused on the sound of it, pulling her back into the world of light, warmth, and love.

She shivered as she took a deep breath, drawing the sweet, pungent scent of pine logs into her smothered lungs. When she moved she experienced a lethargy in her legs that too quickly fled. It was as if she had been dead, and was now suddenly alive again.

"What is it?" he asked, coming off the bed of furs, gloriously real, and gloriously naked. Then his arms were wrapping around her, gloriously warm when she was so cold in spite of the fur wrapped about her.

"Is something wrong?" And then as he reached her and took her in his arms, "By the Prophet, you are cold as ice!"

"The fire has gone out," she whispered from between cold lips as she curled into his warmth. He pulled her back to the bed where he covered her with warm furs.

"I will see that it does not go out again," he told her when she was snuggled beneath them and her skin had begun to warm.

"Do not leave," she implored him.

"Only to put more wood on the fire," he assured her, "then I shall return." He crossed the chamber to the brazier which once more burned brightly. Kneeling before it, he placed two more pieces on so that it would be sure to burn through until dawn. Yet, in spite of the fact that she claimed the fire had burned out, the chamber was not overly cold and he wore nothing as he crouched before the brazier.

He returned to the bed, finding her beneath the mound of warm furs and pulling her close, a dark fear in his heart that he might have hurt her in some way.

"Please, just hold me. It will pass."

London

Vivian awoke suddenly, the warning like a chill across her

skin. Throwing back the thick fur blanket, she crossed the chamber very near the king's, and went to the fire at the brazier.

It had burned low, embers glowing like watchful orange eyes glinting back at her. With a growing sense of urgency, she took a handful of fragrant dried leaves from a basket, and cast them onto the embers.

Tendrils of pungent smoke spiraled into the air, then expanded and grew thicker. Then flames burst to life. She fed in bits and pieces of twigs, gradually adding larger pieces until the fire grew, and she added first one log and then another.

Then, when she had built the flames up until they were once more dancing hungrily about the logs, she extended her hand into the fire.

There was no pain nor was she burned. Instead she seemed to become one with the flames, her features taut with concentration, delicate auburn brows drawn together over eyes the brilliant blue color found at the heart of a flame, her red hair tumbled about her shoulders the bright crimson, gold, and burgundy colors of the fire itself.

Slowly, she closed her eyes, becoming one with the flame, drawing her power from it as she spoke ancient words that opened the portal of light.

"Element of fire, spirit of light, essence of life, awaken the night. Fire of the soul, flame of life, as light reveals truth, burn golden bright."

The flames burned brighter, blending orange, crimson, and yellow light in patterns of visions and dreams. She repeated the words and gradually one vision emerged clearly from all the rest — that of a beautiful golden girl surrounded by a growing darkness.

Her hand clenched as if in sudden pain, and tears glistened at her cheeks. Not for a long time had she seen the young girl. She had prayed to the Ancient Ones that she might be kept safe.

"What is it?" the tall warrior asked with quiet voice as he approached to crouch low beside her. For he knew when the power was with her.

"You have seen a vision in the fire?" Rorke FitzWarren, knight to William of Normandy, asked his wife, Lady Vivian.

She nodded, but when she tried to see more, it would not come to her. She sensed a powerful resistance, blocking her, making it impossible to see anything more.

Finally, exhausted from such intense concentration of power needed to penetrate the boundaries between the mortal and immortal worlds, she leaned against him exhausted.

"I sensed a stirring in the other world and a terrible danger."

His lean features grew tense, his hand curled into a hardened fist, eager to hold the handle of a broadsword as he held her closer, his embrace gentle, protective, sheltering of her and the child that grew in her womb.

"Danger to whom?" he asked with sudden fear, and she could feel his protective instinct that tightened every muscle. She shivered at the portent that even his strength would not be enough.

"Someone I have not seen in a very long time."

"Is the danger near?" he then asked.

She shivered as the coldness returned, a portent of an unknown future. "Much nearer than she knows, and far more dangerous."

He pulled her into his arms, his beard-roughened chin scraping her cheek as he held her and their unborn child close, as if he would physically slay any evil that might threaten them.

She turned in his embrace, holding onto him, wishing with all her heart that his love and fierce warrior's strength was enough to banish the coldness of fear that now filled her soul.

"It grows more powerful with each passing moment," she whispered with the certainty of the gift she had been born with, the all-knowing power of the Ancient Ones.

"Can it be stopped?"

"I do not know," she answered as the first light of a cold and bleak dawn appeared at the edges of the tapestry that covered the window.

"But there is one who will know."

"Merlin?"

She nodded. "I must go to him. He will know what can be done."

Sixteen

The next weeks were frustrating for both Scots and Norman warriors. Mardigan seemed to have disappeared from the highlands, or if he was still there, he had gone to ground in some remote hideout where no one could find him, for there were no recent raids on villages or farms.

The Scots grew restless, for with spring came the need to return to their own holdings and families. Gardens and fields must be planted. The lambing had already begun in the flocks of sheep that had been hidden in the hills for safety along with their families. Some men had new sons and daughters they had not yet seen, but had only heard about through messengers who traveled among the clans.

Perhaps, the chieftains argued, Mardigan had seen their true strength with the Norman alliance and had accepted that he could not take Inverness. Perhaps, he had left the highlands, retreating across the sea. But Brianna argued against them for she knew Mardigan.

"Several hundred men do not vanish in the mist," she told them. "They've taken enough in their raids to last through the summer and longer. And in a few weeks with no new raids, do ye forget the loss of yer family and kinsmen? No," she argued adamantly, "he has not given up.

"He has vowed to have Scotland. If ye lay down yer weapons to take up the hoe, ye seal yer fate, that of yer sons, and every kinsman."

They listened because they had respected Cullum and knew her to possess his same strength and wisdom. Yet, they were torn between what they knew Mardigan was capable of and families that needed to be fed.

Tarek listened to all their arguments. The decision had been made that the Norman knights and warriors would continue to defend Inverness, but without the strength of the alliance they could well find themselves outnumbered in a foreign land when Mardigan struck again. Then he made a proposal by which they could provide for their families and defend Inverness.

Sitting at the table in the large dining hall with Brianna at his side and Malcolm, now very near fully recovered at the other, he proposed a solution.

"There is strength in numbers," he began slowly, thoughtfully, always mindful of the political battlefield he walked through and carefully weighing each word.

"Every man who has ever fought a battle knows this. You have found that strength in the bond of your kinsmen. I propose this: let those who live the farthest distance return to their families and farms. The prize Mardigan seeks is Inverness, for that is the symbolic heart of the north country. Plant your crops, and provide for your families for the coming winter. But band the families together in communities, plant large community gardens and fields of crops.

"Two of every three men will remain here at Inverness in readiness while his family is provided for by the community. Then every two months, an equal portion from among the men here shall be allowed to return home, while another from his community takes his place.

"These communities should be set up within a half day's ride of the next so that word may be spread quickly should there be an attack. Those whose kin live nearer Inverness will form no less than a half-dozen smaller armies whose territory of patrol will also be within a half day of the other, and constantly rotating their area of patrol so that their movements are never the same twice and known only by me. In this way, we will still maintain our strength, your families will be provided for, and we may yet route the snake from its den."

Brianna listened with wonder and pride, for he understood the need of her kinsmen and those of the other chieftains to protect and provide for their families at the same time lessening the protection at Inverness only marginally. And that might be compensated in the bold strategy of splitting his patrols. Yet, she too understood that splitting their strength by even the smallest number left them vulnerable. As Mardigan also would realize it if he learned of it.

The chieftains agreed and a plan was devised by which small numbers of men would leave Inverness, too few to draw attention and under the cover of darkness so they would not be seen. They vowed to return by the same means. Deception became their ally.

The general mood of the men lifted, for they now were assured their families would be protected and provided for during the coming winter. Only Brianna saw him before the fire in the laird's chamber each evening, brooding, the twin medallions clasped in his hand and glinting in the light of the evening fire.

And always there was the unspoken question. What would he do if he could not find the man who had lost the medallion? And if the Scots abandoned the alliance, would he then leave Scotland if he could not hold it with the strength of the army William had sent to the north country?

He grew restless and short of temper. When he returned from the patrols he walked the battlements at all hours of the day or night, his intense blue gaze searching the surrounding countryside for some sign of Mardigan and his men.

One night he returned late, sitting brooding before the fire long after everyone had gone to bed. She had been kept late in the main hall taking care of the myriad details that now fell to her as the daughter of the old laird and wife to the new laird of Inverness.

She had come to rely on Thomas and Enya, for he knew well the daily details that must be taken care of to house and feed the expanded population of the fortress, while Enya had proven herself very capable in overseeing the countless domestic aspects of running such a large household.

As she neared the chamber she saw the door open and Gillie appeared briefly in the light that slivered the opening. Her face was flushed, the laces at the bodice of her gown loose and gaping open as if she had just been with a lover. The sight of her drew Brianna up short.

There had been rumors of course. Even Thomas had warned her that Gillie seemed over attentive to the new laird of Inverness. But Brianna could not believe that he might leave their bed to seek out the whore, although such was not uncommon. Still, Gillie had been most smug of late, completely undaunted by the fact that it was now obvious to all that Tarek al Sharif and the daughter of the old laird now shared a marriage in all ways. Brianna had overheard her speaking with one of the lowland Scots whose family were distant kinsmen of Malcolm's.

" 'Tis said the barbarian beds the old laird's daughter," his voice reached Brianna from the shadows.

"It means nothing," a woman's voice had replied, and Brianna immediately recognized it as Gillie's. "He will tire of her and then look elsewhere for his pleasure. 'Tis said that she has spurned all marriage proposals before, and 'tis equally well known she made this marriage only when forced to it. She has no desire for marriage, there are even those who say she is incapable of it. He will tire soon enough and I will be there."

Now, as she approached the laird's chamber, Gillie saw her. Her expression was surprised, then she flushed with apparent embarrassment as if she'd been caught at something.

"Good eventide, Brianna. Milord asked me to bring his supper." Then she made a very obvious gesture of drawing the two halves of her bodice back together with one hand, as she quickly stepped past Brianna.

When she had gone, Brianna pushed open the door of the chamber and entered hesitantly. So many feelings were new to her. She was still trying to sort them out and deal with them since their relationship had changed. Now, here was yet one more emotion that she vaguely recognized as jealousy.

The chamber was dark except for the fire at the brazier and a large tallow candle set into an iron bowl at the table. A platter had been set out with cold roasted guinea fowl, cheese, fruit, and bread.

He sat silently before the brazier, exhaustion molding his lean body into the chair, long legs spread before him. His boots had been removed, but he still wore his mud-splattered breeches and hand-stitched tunic over an equally mud-splattered woolen shirt.

There had been no private moment for them to exchange even a single word since he and his men returned. As the sun had set and still there was no sign of them, she had begun to walk the battlements, relaxing only when the call finally went out that riders had been seen. Then she immediately saw to the myriad details of feeding so many tired, hungry men.

He had left the hall early with Stephen of Valois to speak of matters in the privacy of their chamber, for he had sent several dispatches to London, and the first had arrived two days earlier just after their departure on this latest patrol.

"You have not eaten," she said, the trencher on the table

in the laird's chamber untouched, the food long since cold. "I will have warm food brought."

"Do not."

"Then perhaps a tankard of wine," she suggested, thinking of the special cask Thomas had procured from a traveling priest who had sought shelter at Inverness on his way north. For it seemed this much at least, Gillie had not provided. As jealousy reared its ugly head and she wondered what else Gillie might have provided he held up a hand, stopping her as she reached for the pitcher.

"I do not care for wine."

She tried to sense his thoughts but found she could not beyond the emotions that were easy enough to guess from his manner and expression. Only in bed had things remained unchanged between them.

There they found a joy of passion in one another that for a time pushed back the restlessness and uncertainty. But of late, even that changed between them. She sensed a remoteness in him even when they came together, that frightened her. She glanced to the medallions dangling from his fingers.

"It weights heavily on you that Mardigan has not been found," she said softly.

"He will be found," he said, as if by willing it alone, it would happen.

"And if he cannot be found? What then will you do?"

His head came up and he looked at her as she stood before the brazier, framed by golden light. His expression was unreadable in the flickering light, as were his thoughts. Yet he seemed to know hers. He reached for her hand, drawing her down onto the pile of warm furs that covered the stone floor at his feet. With his other hand, he swept back the heavy satin of her hair that fell loose past her shoulders, his fingers lightly caressing her cheek.

"I have made promises," he said, leaning forward in the chair so that his face was very near hers. "I hold them sacred."

Promises to her people. But what of the marriage vows they had spoken? Did he now tire of them? Doubt washed through her in spite of his assurances.

"We are not your people," she pointed out. "This is not your land. I know how you hate Scotland, and wish to return to Antioch."

His hand slipped through her hair to curve the back of her neck, drawing her closer. "It is my land now by the vows I have made. If there was no land, I would still remain."

"Because of the medallion."

"Yes," he answered honestly, for he would not lie to her. "And far more." Her gaze lifted to his. He saw there the pain his honesty had caused and sought to ease it. "You brought me to the north country," he told her.

"But the medallion you found . . ."

"I did not know of its existence. But I knew of a beautiful golden creature who saved my life." He brushed his mouth against hers. Then his lips curved into a smile. "And I have found a remedy for the cold."

Longing for more than that brief kiss, she sighed, "Aye, Stephen told me of it." Her soft green gaze glinted with amusement as his kisses banished her doubt.

"Fur-lined breeches? A Scots warrior would never wear such a thing."

"Aye he would!" he remarked, imitating the thick Scot accent. His own eyes glinted with devilment. "Malcolm wears his regularly so I'm told."

"Malcolm?" she replied, delicate golden brows drawing together with her frown. "You are mistaken. He would never wear fur-lined breeches."

"Aye, he does," he insisted. "Most particularly at night, but during the day as well." His arm went around her waist, as he gently pulled her against him in the chair, then nuzzled the softness at the curve of her neck. His voice was husky and muffled as he kissed her there.

"He calls them by name," he added.

"By name?" she exclaimed, part confusion and part growing desire as his mouth lowered to the neck of her gown and she felt a gentle tugging at the laces of her bodice.

"Aye," he remarked still pretending a thick highland accent, as the laces gave way beneath his insistent fingers. She felt cool air on her skin as he pushed aside the fabric of her bodice.

"By the name of Gillie."

"Gillie?"

"She warms him well," he murmured, his lips wetting her through the fabric of her gown.

"But I thought . . ."

His head raised, blue eyes intense as they stared back at her.

"What did you think?"

She struggled to close the front of her bodice, but her hands were slow and clumsy. These feelings were also new to her.

"I saw her outside the chamber tonight, and other times . . . There are rumors . . ."

His eyes glinted with amusement. "You thought that I bedded the woman."

"She has made no secret of her intentions."

"No, she has not."

"Then why did you not . . ." Her voice faltered and her gaze slid away from his. A new frown knit her brows together. His fingers were warm at her skin as he angled her gaze back to his with fingers beneath her chin.

"Because she is not what I want."

"But she offers herself so freely . . ."

"Aye and even tonight would have eagerly warmed my bed," he answered.

"She is pretty," Brianna continued, goaded by more uncertain feelings she did not understand, as his fingers warmly encircled her breast.

"Yes."

With growing frustration that he answered so readily, she commented, "I have heard men speak of her. They say she has very large breasts . . ."

"Yes."

"They say . . ." But anything more that she might have said was smothered by a startled sound of pleasure as his mouth closed over her breast.

"What else do *they* say?" He lightly blew across the peak, the dark rosy nipple puckering and growing taut beneath his lips.

"They say she offers herself to any man . . ."

"Yes."

His mouth was warm and teasing, gently loving until she was wet with his kisses, and wet between her thighs with a response that he seemed to summon from her body so easily. She arched against the hungry heat of his mouth, offering up the taut peak of her other breast as he created a growing hunger within her. Her thoughts scattered, including thoughts of Gillie.

"Milord, you must not. What if Enya or Nel were to see us?" she asked breathlessly.

"Enya would be envious," he whispered with a harsh groan as he suckled her into the wet heat of his mouth.

"But Nel . . ." she protested, her breathing was jerky and

spasmed as she untied the sash that belted his tunic, her eager hands seeking his warm, hard-muscled, bronze flesh as fleeting images of Nel.

"Let the girl learn the true pleasure that can be found between a man and woman." He shifted her onto his lap as he pulled her closer. Through the layers of her gown and chemise, she felt the hard ridge of erect flesh that strained the front of his breeches, her own body responding with an intensity that startled her and made a lie of the protest she made.

"Milord, 'tis not decent," she whispered on a ragged breath, even as her eager fingers sought the pulsing heat of his naked flesh beneath the layers of his own clothing with a growing urgency.

"No," he growled fiercely, drawing up the hem of her gown with impatient hands. "It is not."

The warmth of his hands caressed the bare skin of her bottom, rocking her toward him as they skimmed lower, fingers stroking through tender folds of damp flesh to quickly penetrate her.

She cried out, part startled pleasure at the sensation of his seeking fingers inside her and the aching need to feel that much deeper connection of his body fully joined with hers.

She moved restlessly against him, whispering "Please," as her tongue penetrated his lips and mated with his with a growing urgency at the intensity of desire that swept through her.

"Not yet," he answered, deliberately denying her what she sought, then smiling at her low growl of frustration. She was all urgency and heat in his hands, her nipple taut as he took it between his teeth and gently nibbled, her body pouring sweet rain over his fingers. He felt the tautness that built within her body as she sought a deeper pleasure with each movement of her hips. Then, when he sensed she was at the brink of fulfillment, he withdrew to steady her with both hands at her hips.

Her shimmering gaze met his, green eyes filled with myriad emotions not the least of which was a stunned look that quickly turned fierce.

"Nay, milord," she promised, as her slender fingers closed round him. He groaned at the contact that threatened to spill him into her hand. In the golden glow of light from the fire at the brazier he watched as her pale fingers guided his dark, gleaming flesh to her, the soft, downy gold curls that surrounded the distended and swollen tip, and finally the intensely erotic sight of his flesh disappearing inside her.

She was small and tight and took him slowly, her wet heat gliding down over him like a fist that stroked and caressed him. Fatigue, frustration, and disappointment disappeared with the sweet, stroking heat of her body.

He slowed and steadied her, controlling each movement, slowly withdrawing as she braced her slender hands at his shoulders, then pushing inside her once more, equally slow so that every movement was prolonged, every sense heightened by anticipation.

"Tarek . . ."

"What is your desire?" he replied, fingers closing over her hips, restraining her when she would have quickened the pace of their lovemaking to assuage the ache of need that coiled ever tighter inside her.

"Please . . ."

"What do you wish, Brianna?" His tongue flicked over the peak of her breast as he rolled his hips against hers and then slowly began to withdraw once more.

"No!" she cried out softly, as her hips clenched over his. "I cannot bear the emptiness." Then she gasped as he thrust powerfully inside her.

291

"Aye," she whispered fiercely against his lips as her mouth found his.

Afterward, their bodies glistened. "Are you warm now, milord?"

He rose from the chair, taking her with him, his flesh still snugged within her body as he carried her to the bed. He laid her on the mound of thick furs, tenderly brushing golden strands of hair back from her flushed cheeks, watching the bright fires of passion that burned in her green eyes, hearing the way her breath caught, a sound of surprise that became a sound of pleasure as he grew strong within her once more, feeling himself reborn within the warm sheath of her body.

His own voice broke with the wonder of the feelings she stirred within him as he framed her face with his hands and saw his own image reflected in the brilliant green of her eyes as if he was now a part of her.

"You warm me as no other."

The following morning, Brianna awakened to find him gone. The inhabitants of Inverness still slept as she left the main hall for the stables, certain she would find him there. When some matter bothered him, he either took to the yard with Stephen, or groomed the mare.

Sir Robert of Mortain and several score men had ridden out following rumors of Mardigan a fortnight earlier. There was still no word from them.

The Arabian was in high spirits as she entered the stables, her silver gray head tossing in greeting as she caught Brianna's scent.

"She needs to be ridden," Tarek said as he saw her standing barefoot in the straw. "She becomes restless and unmanageable when she is not exercised."

Brianna stroked the finely boned, sleek head. "I can understand her impatience, for I have felt it, too." Their gazes met across the mare's back.

"The highlands are especially beautiful at dawn," she told him. "You should take her out," she suggested, for she sensed the restlessness in him as well and wondered if he could ever call one place home. "Surely there is no danger, so near to Inverness."

"Are you suggesting that I escape the responsibilities of command?"

"Aye, 'tis most necessary from time to time."

"And where do you escape when you leave Inverness?"

She looked at him, wondering the reason he should ask such a question. Was he thinking of the morning he had found her on the battlements? They had not spoken of it since.

"The lowland hills at the western border of Cullum's landhold. Your landhold now," she pointed out. "There is a lake there. I am always drawn to it." He looked at her oddly.

"I had not thought of it as my home."

"You bargained for it, milord."

"Yes, but home is a place you hold in your heart," his gaze fastened on hers. "I bargained for you."

"At the instruction of your king."

"It was I who insisted upon Inverness, not King William." As the mare side-stepped nervously, he looked at Brianna. "I think it would be wise to ride her before she kicks down the stables. But only if you will ride with me."

"I am not accustomed to riding astride."

"We will ride together."

The sun was just beginning to appear at the horizon as they left Inverness astride the mare. Though there had been no sight of raiders for weeks, still he carried the curved Persian blade, and the shorter blade at his belt.

Brianna sat in the saddle before him, his hand steadying her, his chest solid and warm at her back. It was good to escape the worries and fears, and her own uncertainties of the future that lay before them. By midmorning they reached the lake called Lochonnen in the land to the west of Inverness.

The lake was a dark silver ribbon, still and silent, its gleaming surface like a mirror beneath a cloud filled sky. Brianna slipped to the ground, feeling the ache of muscles in unusual places from the long ride she was not unaccustomed to.

The rowan tree had begun to leaf out, tender buds forming along the branches. She plucked three, reciting the ancient words that she had known since childhood.

"One leaf, two leaves, three . . ."

Tarek tethered the mare and came to stand beside her, staring out over the strange still waters. It was quiet and peaceful, unusually so as before a storm. Yet the clouds overhead moved slowly, like wandering sheep with no particular course. For the first time in weeks, no storm brooded at the horizon.

"I have come here since I was a child. Thomas first brought me here," she explained, as always both drawn to and made uneasy by the lake's ability to somehow reach out to her.

"You seem to have a special connection with Thomas. Has he always been so protective of you?"

"Aye." She did not elaborate on the special connection of thought they shared for she doubted he would understand. She did not understand the gift herself. It was like so many other unanswered questions and disconcerting dreams.

"It was Thomas who brought me to the north country as a

baby," she went on to explain. "He needed a family to care for me. It was my good fortune Cullum and Mirren were childless."

"Then he is not kinsman to you?"

"No, he is more like my guardian."

"And what of your real parents?" he asked, knowing the pain of having lived without both of his.

She shook her head as her gaze was once more drawn to the expanse of shimmering silver water with its mysterious deep shadows, like the shadows within her memory.

"There are times when I think I remember them. I have dreamed of a place, and a woman. I know she is my mother, but the dream ends before I can see her clearly. It is always the same, as if I am not supposed to remember."

"I have only vague memories of my own mother," Tarek said, standing very close beside her. "Her hair was like black satin and her eyes were brown. She was very beautiful, but so very sad. Even her smiles were sad."

He stared out across the lake. But she sensed he did not really see it. She sensed that he saw instead those brief moments spent with his mother — like illusive dreams that could only be glimpsed but never held.

She took his hand and pressed it against her cheek, attempting to take away some of the physical pain in the connection of their thoughts and emotions.

How could he smile and laugh with so much pain inside? she wondered. Yet, she instinctively understood that the laughter and wry humor that was so much a part of him was perhaps what enabled him to survive the pain, just as surely as it was a mask which at other times hid the pain.

Her touch was so tender and gentle, her lovely green eyes misty with tears as she brushed her lips across the back of his hand. He opened his hand and cupped her cheek.

"You are my dreams and my hope," he whispered. "Now, *you* are my family."

She said nothing as she went into his arms. She had discovered that she was capable of that very human emotion, love. But at what cost?

What would happen when he learned her secret? What future could they possibly have? She squeezed her eyes tightly shut, trying to hold back the growing ache of uncertainty. What of the pain she would bring him when he learned of it?

She turned in his arms and leaned back against the solid strength of his chest. She felt sheltered and protected as she never had in her life, almost as if his strength alone could hold back the uncertain future. It gave her hope.

"Do you see it?" she asked as she again looked out across the water. He followed her gaze, but saw nothing.

"According to legend, there is an island in the middle of the lake," she went on to explain. "It is said that it can only be seen in the moments between night and dawn, and then again just as the sun sets. It is called Grail Island. It also said that the Grail is there in the mist, waiting for the one who can claim it. But it is guarded by a great dragon that lives in the depths of the lake."

"Some fishermen say they have seen the creature."

"Another highland myth?" he asked, for he had heard many from Ian and the highlanders at Inverness. Some too incredible to believe, although many others bore amazing similarity to legends among his own people.

She shrugged, her gaze still fastened on the water. "There have been times when I almost thought I could see it. But when I looked again it was gone. It would be a wondrous thing to find it for 'tis said that he who possesses the Grail, rules the kingdom. 'Tis said Mardigan seeks the Grail."

"The cup of truth," Tarek said. "The truth of the ages."

"You know of it?" she asked with surprise.

"The Grail is known throughout all of Christendom. Wars have been fought for it. Kingdoms have fallen in the quest for it. It is said among my people that the Grail is far more ancient than Christendom. It is said to possess the wisdom of creation. It disappeared over a thousand years ago from the middle empire. Or so the legend is told."

"Then you do not believe the legend."

"I have learned to believe in possibility," he said, coming to stand before her. He took her in his arms and drew her very close. "All things are possible." As he brushed his lips across hers rain began to fall.

"By the Prophet!" he swore, pulling her with him up the hill to the pungent pine tree where he had tethered the mare. Rain began to fall heavily as they sought shelter under the fragrant boughs. It pelted the surface of the water in waves until a fine mist rose and the water churned in rippling patterns that washed against the shore of the lake. As if some restless creature stirred in its depths.

"But perhaps your highland rain has its advantages," he said, a far different expression on his face as he pulled her against him in the shelter of the tree. His mouth closed over hers as they sat at the base of the trunk. He drank the rain from her lips, then sipped it from her chin, cheeks, and eyelashes.

The chill from the rain disappeared and was replaced by a fever of need as he pulled her to him. His hands skimmed up her thighs as she loosened his breeches, then down over the curve of her bottom as she nestled against him with a teasing gleam in her green eyes.

"Are you cold, milord? Yer not wearing fur-lined breeches," she teased in a husky voice as she nipped at his lower lip.

He lifted her and settled her over him, and she went breathless at the searing fire of his flesh pushing high inside her. His expression was both dangerous and fierce, and filled with passion.

"I am now," he said lustily, and Brianna broke out into waves of laughter that only heightened the pleasure, until she lay smiling against him waiting for the storm to end.

It was four days past the date Robert of Mortain and his men were supposed to return to Inverness. Tension was drawn to the breaking point.

Both Norman and Scot alike grew somber and silent, tempers flaring at the least provocation, for all knew that a patrol overdue might be a patrol that had been attacked. Then, finally, the signal call went out from the battlements of riders approaching. And they bore the standard of Robert of Mortain!

A knight of many campaigns with William of Normandy across the middle empires, he was an old and trusted friend as well as a seasoned warrior. With him rode a dozen of his men and an equal number of Scots.

The gates of Inverness were opened and they rode through. Brianna watched them from the battlements beneath a midday sun. At the first signal call, Tarek had left the battlements to greet his friend.

The riders were all dusty and dirty, the tunics worn over chain mail stained with grime. Greetings were exchanged though she could not hear from that distance. Their expressions were taut and filled with weariness, yet all had returned. If there had been an encounter, all had survived to tell of it. Tarek's expression was by turns relieved and then grave as he spoke with Mortain.

Brianna tried to sense their thoughts to discern what news

Mortain brought. She sensed Tarek's, fleetingly, as a steeliness of purpose replaced his concern of moments before. From him, she learned that Mardigan's stronghold had been found.

She abruptly turned from the battlement wall, her thoughts already occupied with the additional instructions for Enya with so many additional mouths to feed at the midday meal for all would want to hear of the news. That meant abundant portions of ale to quench thirsts through the council meeting that followed.

"Where is the stronghold?" Tarek asked, leaning forward in his chair as he met that night with his knights and the chieftains.

"Four days' ride to the north," Mortain replied. "It took us a while to find it and we would not have found it at all if not for an old shepherd who stumbled across it during a storm. He took shelter there with his flock, leaving before first light. He told us of it."

Tarek frowned. "The stronghold was not guarded?"

"Apparently all had joined in the latest raid. The old man found bounty taken from raids in the depths of the cave — food, weapons, anything of value that might be used or traded. There was enough to support an army of raiders for several months."

None of the others who had been with him spoke, in spite of their usual outspokenness before at the council table, especially the Scots. Malcolm too asked several questions, each in turn answered by Sir John while the others ate or replenished their tankards. Brianna supposed they were too weary after such a long ride, for none had bothered to take the time to wash but had hastened to the table and the council meeting with the chieftains. Tarek, too, was thoughtful.

While she sensed a great bone-aching weariness in the

others, she sensed a restlessness in Sir Robert.

"We must strike quickly," he urged Tarek for the third time. "Before they realize we know the location. We must take the entire army there at once."

But even Malcolm, always eager for a battle, cautioned, "It would be unwise to take all of the men. What if Mardigan is not there?"

"He will be there," Mortain assured them. "The old man was most specific about it. He watched their movements for several days. He said they return every three days."

"The shepherd risked much. It is fortunate he was not discovered," Tarek remarked.

"He knows the countryside well. He stayed well hidden."

"What is the man's name?" Malcolm asked. "He will be rewarded for this."

"He called himself Davidson," Mortain answered.

"Are ye certain?" Malcolm asked with a faint frown. Across the table his gaze met Brianna's.

"Most certain."

"And you say he's been shepherd in the north mountains for years?" Malcolm asked.

Mortain nodded. "His entire life. He knew every peak and hiding place." Mortain chuckled. "Said he'd climbed just about all of them going after strays."

"Aye, the beasties will do that to ye," Ian commiserated.

Sir Robert continued to urge them to leave at once as Enya and two serving girls refilled tankards about the table.

"Strike while the iron is hot," he persuaded. "They will not be expecting it. Once and for all Mardigan will be stopped."

"We will leave at first light," Tarek decided.

"But each hour we delay is another hour that Mardigan may escape," Mortain argued, coming out of his chair with a vehemence that had all looking at him with speculation, for Mortain was always the voice of caution who argued against haste.

Tarek also frowned at the unexpected outburst. "You and your men are tired. Your horses must be rested as well if they are to carry you back to the north country."

"Someone must remain to guard the fortress," Mortain suggested. "My men and I could remain while you ride to take Mardigan. Your back would be well protected."

"The sacrifice is not necessary," Tarek told him. "I know you would wish to ride at my side as always, now that victory is near. We will ride together in the morning," he said.

"But surely you do not wish to delay," Mortain pressed.

Tarek was surprisingly patient. "You are tired, my friend. Mardigan will still be there and we will take him. But as for your men, you are right. We will find a fresh horse which you may ride on the return north. The others will remain behind for we could not spare fresh horses for all of them."

He signaled for Enya to have more ale brought for the Scots, and wine for his knights, instructing her that all the rest was then to be locked away with the key given to him. He wanted his men sober in the morning.

"A word of caution," Malcolm said as he stopped on his way to attend to his own men. At Tarek's look of surprise, he added, "I owe you for my life."

"Go on."

"I know most men in these lands. Any shepherd would be well known for they are the meat and wool by which our people survive."

"What are you saying?"

"I know of no shepherd by the name of Davidson. It is not a name of anyone in Cullum's landhold."

"Are you saying that Mortain has lied?"

"I say only what I have already told you. You may take it as you choose."

She was not able to hear what they said, but as Malcolm turned away from the table and left, Brianna noticed something she had payed no attention to before. Tankards were refilled all around. Only by chance did Brianna see that Robert of Mortain's tankard was still full, along with those of all his men. Their meals were also untouched.

It was not so surprising. Perhaps they were just tired, for they had obviously ridden hard to reach Inverness, and many had not shown favor with highland food. But the Scots surprising lack of interest in their tankards and platters made her frown.

After the midday meal, Mortain's men returned to the armory while the Scots left the main hall. There was no time to speak with Tarek the remainder of the afternoon, for preparations must be made for the long journey north.

The Norman and Scots were to ride light and fast, carrying only two weapons each. Malcolm was determined to accompany them even though his wounds were not yet fully healed. He would not listen to any objections.

While specific battle preparations were made, Brianna saw to the myriad other details, such as the means to feed such a large army on the march for there would be no campfires to cook their meals.

Long after the evening fire had burned low in the main hall and the last remaining wounded had bedded down on their pallets, she finally saw to the last details and sought the chamber she shared with Tarek.

"Brianna."

She turned at the sound of Malcolm's voice. He had left the main hall where other wounded still recovered days ago and she had seen little of him since the strength had returned

302

to his arm. That evening at the council table was the first she had seen him in days.

There had been an awkwardness then as her gaze met his briefly across the table for it was known to all at Inverness that she now shared the laird's chamber with Tarek al Sharif.

"There has been no chance for us to speak in private," he began hesitantly. "You are well?"

She knew the question that lay beneath the more casual one. "Yes, I am very well."

He nodded, and paused as if struggling with his next words.

"What is it, Malcolm? Surely we can still speak with ease with each other."

"It is just that . . ." He shoved his hand back through his hair in frustration, then blurted it out, " 'Tis said that you share his bed."

She did not wish to answer, but somehow she knew she must. "He *is* my husband."

"Do you love him, lass?"

"I . . ." she hesitated, for in truth she did not know what she felt. It was still all too new between them. Desire? Yes. Lust? Yes, that too for there were times — the most unexpected times — when she felt that ache of longing begin deep inside her, an ache only he could ease. But was it love?

"I do not know," she answered honestly.

"And when Mardigan is finally driven from the highlands?" Malcolm asked, insistently. "What then, Brianna?"

The same question haunted her every waking moment, especially now that the moment seemed to be at hand with Mortain's return and word that Mardigan's stronghold had been found.

Again, she answered, "I do not know."

She pulled her hand from his, even as she sensed his tenderness of friendship. He did not try to stop her. As she turned and fled up the stairs she thought she saw the movement of a woman's skirt at the edge of the shadows and wondered if Gillie waited for him.

But the solitude of her chamber offered no escape from that haunting question. His presence was everywhere — the thick fleece mantle neatly folded across his trunk, the unusual quilted tunic made of dark blue satin that seemed to darken the color of his eyes, and the faintly spicy masculine scent of him that she had smelled on her own skin after they made love and which now seemed to linger in the air within her chamber. As if he was there even now.

Did she love him? In truth she did not know if what she felt was love. Was it love when she found herself at the end of the day turning and waiting expectantly at the sound of the hall doors opening as warriors returned from the practice yard or their patrols?

Was it love that burned across her skin at the simplest contact of his hand on hers?

Was it love that tightened deep inside her at just the thought of the hours shared here?

He seemed to feel it as well, for since their first time together he had sought her out midmornings, middays when the sun was full overhead, and at unexpected times in the evening when she was certain he was still with his men.

There was no need for words between them. All that was needed was a touch — his hand at her cheek, in her hair, at her arm — to rouse a hunger that must be fed.

It had been days since they'd last made love. She'd gotten her monthly flux. Then, he'd been called away on matters of grave importance, returning late the night before.

As they lay together in the bed of soft furs, she could not disguise a deep and profound disappointment that she had not yet conceived a child.

She knew of women who conceived a child their first time with a man. Doubts nagged at her. What if she never conceived? How long would the secret she kept so fiercely guarded remain a secret?

"All in good time, Brianna," he soothed the fears she had spoken aloud, as he had held her close.

"Do you perhaps already have children?" she asked. "And not wish for another?"

He had turned her in his arms, drawing her close against him. "I have no children, for I would not put the label of bastard on any child."

"But surely you have loved other women," she blurted out, for he knew so many things about a woman's body she knew it could not be otherwise.

Always honest, he said without hesitation, "I have found physical pleasure with a great many women. But I have always prevented a woman conceiving a child."

She had heard of such things, although Mirren would never discuss it with her.

"How is that possible?"

Her equally blunt question brought an equally blunt explanation.

"The intestine of a sheep?" she exclaimed incredulously when he explained.

He had laughed at her wide-eyed expression. "It is usually very effective."

"But you do not wear such a thing when we make love."

"No," he said tenderly, pulling her much closer and holding her tight against him. "I do not." Then he kissed her forehead.

"I will give you children, Brianna. We have time. Let us learn of one another first." He had not made love to her. She could feel the exhaustion dragging at him physically and in his voice. Instead he had held her close, banishing her fears with his tenderness.

But just that morning he had sought her out before Mortain's arrival. He had found her in the pantry going over the inventory of food with Enya.

As she called out the count of sacks of grain she was met with silence, instead of Enya's usual reply. When she turned around she found him standing in the doorway, watching her.

He had brushed a smudge of dirt from the bodice of her gown, his fingers grazing her breast. She immediately felt her nipple pucker and harden beneath the soft wool as longing poured through her.

They had come together with a fierce passion that had been stunning and frightening in its intensity. She had been as eager for him as he was for her. There was no patience in either of them.

She had loosened the front of his breeches, freeing his magnificent flesh as it escaped through soft doeskin to spring full and heavy into her hands. With a soft cry she had gone down on her knees before him and loved him the way he had loved her that time before.

He was full and hot as she stroked him with her tongue. She could feel every ridge and pulsing vein, taking him deep in her throat as his hands went back through her hair. In the silence of the pantry, she had made soft, eager sounds, suckling him as he had once suckled her.

"Brianna!" her name was part curse, part desperate longing as he thrust deeper against the back of her throat. And then the powerful spasms of his flesh, and the sweet, hot fire as he exploded between her lips.

Soft, foreign-sounding words whispered in a litany of ancient love sounds as he pulled her to her feet and kissed her, groaning as he tasted himself in the softness of her mouth.

Aching inside, her body flushed and fevered, she had moved against him restlessly, longing to get closer, needing to feel his warm body against hers. But he prolonged her agony as he pinned her against the wall and continued kissing her. Finally, she could bear it no longer.

"Love me," she cried out softly, the sound of his name filled with all her longing and need. "Give me a child."

He took her there against the wall, pushing the hem of her gown up about her waist, lifting her over his engorged flesh and then thrusting inside her.

Afterward, she lay flushed and spent in his arms, her slender body cradled against his, her legs still wrapped about his waist.

"Will it ever cease, milord?" she asked. "This physical longing for one another."

He lifted her chin and tenderly brushed his lips across her swollen ones. "For some it only grows stronger."

"How is it possible to grow stronger and survive it?"

"If we cannot survive it," he answered, "I can think of no other way I would want to die."

Was this soul-throbbing passion the same as love? Surely it was a part of it. But was it more, as it had seemed between Cullum and Mirren? A love so deep that one would die for the other?

She slept restlessly that night. Tarek was already gone from their bed when she awakened before first light. He was in the yard, giving instructions to his men by the light of dozens of torches.

Everything had been made ready the night before. Provisions for the long ride had been packed onto the horses. Weapons had been secured. All was in readiness. His men waited.

"You are leaving so soon?" she said, holding the ends of the fur mantle about her shoulders as she stood barefoot beside him.

"The men and horses are rested," he indicated Mortain who rode to one side of him, Stephen of Valois to the other, and several more who had returned from the north highlands where Mardigan's stronghold had been discovered. The others had remained behind with a small number of his men to guard the fortress.

"How long?" she asked, hating herself as she did so, for it was a sign of weakness.

"As long as it takes."

"Where is Duncan?" she looked among them for the boy. "He wanted to see the men off."

"He is angry with me because I would not allow him to go with us."

"I understand his anger," she said with a sudden huskiness she made no attempt to hide.

He bent down from atop the Arabian mare, slipping a hand beneath the loose fall of her hair. It was still warm from their bed and smelled of her sweetness.

"He was given orders to protect the lady of Inverness in my absence." He kissed her with a rough tenderness.

"And who will protect you?"

"Stephen of Valois, Malcolm, and the strength of Allah."

"Take this," she insisted, removing the warm fleece mantle from about her shoulders. "The ground is cold at night."

He stopped her, drawing it tight about her once more. "I will be warm enough."

"Milord," she said, forcing a smile to her lips, for it was much easier to bear than the tears which threatened. "Do you wear fur-lined breeches?"

308

Beside him, Stephen of Valois choked with sudden laughter. Tarek leaned forward once more in the saddle leaning close to whisper.

"My memories of you will warm me, Brianna. It is all I need."

"I need more than memories, milord," she said, suddenly breathless as she then kissed him. "Return quickly to Inverness."

Then stepping back, she laid a hand at Malcolm's arm. "Safe journey, dear friend."

"I would much rather have the parting words you gave that barbarian," he said, loud enough for Tarek to hear. "But I suppose *safe journey* will have to do."

"It will," Tarek told him.

Then they were gone, dust in the yard churning beneath the hooves of their horses as over two hundred men joined those already encamped beyond the gates. Brianna hitched up the hem of her gown and ran to the battlement steps.

At the battlements above, she leaned far over the wall, watching as they rode past the village, toward the river and the forest beyond, then the far north. And continued watching until the sun was climbing the horizon, casting early morning shadows across the stones, and they were only a dark ribbon of movement in the distance.

One of the men who had returned with Robert of Mortain and the Scots had joined the battlement guards. He too watched as they gradually disappeared.

"Come," she told him. "Enya will have the morning meal ready and you are not yet recovered from so long a ride." For only those who were fully recovered now made the return north. He made no reply. Nor did he make to leave the battlements for the soldier's table in the main hall. Instead he stood stoically, as though keeping watch.

Brianna thought it odd when there were by far enough guards watching the walls. As she turned to leave she squinted against the morning sun.

The shadows of the other guards made them seem eight feet tall. The silent young highlander did not seem to have a shadow, and as he turned toward her, her breath caught. For his eyes were flat, dark, and dead.

Seventeen

"You look as if you've seen a ghost," Enya remarked as Brianna returned to the main hall.

She rubbed her hands together before the fire at the hearth, trying to warm herself against the sudden chill that seemed to have settled in her blood.

She extended her hands before the fire. No shadow fell in their wake and she clasped her hands together, hiding them in the folds of the fur mantle as she struggled to understand.

"In truth, I do not know what I have just seen."

"Mistress?"

" 'Tis nothing," Brianna replied. Yet she was unable to rid herself of the certainty that the eyes she had looked into were not alive, nor were they mortal eyes. And the Scot had no shadow — a disturbing fact she had discovered about herself long ago but had learned to accept. What did it mean that these men also had no shadows?

"Where is Thomas?"

"Gone to the village before the gates are locked while the others are away."

"I would like to see him when he returns," Brianna told her, turning up the stairs. Then she stopped, and asked, "How many of those who returned yesterday remained behind?"

Aware of everything that went on at Inverness, Enya replied with a certainty, "A full score and two."

"Where are they now?"

"Four within the main hall, but most are with the guards

at the battlements. Poor men. They should rest."

"Aye." Brianna nodded with a frown as she sought her chamber. It was almost two hours later when Thomas sought her there.

"Is it possible to withstand a siege if we are attacked?" she asked as she restlessly paced the chamber. His thoughts conveyed his bewilderment at her concern.

"The fortress is well fortified, stronger than before with new stone walls. It will protect those within."

"And if those within are the ones we must fear?" she asked.

"What is it, lass? What has happened?"

"I have seen something that disturbs me — something I cannot explain." She told him then of her encounter with the Scot. In his silent way, he reassured her.

"I will look for the man and learn what I can about him."

The days passed unbearably slowly. By the accounts given by Robert of Mortain upon his return, she charted their daily progress, her uneasiness growing as she knew they drew closer to the location of Mardigan's stronghold.

Inverness had once more become an armed encampment. Those of the villagers who chose to were once again welcomed within the fortress walls. In the first days after Tarek and his men left, several Scots returned from their villages and homes, fulfilling their promise.

Brianna saw no more of the Scot she had spoken to. He and the others stayed outside the main hall, always seeming to disappear when anyone inquired about them, yet stalwart at their duties, taking extra shifts at the battlement walls.

She became increasingly uneasy and restless with each passing day, and resumed her nightly walks upon the battlements. Something was happening. She could feel it like the oppressiveness before a storm. She retreated to the chamber

312

she had shared with Tarek only when exhaustion forced her. There she found a few hours solace in his bed, surrounding herself with his lingering essence while she slept without dreams.

With each morning it became increasingly more and more difficult to awaken as if the night clung to her, like a heavy shroud she could not throw off, trying to smother her. During the day she worked alongside Enya and Anne, seeing to the needs of the inhabitants of the fortress.

"Where is he? He must be here," Brianna insisted one morning when she had tried to find young Duncan. For she wished to begin his studies. Perhaps that might occupy more of her time.

"He is gone," Ian told her. "I suspect he went with Malcolm and the others."

"Milord would never have allowed it. It is too dangerous."

"I do not think he knew of it. The lad was most cunning, said he would disguise himself if he was not allowed to ride out with them. I didna think the lad would do it. But after all, girl, in less than a year he will be as old as me when I drew first blood."

"He is only a boy!" Brianna insisted, coming out of the laird's chair at the council table.

All morning she had been plagued with countless problems, including Gillie who seemed always at her elbow with a comment that only added to Brianna's fears and uneasiness.

"I hope they return safely. It would be a tragedy if something happened to the new laird. You are too young to be a widow, and so recently you and milord seem to have found an accord. It would be dreadful to be alone and perhaps with child. Or perhaps there is not yet a child," she added slyly. "Though milord is a fine, lusty man. His seed will no doubt be well planted when it finds fertile soil."

At that moment Brianna was torn between the desire to tear out every strand of her cousin's hair, and a fearful smothering doubt that closed around her heart. It took every ounce of self-control not to strike Gillie.

"He will be safe," she replied. "He is an experienced warrior and his men will protect him."

"Ah, but who knows who may be trusted and who may not," Gillie replied.

"What is your meaning?"

"Only that Inverness was betrayed once before," Gillie said with an innocent expression. " 'Tis well known that the traitor has never been discovered."

"If the traitor were still at Inverness he has had ample opportunity to betray," she replied and then reminded Gillie, "Everyone must do their fair share of work. If you have nothing to do, I am certain Thomas can find something for you."

Gillie disliked Thomas intensely and it came as no surprise to Brianna when she suddenly recalled several tasks Enya had asked her to do earlier. Still her words ate at Brianna.

She was in a miserable mood as she left the main hall with a desperate need to go to the battlements. Perhaps there she might find some privacy where she could think and sort out these turbulent feelings and for which she had no understanding.

When she reached the battlements she was grateful the guards were elsewhere along the wall. Here she found a measure of privacy and solace as she absorbed the penetrating warmth of the sun and the cleansing coolness of the wind. They seemed to renew her and ease the rage of emotions.

The rolling hillsides spread beyond the walls and gates of Inverness. The sea churned beyond the eastern wall, the arc of the bay curving to the north and south through the misty haze that lay over the water.

The village nestled in the curve of the bay. Fishing boats had been abandoned. The doors and windows of cottages were tightly shuttered, the streets were oddly vacant at the midday hour when they were usually bustling with people at market.

In the vast yard below, within the safety of the walls of the fortress, life went on as usual. Dogs yapped in mock battle over some scrap of food, somewhere nearby a mother called for her child, and the smithy's hammer rang as it struck the anvil. All were safe within the walls of Inverness.

With that thought, her gaze swept the new breastworks and stone walls that both Scot and Norman alike had labored to complete. Then to the stout gates, each timber over a foot thick, the gate so heavy that it required the combined strength of six men to open it. Though only one man was needed to turn the wheel mechanism that dropped the heavy crossbar into place.

But the crossbar was not in place! It was raised into the upright position, and the guards were gone. Her startled gaze scanned the wall that framed the gates. No guards patrolled the battlements. In fact, she saw no guards at all!

As she ran down the steps from the battlements, she cast her thoughts to every corner of the fortress, feeling some small comfort of relief when Thomas' thoughts answered. Her relief vanished as she fell over the body of one of the Norman guards usually posted to that portion of the battlement walls. Beside him lay the body of another guard. Blood pooled beneath their bodies. They were both dead.

She gathered up her skirt, scrambled to her feet, and ran toward the main hall. Here too the guards were gone from their posts. She found Thomas in the large main hall, kneeling beside a Scots warrior. His throat had been slashed.

"Thomas!"

"*Aye, lass. I know,*" his grim thoughts connected with hers. "*I found another in the stables.*"

"There's more," Enya said. Her face was ashen as she brought more news of death. "Three guards at the back entrance are also dead. Nel found them. Poor child. She's wild with fear."

Brianna's gaze met Thomas'. "The main gate is open!"

Their suspicions connected on exactly the same thought — it was exactly like before when Mardigan's men had attacked Inverness. Thomas vaulted to his feet. Seizing a battle sword from one of the slain guards he made for the main entrance of the hall.

"Take this." Brianna thrust a shorter sword into the woman's hands. Enya nodded.

"Aye, mistress." Then she vowed grimly, "I'll not suffer their brutality again. Nor will I let them harm the girl."

Brianna nodded. "Send Anne to warn the people in the yard and find guards who may be trusted. Trust none of the ones who returned from Mardigan's stronghold." Then with a sudden thought, she asked, "Where is Gillie?"

Enya shrugged. "I have not seen her all morning."

"Aye," Brianna replied, then dismissed the woman. "I cannot be worried about her now." With a nod to Enya, she repeated, "When we have left, bar the main doors."

"But what of you and Thomas? How will you return?"

"We'll be safe enough," Brianna told her, praying it was so.

Ian hobbled toward them on gout-ridden legs. He had been left in command of the soldiers who remained behind at Inverness.

"I've alerted my men."

"Be careful who you trust. The ones who returned from Mardigan's stronghold are traitors."

"But some of them are my own men!" he protested.

"They are not your men." At his look of bewilderment she implored him, "Do not ask how I know it. Please dear friend, just do as I ask."

He nodded grimly, his mouth set in a hard line. "And what of Malcolm and the others?"

"I fear they are in grave danger."

Then she and Thomas left the hall.

Chaos filled the yard as word of the murdered guards spread. Families still living within the walls fled for shelter, the men using whatever could be found for weapons. Soldiers who had been left to guard the fortress ran among them, climbing the battlement steps, guarding the wall. She saw none of the other guards among them.

Thomas ran for the gatehouse. He threw his full weight against the wheel. As he strained, with muscles bulging, to angle the bar over the cross members, Brianna saw the warrior who approached at his back with sword in hand. It was the same man she had seen days earlier with Gillie.

She cried a warning as she ran across the yard and lunged at the warrior, grabbing at his sword arm. She was no match for him, but that was not her intention. Her only hope was to divert the blow, giving Thomas a chance to defend himself.

Instead the warrior screamed painfully and staggered backward as though struck by a powerful blow. He stumbled and fought to regain his footing at the same time he tried to throw her off. But it was too late.

To her shock he seemed seized by some dreadful agony of pain, writhing and twisting, trying to free himself from her grasp. Equally stunned, Brianna could only watch with growing disbelief and horror as the features of his face contorted, spasmed, and then transformed, revealing the features of someone she did not know.

Then she felt the muscles of his arm beneath the sleeve of his tunic spasm and wither beneath her fingers until it seemed she held nothing but bone. Unable to comprehend what was happening, she looked up and watched in horror as the flesh slowly peeled away from his face, exposing tissue, blood, and bone, all contorted in a terrifying mask of excruciating pain.

His eyes pulled back in their sockets, staring at her in an agony of dying pain. Then, as she watched, he wasted away to nothing more than a skeleton. His agonizing scream died at his throat. A scull was all that was left of his head. It jerked back, jawbones open and spread in a painful gaping expression. She screamed as his head snapped from the bones of his spine and the bones within his sleeve beneath her stunned fingers snapped and exploded.

Brianna fell to her knees, shaking violently. Her frozen thoughts struggled to comprehend what she had seen. The warrior had been far stronger than she. He could easily have struck her down. And yet, he lay before her. Dead. Or at least all that remained of him.

His clothing and broadsword lay where he had fallen but nothing of the warrior remained except his skeleton stripped of all flesh and muscle. Then it too crumbled to nothing but dust that whirled about her in a sudden, blinding cloud of death.

Thomas was immediately beside her, pulling her away and into his arms as he had when she was a child. But no amount of his gentle thoughts could take away the horror of what she had seen.

"It was horrible," she whispered, unable to banish the images of the warrior's brutal death from her own tortured thoughts. And also unable to rid herself of the certain knowledge she had glimpsed something evil unfolding.

"He is dead because of me," she whispered, horrified.

"He was not truly alive, lass," Thomas said gently, trying to comfort her.

She knew he was right. The creature she had seen was not a mortal, nor was it alive. Then, they heard the terrified scream that came from the main hall. Ian swung the doors open in spite of her orders, a war ax grasped in his hands. His features were grim.

"Look!" Enya cried out as they reached the main hall. Young Nel screamed hysterically as the woman tried to comfort her. Enya pointed to the bottom of the stairs her features pale and taut.

"There are four more in the great room," she said grimly.

Brianna swept past her to the man who lay fallen at the stairs to the second floor chambers. A Norman guard, dead, but it was not the sight of a body that terrified the young girl. It was the horror of the agonizing transformation that took place even now as they watched. The same transformation Brianna had seen.

As with the warrior at the gate, his features altered, revealing the features of someone else in those last moments before the skin peeled back over muscles and tissue and then crumbled to dust. The others had already transformed, familiar features of Norman warriors and kinsmen disappearing to reveal the features of strangers.

Ian's men quickly filled the hall and told of other similar experiences. It was as if all their deaths were connected to the death of the first warrior. With the death of one, all had perished.

But who were they? *What* were they?

Beyond any doubt it had been their purpose to strike the first blows, killing as many as possible within the fortress.

"Take her away from this," Brianna told Enya who held the hysterically weeping girl in her arms. Ian gave orders for what was left of the bodies to be removed.

"Throw their remains over the battlements!" he ordered. "I'll not have their evil fouling the air." As he gave other orders for the defense of Inverness, Thomas' thoughts connected with hers, bringing her back from the horror and confusion of what had happened.

"Aye," she acknowledged, "Tarek and the others are being led into a trap by one they trust. I must find them before it's too late."

He stopped her with a gentle hand at her shoulder. There was no need to read his thoughts for they were revealed as clearly as if he had spoken them in the sad expression at his eyes. She laid a hand over his.

Both knew there was no time for a rider to reach them with the warning of the trap they rode into, even if they could be found. The country where they had gone was remote, difficult for both men and horses. And they had been gone for two days. It would take a single rider equally as long to reach them. By then it would be too late.

She had not gone to the battlements for this purpose since she had given herself to Tarek and discovered the fulfillment to be found in his arms. She feared he might learn the horrible secret she kept from him, and if he knew, she could not bear that he might turn away from her in horror and disgust.

Each time they came together, she turned away more and more from this part of herself, denying it with all her strength, choosing not to return. She had dared to hope she would never have to pursue this path again, turning away from that other part of her that he could never understand or accept, turning instead to the part of her that he had helped discover — the mortal part of her that was flesh and blood, with

320

human thoughts and emotions, and passion.

For every time she turned to that other side, she felt herself slipping more and more away, into that other world. A terrifying unknown place that tore her apart from the mortal world. Now it was the only way to save him — to save all of them.

"There is no other way," she gravely told Thomas, for he alone understood her torment.

He went with her to the battlements. His large hand gently covered hers, offering comfort as he had when she was a child. But there was no comfort to be found now. Only the certainty of what she must do.

She stared out over the expanse of time and distance that separated her from Tarek. The wind pressed against her, filling the folds of her mantle, turning her thoughts skyward.

Could she find them? Would she be in time? But at what price? For even now as she felt the powerful instinct stir within her, tears stung at her eyes. She slowly raised her arms as she turned her thoughts inward to that other part of her, that she had discovered long ago as a child.

Closing her eyes, she felt the cleansing power of the wind against her skin, caressing every nerve ending as ancient words first heard in her dreams long ago whispered through her thoughts.

As the folds of the mantle billowed and caught the wind, she turned her thoughts skyward. She imagined a sleek silver falcon escaping the battlement walls, climbing the sky toward the heat of the sun, escaping the bonds of earth.

Tarek whirled the Arabian mare about at the sound of an approaching rider. His features were drawn with fatigue from the long ride over treacherous terrain, and the increasing uneasiness that settled over him the farther north they rode. His expression was taut as Stephen of Valois reined his warhorse in hard.

"What of Mortain?" he demanded. "Where is he?"

"He cannot be found," Stephen replied tersely. His mail coif was pushed back, sable hair plastered against his head. "Nor any of his men," he added with frustration. "It is as if the earth opened up and swallowed them."

Tarek shifted uneasily in the saddle, his narrowed gaze scanning the steep slopes of heavily wooded hillsides they had traversed since morning, the path taking them deeper into the canyon. They were strung out like beads on a necklace, the Scots afoot descending the slope ahead and partially concealed by heavy tree cover.

"It is like the forest near Hastings," Tarek muttered. "We are like prey waiting for the hunters." He berated himself for leading his men to this place when every instinct cried out against it.

Even now the mist rose from the low places, sweeping up the hillside. They would be trapped, unable to tell enemy from ally, hopelessly doomed.

He made his decision. "Enough of this. We leave now and seek higher ground before it is too late."

But it was already too late.

The battle cry went up among his men. The Scots had been attacked on the trail below.

"We are attacked and Mortain is not about!"

"He would not betray us!" Stephen staunchly defended the knight. "He has ridden with the king through all his campaigns." He added passionately, "he would die before he would betray us."

"Yet he is gone!" Tarek pointed out as he drew his battle sword. "And not about to join the fight!" Then he whirled the mare about, shouting orders.

"Take your men to the rim of the canyon. Seek the high ground."

"What about you?" Stephen shouted.

"My men and I will join the others. If the raiders overrun us and reach this position, save yourselves and return to Inverness."

"I will not. I fight by your side as always," Stephen told him defiantly.

"You have your orders, my friend," Tarek said. Then he whirled the mare back around, and shouting orders to his men, led them down the hillside into the mist shrouded battle below. Only a dozen yards from the battle, he found young Duncan.

"Protect the boy!" he ordered Sir Guy, who grabbed the boy by the scruff of the neck and held him dangling above the ground from astride his warhorse. Duncan kicked and twisted, gaining his freedom as he dropped to the ground.

"Do not send me away. Give me a sword so that I may fight with my kinsmen," he cried out with youthful passion. He pointed to a place where the mist shifted and rolled across the uneven ground, exposing the fierce battle at the bottom of the hill.

"You must let me fight beside them, for my parents and family!" His young face was grim-set, stubborn, and determined. Finally Tarek nodded, handing the boy the short-bladed knife from his own belt.

"Use it as I taught you. And stay with Sir Guy. A good warrior never rides into battle alone."

Satisfied, Duncan took a leg up and swung astride behind Sir Guy, blade clasped fiercely in hand.

"I will protect your back," he vowed to the knight.

"And I will protect yours," Stephen told Tarek as he rejoined them.

"I gave you orders!" Tarek reminded him.

"And I have given them to my men. They ride with Gavin."

With a sharp nod Tarek gave orders to his men. Half were to follow, the other half, led by Sir Guy were to split and sweep the hill from two sides like a pincer.

Sir Guy nodded and sent half his men to each flank. At a signal, Tarek led the rest of his men in a sweeping charge down the slope toward the embattled Scots. Their horses plunged into the heart of the battle.

Heavily outnumbered, the Scots fought with swords, shields made of animal skins, and the narrow-bladed dirks against Norse war axes, round steel shields, and clubs.

Tarek's men speared through the heart of the battle at the same time Sir Guy and his men closed the pincer blades from both sides.

Tarek and Stephen fought flank to flank, protecting each other's back while slashing first to one side and then the other. Over and over, one name filled Tarek's thoughts — Mardigan.

Stephen cried a warning and Tarek blunted a blow that would have severed his leg and cut the mare from beneath him as he was attacked on both sides.

The raider who swung the blow was covered with the blood of battle. As he swung the ax again, Tarek deflected the blow, dismounting before the raider recovered to strike again.

"Yield, and live!" he told the raider, but either he didn't understand or chose not to. He swung again. This time, Tarek deliberately angled his blade high, preferring to wound the man rather than kill him. He wanted one left alive who could tell who had betrayed them. But the raider saw his move, snarled fiercely and drove low with his blade.

With both hands clasped around the handle of the sword, Tarek side-stepped and brought the Persian blade up in a deadly arc. It caught the raider low at the belly, impaling him as it sliced him open all the way to his chest.

Tarek felt the shudder of the blade, then the dragging weight as it sliced through flesh and muscle, the dull scrape against bone, and finally the stunned hiss of air from the raider's dying lungs. He was dead before he fell to his knees and then rolled away beneath Tarek's booted foot.

He swung around to face the second raider. In that moment, across the embattled clearing, Tarek glimpsed something that startled him — a raider who took on two fierce Scots at once.

He was tall and powerfully built, flaxen hair streaming to his shoulders, fierce features wreathed by a thick russet beard. He wielded his weapon as if it weighed no more than a feather, and the deadly gaze that focused on his attackers was an intense shade of blue, like the waters of a northern fjord.

"Mardigan." But even as Tarek knew who the man was, he realized there was no hope of reaching him.

Mardigan outmaneuvered the two Scots, slaying one as he eluded the other, and fought to the edge of the clearing. If Tarek followed, he endangered more of his own men and that he would not do. Grimly, he turned to fight off two more raiders.

We will meet soon, Tarek silently vowed as he turned, cut down one raider, and then gave chase to the second one who fled into the rocks.

This way lay unseen danger. He sensed it in the sudden raising of the hair at the back of his neck like hackles going up as he followed the path the raider had followed.

Then, from the rocks above he caught the sudden gleam of light as the sun reflected off a steel blade. Too late he realized the raider had doubled back and now attacked from the rocks above.

Then just as suddenly as it had cleared, the mist gathered and closed around him once more. He spun first in one direction then the other, blade held before him and ready to strike. But the mist blinded him. Then, he heard the warrior cry out with excruciating pain.

The mist shifted and slowly receded back into the rocks. Less than a dozen paces away, the raider who tried to attack him from the rocks above lay sprawled on the ground.

His sword arm was bloodied and almost severed from his body. His face had been brutally slashed, his features no longer recognizable above the coarse matted beard. A large, sleek cat crouched over the raider's body.

It was a magnificent animal, its rich golden coat tipped with silver that seemed to hold and spin streamers of lingering mist into a glittering mantle that gathered about it, its silken coat marred only by the blood that streaked its left shoulder. It had been wounded as the raider tried to defend himself.

Tarek had seen such beasts in the eastern empire. They were wild, exotic creatures, some black as night, others with spotted markings or stripes on rich golden coats. They were beautiful, elegant, fierce, and feared nothing. They were displayed in palaces for man's pleasure, but possessed such regal bearing that no man could ever truly own them.

The creature's sleek, golden head angled toward him, watchful, golden eyes contemplating him with something that seemed almost like recognition.

Then the mist swirled back over the rocks and the path, like a mantle slowly closing about everything. And through the gathering mist, the cat rose from its kill.

As it turned to leave, Tarek saw something that startled

him. The creature's eyes glowed to shades of green. Then it was gone, fleeing into the swirling mist.

Again, he experienced that sensual awareness at the back of his neck and down his spine. But this time, it was not fear. It was the feeling of having been in a place very much like this before with the mist closing around him — beside a highland pool months ago.

He followed the path through a cut in the rocks, then down the other side as it descended the hill. The way was difficult but not impassable, and the path had been traveled recently, tender shoots of new grass flattened underfoot. Someone, or something, had come this way.

He became disoriented in the mist, sounds muffled so that it was impossible to tell which direction he had come, or which he followed. Then the mist began to lift once more, as suddenly as it had closed in.

Rocks to his left reappeared as the sun pierced the gray shroud, and the path once more lay clear before him. He followed it, darting through pockets of lingering mist that washed warmly against his face. He saw something on the path ahead.

Behind him the sounds of battle had ceased. He now heard horses and knew his men followed. With curved sword held ready before him, he slowly approached.

It was tawny-colored and almost blended with the surrounding rocks. Then, as he approached closer, he saw it more clearly and realized it was the creature who had slain the raider.

A silent warning moved along each nerve ending. Every muscle tensed as he held the sword ready to strike should the animal turn and attack. But as he slowly approached, it made no move either to attack or flee. It lay completely motionless not even responding as his men approached.

Then Tarek discovered that it was not a creature at all, but a warrior dressed in leather-colored breeches and hooded tunic. With the tip of his sword he prodded the warrior's back.

His cautious proddings revealed not the thick, heavy-set muscles of a seasoned, mature warrior but the slender, spare build of a youth who had not yet acquired the thickness of muscles. He cautiously nudged the boy over with the toe of his boot.

Sunlight bathed pale skin across fragile bones and delicate features. Slender golden brows arched over crescents of dark golden lashes. Sensuous, full lips were softly parted, the curve of a slender throat exposed above the swell of breasts beneath the tunic, and with head thrown back amidst a torrent of long white gold hair that spilled free of the tunic.

"Father in heaven!" Malcolm swore as he dismounted and also saw that the fallen warrior was neither man nor boy.

Tarek knelt beside her. As he reached for Brianna the hazy sun disappeared and the mist swirled softly about her like a protective mantle that gently closed round them.

It shimmered in the thick, pale gold of her hair and bathed pale features, making her suddenly seem like a creature of the netherworld. And amid the sounds of other riders approaching and the rising wind that churned the mist, he thought he heard a voice on the breath of the wind.

Flee. Leave this place. There is danger.

It seemed to come from nowhere and everywhere — the rocks, the trees, a warning sighed on the wind as the sky darkened about them like night falling even though it was not yet midday.

Blood seeped through the soft leather of the tunic at her shoulder. Tarek tore open the front of the tunic and discovered the wound at her shoulder.

"Is she alive?" Malcolm demanded.

Tarek gently pressed his fingers against her throat and felt the faint, rapid pulse. He nodded.

Dark gold lashes quivered against her cheek and lifted over soft green eyes. And for a moment the illusion returned — of a slender, golden cat glancing back at him through the veil of mist, blood smeared across the fur at its shoulder as it stood over the warrior it had killed.

"Mortain and his men are all dead," she whispered. "There is great danger. You must leave this place." Then her head slumped against his shoulder.

Stephen rode up. Behind him followed more warriors and knights. His expression was grim, then stunned as he saw Brianna.

"How did she get here?"

"I would like to know that as well," Tarek answered. "What of the raiders?"

"Gone," Stephen said tersely. "Vanished, without a trace, as if they never existed. When I sent my men to follow, they found nothing. And there is more," his mouth flattened into a hard line. "I have found Mortain and his men."

"Where are they?" Malcolm demanded. "I have a few questions I would like to ask of them."

"You will ask them no questions," Stephen replied, the muscles at his jaw taut with anger. "They are all dead."

Tarek's gaze narrowed as it met his. "What are you saying?"

"We found their bodies in a glen not far from here. Or, at least what was left of them. They were caught by surprise and slaughtered," Stephen acknowledged bitterly.

"There is no other way Mortain would have yielded his men or his sword." Then he added grimly, "But it did not happen this morning when they left our encampment."

"What are you saying?" Malcolm confronted him. "It

could only have been this morning."

Stephen's gaze met Tarek's. He shook his head. "They have been dead far longer. It is as if . . ." Once, Stephen had seen exactly the same as he had seen when he found Mortain and his men. It was not something he would ever forget.

"As if what?" Tarek demanded.

"Their bodies were withered and shrunken," Stephen described what he had seen. As if the very life was sucked out of them. I have seen such as this only once before," he added, not wanting to believe it for he bore the fierce scars of that encounter.

"It was in London."

Tarek remembered it well, for it was after they returned from the north country where he first met Brianna and she had saved his life to find the queen in grave danger and Stephen badly wounded as he tried to protect her. Their attackers had not been human, but some evil incarnate.

Darkness closed around them, blocking out the sun, blanketing the surrounding countryside with an oppressiveness that made the air seem heavy. The horses moved restlessly, instinctively sensing danger.

"What of the men who rode with us from Inverness whom we believed to be Mortain and his men?"

Stephen's expression was grim. "We found them wearing the tunics and armaments of Mortain's men. They were still astride their horses, but dead as well. There was very little left. I did not recognize any of them."

Instinctively Tarek knew. "They were sent among us to deceive and lead us here."

"But we saw Mortain at Inverness!" Malcolm argued.

Tarek shook his head. "We saw what we were suppose to see, an illusion. Mortain and his men were already dead."

Malcolm stared first at Tarek and then Stephen. "It

cannot be. What you speak of is impossible."

Tarek's expression was grim as he lifted Brianna. One of his men led the Arabian forward and he eased her atop then swung up and settled her against him.

"She must have a healer," he said tersely. "We return to Inverness."

"What about Mardigan?" Malcolm demanded. "He and his men canna be far."

"He is not here." Tarek gazed about him at the unusual silence that surrounded them. There wasn't a sound, not even a bird or the wind in the trees. He thought of the warrior he had seen across the embattled clearing. Had Mardigan been real?

"We will all return to Inverness," he said with a new urgency that accepted no argument, for he sensed this place was filled with evil.

"You must help her!" Vivian implored. "You cannot abandon her!"

"I have not abandoned her, I have protected her and kept her safe, as I longed to keep you safe."

Brilliant blue shimmered with silver facets in the folds of the robe with each restless movement. With feelings of helplessness and rage, hands gnarled with age yet still powerfully strong punctuated the air emphasizing every word.

"She is safe no longer, father. She is in great danger. You have seen it as well as I. She must be given the knowledge. It is the only way the Darkness can be stopped."

"You could not stop it," he reminded her. "It is too powerful."

"Yet not powerful enough to claim Excalibur," she retorted. "Only a warrior who possessed great wisdom could claim it."

"And now having lost the sword," he added, "the Darkness seeks the power of the Grail." He hung his head as the words of ancient prophecy whispered through his troubled thoughts.

There would be another to claim the throne of Arthur's lost kingdom. It had been promised after Arthur's death when Merlin was banished from the mortal world. But he had not dared believe it, nor that he would live long enough to see it — a king who would possess great wisdom, a true heart, and unwavering courage.

"If I could trade my life for hers, I would," he said passionately. "But I cannot leave. Such is the curse the Darkness has placed upon me. This place is my tomb and I am powerless to leave as long as the Darkness rules the mortal world. Nor can you give her the knowledge, daughter," he said sadly. "For with all your wondrous powers you do not possess that power."

He buried his face in his hands. The air in the white stone chamber high atop the hill with its roof open to the sky was weighted with the grief and pain of a father who could not bear the greatest loss of all — that of a beloved child.

"I am powerless to save her," he said helplessly, "and the cursed Darkness knows it."

"But I am not powerless. I can save her."

Both turned at the sound of that gentle voice. A frown creased Merlin's patrician features for Ninian had not come to the marble chamber since first she entered the world between the worlds so many years ago.

How long had it been? Over five hundred years?

And yet she looked the same to him as she had then, breathtakingly beautiful with fiery red hair that fell to her waist — a gift to the first-born daughter who stood beside him, and with delicate features and soft green eyes. The passage of time had only softened and enhanced her breath-taking beauty.

Ninian had given up all to join him there in the world between the worlds when she brought him the lost sword of the kingdom. What began as devotion in a changeling girl with unique healing powers for the great fallen sorcerer, Merlin, had ripened into a passionate love for which she was willing to sacrifice the mortal world and remain at his side.

"Dearest love," he whispered as he crossed the chamber and took her slender hands in his. "I would've spared you this pain."

"Spared me?" she said incredulously. "How, when my child is in danger? Did you think I would not know? That my powers are so weak?" She glanced at Vivian, the first-born daughter who bore her image so strikingly. "Is there nothing else that may be done?"

"Knowledge is the only thing that can save her," Vivian replied. "The Darkness closes in. She is safe no longer. She must have the knowledge of her powers."

"The Darkness seeks the Grail," Ninian whispered as she slowly crossed the chamber to the open wall that looked out upon the world that had been her home for over five centuries. "Along with all the power it possesses."

Merlin nodded gravely. "It must possess the Grail to strengthen its power. For only by possessing the heart, soul, and mind of mankind can it rule the kingdom, and the universe beyond."

"The future is at stake," she whispered. "Just as the Ancient Ones foretold." She turned to Merlin, her mentor, lover, and father of her children.

"The promise of a new king who must have the power of Excalibur, the Grail, and the Oracle if the Darkness is to be defeated. Brianna knows where the Grail lies hidden. Only she can release its power. But that knowledge along with the knowledge of her powers is locked away.

"She must be allowed to remember. It is the only way, husband, and you know it. In order to save her, we must risk her life."

"If she is given the knowledge, she will be destroyed!" Merlin tried to make her understand. "You do not know the power of the Darkness." He turned to Vivian. "Tell her, daughter. Tell her of your ordeal in the catacombs! Tell her of the ruthless cruelty with no shred of mortal compassion or decency. Tell her what your sister faces if the knowledge is revealed to her."

But Vivian could not do as he asked, even though she knew he was right. "It must be done. It is the only way. I would take her place if I could," she said fiercely. "I would face the Darkness again for I have seen its cruelty. But I do not possess her powers or knowledge. They are the key to the Grail."

She went to him, laying a hand on his arm, the warmth of her power gently soothing. Merlin looked at her suspiciously.

"Do not think to use your powers on me, daughter. I may have been banished to this cursed place but I still possess some of my powers. You are no match for me."

She put her arms around him and laid her head against his shoulder as she had as a child. His heart beat strong beneath her cheek, giving comfort as it had when she was small, making her feel safe. But the sigh he breathed was filled with pain and torment.

"There is no other way, Father."

Beside them, Ninian looked out across the glittering world spread out below, where she had found great happiness.

How could she leave this place? How could she leave the one she loved more than life itself, and for whom she had given up her mortal life?

How could she not?

"I will leave at dawn," she said quietly.

"You must not!" Merlin protested, taking her into his arms as if he could physically prevent her leaving. "You know the curse as well as I. Once you leave, you cannot return. I could not bear to live the rest of my life without you."

She laid a hand against his cheek. "Dear husband, I gave up the mortal world and remained here because of my love for you. I accepted your decision that I must send my children out into the mortal world to keep them safe. I lived with that loss, heartbreaking as it was, cherishing the times when we could all be together."

She framed his face with both hands as her eyes filled with tears of both love and sadness. "But I cannot live in this world knowing that my happiness here with you is bought at the cost of their lives." With a sudden fierce passion that came from a mother's heart, she told him, "I must do this, and you must not stop me."

"You are my life," he whispered. But in her eyes he saw the determination and mother's love that he could never completely understand though he loved all their children as much as she, and for which even a sorcerer was no match. Finally, he nodded sadly.

"Aye, you must go."

Ninian kissed him tenderly. Then she turned to Vivian.

"I will need your help, daughter."

Vivian nodded. "We will return through the standing stone together. I can do that much at least."

"Do you think me so old and feeble that I cannot pass through a standing stone?" Ninian retorted.

Vivian smiled. "It has been a long time since you ventured into the mortal world. At least five hundred years." She

335

shrugged. "It's on my way."

But Ninian wasn't deceived. "One day very soon, daughter," she warned, a smile glowing at her soft green eyes, "you too will be a mother with a child far too smart for her own powers."

Then she became serious once more, glancing at the sky that grew light at the horizon.

"Soon it will be dawn and there are things that must be done. I will need my healing potions, and you must tell me of Tarek al Sharif. I must know what sort of man he is. Then, pray that I am in time."

336

Eighteen

Shouts went out from the guards at the battlements. Wood creaked and ropes strained as the massive gates of Inverness slowly opened. Dozens of torches cast a pall of shifting light across the battle armor of the riders who rode through the gates, dust churning beneath the hooves of the horses.

Expressions were grim as face plates at steel helms were pushed back, blood-stained swords glinting dully in the light of the torches. Their exhausted mounts were lathered, steam rising from their trembling bodies in the cold predawn.

Warriors and Scots who had remained behind emerged from the stables and the armory at a run. Women and children roused from sleep brought water, blankets, and bandages. Amid the confusion and urgency of tending to the wounded, not a word was spoken, nor a question asked. The wounded and the grim expressions of those who had returned told far more than any words.

With great care Tarek handed his slender burden down to one of his men. Then dismounting, he once again took Brianna into his arms and vaulted up the steps to the main hall, shouting orders as he went.

The large main doors were thrown open, Enya waiting with Nel beside her. With a glance at the slender girl in Tarek al Sharif's arms, she told Nel grimly, "Find the healer and send her to the laird's chambers."

Then she turned and ran after him, the torch she carried fluttering wildly overhead as she followed him up the stairs to the chamber.

Where was Thomas? she wondered.

He had been like a caged animal since dawn two days before when the young mistress mysteriously disappeared. Twice she had found him on the battlements, his gaze fastened on the sky as if looking for something, or someone.

He would not be persuaded to come away even when it grew dark and unbearably cold with the threat of a late spring storm. Nor did he accept any food that she brought. She took him a warm fur, watching with him — for what she did not know. Finally, she left him to his silent vigil, certain it had something to do with the young mistress.

Only a short while earlier she had found him still there, watching, waiting. It was then she saw the serpentine column of light in the distance that drew steadily closer, until the long strand of glowing light became separate beads of light and she knew riders approached bearing torches in the unusual darkness.

The call had gone out across the battlements, warriors and knights reaching for their weapons even as the lone rider approached the gates and was recognized — Sir Stephen — his face a fierce, stark mask in the light of the torches as he ordered the gates opened.

No sooner had they swung open than the column of knights and Scots warriors rode through as if all the hounds of hell were nipping at their heels.

Thomas had not followed but remained behind at the battlements, his expression grim, resolute, a faraway look in his dark, gentle eyes.

Where was he now? She knew his devotion to the young mistress and could not imagine anything that would have kept him from her side now.

Enya had kept a fire constantly burning at the brazier in anticipation of her mistress' return. Candles guttered in the iron bowls as Tarek al Sharif swept into the room and carried her to the bed. Bracing a knee at the edge of the bed, he gently laid her among the warm furs. The mantle fell open and Enya saw the blood that splattered her mistress' skin and stained her tunic.

"Where is the healer?" Tarek snarled.

"I am here, milord."

He looked up sharply at the unfamiliar voice. Thomas stood in the doorway. Beside him was a slender figure draped in a flowing dark mantle the color of midnight sky. Light from the fire at the brazier and torches glittered and sparkled across the fabric as though threads of fire were woven through. She was framed by an unnatural light at the darkened doorway.

Then she slowly walked toward him and it seemed with every step she brought the light into the chamber with her.

Slender hands pushed back the hood revealing fair, delicate features surrounded by flame-colored hair that glowed like a brilliant candle in the shadows that steeped the chamber.

"Lady Vivian?" Tarek stared at her incredulously. The woman smiled softly.

"Thank you, milord. I take that as a compliment."

Only when she stepped closer did he discover that he was mistaken. Her features were much softer, the color of her hair shades lighter, and her eyes were not blue like the heart of a flame but soft green.

"Who is this woman?" he demanded. But the question was answered by silence.

"I am the healer," she repeated, stepping past him to the bed. A frown drew slender auburn brows together, myriad emotions shading her eyes darker to the color of forest shadows.

As she laid a hand at Brianna's forehead Tarek instinctively moved to protect her. Thomas stopped him, a powerful hand clasping over his shoulder. Tarek's hand closed over the handle of the knife at his belt.

The green gaze that met his was cool and measuring, the woman's expression making him feel as though he was the intruder. When he refused to sheathe his weapon, Thomas' hand tightened and he felt the powerful strength that could easily have snapped a man's arm.

"Vivian said you were a believer," she said speculatively, her soft green gaze scrutinizing. Whatever she saw seemed to please her. "Perhaps there is hope."

Her words weighted the air within the chamber as if both despair and hope had taken physical form, battling each other in the shadows that dragged at the light from the torches. Tarek stared at the beautiful woman who bore such a striking resemblance to Lady Vivian of Amesbury.

The profile was the same, the full curve of lips that suddenly trembled with emotion as she gazed down at Brianna. But the watery green of eyes suddenly filled with tears, and the softness of her voice as she crooned ancient words in some unknown language, belonged to someone else.

"Who are you?" he again demanded.

"You know who I am," she replied as she sensed his thoughts and knew the comparison he made.

She touched the pulse at Brianna's throat. Then she drew back the heavy mantle, passing her hand palm down over the length of Brianna's body, finally returning to the stain of blood at the shoulder of the tunic. She lifted the edge of the crudely made bandage that had stanched the flow of blood.

"I am called Ninian."

He recalled the name and the ancient legend Vivian had once told him, of the young maid who retrieved the sword

340

Excalibur from the lake and took it to the sorcerer, Merlin.

Tarek looked at her warily, unable to deny her resemblance to Lady Vivian and another who lay on the pallet of furs, yet unwilling to blindly accept what there was no logic for. He thought of Mortain and how easily he believed that the man who returned with news of the location of Mardigan's stronghold was his trusted friend, only to discover that he was not.

For a warrior who had met and conquered many enemies, he learned that day that enemies often wore the faces of friends.

"If you are Ninian, how did you come to be here?"

She waved a hand impatiently. "It does not matter. I am here, and I am in time."

He struggled with the truth. He wanted to deny it, but she bore an unmistakable resemblance to Vivian — the magical creature of fire who was now King William's trusted counselor as her father had once been counselor to another English king.

"Ninian," he repeated her name, as if trying to divine some truth from the sound of it. "The lady of the lake."

"Ah, so you know the story." She smiled faintly. "Vivian was always fond of it. It was her favorite as a child."

"Do you have the Lady Vivian's healing power?" he asked, willing to believe almost anything if it would save Brianna.

"Vivian possesses a rare gift. But what she knows, she learned from me."

"But do you have her gift for mending wounds?"

" 'Tis not the wound that threatens her life, warrior," she answered softly. She rubbed her upper arms as though taken with a sudden chill in spite of the warmth of the heavy mantle she wore.

"Time grows short," she whispered, glancing about the

341

chamber as if she sensed something.

"Then begin the healing!"

"It is not so simply done, warrior. There are things I will need."

"Name them and you will have them."

When she had told him all the things she would need, he sent Enya to bring them even if it meant sending his men to the village or further.

"It will not be necessary," Ninian assured him. "And when the woman returns you must all leave."

"I will stay," he said with a finality that told her there would be no further discussion of the matter.

She sensed something in him, a glimpse of emotion so clear and sharp, and rarely revealed through the protective layers he kept firmly in place. This mortal loved her daughter. But was it enough?

She could have manipulated his thoughts and forced him to leave, but she did not. If he loved Brianna, then he must know all. For that was the true test for what lay before them.

"Very well, warrior," she finally agreed. "But you may well wish that you had gone with the others."

When Enya returned with everything she had asked for, Ninian instructed Thomas and the woman to leave the chamber. Thomas obeyed without hesitation, removing Enya in spite of her protests.

"Bar the door," Ninian told Tarek. "So that none may enter." As he set the bar into place, she began sorting out the things Enya had brought, adding to them several things she removed from a pouch belted at her waist.

"You must do exactly as I say," she told him. "And no matter what you see, you must not interfere. Do you understand?"

She sensed the mistrust in him, sensed too when he yielded to her wishes.

"Now she must be moved," she told him. "Place her on a pallet before the brazier." When he hesitated, she told him, "Do it now, warrior, or leave!"

He did as she asked, gently laying Brianna on a pallet of soft furs. She didn't stir or give any outward indication that she was aware of anything that went on about her. Yet, Ninian sensed her chaotic thoughts, her pain, and the vulnerable life-force that hung in such precarious balance caught between the mortal and immortal worlds.

Ninian went to the window, pulled back the coverings, and threw open the shutters. Tarek thought her mad. It was bitter cold outside. A storm had gathered, the sky dark with clouds churned on a gusting wind. When he would have stopped her, she repeated her warning.

"Do not interfere!"

Hands clenched into fists of helpless anguish, he finally nodded and stepped aside even as it became unbearably cold in the chamber.

Ninian then set out five white candles she had brought with her. One she placed just above Brianna's head. She placed the other four candles, equidistant at the remaining points that formed a five-pointed star about her. As she set out each candle she repeated ancient words.

"Brightness glowing, points of light, protect the one who dwells within." The words whispered across the walls of the chamber. Then she knelt before the northernmost point of the star above Brianna's head.

Her arms were outstretched. Her eyes were closed as she repeated the words. Then she slowly opened her hands. Light, in the shape of a five-sided star, glowed in the palm of each outstretched hand.

"Brightness glowing, points of light," she repeated. "Protect the one who dwells within."

Flames suddenly appeared at the candles and glowed, surrounding Brianna in a radiant pool of light. Beyond the window the sky was bleak. Wind billowed a tapestry at the wall and guttered the flames at the brazier and torches. But the flames at the candles burned bright and true.

"Remember, warrior," Ninian warned. "No matter what you see, you must not interfere."

He expected more ancient words, an incantation or spell perhaps. But she spoke no magical words nor incantations. Instead, she touched Brianna's hand where it lay on the pallet of soft furs.

Her words were tender as she whispered lovingly, "You are safe, daughter. The power of the Light protects you." Then the chamber was completely silent.

No sound reached them, not even from the yard below where his knights and the Scots warriors gathered. It was as if they were cut off from the rest of the fortress — or the real world.

Then mist purled through the window opening. It spilled onto the floor, rippling in waves across the surface of the stones, wrapping around the legs of the table and chairs, slowly spreading toward Brianna.

He had never seen anything like it, not even on the moors. It engulfed everything in its path, tendrils slipping over the toes of his boots, then moving on as though reaching toward her. As if it had a life of its own. His skin tingled.

When he would have gone to Brianna, Ninian stopped him, her hand clamped over his arm with unusual strength.

"It was your choice to remain, Tarek al Sharif," she whispered. "Now you are part of it. If you wish her to live, do nothing."

344

Though logic cried out for him to go to Brianna, he did not. This was something beyond logic. This was something more. Something that caused the flames at the candles to burn higher as the flames at the torches and brazier extinguished, something that went beyond what he knew of the mortal world, and recalled a day long ago when he had stood beside a highland pool and first saw a beautiful maid staring back at him.

Jehara. Mythical, legendary creatures who possessed extraordinary powers — if one believed in them. He had been forced to believe, for Lady Vivian was such a creature.

Sorceress. The English called her. Daughter of the legendary Merlin.

He had seen her powers and knew them to be real. And now the woman, Ninian, stood over Brianna.

Only moments before it had been frigid in the chamber. Now, it was amazingly warm as mist rose and wrapped about his hands. Then he felt it at his face, gentle as a caress.

Brianna's breathing became shallow and rapid through softly parted lips. Her eyes were closed, her lashes dark gold crescents against pale cheeks as the mist slowly continued its journey and moved over her like a shimmering silver mantle.

It spun and wrapped about her, weaving through the pale gold strands of her hair, caressing her face, eyelids, and lips until a glow of misty light surrounded her. Then he noticed a subtle change in her features — the curve of her cheek, the slender arch where neck met shoulder. She stirred but did not waken.

Then suddenly, her slender body spasmed as if she was in great pain. He watched helplessly as her hands clenched into tight fists as if she fought some physical battle. Then she gasped. Her back arched and her head went back, twisting from side to side. She cried out, a painful, sobbing sound that tore at his heart. He was certain she called out his name.

"End this now!" he whispered fiercely.

"I cannot," Ninian replied. "Once it is begun it cannot be stopped."

He tried to free himself from Ninian's grasp but could not.

"Damn you!" he swore softly at Ninian, his eyes suddenly bright with tears of rage and anguish.

She had known only one who allowed himself to shed tears, and he was not a mortal. Now this man, a mortal, whose heart had been carefully protected, whose laughter and wit masked a pain and rage so deep that none ever saw it, wept for a sorcerer's daughter.

Ah, warrior, she thought, sensing the fierceness of his love for her daughter — that he would have taken her place if he could. Perhaps Vivian is right after all.

Perhaps there is that within you to do what must be done, she thought with a faint flickering of hope.

As surely as he felt the invisible bonds that prevented him going to Brianna, he felt the moment they disappeared, releasing him.

He went to her, going down on his knees beside her. She lay on her side facing him. The dreadful spasms were gone, her slender body lying still and slightly curled. Her eyes slowly opened, soft drowned pools of green that stared back at him with a haunted, heartbreaking sadness. Her hand lifted as she tried to touch him. Her lips formed his name.

Forgive me.

The words moved through his thoughts as clearly as if she had spoken them. Then as he watched, her eyes drifted closed once more. Ninian gently pulled him from her daughter's side.

"She must sleep. Go now."

As he walked to the chamber door, the mist slowly gathered and thickened once more. The candles glowed higher about her, bathing her in silver and gold light so bright it was painful to look at.

Eventually the candles burned low once more. The mist slowly receded, disappearing through the window opening. The tapestries hung still against the walls, and the flames returned to the torches and the brazier.

When he turned at the doorway and glanced back at the pallet of furs, Brianna too was gone. In her place, where she had lain only moments before was a sleek, golden cat.

Nineteen

"Damn your spells!" Tarek swore furiously as he turned on Ninian. "What game is this?"

In his face she saw the struggle to deny what he had seen at war with the rational logic of the warrior.

You must help him to understand.

"Yes, yes, daughter. I know," Ninian replied to the voice that spoke urgently through her thoughts. Then another voice joined in.

All is at stake. He is part of it now. You must make him see it. Perhaps with him there is a chance for Brianna.

You must first remind him of the battle in the catacombs and the transformation of the guards at the London tower, Vivian reminded her.

Dear wife, he must be made to realize what is at stake!

"Be still, both of you," Ninian whispered vehemently. "I cannot think with both of you going on." She smiled gently at Tarek.

" 'Tis no game, nor spell, warrior. 'Tis a most serious matter. All is at stake." She saw his gaze go to the creature who lay so still before the brazier and opened her thoughts to his own to try to sense his true feelings.

She sensed the inner struggle, the logical denial that battled the undeniable proof of the creature that lay on the pallet of furs.

"Is Brianna alive?"

"Yes, but there is much to be done. The wound must be healed."

His gaze swung back to her, wary and untrusting, as if he expected her to also transform into some creature.

"Be at ease, warrior. I will not turn into some great fire-breathing monster that you must do battle with." She looked about the chamber as if gauging its size, as she tried for a bit of levity. It was badly needed.

"The chamber is small. It might be a bit crowded."

"Explain this to me!" he demanded angrily.

He did not seem amused. So much for levity, Ninian thought.

Mother, please! Vivian's thoughts beseeched her. *Do not play this game. There is too much at stake.*

Ah, dear daughter, Ninian sighed. *That is your problem, and your father's as well. You must try to find a little humor in everything. Sometimes it is all you have to get you through it.*

Ninian, please! Merlin pleaded. *This is a most grave situation.*

Yes, husband, I am aware of that. But I am also well aware that humor can be very effective. And after all, she reminded him, *I am here and you are not. Now, both of you, leave this to me!*

She heard vague, distant mutterings and smiled to herself as she imagined Merlin pacing about. Her first-born daughter was far more outspoken.

Remind him of the guards at the fortress in London!

In time, daughter. Give me time.

"Be at ease, warrior," Ninian told Tarek as she sorted through the herbal remedies she had brought with her at the same time she sorted through her thoughts, and how best to explain what he must know. She sprinkled a precise mixture over the simmer pot.

"The truth is not so difficult to understand, if you are willing to accept it."

349

Her gaze met his as she gauged his temperament. He was wary, but he did not turn and stalk from the chamber shouting protective words against sorcery and enchantments.

"You are weary. Sit and I will tell you what you wish to know."

"And if I do not wish to sit?" he asked defiantly. Ninian smiled inwardly. Ah, so typical of a man. He felt vulnerable and threatened, and struggled to control a situation he sensed was completely beyond his control. She shrugged.

"Then stand," she said with casual indifference. " 'Tis only that you have ridden far. I thought you must be exhausted, and this will take a while in the telling."

"You toy with me," he accused suspiciously when he could find no other argument to her logic. She sensed the easing of tension within him, and sensed the shrewd workings of his thoughts as his demeanor became less confrontational, if no less wary.

She laughed softly. "No, milord warrior. You toy with yourself. You make it more difficult than it need be. Stand if that is your choice. But I shall sit. It has been a long journey for me as well and I am not as young as I use to be."

She ladled a portion of the simmered brew into a cup and handed it to him. The suspicion immediately returned. She shrugged and set the cup on the table. Then ladled a portion into a second cup which she took with her as she crossed the chamber and knelt beside the sleek, golden cat which slept undisturbed.

"What is this?" he demanded. "Some poisonous brew?"

"It is tea." She took a sip from her cup and bluntly informed him, "If I wished to harm you, you would not have the need or opportunity to question it." Her gaze was faintly amused as she watched him study the cup.

"Tea?"

She nodded. "Very much like that enjoyed in the eastern empires."

He took a tentative sip, found it most pleasant, and took another, though he still remained standing, his feet planted in a warrior's stance as if he expected to do battle with her at any moment.

"You spoke of a long journey," he contemplated her over the rim of the cup.

She nodded. "Several hundred miles," she explained in terms that he might understand. "Not so far as the crow flies," she added with amusement curving the corner of her mouth and reminding him of Lady Vivian.

She shook her head, "A crow would not have been a better choice. Smaller wingspan and all." When he glowered at her, she had cause to wonder if Vivian might have been mistaken about his keen wit. He seemed to possess little humor at the moment. She thought to herself much more seriously, best to get down to the matters at hand.

"I came through the standing stone in the king's wood, although another would have done as well, but Vivian insisted on accompanying me."

"Lady Vivian?"

By his tone and expression she realized he had given little credence to what she had told him earlier. Now he looked at her far more closely.

"There are some who say she favors me a great deal."

"Then the resemblance is no conjuror's trick?" he asked, coming closer.

"I assure you it is not!" she replied indignantly. "I carried her as I carried all my children, in the mortal way because of their mortal blood. For two days she struggled to be born and when she emerged her hair was as red as a flame. After experiencing the ordeal of mortal childbirth I would gladly have done it the next time by any other means were it possible. No," she repeated, "our resemblance is no conjuror's trick but one of blood."

"She is what my people call the Jehara."

"She is what I call a handful! She is willful, stubborn, opinionated . . ." Ninian suddenly experienced a ripple of tension through her thoughts and knew Vivian had sensed them. She smiled as she looked down at the creature beside her and added, "As are *all* of my children in their own way."

"All of your children?" His gaze followed hers to the sleek cat that lay so still beside her. It had been wounded, a deep gash marring the tawny coat across its shoulder.

A thousand images filled his thoughts. Of the mist parting through over the clearing among the rocks; the fallen raider laying across the path before him; and the wildly beautiful creature that stood over it with blood staining its claws; months earlier beside a highland pool and the beautiful maid who appeared through the mist and led him from certain death; when he turned back all that remained was the sleek bird gliding across the water away from him, and then it too disappeared; and Brianna's anguish at the vows they had spoken, "I cannot be wife to you. I cannot feel as others feel"; and finally, the fierce passion they had found with one another as he had made her wife in all ways.

From inside his tunic he retrieved a slender silver feather found on the battlements weeks before. Had he always known but chosen not to believe?

Ninian watched him thoughtfully. She sensed the inner turmoil, and the silent question.

Stroking the silken feather between his thumb and forefinger, confronted with a truth he could not deny, he finally said, "Tell me."

Ninian nodded, "It will take a while, there is much to tell.

Much that she must know as well," she glanced down to the cat who seemed not to be alive at all, except for its shallow breathing. "But first I must heal the wound."

"Will it be painful?"

"There is always pain, warrior. Healing can only come from pain. What was cut and torn apart must be mended."

He glanced at the star-shaped pattern of the candles that glowed warmly about the beautiful woman and the cat. She sensed his thoughts.

"It is a protection spell. As long as the candles burn and she remains within, she is safe." Then, with a surprise of pleasure she sensed his next thought.

"Yes, warrior, you may enter. The spell protects against those who are evil." He hesitated, then stepped inside. When nothing happened, he slowly released the breath he held. She suppressed a faint smile.

"I think we are going to get along very well."

She began the healing, with a simple touch, gently easing together the cut edges of muscle, sinew, and flesh. Beneath her magical fingers blood ceased to flow as if cauterized, muscle mended stronger than before, poisons were drawn, and finally skin closed so that not even a trace of the injury remained except for a faint, pinkish seam amidst thick tawny fur.

When it was done, he leaned back against the stone wall beside the brazier. He had seen Lady Vivian work such miracles of magic when she saved the king's life, when she healed a wound that would have been fatal to Stephen of Valois, and the time she drew the poison from the queen, saving both her and her unborn son.

"Do you possess all the same powers as Lady Vivian?"

In the question she sensed his acceptance. She smiled wearily as she sat back on the pallet of furs. For now, Brianna slept peacefully. The wound was closed and healed, now she must do the rest. But as Ninian glanced at the candles of the star pattern that surrounded them, she realized they burned unusually bright and far too quickly as though they burned higher and brighter against an unusual darkness. The chamber beyond was filled with deep shadows. She shivered as she sensed it again. There was very little time.

"It is different with us all, just as it is different among mortal children born of the same parents," she explained. "One child may have blue eyes, the other green. One will have the father's smile, the other the mother's charm." When he looked at her askance, she laughed.

"Vivian has many of my powers but they are enhanced by those she inherited from her father."

"Merlin." Then he asked, "What of Brianna?"

She chose her words carefully. "What do you know of changelings?"

He recalled Vivian's explanation about Meg, the old blind woman who had been her maid since she was a child.

"Yes, Meg was born to a changeling and a mortal," Ninian replied, sensing his thoughts. At his startled expression she smiled faintly. "That is another gift some of us are born with — the ability to know another's thoughts. Though with some we cannot."

"You know my thoughts."

She shrugged. "Some of them — those that have to do with Brianna, for she and I are closely bound to one another."

Anger drew his handsome features together in an expression any sorcerer might have found intimidating.

"Not *those* thoughts," she assured him. "There are no doubt many, as a mother, I would rather *not* know."

"Then you invade my thoughts when you choose," he said tightly.

354

The conversation was not going in the direction she hoped. "Only when it is necessary," she assured him. "I have to be certain that you understand. There is so much at stake."

For several moments, they studied one another, much like combatants squaring off at each other.

"Go on. Tell me what other powers she has."

Ninian glanced down at the sleek, golden creature that slept peacefully beside her on the pallet of furs, the most obvious of her powers.

"Brianna is also a changeling," she explained. "She has the power to transform herself."

His glance followed hers as he recalled what he had seen only a short while earlier. "The cat."

She nodded. "Because they possess great strength and cunning."

"A bird?" he suggested.

"They possess the ability to travel far and see what others cannot see on the earth below."

"A silver swan?"

She smiled as she sensed the pleasure of his memory of that first encounter with Brianna, a chance meeting that set the future in motion and offered hope.

She smiled softly. "Yes."

He struggled with a new possibility. "Enemies with the faces of my trusted men?" he accused.

"Never!" Ninian vowed. "Those are the forces of evil, the power of the Darkness." Even as she spoke the words, she glanced about the chamber beyond the glow of the star pattern that protected them. The light waned, the candles now burned low. There was not much time left. Could she make him understand all that he must know?

"The Darkness has found her, just as it found Vivian."

He remembered the terror and horror of the evil at the old

fortress in London and the fierce battle Rorke FitzWarren had fought in the catacombs.

"What of the mist that appears as it did when you opened the window?" he asked, recalling how it had appeared other times as if out of nowhere.

"Brianna is a child of the Light. The elements of nature are gifts possessed by those of the Light. Just as Vivian possesses the power of fire, Brianna possesses the powers of the earth. The mist is her special element. She was born in the mist, and she returns to the mist."

"She can summon it?"

Ninian nodded. "It is part of her."

As he struggled to accept it, he then asked, "What does the Darkness want of her?"

"Her knowledge." At his questioning look, she explained, "Only she knows where the Grail can be found."

He scoffed at her. "It is nothing more than a legend. Brianna said as much."

"Brianna does not know the knowledge she possesses."

"How could she not know of it, if she possesses the knowledge? You speak nonsense."

She sensed his mind closing to her, along with his willingness to listen.

"Have you not seen the twin circles on her shoulder?"

She saw the answer in his narrowed eyes as that blue gaze suddenly swung back to her. She had taken a chance and been proven right. So, Ninian thought, it was as she suspected. Her daughter and this warrior had lain together. Brianna was wife to him in *all* ways, she was capable of mortal love. But that brought a new fear, for love made her vulnerable to the destructive powers of the Darkness.

"Twin circles," she explained. "Overlapping, never-ending, life everlasting — the symbol of the Grail. With the

356

mark, Brianna was given the knowledge of the Grail by the Ancient Ones. But her father feared the Darkness.

"We sent Vivian from our world so that she would be safe. When Brianna was born with the mark of the Grail, he knew that she too must be sent away. But there was one more thing he had to do," she said sadly.

"The knowledge of the Grail endangered her. The only way to protect her was to keep the knowledge from her. All knowledge of her true self was blocked from her memory. Thomas was her protector and brought her here to the north country."

"She does not know any of it?" he asked incredulously. "What of the transformations?"

"She knows of them for it is a part of her and could not be prevented. But knowledge of her family, her father and I, and the Grail, are known only in her heart, but not in her thoughts for it would have put her at great risk." Her voice had gone very low and sad.

"Thomas brought her back to us from time to time — a few precious, stolen hours which we could not allow her to remember afterward because it would endanger her. Between those times, I had to rely on the stories he told us of her growing years. That and Vivian's gift of sight helped me know my other daughter.

"It was all that we had because it was necessary for her to believe that her real parents were dead in order for her to love Cullum and Mirren. But her powers are strong. Much stronger than her father realized.

"She has had dreams and visions, many of which are pieces of those memories of our times together. And her visions of you." At his questioning look, she nodded. "She knew you would come and she feared you. For in her visions she felt things she did not believe possible." When she looked at him again his gaze was fastened on Brianna.

"How long does the transformation last?"

"She controls it. It ends as soon as she wishes it to be ended. But this is different. She was wounded while transformed. But because of her fear of your discovering the truth, she transformed back. It was very dangerous. In order for her to be completely healed, it was necessary for her to return to the form she had taken when she was wounded. Even now, the healing takes place within her. When she is strong again, she will be herself once more." She reached out and laid a hand on his arm, propped on bent knee. She sensed both doubt and fear within him.

"She will again be the woman you fell in love with, warrior," she assured him for she could not bear the thought that he would now turn away from Brianna for it would surely destroy her.

"And the Darkness still waits beyond the light of the star," he replied.

His words took the fear from her heart. He accepted what she had told him. Perhaps Vivian was right. If so, then he was a warrior of rare courage.

"Yes," she answered gravely, as her gaze followed his to the looming darkness that seemed to press in on them like a gathering storm within the chamber walls.

"It waits and grows more powerful with each passing moment."

"Is that the reason you came here?"

"I came to heal my daughter's wounds."

His piercing blue gaze met hers — a gaze carried by another. Vivian had foreseen the truth in that as well, a truth he did not yet know.

"I think you came for another purpose as well."

She nodded sadly. Vivian had spoken truly of this as well.

He was shrewd and cunning, and possessed a keenness of thought sharper than most mortals.

"She must know the truth that has been kept from her all these years. Only the truth may save her and the Grail."

How long had they sat there closed within the soft glowing protection of the star pattern? It seemed like hours, and yet the candles which would usually have lasted no more than an hour still burned.

Laying between them, protected by the magic of the star's light, the golden cat stirred. Though he had seen it before, Tarek watched the transformation in stunned fascination and disbelief.

A veil of mist rose amid the light, wrapping around the creature like a silver shroud, glistening in the tips of its fur as he had seen it a hundred times in her hair, so that she seemed a creature of sunlight and mist.

Then the cat's features softened and gradually changed, fading to reveal other features beneath the tawny coat that slowly emerged. A length of slender arm, the curve of her throat, delicate features over fragile bones, the sensual curve of her mouth that he had kissed dozens of times and that had opened willingly and hungrily to his.

How much of her was mortal? How much still the creature?

Jehara. An ancient word among his people for creatures who belonged to neither world and yet were part of both.

Ninian watched him. What would he do now that he had the truth? He believed in the Jehara, but could he accept — as he must — that the woman he loved was one of them?

Or would he turn away in horror and disgust as Brianna had feared. All depended upon him. Brianna would need his help in what was yet to come. Even then, it might not be enough.

He touched Brianna's hand, where it lay curled on the dark fur much the same way as when she slept beside him. Instinctively he understood he could not have one without the other. She and the creature were bound to each other. It was part of her. His friend, Rorke FitzWarren, had spoken of that very thing before Tarek left for the north country.

"I am not certain that I can live with her," he had said of Lady Vivian as an uncertain future lay before them. *"Life with one such as her will be most vexing. Most assuredly it will never be dull."*

With a grin, he added, *"Nor will I lack for warmth with her powers of fire."* Then he had become most serious once more.

"The only certainty, my friend, is that I cannot live without her." It was the reason, Rorke FitzWarren had chosen to remain in Britain rather than return to his beloved Anjou. In giving up the past he had found the future.

Could he live without Brianna? Tarek now wondered.

He traced the curve of her cheek with his finger as he had countless times. Without waking, she turned toward his touch, the warmth of her breath bathing his skin in a memory of countless other ways she had touched him. In that brief contact and the fierce emotions it caused, he knew the answer. He could not.

A pounding at the door shattered the silence within the chamber. The flames at the candles quivered. Beneath his hand, he felt a tremor pass through her body. He glanced at Ninian, but her gaze was fastened on the doorway, her expression intense.

Then the flames at the candles steadied once more. The shadows in the chamber seemed to be held at bay, at least for the present.

"Move her to the bed," she said with lowered voice. "Then you may open the door."

He gently picked Brianna up from the floor and carried her to the bed. In the same order as she had first lit the candles, Ninian carried them to the bed and placed them about Brianna once more, restoring what was left of their protective power.

Her expression was grave. "There is no place safe from the power of the Darkness, warrior. But so long as the secret remains locked within, she is in no immediate danger."

"What will you do?"

"When she is strong enough, I will unlock the memories within her mind."

"And when she learns the truth?"

"Then she must seek the Grail. She is the only one with the knowledge to find it. It is the only way to stop the Darkness."

He nodded. "She will not go alone."

When Ninian had set the last candle in place, completing the star pattern, he went to the door and lifted the crossbar. Stephen of Valois waited anxiously in the hallway. His expression was grim, handsome features taut.

"What news?" Tarek asked.

"The soldiers you left to protect Inverness ended the same way as Mortain and his men. They were not human, and when discovered, crumbled and withered to dust, leaving behind grotesque features not recognizable by anyone at Inverness."

Tarek nodded. "And what of Mardigan?"

"Hundreds of raiders have been seen in the forest. They darken the sky with the black plumes of their headgear, and their blades are the color of night." Then he added in lowered voice, "Gavin de Marte and Malcolm were able to get close to an encampment." His expression contorted with memories of London and the fierce battle fought there against an enemy that could not be seen.

"They saw no faces behind their nose-plates and helms! Nothing, but the cursed darkness."

In the hall flames guttered at the torches making all uneasy. In the shadows, Tarek was certain he saw a movement, but when he pushed past Stephen with torch in hand he found nothing. Nothing but more shadows.

He turned back to Stephen. "Plans must be made." Then he turned to Ninian.

"Bar the door when I have gone. Let no one else inside."

Ninian did as he asked, but even as she lowered the bar into place across the door she knew it was pointless. When the Darkness chose to enter the chamber it would do so and not even the star spell could prevent it. Their only hope was the Grail and its unusual powers.

She turned back to the bed and the slender girl who lay there, with whom the hope for the future of all mankind now rested.

With a mother's fearful heart and a seer's terrible vision, she whispered, "Awaken daughter. It has begun."

Twenty

"Tell me everything about the raider encampment down to the smallest detail," Tarek demanded. "I want to know everything."

"Have you learned something else?" Stephen asked as they returned to the main hall and the large council table where the chieftains now gathered along with his own men. All except for Malcolm of Drummond.

Tarek nodded grimly, and spoke so that only Stephen might hear. "The woman you saw is a healer, sent by Lady Vivian."

"But how is that possible?" Stephen demanded. "London is many days journey from here." But even as he asked the question, his thoughts moved quickly ahead. His hand went to his sword, his amber gaze, like that of a fox scanning the main hall and all those within.

"Sweet Jesu!" he swore softly, remembering the fierce, deadly enemy they had faced once before. "The Darkness is here. The battle has not ended."

Gillie slipped out, escaping by way of Mirren's garden. She had discovered the small crawl space at the bottom of the wall behind a thicket of rosemary weeks ago when forced to work in the garden and now moved swiftly along the outer wall toward the heavily wooded forest that rimmed the rugged coastline.

The growing darkness was to her advantage as she glanced to the top of the wall. She waited and just as she anticipated, a guard appeared. He scanned the ground along the perimeter of the wall and she flattened herself into the shadows.

As he passed by above, she began to count as she moved quickly away from the wall as she had many times before — one, and two, and three, and four, and five, and six — the amount of time she knew passed before the next guard appeared. At the count of six she darted into the thick undergrowth at the edge of the wood.

She huddled there in the thick gorse and pine until her breathing eased. No alarm sounded from the battlements. When she again looked back at the fortress at Inverness, a strange gathering of darkness seemed to envelope it like a pall that slowly closed over everything.

The wind had come up as well and as darkness grew, lightning sliced the sky like dozens of swords, and thunder rolled like the sound of battle. She shivered and gathered her shawl more tightly about her. She was well rid of them all.

She pulled a face as she smoothed her hands over the coarse woolen fabric and thought of Brianna who had taken her in and then expected her to work like everyone else for her food and meager clothing as poor as any peasant might wear; the sharp-eyed Enya who was always watching her, ready to run to Brianna with word of her latest misdeed; and the giant Thomas, who always followed her, those great dark eyes watching, as if he knew what she was about. Her only regret was the new laird of Inverness.

Even now, she grew wet at the thought of Tarek al Sharif and how it might have been between them if not for Brianna — how different her entire life would have been if not for her cousin. She might have been the lady of Inverness.

As it was she was certain that she could have persuaded Tarek al Sharif into her bed if she had more time. And once he was there she was equally certain she would have quickened with his seed instead of the child she now carried.

She shivered again at the thought of a child, but for far different reasons than the cold. Babies were such helpless, needy little beggars. She had seen the young Scots women with their babes, the demands, the constant care that was needed. But there were a few advantages to be had in exchange if one kept her wits about her, and Gillie had always been clever. Especially with a man who had ambitions for a landhold, and lusty sons to hold it.

She cut through the forest, gauging her direction in the fading light that filtered down through the crowning tree tops. It seemed unusually quiet. Not a leaf or animal stirred. Even the water in the stream seemed unusually silent as it tumbled over rocks and through swirling pools. She gathered the shawl more tightly about her as she followed the stream deeper into the forest. Then suddenly, the warrior stepped in front of her from a piney thicket.

She pulled up with a start, for the man had the darkness of the devil about him, a looming shadow with no light upon his features. She wanted to turn and run but she didn't. He was a raider. He had the look of it in his costume with his leather jerkin and leggings, arms bare with hammered gold war bracelets, and metal dome helm. But his eyes . . .

She could not see them behind his helm and it made her uneasy for it was said that those with no eyes were the spawn of the devil.

To mask her fear she demanded, "Take me to him."

The warrior didn't immediately acknowledge her but stood there with short-bladed sword in one hand, and a double-edged war ax in the other. Even his weapons were black as if tarnished with soot. But a sooted blade would cut as deep as a clean one.

When she tried to step past him on the narrow path beside the stream he blocked her. Again she drew up, uneasy at the thought of touching such darkness. Even the air seemed fouled.

"I've brought word," she informed him. "If you don't take me to him, there will be the devil to pay."

Finally, he turned and led the way ahead beside the stream. The forest seemed to close around her. Branches snagged at her skirt and scraped her cheek. Finally they neared a rock-lined clearing and encampment sheltered within the ruins of an ancient stone circle.

She hesitated, uneasy in a place like this for there were those who believed stone circles such as these were the religious temples of the ancient gods whose likenesses were carved onto stones and the gnarled trunks of trees.

A single fire burned in the lee of the largest stone. About it gathered other raiders and the one she sought — Mardigan. Before she was through, he would believe it was his son she carried.

His thick, gold hair fell to his shoulders. His tunic was made of fur over smooth leather breeches and fur-lined leggings. Wide bands of gold, in gleaming war bracelets embossed with a fierce dragon's head, glinted at each wrist in the light of an uncertain moon that appeared briefly and was then smothered by the gathering clouds.

A single torch burned amid the stones, its light feeble and flickering. His expression was fierce and etched with hard lines above the full russet beard. Burnished gold brows angled sharply over blue eyes the color of a northern fjord.

He was a fierce, dangerous warrior who would sell his soul to the devil to claim a landhold in the highlands, and she had thrown her lot in with him. But that landhold had been denied by her uncle Cullum. When he had the information she brought, he would lay claim to Inverness, and she would be the lady of Inverness.

Malcolm had followed Gillie from the main hall, past the laundry, and through the gardens. What might Gillie seek from the gardens with night almost upon them?

She moved unerringly and without the need of a torch in the gathering darkness, as though the way was familiar to her. Then unexpectedly she disappeared behind the thick cover of growth at the back wall.

He found the crawl space, large enough for a good-sized man to pass through and immediately recognized it for Brianna had spoken of it. But he hesitated. If he emerged too quickly he might find Mardigan and his men waiting on the other side and there would be no opportunity to warn his kinsmen.

He listened at the wall for several moments. Hearing nothing, he crawled through and emerged on the outside of the wall. With a glance above he saw the guard as he made his pass along the battlements and none the wiser to Gillie's escape. She had timed it perfectly with the certainty of one who had planned this well, or perhaps done this before.

How many times before had she left Inverness in just that same way? Malcolm wondered. Had one of those times been the night of the raid when so many died? It was almost certain, for Gillie had miraculously escaped uninjured when so many of her kinsmen had been hacked to pieces by raiders who gained access to Inverness through open gates.

There was no time to summon the guard. Each moment that passed took Gillie deeper into the forest where he might never find her. And this was a highland matter to be settled in the highland way. Malcolm unsheathed the blade at his belt and quickly followed her into the forest. Gillie had much to account for.

A skilled tracker as were most of those who lived in the highlands, Malcolm quickly picked up traces of footprints in the soft loam that covered the floor of the forest. Certain that she had gone to meet someone, he kept a good distance between them, following the sound of her footfalls, his own silent as a fox as he moved on a parallel course through the wood.

When she stopped, he stopped. When she listened, he listened as well. And when she angled in a new direction along the course of the stream, he again followed. He was as stunned as she was by the sudden appearance of the warrior as though the man had materialized from the darkness.

Then he heard Gillie's startled gasp of surprise, followed by the familiar edge of anger in her voice. But he knew things Gillie did not, for he had ridden there hours earlier with Gavin de Marte.

Abandoning their horses in a secluded shelter of rocks they had moved afoot, both dressed in the highland way of doeskin breeches and tunics, blending with the shadows in another part of the forest, their faces smudged until they resembled those gnarled faces carved in the trunks of ancient trees, the blades of their swords smeared with mud to prevent them being seen.

For hours they crawled through the forest, listening for sounds, feeling the strangeness of the darkness that thickened and lowered over them. They found and heard nothing and were about to turn back when Gavin saw a movement among the shadows. Moving at an angle and some distance ahead, Malcolm almost blundered into the raider encampment.

There was no warning of their presence so close to the fortress. How had they possibly gotten there so quickly with no campfire, no jangling of harnesses, nor muted conversation that gave away their presence, only the faint shift of shadow within shadow, their darkness blending with the darkness of the night that rapidly closed round them.

They were dressed like raiders, their blades sooted to keep from reflecting any light and betraying their presence. But as Malcolm picked up Gavin's softly whistled warning and went completely still, he saw something that made his blood run cold.

There was only darkness behind the nose plates of the warriors' crude helms such as those worn by Norse raiders. Their features were not stained with mud. He saw no features at all. Only the gaping darkness where faces should have been!

Who were these warriors with no faces? How had they traveled so far in such a short amount of time from the northern hills where Mortain had led them to Mardigan's stronghold? Where was Mardigan? Was he here, too?

Unexpectedly, one of the raiders seemed to take command. No words were spoken. He simply stood, gathered his battle armor and moved off through the forest. The others joined him, like silent wraiths that moved at some unspoken command. Within only seconds — as suddenly as he had stumbled upon them — they were gone.

They made no sound in the forest. Nothing marked their passage. When he and Gavin emerged from their hiding places and tried to follow, there were no sounds or signs of which direction they had gone. No low, swaying tree limb, no broken twigs, no impressions left in the soft, loamy soil underfoot.

They were highly outnumbered and had no notion which direction the raiders had disappeared in, or how they had disappeared. Their only choice was to return to Inverness.

But now Malcolm again felt the same uneasiness as hours before, along with a chilling rage at Gillie's cold-hearted betrayal, and a disgust of self-loathing that he had ever found pleasure between her thighs.

She had come to him when they returned from the ride

north, informing him that she was with child and claiming that he was the father. He had seen the light of ambition in her eyes and turned her away. She had persisted, insisting that he make good by the child or she would go to Brianna and tell her that it was Tarek al Sharif's child. She had much to account for.

When the raider turned deeper into the wood, he followed.

"What is it?" Tarek demanded as he looked up from the council table and the parchment that was spread across detailing the fortifications of Inverness. His voice was edged with the futility of knowing the enemy they faced was not an enemy that could be fought with battle swords and strength alone.

Gavin de Marte entered the main hall. His expression was unlike anything Tarek had ever seen. Not the hardened expression of a warrior who faces the grim reality of the battle to come and the possibility of his own death, but the haunted expression of one who has seen beyond death. Behind him, two of his men carried a third. Or all that remained of him.

A crockery pitcher shattered on the floor stones. Nel screamed as she saw the man they carried.

"It's the same!" she shrieked hysterically, pointing to the dead man. "He has no face!"

Tarek knelt beside the dead warrior. The features were shrunken and withered, the bones of his skull exposed where the skin had dried and fallen away. Beneath his tunic was the same. Except for a grotesque death mask, the skeleton was all that remained.

The jaws were open in a fierce, deadly grin, the last expression before death. All that remained was the thick mane of familiar reddish hair and the ring the man had worn, too small for his own ring finger but worn instead on the smallest finger. A ring of golden amber and malachite which he had once hoped to place on Brianna's finger. Ian recognized the ring as well and wept openly for his dead son.

"It was exactly like Mortain and his men," Gavin said in a tone filled with rage and horror as he spoke low so that Ian would not hear. "He was still alive when we found him at the edge of the forest even as the flesh peeled away from his bones."

"Did he say anything?"

Gavin nodded. "The whore, Gillie, is also dead. It was she who betrayed Inverness to the raiders the night of the attack. She opened the gates. And there is more. She went to meet them tonight. She was with child."

"She had taken a lover among the raiders," Stephen concluded. "And betrayed her kinsmen for her own ambitions."

Gavin nodded. "She had gone to Mardigan, but he would not have her."

"He had no further use of her," Tarek said grimly, remembering Lady Ninian's prophetic warning. The Darkness had found Brianna.

Twenty-one

"Why?" Brianna demanded, her eyes filled with pain, confusion, and anger.

"Why was I not allowed to know the truth? All those years, knowing only that I was not like other little girls, the dreams and visions, the first transformation . . ."

She closed her eyes as she remembered the first time and her terror of this unknown thing that had happened to her. She rounded on Ninian.

"The rumors and superstitions about such things, the things people said. My own doubts. I was terrified of what was happening. I thought I must be going mad. If not for Thomas . . ." Her voice rose again in anger.

"That is precisely the reason we sent Thomas to be with you."

"I needed you," Brianna argued, again close to very human tears, "and you weren't there to explain these things to me."

Struggling for her own composure, Ninian realized how painful the truth could be for both of them. This beautiful golden daughter of hers, her daughter of the mist, was no fey, mild-mannered creature, but as strong-willed, stubborn, and as fierce as her first born.

"I *was* there, Brianna," she said gently, at the same time reaching out with her thoughts, trying to calm her very emotional daughter. She immediately found her thoughts blocked at every attempt.

"Oh, no," Brianna informed her as she clearly sensed the

attempted control. "I will not be controlled or dissuaded to believe otherwise. I want the entire truth. All of it."

"I have told you everything," Ninian replied. "Do you believe you would have been able to accept the transformations if I had not been there in my own way to guide you?" She quickly went on, as Brianna halted her angry tirade and seemed at least to consider what she was saying.

"The transformation is your special power. It could not be stopped or hidden from you. We are alike in that, my daughter," she added, her voice softening as she was able to speak the precious word *daughter* at last, with the comfort that Brianna would now remember it. But it was a small comfort. Brianna was so angry, could she ever bring herself to speak the word Ninian longed and needed to hear in return?

"Though I could not always be with you, I was always bound to you. Here," Ninian laid her fingers against her forehead. "And here." Then she laid her hand over her heart.

"But I was not allowed to remember it!" Brianna angrily accused. "You and my father abandoned me! I thought you gave me up because you didn't want me."

"We gave you into the care of two people who loved you as their own and gave their lives for you, because we loved you! Then I was forced to accept the little time we had together, building a lifetime of love out of stolen moments, watching others receive your love in return, and share your life as I could not!"

The air in the chamber crackled with their combined anger, like that of a storm building within while the storm beyond gathered with equal force.

Do not be quick to anger, wife! she heard the caution of warning in her thoughts. *You must be patient. This is all new to her.*

"Be quiet! You dear old fool," Ninian snapped. "There is

no time for patience! She must be made to understand."

Brianna looked at her with a frown. "You speak to walls?"

"Your father. He is most impatient that you understand everything." Ninian began again to explain.

"You had no memory, while I remembered every painful, empty moment of babies I could not hold or care for, of children's kisses never felt, and the silent void of children's laughter." Tears glistened at Ninian's eyes.

"I remembered every empty moment and wished that I could not," she said fiercely. "For then perhaps the pain might have gone away."

As much as she stubbornly tried to hold onto her anger, Brianna found she could not. Such was the pain of the knowledge she now possessed that she realized hers was not the only pain suffered, nor perhaps the greatest. So deeply was she connected to Ninian — the woman of her dreams — now that her memory had been opened, she felt Ninian's heart breaking.

"You will not understand until you have a child of your own," Ninian said softly. "They are the greatest joy, and the greatest torment you will ever know."

"Is it possible then?" Brianna asked, the anger now completely gone from her voice, and replaced with a longing of hope.

"Is what possible, daughter?"

"To have a child? A mortal child? To live a mortal life?"

In this tentative moment, with both of them so close to tears, Ninian sensed Brianna's uncertainty and fear.

"Your love is strong for him. You will need such a love for what is to come." Ninian nodded. "You are mortal, Brianna. As much as I am mortal, and all my children as well. There is not a hedgehog or crow among them. At least not the last time I checked."

Brianna grinned through her tears. "But perhaps one stubborn mule?" she suggested.

Ninian smiled through her own tears. "Aye, but she will be fine when she has transformed into her true self once more."

Then Brianna's soft green gaze grew somber. "It is very near, isn't it." For she could sense the oppressiveness of evil Ninian had spoken of. It seemed to crowd the walls of the chamber, pressing in, smothering the light of the candles as though trying to smother them out.

"Yes, very near."

"And the only hope is the Grail."

"It must not become an instrument of the Darkness." Ninian held up a hand. "Be patient, daughter. You possess the knowledge of the Grail as no other. In time the memory of it will return."

"Then how will I know where it may be found?"

"That too will be revealed to you. If it were learned all at once, the Darkness would steal the knowledge from you. Such is its power that not even I could prevent it."

"What of my husband?"

Ninian felt the power of Brianna's love for him, a love that made her both strong and vulnerable.

"He is part of it now and can escape it no more than you can." Ninian frowned as she looked down at her clasped hands, trying to find words for the other things Brianna should know even though it would cause her very mortal pain.

"What is it?"

Ninian looked up. Even as she had tried to protect her own thoughts from her daughter until she had time to bring some order to them, Brianna had sensed her emotions about them. The power was strong within her daughter.

It gave Ninian both hope and concern, for though the powers had always been with her daughter, they had been

375

kept safely hidden. No one, including Ninian, knew the true extent of those powers. That was for Brianna to now discover. Her concern was that it was much like a mortal child who is first given a taste of freedom. That freedom could be a wonderful gift or a devastating curse, depending on how it was handled.

"There is something more you are not telling me," Brianna broke through her troubled thoughts. "Something has already happened."

"Much has happened," Ninian sighed sadly. "The Darkness has been regaining strength since its first encounter with your sister. It uses mortals for its own ends."

Brianna frowned "Uses them?" Then she realized what Ninian spoke of. "Aye," she nodded with growing clarity, "the warriors who were transformed into those hideous creatures but with familiar faces of those we believed we could trust."

Ninian nodded. "It is a common transformation frequently used by the Darkness for it is a means for it to work its evil among mortals without being discovered until it is too late." She watched her daughter steadily, then saw the moment of enlightenment when Brianna first knew.

"There were others who were transformed," Brianna said with sudden certainty. "Here at Inverness."

"Yes, daughter."

"Gillie!"

"It was not difficult for the seeds of evil were born in that one. Gillie was here the night your adopted parents died."

Brianna sighed brokenly. "She betrayed Inverness. But why?" Her searching gaze again met Ninian's, but there was no need to ask for the answer came to her with lightning swiftness. Plucked from Ninian's thoughts with the swiftness of a blade.

"Her own greed," Brianna said sadly. "She turned to the Darkness because of her hatred for me."

"There are some for whom the Darkness dwells in their souls from the moment they are first created. The Ancient Ones teach that it is part of the balance that must be kept in the mortal world," Ninian explained.

Brianna nodded. "She cast her lot with Mardigan." Then added with equal certainty. "She is dead." But her look of sadness was matched by a new knowledge. "But not by Mardigan."

Fresh tears welled in her eyes as she said on a single word, "Malcolm." And knew that her friend was also dead.

"Yes," Ninian replied. "He discovered her betrayal and followed her when she went to meet Mardigan only these hours past while you slept and healed from your wounds. For all his anger at you daughter, he was a true and loyal friend."

Brianna nodded, equal to her sadness over Malcolm's death was the anger at the knowledge that he had been slain by the Darkness. No more would she share laughter with him. No more would he tease her. Now, a new fear returned, strong and powerful.

Sensing that fear, Ninian shook her head. "You can not protect your husband from it, daughter. Nor can you prevent his part in this. By what your sister has told me, he is a believer of such things that you and I are part of. He will not allow you to go alone on the journey that lies ahead. I am counting on that, for you will need his warrior's strength and courage. The Darkness has not counted on that."

"I will not risk his life," Brianna said adamantly, stubbornness returning in the clear green of her eyes and steeliness in her voice. "I would die first."

"The risk is his own, Brianna, and not for you to say. For

if you fail, all is lost. Including Tarek al Sharif and the love you have found together."

"But if an army of warriors cannot stand against the Darkness, if my father could not stop it and save Arthur's kingdom, then how is it possible for me to find the Grail?"

"Cunning, true courage, and by the same means the master of Darkness uses so well, my daughter." Ninian's eyes gleamed. "With deception, of course. The true art of a changeling."

"Tell me what I must know, Mother."

Tears welled in Ninian's eyes at the sound of that word she had despaired of ever hearing from this beautiful golden child, her daughter of the mist.

"It will require deceiving your husband."

"Will the deception endanger him?"

"Nay, daughter. It will protect him, just as the knowledge kept from you protected you."

"Where is she?" Tarek demanded as he turned on Ninian. "I left this chamber but two hours ago and she lay near death in that bed. What conjuror's trick is this?"

"A necessary one," Ninian explained in soothing tones as she laid a hand at his arm. He jerked away from her as if burned by fire.

"By the Prophet, I will not stand for your tricks!"

She was not angry, but instead warned, "Your god cannot help you in this, Tarek al Sharif." Then she reminded him, "You vowed she would not go alone."

His eyes narrowed. "Has it begun already?"

She nodded as she turned toward an urn on a wrought iron stand at the table. Through an opening in the bottom a stream of sand sifted steadily into a basin below.

"Time grows short."

"Answer this," he demanded. "Is she safe?"

"For now, yes."

"May I see her?"

"In a manner of speaking. You will accompany her, for the journey must begin."

Then the hardest question of all. "Will I lose her?"

"Only if you lose yourself."

"Damn you, woman! Do not speak in riddles!"

"I speak only the truth." She glanced once more to the timepiece. "For over five hundred years the Grail has been safely hidden until the time when its power might be joined with the power of Excalibur. There was none who could do it with Merlin banished to the world between the worlds. There was no one to challenge the Darkness. Until now.

"The Darkness will use all its power to prevent the power of the Light joining with the power of the Grail." Her gaze held his, intense, and with a longing of hope.

"It will try to stop you. But you must succeed. Brianna must join her power with that of the Grail. If you fail in what lies before you when the last grain of sand has run out, then all is lost."

He did not fully understand the ways of sorcerers, sorceresses, and changelings, but he believed in the powers he had seen. And now Brianna was part of it, and the only way to save her was to help her do what she must do.

"How do I prepare for this journey?"

"You will face three challenges in order to reach the Grail. They cannot be revealed beforehand for the risk of the Darkness discerning and solving them are great. You must meet each challenge. If you fail in any of them, the Grail will be lost to the Darkness."

"How can you be certain I can accomplish this?"

"I cannot. But Brianna is certain. She trusts in you." Then

she explained as much as she could of the tests he would confront. "You will face a challenge of cunning, one of true heart, and one of courage. You must find it within yourself to meet each."

"May I take my sword?"

"For all the good it will do you, by all means. But the greatest battle you face cannot be fought with a sword." Walking with him to the door of the chamber she explained, "There are others who travel with you. They wait in the yard below." She approached closer then and spoke solemnly.

"I know of the medallion you wear. Brianna told me of it. But I would give you another, a talisman to bring good fortune."

A dark brow arched over crystal blue eyes. "Good fortune?" he replied with more than a little sarcasm. "I would have thought a changeling would have no need of such things as good luck charms."

She shrugged and smiled. "I leave nothing to chance where my daughter is concerned. And you will need all the luck you can find, warrior. The crystal contains the greatest power I could send with you."

He snorted, as he accepted the token. "Your confidence in my ability is overwhelming."

The talisman was much smaller than the hammered gold medallion — a remembrance of the father he had searched a lifetime for, and had vowed to kill.

Ninian's luck token was no bigger than the tip of his small finger, a clear crystal teardrop cut with hundreds of facets and suspended from a green satin ribbon.

As he secured it to his belt, Ninian's hand closed over his arm in a fierce grasp. Her expression was no longer amused but deadly serious.

"Once you leave this place, warrior, my powers cannot

help you. Nor can I see the fate that awaits you. You will be guided in the direction you must go. But what you encounter there, you and your companions must face alone. Some will survive, others will not." Then her grasp tightened. "If Brianna should fail, if her heart should turn from the power of the Light to the power of the Darkness . . ."

"She will not," he said, refusing to believe otherwise. "Her heart is true and loyal."

"The heart you know is true and loyal, her mortal heart. I speak of her soul." Her grasp tightened until her nails dug into the muscles at his arm.

"If she should turn to the Darkness, you must stop her. She must not be allowed to return to the mortal world."

His fierce blue gaze met hers. "Explain this to me."

"If the Darkness can turn her, it will use her powers and the knowledge of the Grail. You must vow before the god you believe in and to me that you will not allow that to happen."

He felt a cold rage as he realized what she asked. "She is my wife! I could never harm her!"

"And she is my daughter!" Ninian replied fiercely. "I love her no less. But I understand far better than you what is at stake." Tears welled in her eyes. "If the Darkness claims her soul she will be your wife no longer. She will be a creature of Darkness. I must have your vow!" she insisted. "You must swear it! If you refuse, she must go alone."

"You give me no choice," he said furiously.

"Absolutely none, warrior."

The expression in his eyes was as cold as death when he finally nodded his agreement. "You have my vow."

"Then make ready to leave, warrior."

"How far is the journey?"

"A journey of a lifetime, yet only a day's ride away. In a place you have been before, yet where no other mortal has ever gone." She handed him the Persian blade.

"Where is Brianna?" he asked as he belted it to his waist.

"As I explained, she will be with you." She then handed him the large skin from the bed, still warm with Brianna's touch. Her fingers brushed the heavy gold medallion that hung around his neck.

"You will be faced with a very difficult choice, warrior," she cautioned as she stared at the medallion, "Choose wisely."

As they reached the training yard, he turned on her, "Where are my men?"

"Your men are all here," she assured him, with a gesture that encompassed the yard and the outlying buildings. "They must remain behind, as will I. For none of us may go where you go. 'Tis only that you cannot see them in this place between the mortal and immortal world." She smiled faintly as a dark brow lifted.

"Remember, warrior, you leave the mortal world behind when you pass through those gates. And they may not follow."

"Are they safe?"

"They will remain so, unless you fail."

In her unspoken words, he sensed the rest of the answer. If he failed they would end as Malcolm, Mortain, and the others had ended. He nodded his understanding.

"What of Mardigan? He will surely attack."

Mardigan is also part of this, warrior. You have seen the proof of it in the men who died here."

"Has he turned to the Darkness?" he asked, for he remembered the treachery of the bishop against King William, his own brother.

"The Darkness uses many weapons. You must be prepared to face anything."

He nodded his understanding. It explained a great many things, including why he and his men could never find Mardigan. Like a phantom that disappeared at will.

"What of the companions you spoke of?" He saw only the Arabian mare, saddled and waiting, a water skin and pouch of food tied to the saddle. No other horses awaited their riders. As he swung atop the mare, Ninian whistled softly.

There was a stirring in the air overhead and through the enveloping darkness like an oppressive, smothering pall, he heard the sound of wings.

A falcon appeared in the fluttering light of the torch Ninian carried. She did not seek Ninian's arm, but swept past to light on Tarek's outstretched arm.

She was slender and sleek, her feathers tipped with silver and gold, her eyes a golden green color as she contemplated him with a cunning intelligence. He looked down at Ninian with narrowed gaze.

Sensing his question, she assured him, "She can go where you cannot go and see what you cannot see. You will find her a worthy companion."

"You spoke of three companions. I see only one."

"You see what you want to see, warrior. You must learn to see what is not so easily seen." She made a summoning gesture with her hand. Still he saw no one. Then a stirring movement among the shadows in the yard. A large, tawny cat slowly walked toward him. His furious gaze met Ninian's.

"No conjuror's trick?" he spat out accusingly.

"No trick of mine," she assured him, and then explained, "Remember, warrior, you must look beyond the obvious. You have three companions. One swift and sure footed, capable of bearing you on your journey; one powerful and agile, with the instincts of the hunter; the other capable of seeing what you cannot see. These are your companions." Then as she sensed his thoughts, she nodded.

"Yes, a deception which even you must not know the truth of. Brianna will be with you, but even you must not know which form she has taken."

He nodded, his expression taut at the thought of the task that lay ahead, an ordeal from which neither of them might return. Ninian touched his hand where it lay at the saddle.

"Remember your vow to me, Tarek al Sharif. If her heart and soul are turned to the Darkness, you must not hesitate. For there is another daughter with whom there may still be hope." At his look of surprise, she shook her head.

"I can say no more. Time grows short. Remember this — the greatest strength is not this," she touched the handle of the blade at his side.

"It is this." She laid her hand over his heart. "And remember too," she warned, "the Darkness cannot take from you what you will not surrender. Fear and hatred are its weapons. Guard against them."

With a nod, he set his heels to the Arabian mare and sent her through the gates. When he had ridden several yards past, he reined the mare in and looked back. In the gathering twilight he saw no torches from the battlements, nor at the gates. There were no gates. Nor were there battlements. The fortress at Inverness had vanished as if it had never existed.

You have passed from the mortal into the immortal world, warrior. What you knew before has ceased to exist. The way back lies with the Grail.

Twenty-two

The falcon set their course, soaring ahead, guiding him across a terrain that was unfamiliar, filled with shadows, a foreign land he no longer recognized even though he had ridden through it only hours before.

Or was it days? Or weeks? How many grains of sand had passed through the glass since he had left? A few? All?

In this place, things as he knew them had ceased to exist. There were no familiar landmarks. There were no lush green forests, mountains, or windswept moors.

He had entered the world of the Jehara, the immortal world of Darkness and Light were the powers of good and evil were precariously balanced, where truth no longer existed, and deception was everywhere. Even among his companions.

Which had Brianna used her powers to transform into?

His gaze instinctively went to the cat. It seemed the most logical since he had seen her earlier transformation. The color was there in the creature's coat as well as the eyes with flecks of green among the gold. It would be like Ninian to attempt to throw him off by suggesting it was one of the others.

What fate awaited them?

He would gladly face anything if he could prevent risking her life, but he knew he could not. He remembered vividly Rorke FitzWarren's journey into the ancient catacombs in London. Eventually his friend had been willing to tell of it — the deceptions, his own weaknesses that the Darkness used as a weapon against him, the fear not for himself, but for Lady

Vivian whom the Darkness sought to destroy. The man who had returned from the catacombs was still his friend, but changed in deep and profound ways.

"It was not death I feared," he told Tarek afterward. *"For I have faced death a thousand times on the battlefield. You know as well as I that there is that one moment when fear is gone and only the strength of your belief remains. No,"* he shook his head. *"I did not fear dying. I feared the power of the evil of the Darkness. It is relentless, and it is still with us."*

And when asked how he defeated it, Rorke responded, *"I have not defeated it. That is a battle for another day. But I could not have driven it back into its dark lair without the power of Excalibur."*

But the old blind woman, Meg, Lady Vivian's nurse and a changeling, believed otherwise.

"You were the power of Excalibur, warrior," she had told Rorke. *"Like many before you, you were given a choice. Your heart was true. You chose well and once chosen it was the power of that choice — in your heart — that became the power of Excalibur."*

Choices.

Ninian had spoken of choices which must be made. But could he make the right choice? Would he even know it when confronted with it?

He continued on until the Arabian mare was sweated and lathered beneath him with the arduous climb over rocks and steep hills. Eventually, following the course the falcon set, they reached the top of the last hill. The blackened landscape of a desolate land and the shoreline of a great vast lake spread below.

The sky darkened as they reached the shoreline. The lake was lone and gleaming like a dark ribbon that cut through the land, just as he and Brianna had seen it the day they rode from Inverness.

"I know this place," he said aloud even though there was no one to answer.

"Lochonnen," he repeated the name Brianna had called it that day they had ridden across the highlands, inland to the shimmering lake upon whose shores grew the rowan bush. And in the middle of the lake, sheltered in the mist, was the island of the Grail. She carried the mark of the Grail on her shoulder, those joined circles which symbolized life ever-lasting.

She had not known the meaning of it then. But now he understood. Her fate was bound to the Grail.

He found the rowan, but in a different place than before. It was on the opposite side of the shoreline. Instead of green and lush, its branches were barren of any leaves, like the skeleton of the bush they had seen.

Just as that day, the legend of the Grail whispered through his thoughts, as if Brianna spoke the words again. He gazed out across the murky darkness of the water and in that place where water and sky met was a shimmer of fading light.

Fanciful, he had called Brianna when she had told him to look at that very place. Yet, for a moment he thought he saw something on the horizon across the water. Then it was gone.

It suddenly grew dark, like a heavy curtain drawn over the sky. Light faded at the horizon, sky and water blending into a thickness of darkness that was oppressive in its stillness of silence, and could almost be felt. There wasn't a sound. Not even the water could be heard lapping against the shoreline.

No moon rose on the horizon, bright and clear, its white pearlescent light bathing the land below. No stars winked overhead. It was as if every glimmer of light had been extinguished by some malevolent hand.

It was impossible to continue on without a torch to light

the way. As if sensing this, the falcon settled herself in the up-permost branches of the rowan with a fluttering of wings, her gaze turned toward the water.

The cat too seemed to accept that here they would make their camp for the night, if indeed it was night, as he felt her brush against his leg. Reaching a hand down as he would to a well-heeled hound, he felt the lush velvet of golden fur at his fingertips. The creature's regal head was also turned toward the expanse of water that lay before them as though she too watched for something.

He unsaddled the mare. She was nervous, her ears con-stantly flicking back and forth as she listened for sounds that were not there. He spoke to her softly in his own language, a rhythm of soft clicking sounds and words that usually calmed her.

There was no grass for the mare to graze on, so he gave her handfuls of grain from a pouch he carried then led her to the water to drink.

In the darkness he could not see it, but he heard it. In the vast, pervasive silence, the sudden sound of the water against the shoreline at his feet.

It was not a gentle lapping sound, but more like the sound of a pot boiling and churning at the hearth. Then he was thrown off balance as the embankment suddenly began to crumble away.

It was as if the earth had suddenly disappeared beneath his feet. Water washed over his boots and soft mud sucked at his boots. It dragged at his ankles as though powerful hands were pulling him down, dragging him into the churning water.

With a snort of alarm, the mare lunged backward, the reins suddenly taut in his hand. They became a lifeline.

Tarek called to the mare as he had countless times on a battlefield, relying on her speed, agility, and strength. He desperately needed that strength now for he had never experienced such power as that of the water that steadily pulled him toward certain death.

Twisting the reins tightly about his wrist, he called to her, "Hiyah! Scirocco! Back!"

He heard the frantic pawing of hooves as she struggled for a foothold, and the falcon's shrill, piercing cries of alarm. The embankment crumbled beneath his back and shoulders as he was sucked farther into the water. Again he called to the mare.

The reins slackened then grew taut once more. The mare frantically pawed the shifting shoreline as she dug in, lost footing, and dug in again.

Pain tore through his arm and shoulder, stretched at a brutal angle. He pulled and kicked, trying to free his legs of the dragging weight.

Eventually, he freed one foot, scrabbled for a foothold and attempted to lever himself up the embankment. Twice the embankment gave way beneath him, as if some creature was burrowing in and eroding it beneath him.

Then, he dug in once more. This time his boot heel found solid footing. He called again to the mare and as she strained at the reins, his other foot dragged free with a sucking sound.

As the mare continued backing away, he was dragged high up the embankment and away from the water's edge. He collapsed, cold, wet, and exhausted, the mare standing over him, blowing warm air across him as she nuzzled his shoulder.

"Y'ahla, Scirocco," he praised her, his hand bloodied from where the reins had cut through flesh as she pulled him to safety.

When he finally had the strength to sit up, his gaze fastened on the dark, murky water that had almost taken his life.

Ninian was right. It had begun.

He made his bed beneath the branches of the rowan. The fur Ninian had sent with him provided warmth over his wet tunic and breeches. He was exhausted from the ride and the ordeal at the water, but sleep was long in coming.

The wind came up across the water, silent and brutal. He pulled the fur tighter against a coldness that seemed to move through the fur as though intent on freezing him before morning. It was then, the cat settled beside him, golden-green eyes glowing as she stared off into the gathering of darkness.

She blocked the wind as she curled beside him, her heat penetrating the fur mantle and warming him. In the darkness he could see the soft glow of her eyes as she stared watchfully out across the water.

Instinctively, Tarek reached out and stroked her thick, golden fur. She did not become uneasy at human contact, nor did she lash out at him as other wild creatures might have. Instead, she curled closer, arching her neck beneath his stroking hand, a soft purring of contentment heard low at her throat.

"Brianna," he whispered, uncertain whether she heard or even knew him as he tenderly stroked the sleek creature that lay beside him as she had lain beside him, and as he longed to have her beside him again. And in his agony of longing, he remembered Ninian's parting words as tears had filled her eyes.

"If her heart and soul turn to the Darkness, you must not hesitate."

"She is my wife!"

"And my daughter. But you must swear it."

Wife. Lover. Joy and laughter. Strength and courage. She was all of those to him and more.

When had she come to mean so much to him? But he knew

the answer. It had happened long ago beside a highland pool when a beautiful creature appeared out of the mist and risked her life for his own. A creature who haunted his thoughts and dreams, and now lived in his heart.

His fingers curled in the thick, golden fur as he imagined the feel of her hair in his hands. He had made a vow. He knew it must be kept. But, if it came to it, how could he bear to kill her?

"Curse you, Ninian, and your vow," he whispered fiercely. But he knew his hatred was misplaced as he stared out across the murky dark water. "Curse the Darkness."

The falcon's soft, whistling cry woke him.

He had no idea how long he had slept for there was no way to gauge the passage of time. In this place where so many things now were opposite of what they had been before, he trusted in nothing but the sword at his side and the creatures that had made the journey with him.

The falcon swept from the top of the rowan tree into the air, circling nearby and calling over and over. His gaze instinctively fastened on the surface of the lake. A glimmer of light appeared far out over the water — the horizon as the darkness of sky and water separated. And there in the pale gray dawn, he thought he saw the outline of land.

He quickly rose and walked toward the shoreline, mindful of his narrow escape the night before. The cat too rose and stalked the edge of the shoreline.

The narrow sliver of gray between sky and water gradually widened and grew lighter, the dark shape of land clearly outlined at the horizon. An island.

The island of the Grail, according to the ancient legend Brianna had told him about.

Lightning appeared at the horizon, just over the distant island. Then there were more flashes of lightning that gradually drew closer and closer to the edge of the lake. Was it real, or some illusion? And what of the island? Could it be reached?

The question brought back vivid memories of the night before and his narrow escape from death. Even now the water quivered and moved in strange ways, as if something dark and malevolent stirred in its depths.

The falcon continued her frantic calling, sweeping far over the water and then returning. Waves churned the surface of the lake, rising far above the seething water as if they reached for the sleek, swift huntress. The cat too had grown restless, her gaze fastened on that narrow ribbon of light at the horizon.

The falcon had brought them there. According to legend the Grail lay somewhere on that distant shore. But how was he to reach it? Sprout wings and fly?

"What now, Ninian?" he called out angrily, as if she could hear. "How is it to be done? I do not have the power to cross the water like the Jehara."

You will face three challenges, warrior.

It was as if Ninian's words whispered back in answer.

"I willingly accept any challenge, but this," he gestured across the expanse of water, "it is impossible."

The way is there warrior, if you choose to see it.

"If I choose to see it!" He angrily swung back around toward the water, with dire thoughts about his mother-in-law. If any of them made it out of this alive, he must seriously consider what was to be done about her.

"If I choose to see it," he muttered.

Be careful, warrior, came the warning thought weaving through his own as if Ninian stood just behind him. *You still need my help.*

"I need a boat."

You must learn to see more than the obvious, warrior. Remember, all is not what it appears to be. What need have you of a boat, when you may ride across the water?

"All is not what it appears," he repeated as he stared out across the water, trying to see what more there might be. He saw nothing. It was like staring out across the expanse of desert where his ancestors were once kings. This water was like a desert, shifting, changing, hiding its secrets.

He had been in the western empires so long fighting as a mercenary to any king or lord who would pay him that he had forgotten the ways of the desert. The way one could look at something so hard and not see it right in front of him.

He had no idea what he looked for, only Ninian's words to guide him. He let go of every thought, every emotion, every awareness, opening his mind as he looked out across the water toward that distant island.

In the pale gleam of light that streaked from the horizon to the shoreline, he saw a narrow ribbon of land — a causeway only a few feet wide — that lay just beneath the surface of the water and connected the island to the shore. But was it real or an illusion?

He hesitated. His experience the evening before made him wary. It was too easy. And he had learned, as Ninian had warned, things were not what they seemed. Yet, across the water, he could see the island. Was the Grail there?

Was it also an illusion of the Darkness?

Overhead, the falcon circled restlessly. She flew far over the water, in the direction of the island, then swept back. Tarek whistled her down. She swept low and alighted, her talons gentle as they closed over his arm.

Swift and sure, she could see what he could not. As he spoke her sleek head angled back and forth catching the subtle tones of his voice as if she understood. Then she swept

393

aloft once more and again flew out over the water in the direction of the island, setting the course as she had before.

Tarek cautiously walked down the embankment toward the edge of the water. Unlike the night before, the water was calm. He seized several rocks from the embankment and tossed them onto the causeway.

They plopped into the water that lapped across the surface. None disappeared, dragged below the surface by sucking sand, nor did the water suddenly churn and boil as if some creature stirred in its depths. Instead, he could see them clearly on the causeway just a few inches beneath the surface of the water.

Deception was the tool of the Darkness. He knew well, it was also the tool of the Jehara. Brianna was a changeling, capable of taking different forms. More deception.

He stepped tentatively out onto the causeway. It was solid beneath his feet. The water remained calm. Returning to the embankment, he stripped the mare of saddle and any unnecessary burden.

The cat waited expectantly on the shore, her tawny tail twitching back and forth as if in anticipation of this next part of their journey. The falcon would be safe enough in the air, but the lioness would be as vulnerable as he once they were out on the causeway.

His gaze fastened on that distant shore of the island. How far, he wondered? A thousand yards? More? It was impossible to tell. Seizing the reins in his hand, he vaulted onto the mare's back and turned her toward the causeway. Overhead the leaden sky seemed to be lowering once more. The island was no longer as clear as it had been only moments before. Or was it longer?

"Hiyah, Scirocco!" he called to the mare. "Now you must be like the wind!"

He sent her down the embankment and out onto the causeway. The cat followed alongside, her long, sinuous stride easily matching that of the mare's, while overhead the falcon flew straight toward that distant shore.

The wind came up, churning the clouds overhead until they seemed to lay over the water. Lightning flashed, slicing the sky like white blades as though trying to drive back the darkness. To both sides of the causeway the water became equally restless in waves that swept over the causeway and churned beneath the mare's hooves.

He let the mare have her head, laying low over her neck as the storm built. As it had the night before, the water became dark and murky, like a malevolent force that fought to turn them back.

It swept over the sides of the causeway, sucking at the mare's feet, dragging at her. Tarek felt her begin to tire as the island still seemed hundreds of yards away and drawing no closer.

Through the rain that had begun to fall, he saw the cat not far behind, leaping in great bounding strides as the water deepened over the causeway. Then the mare stumbled. She went down as the causeway crumbled beneath them, struggled for a foothold, and fought her way back to her feet. With each stride the causeway disappeared beneath her hooves, water swirling about her knees, sucking her down. He could no longer see the island.

Then lightning burst overhead, golden white, bright as the sun, illuminating the sky like a torch. The island was only a few yards away. But the mare was played out beneath him.

Water surged past her haunches. She lunged forward, struggling to find the next foothold even as her back legs were sucked out from under her. Still, she struggled and fought, clawing her way to the shoreline, making one last desperate lunge that threw him over her neck without the saddle to hold onto.

He was thrown onto the shore. The coarse gravel tore through his tunic and ripped the flesh from the palms of his hands. Then he was being dragged backward, back toward the water by the reins wound tight about his hand. He rolled to his knees and grabbed hold of the reins with both hands.

The causeway had completely disappeared beneath the churning water. Waves lashed the rocks. Connected by the length of rein, the Arabian struggled to reach the shore. But no matter how she fought for a foothold, she was pulled deeper, sucked down by that same dragging weight that had nearly taken him the night before.

He called to her, shouting to make himself heard over the force of the storm. But it was no use. The harder she fought, the more she was pulled under, dragging him with her.

Some will survive, others will not.

Ninian's prophetic words echoed in his brain even as he fought to save the mare. The reins bit through the skin at his hands. If he held on he too would be dragged under. With a cry of helpless rage he opened his hand and let the reins slip from his grasp.

He struggled back up the embankment, away from the grasping death of the water. When he looked back the mare was gone, dragged beneath the surface of the water.

Twenty-three

Tarek cursed the storm, the darkened sky overhead, and his own feelings of helplessness.

The Arabian had carried him through many battles, saved his life countless times including now, and formed a bond with young Duncan as she had with no other.

Then he experienced a new fear as he recalled Ninian's words about the three companions sent to accompany him. He had been so certain Brianna had again taken the form of the cat, but what if she had not?

The falcon's screeling cry overhead broke through his rage and fear. She swept low overhead, alighting on an outcropping of nearby rock. Her sleek head cocked first in one direction and then another, golden eyes watching him sharply.

Then she leapt into the air once more, sweeping back and forth across the face of the rocky cliff that rose from the shore, extending her flight with each pass she made, once again setting the course.

Nearby, the cat shook water from her thick fur. Glancing over at him with those luminous golden-green eyes she then leapt upon the first shelf of rock where the falcon had perched. She glanced back again, and then bounded farther up the rocky mountain.

Though he sorely felt the loss of the Arabian, his greater fear eased. He was certain Brianna was still alive among his companions.

As he secured his sword at his belt, his fingers brushed the crystal talisman Ninian had given him. He prayed it brought good fortune. He would have need of it.

It seemed as if the island was made entirely of rock. The shore was covered with pieces of crushed rock, and stark, gleaming rock cliffs rose almost straight up.

The falcon had disappeared somewhere overhead. He whistled to her and she reappeared, sweeping low from outcropping to outcropping. The cat leaped impatiently on ahead.

He had no notion how long they climbed. As with the ride to the shores of the lake, time seemed to move out of itself. It might have been an hour, or several hours. It might have been days.

There was no daylight, only the lowering grayness that seemed to smother the sun as the Darkness clung to the peak of the island. Below, the shoreline had disappeared, the murky dark water seething up around the rocks they climbed, closing off any hope of return.

Eventually he reached a ledge. Here the falcon ceased her restless flight to perch on a rock beside an opening into the side of the mountain.

He hesitated, wondering if this was another deception. A trap perhaps. But he saw no other way in.

"By the Prophet," he muttered with a warrior's instinctive uneasiness of such places. "It could not be out in the open, on the shore below, or on top of the mountain. No, we must travel inside the mountain!"

The falcon blinked at him and ruffled her feathers impatiently. The cat stared at him.

He unsheathed the sword, his other hand closing over the talisman at his belt. Ninian had warned him of three challenges that must be met if he was to find the Grail.

"Let it begin," he said solemnly as he held the blade before him, ducked his head, and entered the cave only to discover that it was not a cave at all, but the opening to a passage that led deeper inside the mountain.

There was barely enough room to stand full height, no more than an arm's length distance to each side, and the gaping darkness that loomed beyond. Yet, all about him the passage was strangely lit by countless tiny glittering lights that spread over the surface of the rocks and provided light to see the way ahead.

The cat brushed against his leg. He felt her warmth through his wet breeches and boots. Those tiny lights gleamed in her golden-green eyes. He felt the stroke of the falcon's wings as she flew past into the passage.

There were countless twists and turns, then abruptly the passage ended at a wall. There was no way forward, and suddenly no way back. Only the darkness that closed in from behind, blocking off all light in the passage they had just followed.

You will face three challenges, warrior. As you draw nearer the Darkness will try to prevent you finding the Grail.

He pressed his hands against the wall and leaned his weight into it. It was solid, made of row upon row of cut stones, and immovable. And as far as he could tell, it was no illusion.

"The first challenge!" he snorted, trying to wedge the blade beneath the edge of one stone after another at the wall with the hope of loosening one. Then attempting to find one that perhaps moved — a keystone — like the one in the passage outside Brianna's chamber at Inverness. But he found nothing, only more stones etched with strange lines and markings. Like the ancient runes Brianna had once explained to him.

In the meager light within the passage he saw markings across the face of every stone at the wall; they formed a distinct pattern that repeated in sets of three, and the pattern repeated from side to side, top to bottom at every row. It bore a similarity to the game he had played against Malcolm. Knife, blade, shield.

"It is a game of speed, agility, and memory," Brianna had explained. *"If you make a false move, you lose a weapon to your opponent. If you lose all three weapons, you lose the game, and that is how you must face your opponent."*

"And if I claim all of his weapons?" Tarek asked.

He remembered the surprised look on her face at a possibility she had not considered.

Tarek had been deeply moved by Brianna's fear for him. Yet, as a warrior and the claimant to both her and the landhold of Inverness, he would not refuse the challenge, nor had there been any possibility that he would lose.

They had played long into the night, until drink and recklessness had dulled Malcolm's senses and reflexes. He had refused to drink, preferring to keep his wits about him. And while Malcolm had claimed two of his weapons, he had claimed all of the Scot's.

But the abilities of the opponent he now faced were not dulled by drink. Nor could he be certain the pattern of the game was the same.

The Ancient Ones had created the challenge for any who might try to enter and seek the Grail. Even if he succeeded in meeting this challenge, what other challenge lay ahead?

With each moment he delayed he was aware of those tiny grains of sand running through the glass. Time was running out.

He studied the ancient markings, committing the pattern to memory — the mark of the earth, fire, and water. Then he pressed the first stone in the first pattern at the bottom row. It moved back slightly but the wall remained firmly in place.

He pressed the second stone in the second set. It also moved. And a third in the last set. It moved as well. He pressed a stone at the second row changing the sequence by one. To his surprise and frustration, it did not move.

He studied the pattern of the etchings once more. It should be right. The pattern repeated in a definite sequence without varying by even so much as one pictograph. Yet none of the three stones in the first pattern at the second row would move. He went through the sequence again with the same results. And all the while more time passed.

"How am I to know which it is?" he screamed his frustration and anger, his words echoing back at him through the passage.

"There is no logic to the pattern. Nothing in this cursed place is the same!" Then he recalled the unusual landscape and the shoreline of the lake.

"It is *all* different!"

Then it came to him. Everything was opposite what it had been the first time Brianna had taken him there. Like looking at an image in a looking glass he had once seen in the eastern empire, where everything viewed in the glass was the reverse of the original.

He stared at the pattern on the wall. If the pattern was reversed, then each row must also be the reverse.

He began again, pressing the three original stones at the bottom row, then at the next row he began at the end opposite from his original choice and pressed a stone. It moved.

His next choice was made in exactly the same manner within the next pattern — a mirror image of the one chosen in the first row. It also moved. And the one in the third pattern as well. He moved onto the next row.

It required thinking in complete opposites, creating the image in his mind then reversing it as if reflected in a looking glass. He moved the stones back with increasing speed until he had moved the last one.

No sooner had he pressed the last stone than he heard a grating sound and the entire wall moved back, opening onto a huge cavern.

He had wasted valuable time at the wall and quickly started into the cavern with sword held before him. The cat was beside him. The falcon flew ahead but immediately returned, flying directly at him with sudden urgency. As he stepped back to avoid being struck, he felt the cold rush of air against his face. Instinctively, he grabbed the thick ruff of fur at the cat's neck, holding her back.

Not more than inches away and exactly at the place where he would have taken the next step, the floor of the cavern fell away into darkness.

As it had in the passage, light shimmered on the walls. Overhead, he saw the falcon winging in small circles. If not for her warning he would have plunged to his death, perhaps taking the cat with him.

The walls of the cavern glittered with thousands of tiny lights. By contrast, the bottomless expanse loomed dark and dangerous before him, except for a pathway of stones, like stairs that led upward from the ledge to the opposite wall of the cavern. The wall with its row upon row of ancient pictographs had been the first challenge. Was this then the second?

The first step was a good distance from the ledge. The second an equal distance beyond that, and then another. There seemed to be nothing supporting the stones. Only the darkness that gaped below.

There was no other means of reaching the other side. Nor could they go back, for even now he felt the Darkness all around. Was it a challenge of the Ancient Ones? Or was it a trick of the Darkness?

Several times the falcon flew across the expanse of the cavern to the other side and then returned indicating this was the way he must follow.

A leap of faith. And he a man of little faith. He tossed a pebble onto the first step. It did not disappear into a void of darkness and illusion, but clattered and rolled across the stepping stone.

He was not much in favor of taking a running leap toward the first step only to discover when he got there that it was nothing more than an illusion just before he was hurtled to his death.

"Stay!" he commanded the cat, unwilling to risk her until he knew precisely what he faced.

He secured the sword at his belt, his fingers brushing against Ninian's good-luck talisman. Then focusing all his concentration on the first stone, he took several steps back, and made a running leap.

He landed easily and turned his attention to the second stone. He made the second leap, easily clearing the distance. As he turned to the third stone, the cat followed leaping onto the first stone.

All about as he continued, he felt the cold rush of air. A constant reminder of the death that awaited if he made just one miscalculation or misstep.

The cat did not seem to be bothered by such realities of human logic, but continued to follow with powerful ease. But when they had taken more than a dozen steps it still seemed they were no closer to the opposite side of the cavern.

Tarek turned in the direction of the ledge where they had started. He could no longer see it. Instead, the way they had come looked identical to the way that lay ahead. Not only that, but there were now additional pathways of stone steps leading in a dozen different directions.

Now he could not tell which way they had come, nor which direction he must follow.

The cat stood beside him. She seemed to sense his uncertainty and uneasiness. Somewhere overhead the falcon tried to guide them.

Tarek saw her at a dozen places overhead, each identical to the other, and quickly discerned that what he saw was her image reflected a dozen times over, just as a dozen different stone stairs surrounded him. As if a dozen looking glasses reflected their images.

Illusion and deception. He sensed the Darkness all about them. He saw it at dozens of places, closing in, trying to destroy him with a single misstep that would plunge him to his death.

But which was the real falcon and which was an illusion. Or one of several? Which set of steps was the illusion and which was real?

His hand buried in the fur at the cat's neck to prevent her making a fatal move. There must be a way to determine which was real and which was not, for they could neither go forward, nor could they go back. He was hopelessly trapped. And Brianna was trapped as well.

Desperately he tried to think of a way to determine which was the next stone and which was illusion. He had brought only his sword and the small knife tucked into his belt.

He remembered Ninian's prophetic warning, that the weapons he usually relied upon would be of little use to him. Beside him the cat grew restless.

He removed the knife and tied it to the end of his belt. Then holding onto the other end, he tossed the knife toward a nearby stone. The blade passed through it. It was an illusion.

Twice more he cast the belt with the knife weighting one

end. On the fourth attempt it clattered as it struck the true stone. Reeling in the belt, he quickly made the leap to the stone. The cat quickly followed.

No sooner had they reached it than the illusion changed, images shifting about them, forcing him to begin the painstaking process all over again.

"It is too slow!" he muttered under his breath. "At this rate it shall be an eternity before I have gone five paces."

How many more stones remained in the true path? He had no idea. Overhead the falcon too seemed to sense the growing urgency. He heard her frantic call and saw her image in a dozen places.

Then her flight became more frantic. She flew high toward the top of the cavern, a dozen images of the falcon all converging at a single point. Then all those images suddenly plunged downward at the same time, streaking down the mirror walls of the chamber at a dangerous speed.

Three companions. . . . Some will survive, others will not.

His companions had been chosen for cunning, strength, speed, and the ability to see what he could not. As precious moments slipped through the glass bowl, he watched helplessly, unable to stop the falcon as she flew directly into the wall of the chamber.

The dozen different images shattered in a shower of broken glass. The sound was deafening, an explosion of light and sound as the illusion crumbled in an avalanche of millions of fragments that glittered down the sides of the walls and rained down into the cavern below.

Within seconds it was over, the reflection gone, and the true path was revealed before them. Tarek quickly vaulted to the next stone and the next, climbing steadily away from the treachery and illusion the Darkness had tried to trap him in.

The cat followed, easily leaping from stone to stone

behind him. As he reached a ledge before an opening in the wall of the cavern, the cat leapt up beside him.

This time the falcon was not waiting to guide him ahead. She had sacrificed herself to save him.

Tarek felt the cold fear of doubt. He had been so certain the cat was Brianna's transformation. What if he was wrong?

Three companions.

Some will survive, others will not.

Now, there was only one.

Twenty-four

Tarek pulled himself up onto the ledge and stared about the chamber that opened before him.

It was strangely lit with a pale, shimmering blue light that glittered off the walls, and spiral rock formations that thrust up from the floor and down from the ceiling above.

When he looked back, the stones had disappeared, shrouded in that darkness that seemed to reach upward as if it followed him.

As he entered the chamber there was no opportunity to ponder the next challenge of Ninian's prophecy. He was struck with a brutal blow that drove him to his knees and loosened the sword from his stunned fingers. The sword was sent clattering across the stone floor. A second blow caught him at the shoulder and sent him sprawling.

As his attacker closed in, he quickly rolled out of the path of a third blow, pushed painfully to his feet, and whirled to meet the next blow.

His attacker was tall and powerfully built, his body protected by a black metal breastplate and leggings, his head encased in a black helm, with a gleaming war ax held before him. A formidable warrior, he relied neither on agility nor speed, but instead on brute strength as he maneuvered between Tarek and the sword. It lay no more than a dozen feet away on the cavern floor. If only he could reach it.

Tarek launched himself across the floor of the cavern. He landed with a grunt of pain and rolled several times. Seizing the sword on the last roll he quickly came to his feet, anticipating the next blow. Instead, he heard a fierce animal scream.

The cat leapt from the shadows where she had been crouching and launched herself at the warrior's head. Deadly claws tore through the exposed flesh at powerful arms as she sank her teeth deep into the warrior's shoulder.

He screamed in agony, his arm bloodied as he attempted to throw the cat off. Finally, he succeeded. She rolled, leapt to her feet, and crouched low to spring again. When she attacked, he brought the war ax up in a gleaming arc.

The blade caught her in the vulnerable underbelly, sinking deep as her claws raked his forearms. She screamed, a painful, dying sound, as the warrior staggered backward beneath the weight of her attack and threw her off.

The cat landed with a dull, sickening thud, and did not move. Then the warrior whirled around, his mouth curved in a gleaming deadly grin beneath the nose-plate of his helm.

"Now we face each other, warrior," he said, the blood-stained ax held before him. "To the death."

Before the challenge was even spoken, Tarek struck the first blow.

"Damn you to hell!" Bloodlust burned through him, driven by the sight of the cat, blood soaking the silver-tipped fur of her lifeless body.

He struck again and again, thrusting, blocking a strike, then slashing again in blow after blow. He felt none of the blows the other warrior struck, moving out of striking distance, sidestepping a blow that could have been fatal, then bringing the sword around in another slash.

The warrior met him blow for blow, but his lack of speed and agility began to tell as again and again, Tarek drove against him, thirsting for blood to quench the rage of hatred that burned through him.

Brianna lost! Dead. Sacrificed to save his life!

He struck again. And again, not even feeling the shudder of metal against metal as he relentlessly drove the warrior back, and back farther still with a strength of rage, hatred, and vengeance.

The warrior staggered under the next blow. He began to falter and show signs of weakness as more and more strength was needed to lift the war ax and counter each new blow. He was weakening, gradually moving backward, trying to seek a better vantage point and finding none — finding there was nothing he could do but meet each new blow or be cut down.

Finally, he stumbled. A more agile warrior might have recovered. But his movements were now clumsy, and he was weighted down by his protective armament and his size. He went down, pummeled by more blows, barely able to keep from being hacked to pieces. As he raised the war ax to protect himself, his helm fell back, the next blow poised above his head.

Tarek stared in disbelief at the warrior who lay at his feet, and who in the next moment would lay dead beneath his blade — the dark features that hinted at his Persian ancestors, the sharply angled bones of his face, the hard mouth, and startling blue eyes as clear as a northern fjord.

Tarek al Sharif stared down at the man he was about to kill.

Himself!

He hesitated, sword poised to strike. Impossible as it was to believe, the man who lay before him with hand raised to protect himself against the next blow had his own features.

What trickery was this? An illusion made it seem as if he stared into that looking glass and saw his own reflection?

But this was no reflection. Though the features were exactly the same as his own, the costume was different, as was the weapon the warrior held in his hand. And his posture, sprawled on the stone floor of the cavern was not a reflection either.

Illusion or trickery? Whichever it was, the surprise provided a momentary advantage. He was startled at the sight of himself sprawled beneath the blade he held in his own hands.

Tarek was slow to react when the warrior brought his ax up and deflected the tip of his sword. He leapt back, just beyond the deadly blow of that war ax as the warrior sprang to his feet and launched a new attack.

As he countered each blow, Tarek fought off the uncertainty of looking at himself with each strike.

The warrior maneuvered out of striking distance and swung the war ax about in a new attack. His features were hidden and then revealed in the play of shadow and light about the chamber. He fought with renewed strength as he drove Tarek back. But now the warrior's face revealed different features.

Mardigan!

So great was Tarek's surprise that he barely deflected the next blow. Then he was almost driven to his knees by the relentless hammering blows from that war ax. Mardigan's expression was fierce and triumphant with the victory he sensed close at hand.

Tarek countered the next blow, and the next, fighting back to his feet as he struggled to understand the transformation. But one truth remained. Whatever face his adversary now wore he was responsible for Brianna's death.

Rage and pain focused Tarek's concentration and the power behind the next blow, and the next, and the next. He drove Mardigan back.

He fought relentlessly, beyond the point of exhaustion until he felt nothing, except the rage, hatred, and pain over what had been taken from him. Brianna.

Mardigan stumbled, fell back, and rose to his feet. But he was slow to recover and the next blow was already there, driving him back, blows pummeling the metal breastplate, slicing away at thick leather padding over his forearms, until blood ran from a dozen different wounds.

When he raised the war ax again, Tarek brought the blade down at his shoulder, slicing through leather, the breast-plate sagging away and exposing vulnerable flesh across the chest, and a gleaming golden medallion.

Tarek swung the sword for the next killing blow, then suddenly hesitated at the sight of that medallion.

It was hammered gold, the size of a man's fist, with the image of a dragon's head embossed in the gleaming yellow metal, and identical to the medallion given years ago to a small boy. The only legacy of the man who had sired him, and then abandoned Asmari to a shame she could not live with.

For a score of years he had worn an identical medallion. Across the span of countless empires and equally countless wars, he had sought a blue-eyed Viking warrior who wore that medallion like a family crest or tartan of colors.

For just as long, he had sworn to kill him — his father. And now, in a cruel twist of fate, the man who was responsible for Asmari's disgrace and death, was also responsible for Brianna's death.

He stood with sword poised to strike. He gripped the handle of the sword so tight his hands shook. Hatred poured through him, turning his mind, heart, and soul, filling them with anger, rage, pain, and only one thought, only one desire. Mardigan's death.

Fear and hatred are the weapons of the Darkness.

Ninian's words whispered through his thoughts as if she stood beside him and spoke them.

"Curse you," Tarek whispered savagely, as if she stood beside him and could hear. And as if she had heard, her words whispered in reply.

The greatest battle you face, warrior, will not be fought with a sword. You must choose wisely.

With a fierce war cry, Tarek brought the sword down in a powerful deadly arc.

Twenty-five

Mardigan cried out as the blade sliced through his right shoulder, the war ax falling from his stunned fingers.

"That is for Asmari," Tarek told him. "A gift from her son!" Then he tore the medallion that he'd worn for twenty years from about his neck and flung it at the wounded warrior.

Mardigan slowly reached out with bloodied fingers and scooped up the medallion. His breathing was ragged, the look in his eyes filled with disbelief. When he looked up — his gaze that identical shade of blue — met Tarek's.

"You are Asmari's son?"

Until that moment Tarek had not even known whether his father knew the name of the beautiful Persian captive he had taken at Antioch and then ransomed to the emir.

The expression on Mardigan's face, a mixture of pain, shock, and disbelief, slowly gave way to a new agony, and brought almost as much satisfaction as his death might have.

"My son?" Mardigan whispered, staring at him through the glaze of pain, and then as a slow fierce smile forced its way through the pain.

"I have a son! You have my mark in the color of your eyes and in your strength. I should have known. I should have seen it." He struggled to get to his feet.

All these years Tarek had wanted revenge for his mother. It had driven him relentlessly, like an obsession, to find the Viking warrior who had ransacked Antioch and disgraced a daughter of royal blood. But more than anything he wanted

413

to see fear in his father's eyes. He wanted him to grovel at his feet and beg for his life.

He realized now he would never have that. Not from this proud, cold warrior. He also realized how the forces of Darkness had used Mardigan. It used him still, in all those old feelings of bitterness and loneliness experienced by a small boy who had lost his mother and never knew his father. It used his own hatred against him. And it had taken Brianna from him. Did anything else matter?

The Darkness cannot take from you what you will not surrender.

Once again, Ninian's words whispered through the hatred and pain. The Darkness could not take what he refused to give it.

His fingers closed around the talisman. He tore it from his belt, cradling it in his fingers. The facets of the crystal sparkled in the shifting light. The rage eased to a dull ache as if the simple touch of the talisman assuaged the hatred.

"You will not kill me," Mardigan said with satisfaction, his eyes gleaming with the certainty of it. "You cannot kill your own father."

Tarek slowly looked up. "You are right," he said, the bitterness and anger giving way to a coldness of indifference he would not have thought possible. He lowered the sword and shoved the wounded warrior away from him.

"Your death no longer holds any meaning for me." His fingers closed protectively around the crystal. The only pain came at the thought of Brianna.

No matter what happens, you must find the Grail!

He drew no comfort from Ninian's final words, only a sense of purpose. He did not know why it mattered any longer, now that Brianna was lost to him. But he had made a vow and he would keep it.

414

"You cannot leave me like this!" Mardigan shouted after him. When Tarek made no response but turned to leave the chamber, he cursed fiercely.

"This is no way for a warrior to die! I will not be left like this! Do you hear me? You are my son! I forbid you to leave me like this, groveling about with my lifeblood spilling out. If you will not help me, then I demand that you give me the means to end it quickly!"

Tarek whirled back around, his eyes as cold as Nordic ice. His expression was bleak as he stared at the barbarian who had sired him. He slowly shook his head.

"I leave you as you left my mother," he said coldly. "You may live or die, that is your choice. But until the moment of your death, I want you to remember the fate you gave her, and that I spared your life so that you could remember it.

"That will be my revenge upon you, and the satisfaction of denying you the one thing you wanted more than anything else. A son."

Then he turned and left the chamber, ignoring the enraged cries and fierce oaths that echoed after him as he followed another passage that rose steadily up through the center of the island.

He followed that shimmering pale blue light through shifting patterns of Darkness, Mardigan's curses echoing after him, Ninian's talisman clutched tight in his fist. Abruptly the passage ended at the entrance to a large grotto.

Pale blue light filled the grotto. It glistened at crystal formations that lined the walls and hung from the ceiling as tall as any man, across the dark surface of water that filled the grotto, and an unusual crystal monolith that thrust up from the water like a jewel in a magnificent crown of crystal spires. Atop the crystal monolith was a gleaming golden goblet.

The Grail.

It was made of solid gold and etched with markings although he could not clearly see them. But he knew what they
were — the same as those at Brianna's shoulder. The twin, in-
terlocking circles. Symbol of the grail.

*No matter what happens, you must find the Grail. All depends
upon it.*

The water in the pool splashed over the edge of the stone
ledge where he stood, lapping at the toe of his boot. It was
dark and murky, moving with unseen forces. It slowly rose
higher, exactly like the water of the lake that had flooded the
causeway.

If it continued to rise, it would eventually flood the grotto.
In very little time it would reach the top, and the Grail.

You must not fail.

There was no causeway this time. Nor could he approach
from another direction for the ledge ended only a few feet to
either side of where he stood. There was only one way to
reach the crystal monolith and the Grail. He stepped into the
water.

Several yards away, the surface rippled as if something
stirred beneath. He took another step. Again the water stirred
it something moved steadily closer. He dove across the water
toward the crystal rock.

He broke the surface, arms stroking powerfully. Just as it
had at the causeway, he felt the water pulling at him and dragging him under. Something brushed against his leg in the
water. He stroked harder.

Waves churned and pulled at him, dragging him away
from the crystal monolith. Again something brushed against
him, breaking the surface nearby. Another wave rose, dragging him under. He kicked savagely as the creature turned,
passed by much closer, and then struck.

He was rolled beneath the surface of the water. As he

stroked his way back to the surface, the creature attacked again. This time the blow rolled him through the water, slamming him against the rock island.

Jagged edges cut at his back and shoulders. Overhead, through the shifting shadows of the murky water he saw a shimmering golden light. The Grail.

Just before the creature struck another crushing blow, he propelled himself upward. He broke the surface and launched himself up out of the water at the same time the creature's next blow lifted and thrust him against the side of the monolith. Jagged edges of rock cut into his palm as he fought his way up the side of the small island to the base of the crystal monolith. As the creature broke the surface of the water, Tarek drew his sword and turned to face it.

It was huge, rising out of the water and towering over him, its large head supported by a long, slender neck the size of a tree trunk. The massive body barely broke the surface, the creature's long tail arching as it maneuvered with surprising agility. But above the surface it was slow of movement, forced to rely on brute strength rather than speed.

It was covered with scales, huge fins churning the surface of the water, as it swung that massive head like a battering ram. As it swung toward him, Tarek maneuvered out of the path of the blow then attacked with the sword.

The curved blade sliced through scales and thick tissue. The creature bellowed with pain, that huge head whipping about. As it turned to attack, Tarek struck again with the sword, plunging it deep into the beast's neck. That huge head snapped back and forth as it tried to throw him off. Pulling the blade free, he jumped down on to the rocks at the base of the crystal monolith and scrambled for a better foothold.

When the creature lunged, he maneuvered out of the way on the slippery rocks and slashed a new wound across the beast's glaring eye, blinding it. The beast screamed in pain and tossed its head, angling that massive head back and forth now with only one eye to see. Its painful bellows echoed in the grotto as it plunged once more beneath the surface.

The water became unusually calm, the surface flattening like a looking glass. No movement stirred in its depths.

Tarek scanned the surface warily. The blow had not been a fatal one. The creature was still alive, he was certain of it. It was a trick, and he wondered what the Darkness would confront him with next. All the while, he was aware that time was running out.

Atop the crystal monolith the Grail waited in golden splendor. As he climbed the rocks, he heard the water churn as the creature broke the surface. The blow caught him across the back.

He was slammed down onto the rocks. Stars exploded behind his eyes. The air was driven from his lungs. The crystal talisman Ninian had given him, shattered beneath his hand.

He had refused to believe it possessed any magic. Still, it was all he had left. Now, it, too was gone. Taken from him by the Darkness. He rolled to his feet and brought the sword up as he turned to face the creature once more.

"I am not afraid of you!" His gaze searched the grotto, skimming the surface of the water.

"Come and we will end this now!" He whirled in the opposite direction, sword held before him. But there was only his own voice echoing back at him, and the mist that swirled about the crystal monolith.

He stepped back cautiously, sword still held before him as the mist gathered, thickened, and closed around him. It brushed his cheek warm as a caress. He whirled back around, straining to see through the misty shroud that wrapped about everything, making it impossible to see his hand before his face, making it just as impossible for the creature to see him.

He heard the beast thrashing through the water, searching for him, the sounds muffled by that cloud of mist. Water lapped about the rock island as the creature passed nearby, yet could not find him.

Again he felt something, warm and tender like a hand at his shoulder. He spun back around, sword drawn, wondering what new game the Darkness played.

At first he saw nothing. Then, the mist slowly swirled and shifted. It gathered in long streamers and tendrils. Like the silken strands of a chrysalis wrapping about a slender figure as a shape began to take form — head, body, arms, and legs — until it had taken human form.

The creature of the mist lifted its head, like that of a butterfly slowly emerging from that silken chrysalis as the remnants of mist slowly disappeared.

White gold hair spilled about slender shoulders and swept back from beautiful, fragile features. Eyes slowly opened. They were the color of a highland glade.

Sword drawn, he took several steps back as he demanded, "What trick is this?"

Brianna reached out to him, but found the way blocked by that deadly blade.

" 'Tis no trick," she assured him. "I am very much alive." Again she reached out to him, but he backed away, leveling the tip of the sword at her heart.

"It is not possible. I saw you die."

"You saw what was necessary to protect the truth. I assure you, I am very real." Again she held out her hand. "Touch me and you will know that I am real."

"Or a creature of the Darkness?" he suggested, unconvinced.

419

"Never!" she said vehemently. "You must believe me. We waste precious time."

"If you are not a creature of the Darkness, then, how is it possible that you are here?" he demanded. "My companions are all dead."

She nodded. "Aye, you lost three companions and believed I was one of them. That was the deception. It could not be otherwise. For if you had known the truth, so too would the Darkness have known it, and I could never have reached this place." Her voice grew tender.

"You brought me here, in the crystal Ninian gave you."

He felt the tiny cuts at the palm of his hand from the broken crystal as Ninian's words whispered through his thoughts.

Some will survive, others will not . . . The crystal contains the greatest power I could send with you . . .

Brianna. Safely hidden within the crystal while he had been led to believe she had transformed into one of the creatures that accompanied him.

The Darkness cannot take from you what you will not surrender . . .

He seized her by the wrist in a powerful grasp. She winced as though in pain, but he was unconvinced. That too might be an illusion of the Darkness.

Rorke FitzWarren had once confronted such a beautiful creature he at first thought to be Lady Vivian in the catacombs below London fortress. But she had been a creature of illusion and darkness, without a soul, sent to deceive and destroy him.

And what of Mortain and his men?

Those who had ridden with him had been illusions of the Darkness, soulless creatures with death in their eyes who when slain had withered and crumbled to dust. No human blood flowed through their veins, no mortal heart beat within their chests.

He brought the tip of the sword up and pressed it against her throat. If she was real, then he would know it. But if she was a creature of the Darkness, then he would fulfill his promise to Ninian.

As if she knew his thoughts, she faced him unafraid. There was no darkness in the gaze that met his, no shadows of evil lurking there.

Her eyes were clear, brilliant green and open to her soul as she placed her other hand over his at the handle of the sword and willingly leaned into that deadly gleaming blade.

"In all ways we shall be as one."

When he tried to pull the sword away, she pressed the tip deeper. A single drop of her blood slipped down the blade as she repeated the marriage vows they had spoken to one another — a memory that they both shared.

"One life," she whispered, "one heart, one soul for all eternity."

He jerked the blade away and pulled her against him. His hand went back through her hair. He twisted it about his fist as he angled her head back and looked down into those clear green eyes.

"You are real!" he said fiercely.

"Aye, milord . . ." she whispered. Anything more was smothered beneath his kiss.

The mouth that opened beneath his was both tender and sweet, filled with longing and passion.

As the kiss ended, he laughed. A sound that was part agony, part disbelief, and no small part anger.

"Ninian's deception! Good luck token!" he snorted with contempt. "I will repay her for this."

"It was my deception too," she reminded him. "But it will

matter little who thought of it. Time grows short. We must hurry. My powers must be joined with those of the Grail and then we must leave this place before it is too late."

As she spoke, the small rock island shifted beneath their feet. The water continued to rise steadily. The entrance at the passage was already sealed off. A powerful wind came up like a storm gathering. Beneath the surface of the water, the creature returned, its powerful movements sending waves washing about the island.

Tarek turned to face the creature, seeking higher ground as the island continued to disappear beneath the surface of the water. All about them, the grotto seemed to be disintegrating. Pale light that had shimmered at the walls had been swallowed by dark shadows. Pieces of rock fell as the walls crumbled.

"I hate places like this," Tarek muttered, as he brought the sword up, ready to face the creature.

"You cannot stop it," Brianna cried above the rising storm that built within the grotto as the Darkness gathered its strength to prevent her reaching the Grail.

"No," he admitted, recalling how the water and the creature in its depths had claimed the mare. "But, it cannot go after both of us at the same time." He pushed her behind him as another wave lashed the island, driven by the powerful strength of the creature.

"Now!" he shouted to her as the creature broke the surface of the water. He lured it away, as she scrambled toward the crystal monolith.

Wind and water swirled around the rock island as the storm grew and the Darkness unleashed all its power. Wind lashed and pulled at her. A wave caught her and dragged her back toward the churning darkness of the water.

Brianna sensed that it was pointless to fight it. Her mortal strength was no match for that of the Darkness. Instead she used the forces of the storm it had created.

She turned her thoughts inward to that place deep within where her newly discovered powers drew their strength. As the storm whipped about the crystal monolith, she transformed once more.

Mist rose over the rocks as the storm exploded over the tiny island. It lashed at the crystal trying to engulf the golden light that glowed about the Grail. The mist was drawn upward, carried on the swirling wind as it wrapped about the Grail.

A deafening sound exploded in the grotto, a violence of anger so powerful it drowned out the roar of the wind as the power of the Grail was joined with hers.

The beast violently churned the surface of the water, sending waves crashing over the tiny island even as the water continued to rise steadily higher. Beneath his feet, Tarek felt the island breaking apart. He shouted a warning to Brianna, but there was no answer.

As the creature rose out of the water, he raised the sword and turned to face it.

"Come taste the sweet death of my blade, you spawn of the Darkness!"

As the creature struck, he lunged out of the way of those powerful jaws, and plunged the blade deep into the creature's massive neck.

The beast writhed and spasmed, whipping that head about in pain. Again, he plunged the blade deep even as mist began to gather and close around the island.

Waves lashed the island as he crawled to the top. The crystal monolith and the Grail were both gone. What little remained of the island steadily disappeared as it sank beneath the waves. And Brianna was also gone.

Had she transformed and somehow escaped? He drew

comfort from that possibility as he heard the creature churning through the water much closer now.

The walls of the grotto crumbled as the island disappeared completely beneath his feet. Darkness closed around him. As he raised the sword to meet the beast one last time, he held onto one last memory — Brianna as she had been when he first saw her beside a highland pool so long ago. A creature of sunlight and mist who held out her hand to him.

As the beast struck, the island exploded in a brilliant flash. Then he was hurtled through the light.

The sun had broken through the clouds. The water was smooth as glass. The warmth of the sun on the surface of the pool caused a mist to slowly rise. It spread across the water and up the embankment.

Tarek knew this place. He had been here before. The highlands near Inverness months ago. It was both a memory, and his last thought in the grotto.

She appeared out of nowhere, slender and graceful as a doe. Her face was heart-shaped with flawless skin across high cheekbones. Her mouth was full above a small, firm chin, her eyes a startling, clear shade of green.

The hood of her mantle had fallen back to her shoulders revealing a green satin lining as brilliant as her eyes, and a thick cascade of hair the color of sunlight through mist.

She reached out as she slowly walked toward him. And as he had that morning long ago, Tarek took her hand. It was pale and slender, yet warm and strong, filled with life and the amazing power of the Light from which she drew her strength.

Brianna smiled as she stepped into his arms.

"I have been waiting for you," she whispered as her mouth met his with a fierce sweet passion.

"Welcome home, warrior."

Epilogue

Tarek stood high on the battlements, his narrowed gaze fixed on the churning gray water of the firth of Moray off the coast of Inverness. Beyond, lay the cold, vast openness of the North Sea.

"What word is there?" he asked grimly.

"Many of Mardigan's men fled to the open sea rather than be taken prisoner." Gavin de Marte shrugged. "Many perished. Their bodies have washed ashore."

Tarek's thoughts churned, as dark and fierce as the waves of the firth, for there was no mention of the one warrior whose fate he most wanted to know.

"And those who did not take to the sea?"

"They have been hunted down. They will not bother the people of the north country again."

Their forces splintered and fragmented, and without their leader, the raiders had been vanquished. But it was a hollow victory.

"What of Mardigan?" The name came low in Tarek's throat, a painful sound laced with old hatred.

Gavin shifted uncomfortably, the wind that swept the cliff, bitingly cold. "Our men constantly watch the lake. No one has been seen. 'Tis doubtful he survived."

Doubtful, but not certain. Tarek nodded as Gavin left to rejoin the others in the main hall below in celebration.

He felt no desire to celebrate. There was no satisfaction in the outcome, only a lingering sense of something left unfinished.

His head lifted at the sudden warmth carried on the chill breath of the wind, like a caress that moved across his senses. Then he heard the faint stirring of wings in the air.

A shadow swept across the battlements. Then absolute stillness as streamers of mist swept up the rugged cliffs below and slowly curled over the walls. The pain and anger eased as he turned, and smiled at the beautiful golden creature who stood and slowly walked toward him.

A smile curved her mouth as Brianna moved into his arms. "How did you know I had returned? Not even Thomas is so aware, and he has had many years' practice."

Tarek pulled her against him, folding her into the warmth of his mantle. He would have pulled her inside him if he could. Perhaps in that way he could banish the cold ache that seemed to have permanently settled there.

"I know whenever you are near," he said with a far different sound low in his throat as his mouth hungrily took hers, seeking the fire that leapt so easily between them. "I can feel it in my blood."

"Aye," she whispered with a sudden breathlessness that had nothing to do with the long journey she had just made. Her green eyes shimmered with desire.

She laughed, a sultry sound that caught suddenly as his hands moved low at her back and he angled her hips against his. Her eyes widened and grew dark with passion. "I feel it too."

He tucked her head beneath his chin as the cold eased inside him, like the first breath of spring after a bitter winter. He had begun to believe that spring might come even to this frozen land.

"Is it done?"

"Aye," she rubbed her cheek against the open place at his tunic where dark skin gleamed golden with the warmth of the desert sun of his ancestors.

"And the Grail?"

"Safe with Merlin." Her head angled back so that she could look at him. "It meant so much to see him, now that the memories have returned and I know who my real parents are." Tears welled in her eyes.

"Ninian paid a high price to bring me that knowledge for she cannot go back, nor can my father leave to be with her unless the curse is broken." A tear spilled over her lashes and slipped down her cheek.

"All she has left is the bond of their thoughts." Her voice caught as though drowning in those tears. She laid her hand tenderly against his cheek, her fingers trembling.

"I could not bear to have only your thoughts, knowing I might never touch you again."

"Is there no way?" he asked.

"Not as long as the curse remains. Not even the power of the Grail was strong enough to break it. My father had so hoped that it would be. He longs for her so."

Tarek's mouth thinned. "Then it is not finished."

"Nay, 'tis not." She brought her other hand up from inside the folds of his mantle. In it she held a richly colored, rolled fabric.

Tarek recognized it for he had seen it many times on the loom in Rorke FitzWarren's chamber in London. It was the tapestry Vivian had been weaving. As he unrolled it, sunlight speared through the clouds overhead and shimmered across the vivid images woven in the tapestry.

Warmth shimmered through the heavy fabric as if the tapestry were alive. There were other images as well, fleeting shadows not woven through the fabric that played across the surface, illusive as dreams. In those faint shadows he thought he saw something familiar — the chaos and destruction of

427

some great battle. His gaze met Brianna's.

She sensed his thoughts. "Vivian saw it as well," she said solemnly. " 'Tis the reason she sent the tapestry back with me."

"What does it mean?"

Her slender fingers moved over the shimmering images woven within the threads. That which had already come to pass — the battle at Hastings, countless warriors and knights, William's near death, a fierce knight whom he recognized as his friend Rorke FitzWarren and the beautiful flame-haired weaver who sat before a loom and spun the threads of the future. His own image was there as well, along with Brianna's and a gleaming golden cup — the Grail.

" 'Tis the future that now lays ahead," she explained solemnly.

"War," Tarek concluded with a heaviness of heart.

"Aye, but unlike any that has ever been fought. The battle for all mankind. Even now the forces of evil gather. My father spoke of it as I placed the Grail in his hands."

"Will it be fought in the highlands?" he asked, his thoughts once more those of the warrior who knows all too well that peace is fragile and fleeting.

Once, all he wanted was revenge. Now he wanted so much more. More time — time with one another, time for the child he had promised her. A child born to loving parents who had spoken vows with one another, home and family.

She shook her head. "It ended here when the Darkness lost the Grail and its powers. Now its only hope lies with the Oracle of the Ancient Ones, through which it may seize the powers of the Light."

"Where can this oracle be found?"

"According to legend, it lies in the western lands where my father was born."

428

He did not question, but merely nodded for he accepted without question. After his battle against the forces of Darkness at Grail Island, he no longer doubted what was at stake.

"I will give orders for the army to make ready. We will ride for London at first light. Rorke FitzWarren will join us for he understands the danger was well as I. We must find the Oracle."

Brianna laid a hand at his arm. " 'Tis not so simply done for it is not your fate that is woven among the threads. 'Tis the fate of another and only he may make the journey and seek the Oracle."

Her fingers moved across the newly woven threads of the tapestry, the last images Lady Vivian had woven — a portent of the future. One was that of a warrior. He was young and fierce. The fire and passion for battle burned in his amber colored eyes. He wore a warrior's armor but the shield he carried bore no emblem. Instead, it was solid black and inscribed with the letters of a Latin word — *Desdicado*. A man of no honor and no name, born a bastard. Stephen of Valois.

The image entwined with Stephen's in an explosion of darkness and light was that of a slender young woman with beautiful exquisite features, hair the color of the night sky, and violet eyes.

"Who is she?"

"Her name is Cassandra. She is my sister."

Ninian had spoken of another who might hold the hope for the future if he was unable to save Brianna from the powers of Darkness. But there had been doubt as well as great sadness in her voice as she spoke of it. Now he realized who it was she had spoken of. But the scene was incomplete, unfinished.

"What of the outcome? Surely Lady Vivian has seen it."

Brianna shook her head as her fingers tenderly traced the threads that formed Cassandra's image at the tapestry.

"It is impossible for anyone to know for certain." Her green gaze was filled with sadness. "Cassandra chose long ago not to return to Merlin's world." Her soft green eyes glistened with tears as she looked up at him.

"I cannot imagine that she would not wish to return. Though I did not know of my true mother and father for so long, still I had Cullum and Mirren." Her fingers brushed his lips. "And then even after the pain of their loss . . . But to have no family, no one whom you loved and loved you in return . . ."

He understood far too well. They each had suffered similar loss, yet not of their choosing. The pain of that loss had been assuaged by the love they found with one another. He took her into his arms, closing the fleece mantle about them. He felt her shiver.

"The tapestry is not yet woven," he reminded her. "There is still the future. Perhaps that which has been lost in the past, may be found there."

She knew he was right, for they had both lost much, and then found each other in an uncertain future. She brought her hand up from the warm cocoon their bodies made, pressed tightly together within the fleece mantle. She traced the curve of his mouth with her fingertips.

"Aye, milord," she said with growing huskiness. She shivered again, but for far different reasons as his hands swept down the length of her spine, gently cupping her bottom as he pulled her closer. She closed her eyes and closed out the darkness that lurked at the edges of her thoughts.

"The future," she whispered against his lips.

BUMP IN THE NIGHT

BY ISABELLE HOLLAND

BUMP IN THE NIGHT

ISABELLE HOLLAND

Doubleday

NEW YORK LONDON TORONTO SYDNEY AUCKLAND

Published by Doubleday, a division of
Bantam Doubleday Dell Publishing Group, Inc.,
666 Fifth Avenue, New York, New York 10103

Doubleday and the portrayal of an anchor with a dolphin
are trademarks of Doubleday, a division of
Bantam Doubleday Dell Publishing Group, Inc.

BOOK DESIGN BY TASHA HALL

Library of Congress Cataloging-in-Publication Data
Holland, Isabelle.
Bump in the night.
I. Title
PS3558.03485B84   1988   813'.54   88-3732
ISBN 0-385-23891-6

Printed in the United States of America

November 1988

First Edition

BG

To Wolff Computer
Where it all started

BUMP
IN THE
NIGHT

1 The child disappeared on October 14. Martha woke up late, called her son, and then, when he didn't answer, slowly and groggily got herself out of bed.

"Jon, where are you? Why don't you answer me?"

She paused, sure that she would hear his rather alto voice if she just waited. But there was no sound except the drip from the bathtub. The washer was old and she had meant to have the plumber fix it, but somehow the days passed and she forgot to call him.

"Jon!" She waited, slowly walking to the door.

"Jonathan, goddammit! Answer me!"

Suddenly the silence seemed to have a threatening quality. Martha stood on the duplex landing orienting herself. It was Saturday, she told herself; therefore her son, Jonathan, age eight, should have been in his room. It was only— She glanced at her watch and then stood looking at it unbelievingly. It was ten-thirty. It should be only seven-thirty. What had happened to those three hours? She had waked at five with a blinding hangover and taken both an Alka-Seltzer and a . . . a sleeping pill—

Oh my God! she thought. Then panic seized her. Stumbling down the rest of the steps, she glanced into the living room, the kitchen and the small study. Jonathan was nowhere.

Of course, she could have missed him upstairs, if he had decided to have a nap. An eight-year-old? Deciding to take a nap in the middle of a Saturday?

I must think, she told herself, continuing to stand there. Her head felt thick, as though her thoughts were trying to operate in some kind of congealed substance. "Coffee," she said aloud. Quickly she went into the kitchen, put on some water to boil, then came back to the living room.

Suddenly it occurred to her that Jon might be in the street, playing, something he was strictly forbidden to do unless he had asked permission and she was where she could keep an eye on him from the window.

"He had no right," she said aloud. And then grew self-justifying. "No right at all. He knows he's not allowed to play outside unless I've told him he can."

The phone rang, and at the same time the kettle started to scream. She let the kettle go on and plunged for the telephone, falling over Jonathan's cat, Susan.

"Get out of my way," she yelled, kicking out.

The cat gave a cry and rushed behind the sofa.

Martha snatched up the receiver. "Is that you, Jon? I want you to know—"

"Mrs. Tierney, please, this is Sarah Jennings."

"I'm sorry," Martha said, and made an effort to lower her voice. "I—I—" A sense of instant humiliation filled her. "I was back in the kitchen with the radio playing—"

"Mrs. Tierney, where is Jonathan? He's supposed to be in school. He should have arrived more than two hours ago."

"But it's Saturday." That reality seemed immensely important.

"It's Tuesday, Mrs. Tierney. And Jonathan should be in school. He should have been here at eight-thirty."

"But I thought—" Martha found herself staring straight at the wall calendar in the kitchen. Then she glanced at her watch, whose dial had a tiny square indicating the day. The little figure was twelve. The calendar straight ahead showed the twelfth to be Tuesday. Why on earth had she thought it was Saturday? Had the weekend disappeared in an alcoholic blackout? Couldn't she remember anything about it? Further humiliation washed over her, followed by fear. The fear rapidly became anger. She went instantly on the offensive.

"You mean to tell me that you—or at least his classroom teacher—have known for nearly two hours that Jonathan wasn't in school and you've only just got around to telling me?"

"She's a new teacher, Mrs. Tierney, and when Jonathan didn't answer to his name, one of the other kids said he thought Jonathan was visiting his father. I'm sorry."

"When I think of the fees I've paid to your school—" Martha could hear her voice, going on about their carelessness, the iniquitous amount of money the school charged per term, and her own anxiety provoked by their lack of efficiency and organization.

And then the ground was pulled from under her.

"Mrs. Tierney, we tried to call half an hour ago, but the phone didn't answer. We let it ring ten times."

Where had she put the phone in the bedroom? she wondered, and with a sick feeling remembered the times when she had got up, put a cushion over the telephone or put it in

5

the closet or even in a drawer to keep it from waking her. Or perhaps it was just that the pill was still working powerfully.

"I forgot, I had to go to the doctor," she said haughtily.

"The main thing is," the headmistress of the little private school said, "where is he?"

Martha was silent as she fought with nausea and with guilt, both overpowering. "Of course it's the main thing," she said. A terrible need to cry filled her, and she knew in one part of her mind that all of this was just a device for not letting the fact that Jonathan had disappeared get through to her. Because if it did . . . And then the full horror of what the headmistress was saying, of what she knew in her gut, hit.

Jonathan, her beautiful eight-year-old son, was missing, here in a city filled with criminals, sexual perverts. . . .

"Oh my God!" she said, and started to sob. "What's happened to him? Where's my little boy?"

"Are you alone?" The calm voice at the other end of the phone had its effect.

"Yes."

"Do you have a neighbor you can call? Or I can call for you?"

Beulah, the woman who lived in the apartment downstairs, worked during the day. So did both members of the couple upstairs. Several doors down there was Katie. Katie would be home.

"Yes. There's Katie Leonard. I'll call her."

There was a slight pause at the other end. Then, "All right. Call her. If she's not there, or . . . or not well, let me know. I'll send over one of the teachers. Now I'm going to see how much I can find out, and to question that child who thought Jonathan was with his father."

. . .

6

As she hung up, Sarah Jennings repressed a strong inclination to say, "And get dressed, have some coffee, and above all, don't have a drink." She didn't for one minute believe that Martha Tierney had been up long enough to be dressed and out. There'd been too many times when someone from the school had called only to get the same slurry, sleep-thickened voice, uttering similar unlikely excuses. But she was a woman who liked to choose her own time and place for a major battle, and the morning when Jonathan Tierney was missing was not it.

And besides all that, Mrs. Patrick Tierney was a fee-paying parent. At a time when costs were going up, such were not to be insulted lightly.

St. Andrew's School, located on Remsen Street in Brooklyn Heights, was vaguely church-affiliated, small and coeducational. It had a good reputation and took its students up through the ninth grade. After that almost all the boys went to boarding school and the girls either did likewise or passed into one of the elite private high schools scattered over the Heights and the Upper East Side of Manhattan. Occasionally a particularly bright student with parents who were either financially limited or staunchly liberal or both sat for the tests to enter one of the competitive public high schools, such as the Bronx High School of Science, or Music and Art, or Hunter or Stuyvesant.

Sarah Jennings was always especially pleased when one of her stars went to one of those prestigious places, although she rarely recommended it. It took not only brains and scholarship to survive there, it also, in her opinion, required stability and toughness of spirit. The competition was—or had been before the recent, politically motivated relaxation of standards—fierce. And the bright city kids were not always noted for their civility or delicacy of feeling.

Jonathan Tierney would not be one of those she would expose to the city schools. He was a sturdy little boy, but she considered he had more than enough to cope with with his divorced and frequently absent father and alcoholic mother. He was also a child of great beauty, and the thought of that made Sarah's heart miss a beat. The list of children who had disappeared or been abducted was never far from her mind.

The main school building had been constructed in the earlier part of the century especially for St. Andrew's. But as the student body had grown, the need for more room had forced the school to take over brownstones on either side and renovate them for class use. Preschool, kindergarten, and the first two grades were housed in the brownstone to the north of the school. The third and fourth grades were in the brownstone to the south, and the remaining grades in the main building in the middle. The school stood flush with the street, which meant that the athletic field was three blocks off in a small private park.

Walking briskly now along the main downstairs hall, Sarah pushed open the connecting door to the brownstone containing the smallest children and went looking for Jonathan's homeroom teacher.

The third grade was on the second floor in the biggest and sunniest classroom. Sarah opened the door and went in. Fifteen eight-year-olds turned and looked at her and said, as they were drilled to, "Good morning, Miss Jennings."

Sarah knew that Hilary Babson, the new third-grade teacher now standing in front of the blackboard, encouraged such English-school-inspired manners. She wasn't quite sure how she herself felt about them. Part of her thought they were a phony import that sat ill on American children and that good manners involved more than these rather showpiece displays. On the other hand, she was astonished at how much pleasure the sound of the children's voices in their choral good-morning gave her.

"Good morning, children. Miss Babson, may I speak to you for a moment?

"Miss Babson," she said, when the young woman emerged from the classroom, closing the door behind her, "I'd like to know again just how soon you realized Jonathan Tierney was absent. I know," she went on hastily, not wanting the relatively unknown quantity in front of her to take umbrage and become uncooperative, "that you informed me as soon as you knew yourself, but Mrs. Tierney is not an . . . an easy woman, and I don't want to give her any more reason for complaint than I have to."

"I'm sorry, Miss Jennings," Miss Babson said, a defensive note in her voice. "I would certainly have told you sooner, if I had not been assured by Stephen Morgan that Jonathan would most likely be with his father. In this day of almost universal divorce—"

Sarah had not known Miss Babson long, but she had known her long enough to have a fair idea of her prejudices and preoccupations, since the younger woman was not hesitant at the lunch table or in the common room to voice them. So she interrupted now.

"I know how you feel about the breakdown of the family and the frequent separations. However, the main thing here is that the child be found."

"But why shouldn't Stephen be right? Why shouldn't I have believed him when he said Jonathan was with his father?"

"I understand why you assumed Stephen to be telling the truth. The trouble is, Stephen's parents are good friends of Jonathan's father, and rarely have a kind word to say about his mother. As far as they're concerned, custody of Jonathan should have been given to his father in the first place."

"Considering that she's a notorious drunk—"

"We're not discussing moral issues right now. Please call Stephen out."

"If you're going to punish him—"

Miss Jennings suddenly lost some of her patience. Opening the classroom door, she interrupted a low ripple of chatter and went in. "Stephen, would you please come out here for a moment."

"Told you it'd be about Jon," a girl said.

"And you, Marguerite," Miss Jennings said. Marguerite Stanley was bossy and pushy, but she was also bright and a good observer.

"Now," the headmistress said when both children came out, "why did you, Stephen, say you thought Jonathan was with his father?"

Stephen sighed and looked down at his feet. "I just thought . . ." he said. His voice drifted off.

"You mean you had no actual reason for saying so?"

"No."

"You hadn't heard anybody—like your parents—say anything? I know they're supposed to be good friends of Jonathan's father."

Stephen went on staring at his feet. Overwhelmed with the harm he could have done to the cause of getting Jonathan back to his father, he added, "He's a really super guy, and Jon'd a lot rather be with him than with his mother."

Miss Babson spoke with some indignation. "So because you wanted to believe something that we now know is not true . . ." She glanced at her superior. "It isn't true, is it?"

"No. No one has seen or heard of Mr. Tierney in some while."

"Yeah," Stephen said. "But he could be here couldn't he? And it'd be so much neater for Jon—"

"Wishful thinking is not reality, Stephen, and your saying

10

what you did may have delayed our efforts to find him by an hour or two." It was also true that Mrs. Tierney wouldn't answer her phone for an hour, but Miss Jennings decided not to mention that.

"You mean he's really lost?"

"I mean that he's not at home, he's not here and no one knows where he is. Do you? I mean, do you really have any knowledge—not just fantasy—where he might be?"

"No." The little boy sounded desolate. I don't. For real."

"All right, Stephen." The headmistress turned to Marguerite, a rather square child with a round face, bright green eyes and two stiff pigtails. "What about you, Marguerite? Do you have any idea at all where Jonathan might be?"

There was a pause. "No," she said.

Miss Jennings was fairly sure that Marguerite was not telling the entire truth, but when Miss Babson said, "Marguerite, I don't think—" the headmistress broke in.

"Forgive me, Miss Babson." She turned back to the stocky child. "I have a feeling you might have an idea of where Jonathan is. It's important, for his sake, that we know where to look."

Marguerite sighed. "Sometimes he goes to . . . to an animal shelter."

"An animal shelter?" Miss Babson's voice rose with astonishment. "Why should he go there? Does his father—"

"Why, Marguerite?" Miss Jennings said.

"Well . . ." Marguerite hesitated. She looked at Miss Jennings and then at Miss Babson.

Miss Jennings opened her mouth to say, "Please help us." But she didn't get the first word out.

"Well really, Marguerite," Miss Babson said, "I can't believe that that is where Jonathan would be when he is supposed to be in school."

Miss Jennings watched Marguerite's face close down.

"Marguerite?" she said gently. But she knew it was no use. To herself she cursed the clumsy teacher whose one approach seemed to be coercion.

"I dunno," Marguerite said.

"I think—" Miss Babson said.

"Miss Babson, I mustn't keep you here in the hall when neither of us knows what the children could be getting into."

It was not a statement laden with tact. But Miss Jennings was angry with the teacher and didn't mind showing it.

"Very well, Miss Jennings." And she swept past Stephen and Marguerite to open the classroom door.

"Stephen, is this something Jonathan talked to you about?"

"No. I think that's crazy. Why'd he go to the animal shelter?"

"Perhaps Marguerite can help us."

But Marguerite had been warned off any further cooperation. "I dunno," she said, and shrugged.

"Does either of you have any other idea?" she asked them.

They shook their heads.

It was wisdom to recognize defeat, and Miss Jennings was a wise woman. "All right. Go on back, both of you." She was about to turn away when she suddenly thought of something. "Wait," she said. And then, when they had turned back, "Which animal shelter?" When there was no answer she said, "Marguerite?"

But Marguerite shook her head. "I dunno," she repeated.

"Please help us, Marguerite. Because it would be helping Jonathan."

Marguerite shook her head. "Dunno," she said.

"I don't know," Miss Jennings, frustrated, corrected.

. . .

Miss Jennings went back to her office and rang for her secretary.

"Joanna," she said, when that young woman appeared, "how many animal shelters are there in the Heights?"

Joanna Weldon was an attractive young black woman who was working her way through college, taking most of her classes at night. She could, Miss Jennings had told her often, have obtained a loan for daytime attendance, which would have cut short her time in obtaining a degree. But Joanna had an admirable and stubborn desire to graduate without a debt to be paid off. "And I'm not that much in a hurry," she said. "I'm not even sure yet what I want to do. And I like working here."

So Miss Jennings, feeling that she had paid enough tribute to her conscience, accepted Joanna's statement and rejoiced that she had someone as bright and well organized to keep her office functioning.

"I'm not sure there are any shelters in the Heights," Joanna said now. "I think the nearest city shelter is in the Flatbush area, or maybe Park Slope."

"I gather there are other than city shelters."

"There are various private types who pick up strays and try and find homes for them." Joanna looked with sympathy at her boss's worried face. "Why are you interested? You're not thinking of giving up Alcibiedes, are you?"

Alcibiedes was Miss Jennings's cat, a large black neutered male.

"Of course not." She glanced at Joanna. "Are you aware that Jonathan Tierney is missing?"

"Yes. I think that's pretty much around the school now."

"When asked where Jonathan might be, Marguerite suggested an animal shelter."

"But she didn't say which one?"

13

"I'm afraid she got interrupted before I was able to ask her that."

"Marguerite's aunt, the one she lives with while her parents are abroad, sometimes takes in strays."

"Not, I hope, like that crazy Beauchamps woman. Doesn't she live in the same area?"

"Yes, she does. But Meg Stanley's not as bad as that. Nobody knows how many cats Miss Beauchamps has; she won't let anyone in to see. Meg isn't nutty. Just a little soft in the head about animals."

"Well, she'd obviously be a good person to talk to. Let's get her on the phone. Or does she work?"

Joanna was about to answer when Miss Jennings glanced towards the window. "Oh Lord!"

"What's the matter?"

"Mrs. Tierney is here."

Martha had somehow got herself dressed. All the while she was putting on her clothes and at the same time trying to control the shaking of her hands, she told herself that this once she would not take an early morning drink. She would not take it because Jonathan was missing—temporarily, she assured herself—and because she was sure that when she got to the school that nosy, self-righteous headmistress would smell it on her.

But then, just before she left the house, she knew that she wouldn't be able to get through the coming hours without a little something to hold her together. The shaking of her hands was so bad she could see her purse jumping around. So she had two shots of vodka, because vodka wasn't supposed to have any odor.

As she waited after swallowing the second shot, anticipating the sense of calm and control that would come, the voice of her divorced husband, Patrick, sounded in her mind, as it often did. "Why the hell do you think I'd want to leave my son with a woman who can't stay away from the bottle?" His voice was so clear she turned her head, expecting him to be there. But he wasn't.

Oh God! she said to herself and shivered, even with the reassuring warmth of the vodka. Custody of Jonathan had remained with her because of Patrick's constant traveling. A former journalist, he still spent months abroad each year on research for his books. But one day, book or no book, he might decide to stay home, especially if he became convinced that she hadn't managed to put some kind of hold on her drinking as she had sworn to him—and to the judge in the custody case—she was going to do. She shivered again, reminding herself that Patrick was due back in two weeks. As soon as Jonathan was home safe she'd really come to grips with her drinking.

The thought of AA drifted across her mind. Who had first brought it up? Maybe it was that interfering brother of Sarah Jennings, David Jennings, whom she had met somewhere. A member himself, he had suggested she might like to go with him to a meeting. She had refused flatly. "I'm not an alcoholic," she had told him. She repeated it aloud to herself now. "I'm not an alcoholic!" Her drinking, she reminded herself, was the immediate result of Patrick's scurrilous behavior. Even before they separated he had made no secret of the women he wined, dined and bedded. She'd have it under control by the time he got back. Her hands had stopped shaking, so she wrote a quick note to Jonathan, telling him that Katie Leonard three doors down had the apartment keys, then spent a few minutes frantically looking for her own set that she normally kept in her handbag. This time she found them in her sewing box. Then she called Katie.

The phone rang eight times, but Martha let it ring, since she knew that Katie, like herself, had a hard time getting up in the morning, and for the same reason. A rush of affection for Katie filled her. It was good to have a friend who wasn't always criticizing her and suggesting she had trouble with alcohol.

"I'm not an alcoholic," she repeated aloud. And at that moment Katie picked up the receiver.

"Hello," she said foggily.

"Wake up, Katie," Martha said. Then she added, "Jon's missing." And started to cry.

"There now," Katie said. "I'm sure you've just forgotten where he is. Now think!"

"He's not at school, and that moralistic beast Sarah Jennings called to tell me. I'm on my way there. I've left a note on the door telling Jon, if he comes home while I'm at the school, to come over to you. Is that all right?"

"You know it is, Mart."

"So don't go back to sleep on me, will you?" She added, "Have a shot of vodka."

"I might do just that," Katie said, sounding brighter.

Martha left the note on the door and walked over to the school as fast as she could. She had put on high heels, because she always felt more formidable in heels, but they kept her from moving too rapidly. Her ankles turned easily, and on the uneven pavements of the Heights she had to be careful.

"But why would he go to an animal shelter?" she protested when she was in the headmistress's office.

"I don't really know, Mrs. Tierney. I was hoping you might cast some light on that. But Marguerite Stanley is a friend of his and she seemed to think it was a possibility."

Miss Jennings was fully expecting a stubborn argument,

so she was surprised and pleased when Martha said, "Which one? There must be dozens." Obviously, the quick mind that had once made Martha Tierney one of the city's best journalists was still—occasionally—functioning.

"We don't know. Joanna, my secretary, says that Marguerite's aunt runs a sort of unofficial shelter herself. Maybe we ought to start there."

Martha sat down and rubbed her forehead. "If Jon were at the Stanleys', then Megan Stanley would have called either you or me." Sarah was about to reply when Martha said, "We might as well call her anyway." And before Sarah could move, picked up the phone in Sarah's office. "What's the number?" she asked.

Silently, Sarah turned the Rolodex to Mrs. Stanley's number and watched Martha punch out the number.

"Yes," Mrs. Stanley said cheerfully, "Jon was here."

"When?" Martha shot back, her voice hostile.

"Around twenty to eight. He said he came to look at the new kittens."

"And then he left?"

"Yes."

Sarah, who had gone to Joanna's extension to listen to the conversation and add her two cents if she thought it was necessary, said, "I have one more question. Did he say what he was going to do when he left?"

"He said he was meeting his friend before school."

"Which friend?" Sarah and Martha said together.

"How should I know? He simply said it was a nice man he'd met, a friend of his father's, who was going to buy him breakfast. I figured that, as usual, he didn't get any."

"What time was that?"

"Around five to eight. Isn't he there yet?"

"No."

"Well, maybe he's enjoying his breakfast for a change."

"And you didn't think to call and check, or at least tell me?" Martha shouted.

"What good would that do? You probably wouldn't be out of bed, and if you were you probably wouldn't be sober." And she hung up.

Sarah noticed that by now Martha was a ghastly color, a greenish white. Below her eyes were purplish brown shadows, made all the more obvious by puffiness. Many years ago, Sarah reflected, when they were both at Smith, Martha as a student, she as an assistant in the English department, Martha had been a beautiful young woman, tall, leggy, with auburn hair and an enviably slim body. She was still tall and leggy, though the bulging abdomen above her thighs made her look fat and cumbersome. Even her hair seemed to have faded to a dull brown, periodically streaked with brassy blond stripes. How are the mighty fallen, Sarah thought, and reflected wryly on the long reach of her biblical upbringing. "Do you have any idea, Mrs. Tierney, who this friend of Jonathan's father could be? This, quote, nice man that he was supposedly going to meet?"

Numbly, Martha shook her head.

"Not a cousin or brother-in-law or uncle or anybody who could be reasonably considered to have connections to you and Jonathan?"

"No."

"Is there the slightest chance it could have been Jonathan's father?"

The familiar fear shivered through Martha. There was so much she had to do before he was due back. She moistened her lips. "He's in Europe. My lawyer told me that and said he'd return in two weeks." If not— But she didn't want to think about that, and besides, nothing mattered until Jonathan came home.

"In six hours, let alone two weeks, he could be back in New York. Have you heard anything of him since you talked to the lawyer?"

Martha shook her head again. "No."

"So it could be his father."

"Why would Jon call him a nice man?"

Sarah answered slowly, "Maybe he did it deliberately to keep anyone from knowing he was going to meet his father." She added, "I take it you have complete custody of Jonathan."

Martha gave a sob and buried her face in her hands.

Sarah stared at her with a mixture of compassion and contempt. "Does that mean yes or no?"

"It means," Martha said, raising her head and speaking with a forlorn dignity, "that we share custody. But because Patrick travels the agreement was that Jonathan would live with me—unless I got drunk again."

"And then he would live with his father."

Martha nodded. "Yes. If he stopped traveling and came back here permanently."

"Then we have to assume it was his father he was meeting."

There was a pause. For Martha, the thought that Jonathan might be with his father—the man who had so contemptuously rejected her—was unbearable. "I still don't think so."

"Why?"

Martha was too fuddled and frantic to give a rational answer. She just shook her head.

"That's a big help. I'm going to call the police."

2 Patrick Tierney sat in the doughnut shop on Court Street drinking his fourth cup of coffee. It was, he decided, probably the worst coffee he had ever tasted, including the bilge handed out in second-class English hotels, with which, as a writer doing research that took him to some of the smaller towns of Great Britain, he had intimate acquaintance. He stared down at the watery liquid. He preferred his coffee black, but with this brew he had added milk on the theory that any change could only improve it. His theory was wrong. If this were one of those English hotels he would now order tea. English tea was as magnificent as some English coffee was dismal, but American tea vied with the worst of English coffee. He pushed the cup away and looked at his watch for the umpteenth time.

Jonathan had said he would meet him here at eight. The words of Patrick's lawyer, spoken almost every time they talked and most recently yesterday afternoon, filled Patrick's mind. "Whatever you do, don't, I beg you, *don't,* try to see Jonathan without asking his mother first and setting up the date with her permission."

"His mother's a drunk," Patrick had said savagely. "Trying to have a sensible conversation with her—one that she'll remember the next day—is like catching air in a—a sieve."

"I don't care, Pat. The name of the game is your getting custody—that is, if that's what you still want and you're going to stay put for a while. You can't have custody if you're out of the country three quarters of the time. It's not fair to the boy. But after the last report from the detective agency, your chances are excellent. Martha's drinking has escalated in the past six months, and, according to her neighbors and the school, Jonathan goes around alone as though he were twelve, not eight. She's not fit to have him, and we can make a strong case for your having custody. That is," the lawyer went on, underlining the words, "if you behave yourself. Having titanic fights with Martha is not the way. You remember what happened last time you were home!"

Patrick winced. A year before, he had called on Martha to suggest a) she cut down on her drinking, b) she try a rehab and c) while she was there he'd take Jonathan abroad with him.

He had barely mentioned his first suggestion when she exploded in fury. He raged back. Almost everyone in the entire house heard, and Jonathan, after screaming, "Stop! Stop!" had fled from the apartment.

When the battle was over and Jonathan had finally been located at Marguerite's, Pat had appealed to his lawyer.

"Public arguments aren't good for anyone's cause," the latter pointed out.

"It wasn't public," Pat said stiffly.

"It might as well have been, and making Jonathan run away did nothing for your side."

"She was drunk."

"You don't even have that excuse."

After that, Patrick had (reluctantly) promised to be good, which included his not trying to get in touch with Jonathan without first talking to Martha. "In the long run you do yourself more good that way," the lawyer explained patiently. "Technically, you have the right. Realistically, it's better to get Martha's cooperation when you want to call Jonathan and talk to him or take him out. You'll get further that way."

Since then, Patrick had been in England and France. But the previous day, fresh from Europe, too beaten down by jet lag (he told himself) to embark on careful negotiations with Martha and yearning to see his son, he had succumbed to temptation and telephoned Jonathan in the hope that it would be he who picked up the phone.

And that time he had.

"Son, don't say anything."

"Hi!" Jonathan said with such warmth and enthusiasm that Patrick felt tears spring to his eyes.

"Hi, Jon," he said, and was embarrassed to find his voice shaking.

"Are you okay—er, okay?" Jonathan had almost let slip the fatal word, "Dad", but caught himself just in time.

"I'm fine. Don't you worry about it. Listen, can you meet me sometime? Anywhere. Just say the place."

Jonathan was no stranger to guile. Living with his mother had taken care of that. But at that moment he heard her coming slowly down the stairs. He could often tell to within an ounce how much liquor she had had by the sound of her voice or her steps, and he was quite sure now she had had enough to be drunk but not enough to pass out.

"Meet you at the doughnut place on Court Street at eight tomorrow," he said quickly, and hung up.

"Who were you talking to on the phone?" Martha said.

"Just Joey."

"Oh." She seemed to search her mind. "What did you say you were going to do at eight?"

"Go to gym class together."

"Oh. All right."

Patrick now glanced at his watch. It was eight-fifteen. He had taken the trouble to make sure that this was the only doughnut place on Court, though he remembered there were several on Montague. And, of course, there were any number of things that could have delayed a small boy who was trying to get away from a difficult mother and perhaps avoid other nosy adults or children. To distract himself, Patrick eyed the obvious renovations in the doughnut shop, to which his attention had been drawn by the smell of paint.

At nine Patrick was still sitting at the doughnut shop table, holding his newspaper clenched in his hand as though it were a weapon.

At nine-thirty he tried to call Martha. There was no answer.

He had several times considered phoning the school. But he had learned from bitter experience that calling the school without talking first to Martha produced wild scenes when Martha found out about it, which she always did. He gave as good as he got in those scenes, but with his lawyer's advice ringing in his ears he preferred not to precipitate another— at least not for the moment. And it was always possible that, unknown to Jonathan, Martha had made an appointment for him this morning with his doctor or dentist, and, given the secrecy with which Patrick himself had wrapped this morning's date, Jonathan would not be likely to tell his mother.

Then another thought intruded, frightening him. Could Jonathan have been in an accident on the way to the doughnut shop?

Patrick got up abruptly, started to leave the shop, then went back to speak to the counterman.

"If a little boy, eight years old, reddish hair, comes in, tell him I'll be back. I'm his father."

The man looked up from his paper. "Sure."

Patrick walked the length of Court Street and back and then went to Montague. Could Jonathan have meant one of the doughnut places there? Half an hour later he had gone into every doughnut place. No one had seen a boy answering to Jonathan's description.

At ten Patrick headed for the nearest phone to call the school, scene or no scene.

Jonathan Tierney had gone to the doughnut shop on Atlantic Avenue.

After he had hung up the phone, he was so excited over the prospect of seeing his father and also so frightened that his mother might have heard his part of the conversation and guessed whom he might be talking to, that when the morning came he left a little early and decided to stop by and see the Stanley kittens on his way to Court Street. There he found Mrs. Stanley distracted with worry about Simpson, her big ginger male, who had taken to hiding under the bed for absolutely no good reason. She was also fairly sure he was not eating much.

"I wonder if I should take Simpson to the vet right away," she said.

"Why don't you?" Jonathan asked, sitting cross-legged

among the kittens. Gently he removed one of the kittens from his head, where it was playing with his hair, and got up to leave.

"Because he loathes the carrier and I sometimes think that no matter what's wrong with him, he's more traumatized by being put in it than by whatever ails him." She glanced up and took in the fact that Jonathan, uncharacteristically, was departing almost as soon as he had arrived. "Off so soon?"

"Yes."

"To school?"

"Actually . . . I'm going to the doughnut place on Court Street."

"At this hour? Why didn't you say you were hungry? There're some muffins in the kitchen. Anyway, the place on Court Street is closed for renovations."

"Are you sure?"

"Of course I'm sure. I passed by there a couple of days ago. Were you going to meet somebody?"

Jonathan was overcome with an urge to mention his father. With a huge act of will he pushed it back. "Yes."

"Anybody I know?" Her eyes were back on Simpson, who had opened his mouth and seemed to be panting. "There *is* something wrong with him. Oh God, the last time one of my cats did that it was Amanda, and she died the next day. I'll have to take him to the vet now. Help me, Jonathan. He likes you. Hold him and talk gently to him while I get out the carrier. Oh, he's going to hate this!"

For nothing else would Jonathan have delayed his departure, but a cat was an animal and therefore more important than any person, except his father, and he'd just have to run when he finally got out.

They eased the protesting Simpson into the carrier and Jonathan helped Mrs. Stanley lug the carrier to her car parked on the street. "I'd offer to give you a lift, Jon, but I think the sooner I get Simpson to the doctor the better. It's not Marguerite you're going to meet, is it? She didn't say anything."

"No, it's a nice man." The need to mention his father became overpowering. "A friend of my father's."

Mrs. Stanley was placing the carrier gently on the passenger seat, her murmured words to the cat drowned out by Simpson's loud protests.

As she started the car and turned away from the curb she knew that something about their conversation had bothered her, but she couldn't concern herself now with digging it out. Simpson was making ominous sounds that usually meant he was about to throw up. Fretting and worrying over Simpson, she forgot about what had disturbed her in Jonathan's comments until she found herself talking to Sarah Jennings.

Jonathan ran, zigzagging towards Atlantic Avenue in the hope that when he discovered the place on Court Street closed, his father, who hadn't lived in the Heights for three years, would have inquired as to where the nearest doughnut shop might be and then gone there. Of course he might just stand in front of the closed shop and wait. But it seemed much more likely to Jonathan that an important and highly intelligent man like his father would not do the obvious thing that any ordinary man would do. He'd figure out that Jonathan probably meant another place nearby and would find out where it was and go there.

Martha had often accused his father of fiendish subtlety— a quality she particularly disliked, especially when she had a hangover. And there were times, when she was displeased with Jonathan, that she suggested he had inherited that unlovable characteristic. Jonathan was extremely proud of it. He tried to be as subtle as he knew how.

Jonathan's only watch was on the fritz, so he had to guess how late he might be by checking clocks as he ran past drugstore and other windows. Unfortunately they didn't agree. According to one he'd be exactly on time. To another, he'd be ten minutes early, and to two others, a quarter of an hour late.

He slid into the doughnut shop on Atlantic Avenue and looked around. The clock there reassured him. He was only five minutes late, and given the fact that his father didn't know Brooklyn Heights well, he couldn't be expected to be on time. Jonathan sat down and started shredding a napkin that had been left there.

Time passed. Jonathan stared at the clock, which seemed not to have moved. This proved, he told himself, that he had not waited as long as he thought. A watched pot never boils.

"You waiting for somebody, son?"

Jonathan stared at the man standing beside his table. He was dressed like most of the men around the Heights, including the men teachers at the school, in tweed jacket and jeans. If he had had on a pinstriped suit, Jonathan would have been instantly on his guard. He did not consciously take on his mother's opinions and prejudices. But as far back as he could remember, his mother was given to talking with scorn about corporate Nazis in pinstripe suits.

"Yeah, my dad."

The man had a thin face that in some way reminded Jonathan of his father's, although his father had brown hair and this man's was black and his father had blue eyes and this man's were brown. Maybe, Jonathan thought, it was the nose, a prominent beak with an aquiline bend. Whatever it was, it gave Jonathan a slight feeling of reassurance.

"I think," the man said, "he was here looking for you. He hated to have to go, but said to tell you he'd be in touch."

"What time is it?" Jonathan cried. Disappointment flooded through him. He felt sick.

The man looked at his watch. "What time were you supposed to meet him?"

"At eight. But the clock there says it's only—" The obvious fact that the clock wasn't moving now struck Jonathan with stunning impact, along with his own stupidity in wanting it to be right. "Oh no, oh no!" he said, hitting the table.

"I'm afraid it's long past eight. I'm really sorry."

Jonathan sat there with his arms on the table, flattened with misery. He had been less than six when his parents split up. Since then he had seen his father only half a dozen times. The main reason, he knew, was that his father was so often out of the country. But even when he was there, Jonathan didn't see him as much as he would have liked to, and this he blamed on his mother who, while she couldn't prevent their getting together, would frequently be deliberately obstructive.

"Jonathan, that's the afternoon we're going to the pediatrician, don't you remember? You can't go out with your father then."

"Can't we change it? You already said I could spend the day with him."

"Well, I forgot. We're going to have to make different arrangements for you to go out with your father. It's almost impossible to see Dr. Penrose."

Eventually, he'd get to see his father. But eventually usually included a fight, and while his mother would not drink the day he was to see his father, she would the next and the next to make up for it.

After the divorce he was content to live with his mother. At that time her drinking had not damaged the early closeness between them, those years when she read to him, played with him, and took him to the zoo and the aquarium. His father, brilliant, impatient, was somebody to adore, but not somebody to count on as being there when Jonathan needed him. He'd be likely to be off in Africa or Asia pursuing some story. Having his parents divorced, Jonathan told himself again and again, wouldn't be different.

But it had been. Not because his father's pattern was any less erratic, but because his mother's drinking had suddenly escalated. The woman who had read to him after school and at night became a sullen, silent creature, glass in hand, staring at the television set, erupting in anger whenever his father returned to New York and wanted to see his son.

Now, numb with disappointment at his father's failure to show up at the doughnut shop, he directed his anger towards his mother, because it was unthinkable that this disaster could be his father's fault. If there was any way his father could have waited for him, he would have. If he, himself, hadn't stopped to help Mrs. Stanley with Simpson, he would have been on time. . . . But Simpson was a cat, like Jonathan's own Susan. If her cat was ill, then she was right to do everything to help him, including delaying Jonathan. His mind veered back to the acceptable target. If his mother weren't such a—a rotten person . . . Aware that tears were trickling down his cheeks, he got up from the table and stalked out of the doughnut shop. Once outside, he furtively wiped his cheeks with his hands.

"What do you plan to do now?" asked his father's friend, who must have come out with him.

Jonathan shrugged. He could, of course, go to school. He'd be late by now, and there would be questions. And the headmistress, Miss Jennings, would call his mother. Jonathan rather liked Miss Jennings, but he knew that he couldn't stop her from getting in touch with Martha if that's what she thought she ought to do. And his mother would almost certainly berate him in the alcoholic rage that seemed to have been so frequent in the past six months.

"I think I'll go to the zoo," he said. As always, animals would comfort him. He had fought a long, hard battle to have Susan, and his mother had given in only when the pedigreed Siamese had arrived as a present with a full batch of papers. Martha still didn't like animals, but insisting that an expensive pedigreed animal be given to a shelter was more than she could do, particularly as the cat came from her own sister.

"I think the zoo is an excellent idea," the man said to Jonathan. "Where is it?"

"Prospect Park."

"Of course! I'd forgotten there was a zoo there. Would you mind if I go with you?"

Jonathan had a vague feeling that it was not a good idea to let this man get friendly. There had been lectures at school about the dangers for young children in talking to people they didn't know, let alone going somewhere with them. On the other hand, he had been chosen by his father to carry a message to Jonathan.

"Where did you know Dad?" he asked, instead of answering the question.

"From business."

"You mean you're with his publisher?"

"Yes." The man put his hands in his pockets and strode beside Jonathan, his long legs making the strides look easy.

Detective Sergeant Pete Mooney listened to Sarah's crisp voice on the other end of the telephone giving him the outline of Jonathan's possible disappearance.

"I say possible, Mr. Mooney, because of course Jonathan could come walking in at any moment, having decided to skip school this morning. But it's not like him. His mother is"—she glanced at Martha's face across the room—"distraught, and I wondered if you had any people who could help organize a search."

"You say he just failed to show up this morning at school?"

"Yes. But as I said before, it's not like him."

"What time did he leave home?"

"I'm not sure. But he was at a neighbor's before he was due to show up at school."

"Do you or his mother have any idea who he might have skipped off to meet? I mean, if the parents are divorced— By the way, are they?"

"Yes, they are, and I asked his mother that question. The answer is, she doesn't know. The last she heard from anyone about her husband was two weeks ago when she talked with her lawyer. At that time she learned her husband was in England."

"Well, he could have come back here the next day."

"That's what I told her."

"So this kid could have gone to meet his father."

"Yes."

Mooney doodled on a pad beside his phone. When missing children were involved, it had been his observation that in nineteen out of twenty cases a missing child could usually be found with the divorced or separated parent. That didn't mean that the anguish of the parent who had been left was any less. A missing child might very well be with the noncustodial parent, who meant nothing but good. But the parent left in the dark struggled against the savage mental picture of the twentieth time, when the child had been kidnapped or lured away by a stranger. Those were the heartbreak cases.

Because he was a divorced parent whose only child lived with his former wife and in some respects seemed lost to him, he dreaded those more than anything else, and had to fight against an unwillingness, as each case came up, to acknowledge the possibility of the stranger involvement. It was so frequently hopeless and, in his opinion, worse than death, both for the parents and for the child.

He said now to Sarah, "The first thing is, don't panic and don't decide the worst right now. Give me a description of the kid and I'll get it on the radio right away. What's his name?"

"Jonathan Tierney."

"Age?"

"Eight."

"Height?"

"About four feet and three or four inches."

"Weight?"

"Seventy pounds."

"Coloring?"

"Red-blond hair, gray eyes."

Mooney wrote down the answers, a mental picture of the child Jonathan forming in his mind. Almost angrily he thrust it away. Just because it was a child he must not allow himself to sentimentalize the case. For one thing, it would impair his judgment.

"Why did he stop off at this neighbor's, and who is she?"

Sarah sighed. Along with her anxiety was a growing irritation at Martha Tierney and her uselessness. It was worse than pointless to turn on Martha and berate her for her poor care of her son—for not knowing what time he left the house and where he was going. Not only would it not find Jonathan, it would probably muddle what little common sense and powers of observation Martha had left.

"I think he wanted to see some kittens she had. Her name

32

is Megan Stanley. She also lives on Sidney Place. Her niece, Marguerite, is in the same class as Jonathan."

"I'll have to talk to his mother. You say she's distraught. Is she there with you?"

"Yes. Do you want to talk to her?"

"Yes."

"All right." Sarah turned, holding out the receiver. "Martha? The policeman wants to talk to you." A conscientious woman, she reproved herself for harboring a tinge of malicious pleasure in the fact that for once, in talking to the policeman, Martha Tierney would have to cope with something herself. As Martha came forward she handed her the receiver. "You can sit here."

"Hello," Martha said.

"Mrs. Tierney, I'm sorry about your son. Do you know at about what time he left your house?"

From Martha's viewpoint it was the worst question he could have asked. If answered truthfully, it would reveal the hangover, the drinking the night before that had brought it on and the sleeping pill early in the morning. She hesitated. The simple truth, "I don't know because I was still asleep," formed in her mouth. But she couldn't bring herself to say the words. "I guess around seven-thirty. He wanted to see the kittens at the Stanleys' before school."

"But you don't know the exact time."

"No." She found her tongue adding, apparently of its own accord, "I was in the shower."

"All right. I'm coming by the school now and would appreciate your staying there."

Mooney put down the telephone and glanced up at his partner. "I'm going around to St. Andrew's School. One of their kids hasn't showed up."

33

"Lucky you. Divorced parents?"

"Yeah."

"He's probably halfway to somewhere else with the parent he isn't living with."

"Yeah. That's what I think." Or what I hope, he thought.

Lawrence Miller walked beside Jonathan fighting the internal battle that always seemed to be with him and that escalated the moment he became in any way involved with a male child. One side insisted, I mean him no harm. He wouldn't be sitting in a doughnut shop by himself at eight in the morning if he was decently looked after. Kids today are neglected. Parents don't care. If Michael had lived . . . The other side, the side that never seemed to express itself in words, was drinking in the beauty of the little boy, the red-gold hair, the sensitive features, the guarded look in the widely spaced gray eyes.

"Do you have any animals of your own?" he asked when Jonathan, who had been chattering on about the tigers in the zoo, had run down.

"Yes, Susan. She's a Siamese."

"Seal point or blue point?"

"She's a lilac point," Jonathan said proudly. "She was almost completely white as a kitten and her ears and nose were pink. For a while I called her Miss Pink."

"How old is she?"

"She's two. She has blue eyes that are slightly crossed and a loud voice. When Mother—" He stopped. He was about to say, "When Mother trips over her . . ." But a vestigial sense of loyalty stopped him.

Lawrence's senses quickened. He was sure that midsentence brake meant that the boy was probably going to give out with some candid and uncensored information about his mother. Lawrence had a profound conviction that old-fashioned, caring motherhood had gone out, if indeed it had ever existed. And that children, especially boy children, were neglected.

"When Mother what, son?" he asked gently.

"Well, sometimes Susan stands in front of her and Mother trips." Technically, this was true. But saying it that way angered Jonathan. Loyalty was loyalty, and what about his loyalty to Susan? "I mean, Susan doesn't mean to stand in front of her. Anyway, she has a loud voice."

"Siamese often do. They're famous for it."

"Do you have a Siamese?"

"No. As a matter of fact, where I live now, I'm not allowed to have a pet."

"That really stinks."

"I agree with you."

Lawrence had a sudden mental picture of the seedy single room he was now occupying. Once his home had been a house in a college town with a garden and a dog and, yes, two cats wandering around. But they weren't Siamese. One was calico, one was black. "I had two cats once," he said now. "But neither one was a Siamese."

"What were their names?"

He could hear Michael's voice: "Let's call the kittens Scylla and Charybdis." And Donna's amused voice: "Do we have to be so literary? Why not Blackie and Smudge?" It was true that Michael was precocious, and he'd just been telling his son about the legend—

"Maybe we ought to get a bus," Jonathan said, suddenly interrupting his memory. "The park's pretty far."

Lawrence was flung out of his dream into potential danger. Buses contained people who had nothing to do but sit and remember those around them.

"It's such a nice day, why don't we walk? It's not that far.

And we'll be all the hungrier for a hot dog when we get there." He watched the boy's face closely. Michael had loved hot dogs. This boy's expression didn't change, didn't show pleasure. "Or an ice cream." This time there was a slight lifting of the boy's mouth. But he didn't say anything.

Lawrence didn't trust silences. They gave people—like this boy—too much time to think and remember warnings against talking to strangers. Casting around rather desperately for something casual yet personal to say, the teacher in him came up with, "By the way, there are several spellings of your name and I forgot to ask your father which one you used. Which is it?"

"I never heard of any except mine," Jonathan said.

"Really? As I said, I can think of three." He could feel the moisture breaking at his hairline. Why the hell did the kid have to be so seemingly poised, so plainly—from the way he spoke and acted—from an educated background? Why couldn't he have been an ordinary street kid from a working-class area? And if, Lawrence asked himself, he had wanted a kid from the working class, what was he doing in Brooklyn Heights, probably the richest neighborhood in all New York except the Upper East Side of Manhattan?

I didn't want—I wasn't looking for—a boy, one of his internal warring parties seemed to scream in his head. Liar! the other side mocked. You were looking for this boy, the boy in the pictures that seedy man, Ben Nicolaides, in that squalid hangout sold you, this beautiful kid with the troubled eyes that you've been stalking for days. . . . And then this morning he finally saw him come out of one of the houses and talk to a woman before she drove off. The boy looked, Lawrence told himself, as though he might need a friend. Also, in some way, he reminded Lawrence of Michael, though Michael was dark and taller. . . . He snapped to as he heard the boy spelling his name. "What was that?" he asked quickly.

"Like I said, J-O-N-A-T-H-A-N. What are the other spellings?"

Relief made him weak. "Oh, an *o* in the final syllable rather than an *a*," he said.

"What's the third?"

"An *o* in the middle instead of an *a*."

"I never heard of that."

"They're not really common ways of spelling it," he improvised rapidly.

Jonathan, the man thought, Jonathan. *I am distressed for thee, my brother Jonathan: very pleasant hast thou been unto me: thy love to me was wonderful, passing the love of women.*

The ancient words brought a sentimental ache. Watch it! he told himself. Soon, but not now.

"Do you happen to have a picture of Jonathan with you?" Sergeant Mooney asked Martha.

She pawed in her large handbag. "I never can find anything," she muttered, still heaving things from one side of the bag to another.

"Maybe a school picture?" Mooney said, turning to Sarah Jennings.

Before he even asked she had pulled the most recent yearbook from the shelf. "I'm not sure— No, we didn't get one of him. He had flu the week the children were getting their pictures made. I told him to bring one in, but he never did."

Martha was strongly tempted to say, "He never asked me about it." It was true, she had no recollection of his ever mentioning the matter, but she knew she couldn't be sure that her memory was reliable, so she decided to say nothing about the school picture. Instead, she finally and triumphantly pulled a wallet out of her bag and flipped it open. "Here it is. Taken only . . . well, only three years ago. I've been meaning to get another one."

Three years, Mooney thought, would bring the eight-year-old back to five years. What could you tell about an eight-year-old boy from a picture taken when he was five?

"Let me see," he said, reaching out for the wallet. There, in its plastic envelope, was the photograph of a small boy with straight red-gold hair falling over his forehead. The face underneath the hair was round and serious. "Do you think you have a more recent one at home?"

Did she? In her desk drawer there were boxes full of snapshots, unless those were the boxes she had put on the top shelf of her closet, or maybe they were among the boxes that she had persuaded her landlady to let her store in the basement.

"No," she said loudly, because it was easy and wouldn't ambush her with sudden demands on the part of other people who wanted to see pictures she might or might not have. "No. I sent all the photographs of him to my sister who wanted to see them." Then, because she felt that everyone in the room was silently accusing her of lying, she said, "That was last year."

"So neither of you has a recent picture of Jonathan," Mooney said. He tried not to sound judgmental, but it was, in his opinion, a hell of a note when neither of the two people most intimately connected with the missing boy had a photograph that could help him in the search.

"I'm afraid not," Sarah Jennings said.

"No," Martha said more baldly.

"I guess I'll have to ask his father," Mooney said. "Do you know where I can reach him?"

It was at that moment that the buzzer on Miss Jennings's telephone sounded. She went over and picked up the receiver. "Yes, Joanna? Oh, all right." She pressed down a button on the telephone and said, "I'm glad you called, Mr. Tierney. We were about to try to get in touch with you." She glanced towards Martha. "No, I'm afraid he's not here."

3

The look of disgust on Patrick
Tierney's face when he walked into Sarah's office and saw
his former wife was like a slap in the face.

"Still on the bottle, I see," he said. "Couldn't you at least
lay off enough to get my son safely to school?"

"You have no right—" Martha started shrilly, when
Mooney interrupted.

"Let's leave the accusations for the moment. We have to
locate a child."

"We wouldn't have to if he'd been halfway looked after—"

"Mr. Tierney." Mooney addressed himself to Patrick because he felt there was a greater chance of progress there
than with the befuddled woman who was Jonathan's mother.
"Right now we don't have time to waste. Whoever's fault it
was, the important thing is to find out where your son is."

40

He paused, then added, underlining the words, "Everything else has to be postponed—no matter how you feel. Okay?"

Patrick stared at him. "Of course," he said. "For now."

Mooney went on, "When were you last in touch with Jonathan? I take it you were supposed to meet him this morning." Out of the corner of his eye he saw Martha about to speak and turned towards her suddenly. She closed her mouth.

"I called Jonathan last night, around nine," Patrick said. He told me to meet him at the doughnut shop on Court Street at eight this morning. I got there at about five minutes to eight and waited for him until nine-thirty. Then I thought he might have meant one of the doughnut shops on Montague Street and checked all of those. Nobody'd seen him. So then I called here."

"Do you have a recent photograph of your son with you?" It was a long shot, Mooney thought. If the boy's mother, who had custody of him, couldn't rustle up a recent picture, where would his father get one? Still, you never knew.

Patrick hesitated a second, his lawyer's words still sounding in his brain. But Jonathan was missing. Beside that, nothing mattered. "Yes. Here." He reached into his coat for his billfold and opened it. There, behind the plastic frame, was a snapshot. He pulled it out and handed it over. "It was taken six months ago."

Mooney looked at the photograph. It was a head shot and almost certainly enlarged. The five-year-old's round face was now thin, the cheekbones high, the eyes wary. An astonishingly good-looking boy, he thought, though not a happy one.

"You don't have custody of your son, do you, Mr. Tierney?"

"We share custody, but I travel a lot so he lives with my former wife." His voice hardened. "For the moment."

"But when you're home you can see him freely?"

"When obstacles aren't put in the way."

"What obstacles?" Martha snapped.

Patrick went red and then white. "You have one hell of a nerve asking that!"

"Shall we keep to trying to find your son, the son of both of you?" Mooney interrupted coldly. "Time is passing. If he has been . . . has fallen into the company of a—a stranger, the sooner we can figure out how to find him, the better." He paused, letting the pictures his words summoned up have their effect. "All right," he went on. "How did you get this picture, Mr. Tierney?"

"I bribed a kid who works in my agent's office to hang around the school and take it and send it to me."

Mooney stared down at the photograph. "Was this the only picture he took, or were there others?"

"There were others. This was the best."

"Do you think you could get hold of the others?"

"Sure. Why? I mean, will more be better?"

"I'm not sure I can tell you why. But I'd still like to see them." He turned to Martha Tierney. "When did your son leave the house this morning?"

"I told you. I was in the shower."

"Approximately?"

As Martha continued not to answer, Mooney was fairly sure of the reason. He had seen too many alcoholic women not to be able to identify one. There were the coarse pores on the skin, the body appearing bloated without being actually fat, the uncared-for look, the bloodshot eyes. . . . Despite everything he felt sorry for her.

Martha raised her head and looked at him with despair. "The truth is, I overslept. He . . . Jonathan left the house before—before I got up. I wasn't well during the night." The pathetic lie lay there, obvious to everyone. "Oh God!" she said and put her hands up to her face. "Oh my baby."

Mooney glanced back at Patrick Tierney. If looks could murder, Martha Tierney would be dead. And Mooney could understand that, too. He turned to Sarah. "You say that this Mrs. . . ." He looked at his notebook. "Mrs. Megan Stanley said that he had arrived at her house to see some kittens. What time would that be?"

"She said about seven-thirty. And left about five minutes to eight. She also said . . ." Sarah hesitated briefly. "She said Jonathan said he was going to Court Street, where he was going to meet a friend. He described him as a, quote, nice man, close quote. He said he was a friend of his father's."

"What?" Patrick said.

Mooney turned. "Did you tell him it was all right to say where he was going? Or did you tell him to keep it to himself?" He knew that in these ugly custody cases parents were inclined to be secretive and paranoid.

Patrick's mouth clamped together for a moment. "I told him to keep it to himself because I didn't know what trouble his mother might raise. Yes, I know, Martha, I'm not supposed to make any inflammatory statements about you, but if your attitude hadn't been a factor I wouldn't have had to tell him to keep his mouth shut."

"So it's all my fault, as usual. You're the one who made dates with him when you knew he was supposed to be in school, who hired people to spy on him and photograph him—"

"Which I wouldn't have had to do if you had had the decency to send me copies of his most recent pictures."

"Okay, you two," Mooney interjected. "I wonder why Jonathan felt impelled to say anything about, quote, a nice man. That seems a pretty odd thing to me."

"Maybe . . ." Sarah started.

He turned. "Maybe what?"

Sarah hesitated. "Maybe he just felt impelled to mention his father and, knowing he shouldn't, said something less dangerous but still satisfying."

"Why should he do that?"

"Children like to talk about something they're excited about. So they'll sometimes go at it sideways."

They were all silent for a moment. Mooney put away his notes and faced the parents. "I think you both ought to go on home in case your son tries to reach you." He turned to Patrick. "Would he know where to get in touch with you?"

"Yes. I gave him the telephone number in the last letter I wrote."

"Okay. Then I think you'd both better be at home. I'll talk to you later."

"I'd like to know what the kids here say," Patrick said.

"So would I," Martha joined in, in rare agreement.

"If there's anything, I'll tell you. But I'd rather see them alone." He turned to Sarah. "Could you send for them?"

Lawrence Miller walked slowly beside Jonathan as Jonathan stared into the cages they passed and commented on the animals.

"Those tigers look sad," he said, peering between the bars at a huge tigress spread out on the ground, head on her paws. "Do you think she hates to be in the cage?"

"She has some space outside, where the tigers roam around the field over there. Maybe she's here because she wants to be." Surreptitiously he glanced at his watch. It was now ten-thirty. Experience told him that with a boy of Jonathan's age missing, the police would already be informed. Descriptions of the boy would be broadcast to every police car. In the zoo they were better off than in the streets, at least for the time being. But that could change as the news of

Jonathan's disappearance got out. He'd better hurry things up.

Once again doubt overwhelmed him like a subtle enemy. It's been so long, he told himself. Self-pity flooded through him. So much had been taken away. He meant the boy no harm.

"Look," he said. "I didn't tell you this before because I didn't want to get you too excited. But your father told me that if he had not joined us by now, we were to go to him, and I think we ought to find a cab and go."

"Why didn't you tell me before?" Jonathan cried.

"I told you, because I didn't want for you to be too excited and start insisting we go to him right away."

"I'm not a baby!" If there was anything that enraged Jonathan it was someone, usually his mother, treating him as though he were younger than he actually was. "I'd have understood. Where are we supposed to meet him?"

Lawrence had prepared himself for this question. "At a house where he and his agent are going to meet another writer and another agent. They're there to discuss a special writing project they're both engaged in." Silently he thanked the fates that Ben had been able to tell him about the father's profession.

Jonathan frowned. "Dad always said he'd never go in with another writer on a book. He says it almost never works. And anyway, how did he know we were going to be at the zoo?"

Sweat started to break out again on Lawrence's hairline. Why couldn't this boy have been stupid? "Because he was quite sure that the zoo would be the place you'd want to go. You always go there when you're disappointed and upset."

"Yeah, I guess." Jonathan then added proudly, "He knows me pretty well, doesn't he? Even though he doesn't see me a lot. He knows me a lot better than—" Again he stopped.

"Than your mother?"

"Yeah."

Lawrence felt an upsurge in self-justification. Here was obviously a mother who didn't care, and her neglected son who needed someone to love him. . . . "Let's head to the gates, okay? I'm sure we'll find a cab there."

But when they approached the gate there were no yellow cabs in sight, and as Lawrence looked around he saw what he had been too preoccupied to notice before: the area was poor and almost entirely black. No wonder there were no yellow cabs. Then a dark car with the word LIVERY stuck in the windshield approached. "Here," Lawrence said, "We'll take this."

"That's not a cab," Jonathan objected.

"Yes it is. It's just a different company. In with you!" He pushed Jonathan into the back of the car, went to the driver's window and said quickly and in a low voice, "102nd Street and West End Avenue in Manhattan." Then he got in himself.

Sergeant Mooney faced Stephen Morgan and Marguerite Stanley in Sarah Jennings's office. He was sitting in the chair beside the desk, Sarah was sitting at her desk, and the two children were on the small neat sofa against the wall.

"Now," he said. "Could you please tell me, Stephen, why you thought Jonathan might be with his father?"

Stephen felt himself caught between a rock and a hard place.

When Miss Babson, whom he rather liked, had inquired about Jonathan, he had, without thinking, offered his opinion based on a conversation he had overheard between his parents, two of Patrick Tierney's best friends. The previous evening Stephen, sitting on a stool beside the refrigerator in the family kitchen eating some ice cream, had heard his parents talking on the other side of the kitchen, from which he was invisible. The conversation went like this:

Stephen's mother: "Do you think Pat's got a snowball's chance in hell of getting custody of Jonathan? Not that he shouldn't have it, considering Martha's alcoholism."

Stephen's father: "Yes, for the first time I do, if he can manage to stay cool. He said he was going to try and see Jonathan, but for God's sake don't blab that around for Martha to hear. . . ."

And then the conversation veered to the trouble Stephen's mother had in keeping things to herself.

The moment Stephen had said his piece to Miss Babson in class, he had felt guilty that in some way he could have threatened Jonathan's chance of living with his father. It was not a mistake he was going to make again. There was no question in his mind that Jonathan and his father were now together, and this fact must remain a secret until the time was right for Mr. Tierney to make his move.

"Well?" Detective Mooney said patiently.

"I don't know. I just thought maybe he might be."

"You know that Jonathan's parents are divorced and that Jonathan lives with his mother, don't you?"

"Sure. Everybody knows that."

"Then why did you think he might be with his father?"

"Well, sometimes he is. On some holidays."

"But today isn't a holiday, is it? I mean, you're all here in school, aren't you?"

"I guess so—I mean, sure."

"So why, if it's not a holiday and Jonathan mostly visits with his father on holidays, would you think he might be with his father now? Did you hear somebody say that he might be?"

That was so near the case that Stephen was suddenly afraid that the cop was reading his mind.

"No," he said. "I didn't hear anybody."

Mooney looked thoughtfully at the boy's face that had now gone pink. "The reason we want to know is that if Jonathan is not with his father— And he isn't. His father's just been here. Jonathan was supposed to have met his father, but he didn't show up. So, as I say, since Jonathan's not with his father, he could be in serious trouble. You know about that, don't you?"

"Yes." Doubt entered Stephen's head. But his father was sure, and his father had told his mother to keep it to herself. So it was now up to Stephen to keep this policeman from forcing something out of him. He stared at Mooney.

"I have a feeling you know something that you're not telling," Mooney said gently.

Stephen went on looking at Mooney and made himself think about some homework he would have to hand in tomorrow at class. Although he didn't entirely believe that somebody could read somebody else's mind, he wasn't going to take any chances. He concentrated on thinking about the book on Lincoln that he was going to have to report on.

"Isn't there something you know that you're not telling us?" Mooney asked.

"No," Stephen said. Abraham Lincoln was born in Kentucky, he recited to himself.

Mooney was unconvinced, but he knew enough about children and about questioning them to realize he couldn't get any further for the moment.

"What about you, Marguerite? The principal tells me that you said Jonathan often goes to an animal shelter. Do you know which one?"

"Well, there's the one in Park Slope."

"You mean the shelter run by the Animal Welfare Society?"

"Yes."

Mooney flipped open his book. "We've already been in touch with them and described Jonathan. They recognized him from the description, but said he hadn't been there for a while." He closed the notebook. "I believe there are private people who pick up stray animals and then sometimes try to find homes for them. Do you know of any?"

"No," Marguerite said. "My Aunt Megan has a lot of cats, but I wouldn't exactly call her a shelter."

"But you don't know of anyone else?"

"Not really."

There was something so truthful about the rather stocky child that Mooney automatically felt she might be lying. He stared at her and she stared back. "I don't have to tell you, do I, how important—for Jonathan's own safety—it is for us to find him."

Marguerite pushed down a feeling of guilt. She, too, had persuaded herself that Jonathan was probably with his father. She knew very well that that was what Stephen thought, and if he thought that, as far as she was concerned, it was true. Stephen might be stupid enough to like that bossy Miss Babson, but he didn't exaggerate or fool around with facts. Furthermore, the private shelter that she often visited, with Jonathan, was a secret. According to the crazy woman who ran it, all her dozens of cats would be taken out and killed if the enemy—she called them "the authorities" —should ever find out. She and the animals lived in her tumbledown, dilapidated house across the street from Marguerite and her aunt. "She's the Mother Teresa of the animal world," one admirer and occasional worker in the house had said.

No one, including or perhaps especially this policeman, must ever discover the number of creatures that lived in the crazy woman's house. Marguerite and Jonathan had been sworn to secrecy. So when the policeman said to her, "Are you positive you don't know of any other shelters around here?" Marguerite was able to look at him with a child's candor and say, "Positive."

Detective Mooney was stymied. He was certain that each child was hiding something, but if so, he hadn't been able to get it out.

"All right," he said. "I may come and talk to you again here at the school, or maybe at your homes." As he spoke he looked at each little face. But neither one altered in any way. For a moment he wished he could have shaken them.

Barry Pinkus waited for Cheryl outside the college, leaning against the wall of the main administration building. Sometimes he thought it wasn't such a bad old place. At least for the minimum outlay of money he would one day, sooner or later, emerge with a degree. It wouldn't be a distinguished degree from a prestigious university. Urban cow college, he called it to himself. But a degree was a degree, and while he was pretty sure he'd get ahead with or without it, a B.A. from anywhere dressed up a résumé. As he leaned there, his mind slid to a familiar and pleasurable fantasy. There he would be, in Hollywood, an agent of incredible influence and power. Studios would court him because of his notable clients. The would-be stars would do everything in their power to persuade him to represent them. But everybody would know that Barry took only the best, the best that he knew he could place and push on their way up. . . .

"So why couldn't we meet at the Shamrock?"

Jarred out of his daydream, Barry reflected again on the sharp edge in his beloved's voice—something he managed to forget most of the time. He straightened. "Because we said to meet here. Remember?"

"Only after you said you didn't like the Shamrock. What've you got against it?"

The Shamrock was not the kind of bar featured in Barry's fantasies. The latter summoned up comparisons with the King Cole Bar in the St. Regis, or the Oak Bar at the Plaza, cocktail lounges where his boss's secretary was constantly telling clients to meet her employer. "Mr. Fremantle said to meet him in the Oak Bar at five-thirty," she frequently said over the phone to a privileged author or an important Hollywood contact. "He usually sits in one of the corner booths. Just say you're meeting Mr. Fremantle and the headwaiter will take you there immediately."

Barry had been to the Oak Bar himself now twice. The first time was when a hand-delivered letter Mr. Fremantle was waiting for arrived just after he left the office to meet a client for dinner. "Take this to Mr. Fremantle in the Oak Bar, Barry," the secretary said. "He wants to get it tonight. Do you know where it is?"

"Sure. Plaza Hotel."

"Okay. Here it is. Get moving."

Just going to the Plaza had set his heart beating. As he neared the sacred premises of the Oak Room he thought he'd suffocate. A headwaiter bore down on him with a chilling look, but when Barry said he was there to deliver a letter to Mr. Fremantle, the waiter's face thawed and he waved a hand towards the agent's table.

The literary agent, a well-mannered man, thanked him and then introduced him to Patrick Tierney. "As I'm sure I don't have to tell you, Barry, Mr. Tierney is the author of *Focus,* one of the most successful books we've handled. And this is Barry Pinkus, who messengers for us while he's getting his degree."

"Hi!" Patrick said. "Where are you studying?"

"Baruch."

"Good for you."

Focus, an intricate and riveting story of international intrigue, had not won the Pulitzer Prize, but it had been made into a successful movie. For Barry, meeting Patrick Tierney was almost the equivalent of meeting the Pope for a devout Catholic.

"You worked on the screenplay, didn't you Mr. Tierney?"

Patrick smiled, and his intense, rather bony face, relaxed. "For my sins. Writing the novel was a picnic by comparison."

"Don't let him fool you, Barry," Fremantle said. "He turned out to be a born screen writer. I'm going to scribble a note on the back of this envelope and I'd like you to take it back to the office. I think Janice will still be there."

Speeding out of the Oak Room he had not heard Fremantle say to Patrick, "The kid has enough ambition for a killer whale, but what he's really good at is photography. He ought to go into that instead of dreaming of Hollywood."

But by the next day Barry knew such an exchange had taken place, because while he was chewing his sandwich in his cubbyhole near the reception office, Patrick Tierney had strolled in and offered a proposition: an assignment to take some photographs of Tierney's son, Jonathan. "Look," Patrick had said, taking out a map of Brooklyn Heights. "Here is where Jonathan lives, and here is where he goes to school. The name of the school is St. Andrew's, and it's on Remsen Street. You could snap the shot there either in the morning or at the end of the school day. It'd be easier, of course, to take him coming out of his house, but . . . well, I'm afraid his mother might see you, and there'd be hell to pay."

So Barry had taken his camera to Remsen Street early one morning, had fixed it with a telescopic lens, and had snapped away while Jonathan loitered talking to various friends. Barry, hiding across the street in a doorway, had not been noticed. Taking the camera back, he had developed the pictures himself and carried them into Fremantle & Coe the next day. Patrick had been delighted. With his pencil he had drawn frames around the parts he had wanted enlarged, and when that was done, had paid Barry handsomely.

On the strength of that money, Barry had taken Cheryl to the Oak Bar, cautioning her to dress properly.

"What're you talking about? I always dress right."

"Well, no punk stuff," Barry had said. "That place is full of class."

For all her defiance, Cheryl had been impressed. Finally she asked the crucial question: "Where'd you get the money for a place like this?"

Barry had never boasted about his photography because that was not where his ambition lay. But he knew he took good pictures and told her about his assignment from Patrick.

"You sure it was his kid?" Cheryl asked. She was older than Barry and her professional life had lain along paths he had hardly dreamed of.

"Sure I'm sure. Why else'd he want the pics?"

"He might be one of those men. Men who like boys."

"I told you, this is his son. He took out an old photo of the kid and showed it to me. It was all he had, but it was about three or four years old."

Cheryl shrugged. "So you could recognize him?"

"Yeah. A good-looking kid. Maybe a little, well, sensitive. But you couldn't miss him even in a crowd of other kids."

"Got any copies of the pics?"

"No, I gave him all the positives. Why?"

Cheryl lied. "I'm thinking of taking drawing lessons again. I used to do it in school. A picture of a nice-looking kid'd be something to help me. Better than a real kid, because they're never still."

"Okay. I still have the negatives. I'll bring you some glossies next time we meet."

Cheryl had looked at them. Barry had been right. The kid was good-looking, almost beautiful. She knew who'd pay good money for those photos. "Gee thanks, Barry. These'll help a lot."

For all his smattering of street smarts, Barry had a broad streak of naïveté. He liked to call himself a New Yorker, which was accurate in that he came from New York State. But he was not from the city. Barry had grown up in a small town outside Rochester. What Cheryl saw immediately she could do with the photographs was something that would not have occurred to him in a thousand years.

Now he said, "I thought we said we'd meet in front of the administration building. It's near Joey's, where they have great beer and sandwiches." In fact, he was embarrassed to admit to his dislike of the Shamrock. But he found the people there sleazy and a little frightening, and he didn't care for the way some of the men looked at him. Not for anything, though, would he have said this to Cheryl. She had an uncomfortable way, sometimes, of looking at him and pronouncing judgment on some of his statements. "That's not cool, Barry." One of the things he liked about Cheryl was her air of having been around.

As they munched their sandwiches at Joey's, Cheryl asked casually, "Hey, you got any more pictures of kids? I mean, the photos you gave me really help. I was thinking I oughta have more. Like, they're different and it'd give me more experience."

"No. I once thought about going into photography, but agenting is the place to be now."

Cheryl chose her words carefully. "Y'know, I think you could make some money with pictures of kids. I mean, like, agents are always looking for them for commercials and so on. I know a couple of people from work who do photos for them."

"Yeah? Well sure, if you know any kids who want to break into television or Broadway, I'd take their pictures."

This wasn't exactly what Cheryl's business partner had in mind. What he actually said was, "Tell your pals I'll buy pictures of kids this good-looking anytime. There're never enough for the market."

The business partner worked in a filthy-looking walk-up in one of the side streets between Broadway and Seventh Avenue. Ostensibly it was a place that developed ordinary snapshots at a discount, and tourists, attracted by the SAME DAY, 40% OFF sign, dropped film off there constantly. But behind the cut-rate front and up one flight was a full floor, divided into cubicles and a couple of studios. Clients came there for something else. Painted on the windows facing the street were the words BALLET SCHOOL, and music—usually familiar ballet music, but sometimes rock—sounded constantly. This explained the children, both boys and girls, but mostly boys, going in and out of the doorway.

For the umpteenth time Cheryl wished Barry weren't such a square. He was a sweet guy and better in bed than most of the men she'd slept with. But she stuck to him because there was something about him that gave her confidence in his ultimate success. If, in the meantime, somebody with more success up front happened on the scene, she'd leave Barry in a minute. Barry was a good-looking boy, and sometimes she wondered why he stuck with her. She knew she wasn't pretty. What she didn't fully realize was that in her almost anorexic thinness she had an entirely false air of fragility, and it appealed to a romantic streak in Barry that still existed under his layers of hastily acquired sophistication.

Cheryl now tried to figure some way to get Barry to find handsome boys, photograph them and bring the pictures back to her.

"You know, you could just take your camera along in the street, snap good-looking kids, get their names and addresses, and if the people at the commercial agencies want them, well, then it's a nice surprise for them."

Naïve as he was, this suggestion rang some faint alarm in Barry's mind. "Just take pictures of kids whether or not they want it?"

Cheryl pushed her empty dish back and got up from the table. Barry might be a pushover, but she had to be careful. One push too many and she might be in trouble. "It's up to you. Just thought you could use the money. Commercial agencies are always looking for cute children for their ads. And some of them would kill to get on television. I have to get back now. Thanks for the lunch." And she marched out of the restaurant, confident that Barry would be so upset if she seemed displeased that he wouldn't think of anything else. She was right.

"Hey!" Barry said, throwing some money down on the table and going after her. "Maybe you're right. Maybe it is a good idea!"

He was behind her so he didn't see the look of satisfaction that crossed her face.

Neither did he see the man who rose up after they did. The man had been stalking Cheryl all morning. Now, also leaving money on the table, he followed them out.

4 Martha paced back and forth in her living room. It was a few minutes past one. She had been at home an hour, following the suggestion of that sadistic policeman, Mooney, that she should be there in case Jonathan came home, or in case he or someone else called. It was the "someone else" part that she found sadistic.

Actually, Mooney had said, "Maybe you ought to go on home. Jonathan would go there if he were just coming back from some outing or adventure or spree, or some—someone might call about him." He made an effort not to sound punitive or threatening. Martha heard the slowing of his words as a deliberate effort to inflict pain.

"Bloody sadist," she said aloud, and then, again, "Bloody sadist."

The words served for a moment to buoy her up. Then her spirit caved in. If she had just not overslept. If she had just not drunk herself into a zombie state last night, sitting in front of the tube. What was it she had been watching? She couldn't remember. She passed out around eleven and then woke up around four with the dry heaves. She retched long past the time when there was anything left to bring up. That was when she had taken an Alka-Seltzer and a pill and had slept until . . . until Jonathan was gone.

"Oh God!" she whispered, and, as though pulled, her eyes went across the room to the cabinet where she kept the liquor and where two bottles, one of bourbon and one of vodka, were sitting on a tray on top of the cabinet.

The desire—no, far more than that—the craving for a drink blotted out everything else, even, for a moment, the pain about Jonathan. The drink would unquestionably make her feel better, think better, function better. . . . She was almost across the room when something within her, something new and implacable, said in her mind, as though somebody else had uttered the words, You Cannot Drink Now.

It was not a decision she was making. It was a decision that had been made.

She turned away and started pacing again. Then the phone caught her eye. She could call the school to see if any news had come. . . . She could call— Who else was there for her to call?

"Please bring him home!" The words came out of her like a cry. And then, "Please let him be all right!"

To whom was she praying? She had gone from being a devout believer to an angry agnostic. "All religions are the same and they're all crap!" That had been a line used more than once in some of her barroom arguments.

Always when she was slightly drunk any conversation turned to cosmic issues. Why I Believe in God. The God I Believe In. Finally, The Belief in God Is the Longest-Running Myth in the History of the World. It was a long title, but it had style, and many of the evenings in front of the television set were spent polishing some of its arguments. Not on paper, just in her head. It was a talk she would deliver one day when she was finally recognized as one of the better writers and thinkers of modern journalism, one of the victims of the sexism that continued to rage in the world of newspapers and news magazines. . . .

"Please let him be all right. Please let him just be playing hooky."

She found herself once again within feet of the liquor bottles. One drink would make her think more clearly, feel better, be better able to help in this awful crisis, help her perhaps remember something that might yield a clue—

Her hand was reaching out when the phone rang. Obviously God had stepped down and prevented her from picking up that drink. She ran over and lifted the receiver. "Hello?" Her voice came out high and panicky.

"Martha?"

"Pat. Have you heard anything?"

"No. That's why I'm calling. You'd be more likely to hear than I. Have you heard from Jonathan or from anybody about him?"

She shook her head and then realized that he couldn't see her. "No."

"It's no use asking you about anything he might have said this morning. What about last night? Do you remember anything?"

"Last night? What kind of thing?"

"Use your head, Martha. Anything at all he might have said if he planned to go somewhere today."

What did they do yesterday evening? The last part was pretty much a muddle. But in the earlier part . . . She remembered pan-frying some chicken legs for a casserole and then chopping tomatoes and celery and thawing some peas.

. . . A picture of her kitchen appeared in her mind. Where was Jonathan? She saw herself, a big knife in one hand, holding the tomato in the other, and off to one side, a glass with dark gold liquid. And lying full-length on the other end of the table, Susan, hoping for a handout.

"Jonathan and I had dinner here." She wanted to add, "I cooked it." But it would sound ridiculous.

"And he was there all evening?"

The sharp impatience in Patrick's voice, a sound that was once all too familiar but which she hadn't heard for a while, provoked anger and self-pity. "Yes, he was here all evening."

Was he? She remembered his helping her put the dishes in the dishwasher. She remembered his going back to his room to work. What did they talk about at dinner? It was a blank.

"I can't think of anything he said that had any bearing on where he is now," she said. There was a silence. Then Martha asked timidly, "Have you heard anything? What— what does the policeman say? Mooney, what does he say?"

"Nothing. You and I left at about the same time because he wanted to talk to the children alone. Remember? I came home, and I haven't heard from him since and neither has Miss Jennings. I called and asked her. Look, here is the phone number you can reach me at. 555-4766."

"That isn't the number to your apartment."

"No. My apartment is sublet and will remain so for the next month. Right now I'm subletting one myself. If you hear anything at all, call that number. If I'm not there, there's a tape. If there's any problem you can always call Roger Fremantle."

He was about to hang up when Martha said, "Pat—"

"Well?"

"Do you think Jon's going to be all right? I mean, a kid

often goes off this way, doesn't he? You were a boy once. Boys do this more than girls, don't they?"

Even as she talked, Martha knew that she was pleading subserviently, begging for reassurance, and hated herself for it. "I mean——"

"You mean you want some reassurance that everything's going to be all right. I'd like that, too, Martha. But I'd like it even better if I could have the reassurance that by some magic you'd become a responsible mother, somebody with whom I'd feel safe leaving my son, since the idiot courts seem to feel that a mother—any mother at all—is preferable to a father. If I hear anything I'll let you know."

The moment he hung up Patrick was sorry for his next to last comment. For one thing, it wasn't entirely true. As he well knew, his own absences had a lot to do with Martha's having custody. And there was no point in weighing in on his former wife at this point. Furthermore, reproaches would probably wipe out what little memory and ability to think she had left. But his anger, that had lately seemed bottomless, bubbled up when he least expected it.

He was in a small flat sublet to him by a friend who was spending the season in L.A., and for a moment, to his intense surprise, Patrick wished he were in the Brooklyn Heights apartment. He and Martha had lived there for eight years—three before Jonathan was born and five afterwards. And he would have sworn that its bitter memories for him had erased the good ones. But there *had* been good ones, before Martha had crossed some invisible line to alcoholic drinking, before he started staying out the night with somebody else. For a moment he saw Martha as she had been four years previously—bright, articulate, funny, sexy—a woman who could still excite him. There had been some good years, before and especially after Jonathan was born, years when the three of them did things together—had picnics, went to the zoo and the aquarium, strolled on the promenade opposite the soaring jumble of downtown Manhattan. Both he and Martha were making good money, and the duplex on Sidney Place, although expensive, was well within their combined income. Now he had to maintain it for Martha and their son. Fortunately, he had made money on his most recent book so it wasn't much of a strain.

He got up. Waiting was godawful. He stared at the photograph of Jonathan in a leather traveling frame that was now beside his bed. It was another of the ones taken by that kid, Barry something, employed as a gofer by Roger Fremantle.

Pat stared at the phone, then jerked up his arm to look at the time. Nearly one. The kid was probably on his lunch break.

Patrick was downstairs trying to hail a cab before he knew what he was doing.

Actually, Detective Mooney was ahead of him. Armed with Barry's name and the address of Patrick's agent, he had got into his car and driven into Manhattan. Fremantle & Coe were on Greenwich Avenue in Greenwich Village, an avenue that lay athwart the strict rectangular grid that marked the midsection of Manhattan, slanting from Sixth Avenue and Eighth Street to Eighth Avenue at Fourteenth Street.

The Fremantle office was on the fourth floor of what had once been two brownstones that had been joined together. In the front was a reception office and off it a room not much larger than a closet, where the messenger sat and which also served as a mailroom.

When buzzing from below, Mooney had, on impulse, simply given his name. No need, he thought, to announce that he came from the police. He had no reason to think there was anything amiss with the gofer who took the pictures of Jonathan, but who knew how the boy might react? And who knew also how many back doors there were to such an old place?

Fremantle's secretary, who also doubled as the office receptionist, pressed the bell to let him in without demanding credentials—not, Mooney thought, the safest practice in a city like New York. On the other hand, a literary agent could very well have clients, authors, and assorted others coming in at all hours and couldn't always demand they wait at the door to be properly identified.

When he got in, he asked the receptionist, "Do you have a messenger named Barry Pinkus here?"

"Sure. He's out now with some packages, but he ought to be back soon." She eyed the policeman. "Who wants him?"

Mooney took out his identification and showed it to her.

"Wow! What's Barry been up to?"

Mooney smiled a little. "Nothing, as far as I know."

"Well . . . you can sit there if you want to. He shouldn't be too long."

Mooney sat down in the chair in the waiting area and tried to be patient. The boy, Jonathan, had been missing only a few hours. Mooney reminded himself that the chances that there was anything wrong were a hundred to one. Dozens of children in New York wandered off every day, giving their parents and their schools the fright of their lives. And then they came back wondering what the fuss was about, or were found playing hooky.

But there were the others, the ones who did not come

back. Mooney knew their names, and they filed past in his mind.

Roger Fremantle, on his way from the men's room outside the office, came through the reception area and saw a tired-looking man in his forties in a poorly fitting suit sitting there patiently, looking at a notebook in his hands.

"May I help you?" Fremantle asked.

Mooney stood up. "I'm waiting for your messenger, Barry, Barry Pinkus, to come back." He paused. "I'm Detective Pete Mooney." And he took out his identification again.

Fremantle glanced at it. "Why do you want Barry?" He was surprised. Barry had seemed a squeaky-clean kid, surprisingly so in the late eighties in the city of New York.

Mooney was taking in the handsome, rather nattily dressed literary agent. About forty-five. WASP. Such classifications were inevitable and meant nothing to Mooney except as a filing system.

"I believe he took some photographs of Patrick Tierney's son, Jonathan, for Mr. Tierney. Did you know anything about it?"

"No. But that doesn't mean anything." He paused. "I do remember mentioning to Pat that Barry took excellent photographs."

"Have you talked to Mr. Tierney in the last couple of hours?"

"No. Why?"

At that inopportune moment Barry burst through the front door. Seeing his boss and another man talking in the small area, he skidded to a stop.

"Why?" Fremantle persisted.

"Just a moment, sir." Mooney turned to Barry. "You're Barry Pinkus?"

"Yes."

"I'm Detective Mooney." Mooney pulled out his identification again. "Did you take photographs of Jonathan Tierney during the past week or so?"

Oh God, Barry thought. Some nosy, interfering neighbor of the school had complained. Was it against the law? "Yes. I did. Mr. Tierney asked me to. What's wrong with that?"

"Nothing, as far as I know."

"Detective Mooney, why are you asking these questions?" Fremantle asked sharply.

"Because Jonathan's father and mother and the school are concerned. Jonathan hasn't been seen since about five to eight this morning."

"My God!" Fremantle said. "You mean he never turned up at school?"

"No. A neighbor saw him when he came to look at some kittens in her apartment around seven-thirty. Then he left at five to eight, saying he was supposed to meet a friend at a doughnut shop on Court Street. It seems the so-called friend was his father, who had made a date to meet him at the doughnut place at eight. Mr. Tierney was there, but Jonathan never showed up."

"Oh Christ!" Fremantle turned to the receptionist. "Get Patrick on the phone for me, Sheila."

Mooney turned back to Barry. The boy had gone completely white. Mooney cursed the fate that had brought Fremantle out to the reception area when he did. Mooney would have led up to the subject in a more circuitous way.

"No reason to be frightened," he said. "You didn't do anything wrong in taking the photographs. Did you, by the way, show them to anybody?"

"No," Barry said. In the few seconds between the cop's first question as to whether he had taken the photographs and this last one Barry had come to a difficult but necessary decision. He had to protect Cheryl. He knew there'd been vague trouble in Cheryl's young life. She'd never been too specific about her reasons for mistrusting police, but one thing was clear: she was in no way to blame.

"Just because you stick up for your boss," she said once to Barry, "they look on you like a . . . a criminal."

"Police are as corrupt as anyone else in New York," Barry had said, quoting Pinkus senior, who found paying the mob for protection for his small cleaning establishment was in no important way different from paying the local police, which he also had done. Anyway, Cheryl must be protected against unfair pressure.

"No," Barry said firmly. "I didn't show them to anybody. And I developed them myself."

"I thought Dad's agent lived in Greenwich," Jonathan said. There was an edgy note to his voice.

"His house is there," Lawrence said quickly. "This is just an apartment where he entertains clients—he keeps it for business."

Lawrence could feel Jonathan's rising anxiety. The boy was becoming suspicious. Once again Lawrence asked himself bitterly why he couldn't have been interested in a slower, less sophisticated child. He had to get Jonathan to the apartment soon. Fortunately, there were only a few more blocks to go until they reached 102nd Street and Broadway. (He had not dared to give the driver the exact address. Cab drivers were required by law to record such addresses, and he didn't want it noted down anywhere.) Once they reached the corner, they'd be almost at the apartment, the address and keys of which had been given him by Ben Nicolaides, the man who sold him the pictures of Jonathan. Lawrence didn't like Ben, and he didn't want to take Jonathan to the apartment Ben was supplying. He wanted Jonathan for himself for as long as he wanted him. He would treat him like a son, a much loved son. . . .

But there were practical problems. Lawrence no longer had a place where he could take a boy like Jonathan, a place where he and the boy would be safe from prying neighbors. Even in a city like New York, neighbors could be a nuisance. But Ben, who owned the studio off Broadway that Lawrence patronized from time to time, had offered this apartment. "It's an old place," he'd said. "We use it for filming some of our deluxe stuff. The walls are thick. You and the kid could be there for a while and nobody'd be the wiser. Then I'd know where to find him when I needed to start some work."

"All right." Lawrence tried not to think about how much he disliked this particular man, his dirty fingernails, his leering eyes and heavy mouth. He wore a diamond ring on his little finger and his clothes emitted a musky perfume. Lawrence's feeling for this boy had nothing in common with the sleazy traffic the man specialized in, Lawrence assured himself again and again.

"You mean Dad's agent has an apartment up here?" Jonathan asked as the taxi passed through a particularly run-down block. Astonishment and doubt filled his voice. He was a New York City boy, born and bred. He knew about neighborhoods, whether in Brooklyn or Manhattan. And there was nothing in the neighborhood of Amsterdam Avenue and Ninety-ninth Street, through which they were now passing, that indicated it might be a place where the elegant Mr. Fremantle would live. Almost everyone in sight was either Black or Hispanic and all were plainly poor. Jonathan was free from racial and ethnic prejudice. But, like most New Yorkers, he was snobbish about neighborhoods.

"We're just going through it," Lawrence said. Again he could feel the sweat on his face and under his arms. Then, as so often happened in the city, the cab traversed a few blocks and they were among the old, beautifully built apartment houses of the Upper West Side.

"Here y'are," the driver said. He had been listening to his radio most of the time and ignored the conversation behind him.

"Come along now," Lawrence said, pushing Jonathan out of the taxi ahead of him. He thrust some bills through the window. The tip would be obscenely large, but he didn't want that nosy driver looking at his face any longer than necessary. His photograph hadn't appeared in any newspaper for several years. But once it had been in every paper and news magazine in the country. And he was afraid of long memories.

"Just along here," Lawrence said, walking quickly west. His hand was around Jonathan's arm.

"I don't understand Dad's wanting me to come up here," Jonathan said. He sounded both angry and afraid and pulled against the man's hold.

"He'll tell you himself in just a minute." Lawrence stopped about halfway along the block in front of a narrow gray stucco house.

Jonathan had a glimpse of the Hudson River seen through the trees of Riverside Park, of a brownstone house next door, where a Siamese cat, like Susan, was in the window, sitting beside a yellow flower in a potted plant. The next moment they were walking up the steps of the apartment house. Lawrence, his hand retaining its hold on Jonathan's arm, smiled down at him. "Any moment now you'll be with your father." Jonathan stared at the doorknob, a leopard's head with a ball in its mouth. He wondered if they were going to use it. But the man inserted his key and the next moment they were in the elevator.

Patrick Tierney burst into his agent's reception area to find Fremantle, Barry and the detective, Mooney, all standing there, looking tense.

"You're sure you didn't show the pictures to anyone?" Mooney was asking Barry.

"I'm sure," Barry said. His eyes slid to Patrick. "Hello, Mr. Tierney. Will you please tell the detective here that you asked me to take those pictures of Jonathan. And I'm sorry about his not . . . about his being missing."

Fremantle turned. "Patrick, for God's sake. This is a hell of a thing! I'm sorry! I'm sure he's going to show up, having decided to take French leave of some kind. But I know how you must feel. Anything at all we can do—just tell us!"

Patrick was fond of Fremantle and knew that he owed him a lot, but for a moment he wanted to throw back, "No, you can't know how I feel!" Because Fremantle, thrice married and busy courting number four, had never had children.

Instead, Patrick said, "Thanks." And to Mooney, "Have you found anything?"

Mooney shook his head. Then he asked, "Did you show your pictures to anyone at all?"

"No. I didn't have anyone to show them to. I used another of the shots to put in a leather traveling frame I have. The rest are in my file drawer." Patrick turned to Barry. "Did you show them to anyone?"

If Patrick had asked that question before the arrival of the detective, Barry knew he would have gladly told him that Cheryl had seen and admired them. But the cop's interest changed everything.

"No, Mr. Tierney, like I told the detective here, I didn't show them to anybody."

"Okay." He paused. "Where you had them developed, would somebody there have seen them or borrowed them?"

"No, like I said, I develop my own."

"Well," Patrick said, "I guess that's that."

"What are you thinking might have happened if he did show the pictures to somebody?" Fremantle asked. He was far from naïve, but long work with contracts and familiarity with the world of words made him prefer to have things spelled out when possible.

Mooney hesitated. He was a compassionate man and didn't, at this point, want to present to Patrick's imagination some of the more frightening things that could happen to an eight-year-old boy. But moving quickly was right now more important than compassion.

"Jonathan is a good-looking boy—an unusually good-looking boy. There are markets for such kids. I'm sure you know that, Mr. Tierney. And there are people whose chief job is to find them, which they do by any means they can, including looking at pictures—anybody's pictures."

"Well," Fremantle said after a silence, "no one has seen Barry's. So I guess Jonathan's all right from that point of view."

Mooney turned to Barry. "Do you have the negatives?"

"Yes."

"I'd like to have them."

"Sure." There was a sick feeling in his stomach. Into his worry for Cheryl a seed of doubt had entered. He refused to acknowledge it. But it did not go away. "I can bring them in tomorrow."

"Why don't I go along with you and pick them up. Where do you live?"

Barry's spirits sank even further. He was ashamed of having anyone see the rathole in the West Fifties which he shared with two other boys. It was a studio containing one pull-out bed and a narrow cot. They had to share the only bureau. But Barry had bought a steel file cabinet which he had placed against the one remaining wall space that wasn't occupied by the sofa bed, the cot, the bureau or the television set. It was in the file cabinet that he kept his photographs and negatives.

"West Fifty-third," he said resignedly.

"May I come along?" Patrick's tone indicated that he did not expect no for an answer.

"If you want to," Mooney said. He turned to Fremantle. "Can I use your phone?"

Fremantle indicated the telephone in the reception area. "Or you can go into any of the offices if you want to be private."

"This is fine." Mooney murmured into the phone for a few minutes, then put down the receiver.

"Any news?" Patrick asked when he was through.

"No." Mooney strove for a reassuring note. "It's pretty early yet, you know. If Jonathan decided to play hooky, which is what it looks like, he's probably not going to go back home before the usual hour."

"But surely he'd guess that when he didn't show at school, the school would be in touch with his family. Where was he when he was supposed to be meeting me?" Patrick hit the table with his open hand.

"How did he sound when you talked to him, Mr. Tierney? Excited? Pleased? Fearful? Resigned?"

"He sounded the way he always sounded when there was a prospect of our getting together. Excited, yes, pleased, yes. Resigned, no, although he ended the conversation quickly because I gather his mother came into the room." He paused. "Have you talked to Mrs. Stanley?"

"No. I called her but there was no answer. I'll try again. We'd better get going after those negatives."

"Yes."

Patrick and Barry went with Mooney in his car to Barry's

address. "This whole area used to be called Hell's Kitchen," Mooney said as they got out of the car and he locked it.

Five flights later they were ushered into the small apartment by Barry. The sofa bed was folded, but a swatch of sheet stuck out from behind one of the cushions. The cot, unmade, was shoved in front of it. "Sorry about the mess," he said. Going over to the file cabinet, he unlocked it with a key he took out of his pocket. He rummaged quickly through the folders, then went through them again. After that he paused and stared at the drawer.

"What's the matter?" Patrick asked. Somehow he knew the answer.

"The negatives aren't here," Barry said. "They're gone."

5

Martha sat on the high stool in her kitchen, drinking her sixth cup of coffee. Although she was an inveterate user of saccharin, dim memories of books she had read on nutrition made her decide at the fourth cup to use sugar to counteract the caffeine. The reason she was sitting on the high stool thrust against the counter instead of in a more comfortable chair was that, because of her shaking hands, she couldn't hold the cup. From where she was sitting, she could sip from the cup resting on the counter without attempting to pick it up. Her body was alternately hot and covered in cold sweat. The demon in her head kept telling her that if she had a drink—just one drink—she would feel better and cope better and be better able to help Jonathan.

"Get thee behind me, Satan," she said aloud. She prayed aloud, too. "Lord, just bring Jonathan back safely and I won't drink again."

Unfortunately, she had attempted this bargain several times before, had been given what she asked for, and in due course picked up a drink.

"I mean it this time," she said aloud, and started to cry.

At that moment the telephone rang.

"Have you heard anything?" Megan Stanley asked.

"No," Martha said.

There was a pause. Then, "Would you like me to come over?"

"No, I'm all right. It's not necessary." Martha knew very well what Megan thought of her. Her answer was dictated by pride and resentment.

"All right. Let me know if I can do anything."

Martha's hand was shaking so badly she could hardly get the receiver back onto the phone. "Moralistic bitch!" she said to herself. And then she forgot to sip from the cup resting on the counter. Instead she picked it up. The cup, shaking in Martha's trembling hand, splashed coffee in every direction, including on her blouse and suit and on Susan, who was lying on the floor a few feet away. Susan gave a wild Siamese cry, sprang up and shook herself.

"I'm sorry," Martha said. "I'm sorry." Sober, she acknowledged to herself that when drinking she had often kicked Susan out of the way. And it was Jonathan's cat. Guilt flooded through her. She slid off the stool and tried to approach Susan. But Susan had learned early not to tangle with Martha. With another cry she sped out of the kitchen.

"I said I'm sorry," Martha cried, running after Susan. But she tripped over a garbage can and went sprawling.

Lying on the floor, she burst into tears and was still lying there when the phone rang again. Getting up was painful, but she moved as quickly as she could and snatched up the receiver.

"Hello?" she cried.

"It's Sarah Jennings. I just called to see if you're all right and whether you'd heard anything."

Martha stared at the wide run in her pantyhose and the scraped skin on her knee. "I haven't heard anything and I haven't had a drink, if that's what you mean."

"That's wonderful!" Sarah said. "Is there anything I can do? I can't leave the school for several hours, but short of that—"

"Just let me know if you hear from Jonathan or the detective or even my husband—my former husband."

"Of course I will." And then, "Try some broth, it's very soothing to the stomach."

The moment Sarah said that, Martha knew that Sarah was referring to her hangover and she bitterly resented it. "How would you know?" she snapped. She didn't really expect an answer.

"My older brother, David, is a member of AA. When he was newly sober and shaking to pieces he drank quarts of soup, more quarts of sweet tea, and lots of ice cream and candy. Your body loses a lot of sweet when you cut out alcohol. I'll call back later." And she hung up.

"Asshole!" Martha said to herself. Then she put her head in her hands. "I must *not* drink," she said aloud. After a while she looked at her half cup of muddy coffee, picked up her cup and saucer and took them to the sink. They rattled in her hand as she carried them and seemed to fly into the sink of their own accord. The cup broke, splashing more dregs onto Martha's skirt, which was already stained from the previous mishap.

Martha stood and stared at it. Where was Jonathan? What would they do with him? Mental pictures drawn from lurid newspaper and tabloid stories filled her mind. As a sometime writer on a news magazine she had also read her share of police stories of their raids on centers of child pornography and graphic accounts of what child abusers and pornographers did to the children they seduced or kidnapped.

"Oh God, oh God!" she cried, her head down between her arms resting on the drainboard.

The phone rang again. Again, it was Sarah. "Listen, Martha, I just called my brother. He said he thought it would be better—less dangerous—for you if you went into a detox center. He'd be glad to call the one he was in to see if they have a bed."

"I'm not going anywhere away from this house as long as Jonathan might be trying to get in touch with me, or the people who kidnapped him—if they did."

"All right," Sarah said slowly. "I can understand your feeling that way."

"That's hogwash, Sarah. You're not a drunk and you're not a mother. It's impossible for you to understand how I feel. And don't patronize me."

"All right, Martha." Sarah was reining in her temper—not an easy thing to do. "I won't bother you."

"Unless you hear about or from Jonathan," Martha screeched as Sarah slapped the phone down.

It rang again immediately. "Hello," Martha said breathlessly.

"Hi! Found Jon yet?" There was a slur in the words.

"Hello, Katie. No." She added, "You've been drinking."

"You told me to have a drink when you called this morning."

"Well, you've had more than one." A small voice within reminded her that alcohol was the main element in their friendship.

"If that isn't the pot calling the kettle black! What have you done since this morning? Taken the pledge? Gone to AA?"

"Oh shut up!" Martha slammed down the phone.

At the other end Katie replaced the receiver and stared at it angrily. "All right, Mrs. Pure and Holy. If you want to find out about that man I've seen lurking around the street then you're going to have to come off your high horse and apologize." Weaving towards the kitchen she poured herself another vodka on the rocks and took a swallow. "Dry. Very dry," she said. And then, "That'll teach her."

For a moment she thought she should call Martha back anyway and force her to listen to her report on the loitering stranger. But her ego was hurting. When the Tierneys first moved into the apartment in the brownstone three doors down, Katie had called, bringing them a bottle.

But she didn't see much of them at first. In fact, she was convinced they looked down on her. After Patrick left, she saw more of Martha, although not much while she was still working. When she quit (or was fired) Martha had taken to dropping in on Katie. As her drinking grew, so did the friendship. But Katie always had the idea that Martha condescended to her, and she resented it.

It was only in the last hour that she had remembered the man—tall, with a bony face and intense dark eyes under a shock of dark hair. He was, in a weird way, attractive, which was why Katie began to watch for him. She thought about him a lot, which was one reason she was a little hesitant to bring him up. Katie liked men, especially attractive ones. Once, when they had been drinking together, Katie had regaled Martha with some of the romantic tales of her life. Martha, far from sober, had giggled and said, "You seem to go for the wounded-hero type."

Katie felt she was being made fun of, and regretted saying anything about the matter. She had not brought up the subject of men since.

"Bloody snob," she said now. Sinking into her favorite chair, she pushed the On button in the remote control of her television set. Her favorite soap opera was about to start. Mrs. Saintly Tierney could just come hat in hand if she wanted any information from Katie. With another press of her finger she turned up the volume. She liked everything loud. That way it blotted out reality. And anyway, the neighbors weren't home in the middle of the day or—Katie checked her watch—the early afternoon.

The self-service elevator opened and Lawrence and Jonathan got out. There were only two doors in the small foyer. The silence was total.

Fumblingly, Lawrence got out a key and opened one of the doors. "Run on in," he said to Jonathan.

Jonathan hesitated, his fear stronger. "Are you sure Dad's here?"

Lawrence felt panic clawing at him. The walls were thick all right, but that would not prevent the people in the apartment opposite from hearing if Jonathan took it in his head to scream right outside their front door. Then inspiration struck. He put on a performance of studying his watch.

"We got here quicker than I thought. It's still a little before the time when your father said he'd be here. But let's wait inside where we can sit down."

"What time is it?"

"Around noon."

"What time were we supposed to meet Dad?"

"Twelve-thirty. Let's go in."

Jonathan might still have balked if the phone hadn't started to ring in the apartment.

"Come on," Lawrence said. "That might be your father now."

Jonathan ran in and picked up the phone. "Dad?" he said.

A male voice said, "Is Mr. Miller there?"

Jonathan, let down, said to Lawrence, "Are you Mr. Miller?"

Lawrence took up the receiver. "Ben?"

"I called to see if you had the boy yet." The voice at the other end gave a gravelly laugh. "I guess the answer's yes."

"Yes," Lawrence said.

"I want him ready to film when I get there later today. Until then, well, he's yours. But don't lose him."

"I won't."

When Lawrence hung up, Jonathan said, "Dad's not here."

"I told you. He will be soon."

"You said this was his agent's apartment. Will the agent be here, too?"

"Of course. Now, why don't we have some soda. Would you like a Coke?"

"Mom doesn't approve of my drinking Cokes. She said it's bad for my teeth. But I'll take one."

"All right. Why don't you go over and look at the river? You can see a little of it from the bedroom window. Sometimes sailing ships go past."

Jonathan wasn't a sailboat enthusiast, but he was liking Lawrence less and less. He even admitted to himself that he was afraid of him. So he'd rather watch boats than hang around the guy. "All right. Where's the bedroom?"

"The one that has the view is through that door." And Lawrence pointed towards the back and right of the apartment. Once he was in there, Lawrence figured, the boy's retreat would be cut off. If worse came to worst Lawrence could lock the bedroom door. And Ben was right. This was an old building. Jonathan could scream his heart out and nobody would hear him. "You look at the boats," he said to Jonathan, "and I'll get the sodas."

When Lawrence came into the bedroom carrying two sodas, Jonathan was staring out the window at the Hudson River. "There aren't any boats," he said crossly. An enormous sense of unease was welling up in him.

"Sometimes there aren't any for a few minutes, but usually one or two come along." Lawrence sipped his gin and tonic, which was more gin than tonic. Generally he preferred drugs to alcohol, but money had been short of late. Once Jonathan had been delivered, there'd be more money. So, much as he hated the thought of having such a short time with Jonathan himself, he felt that his personal needs came first.

"Don't you want your soda?" he asked.

"Sure." Jonathan was busy watching a sailboat and two tugboats that had appeared. Absently he sucked up some of the ice floating at the top of the soda. "What are those things for?" He turned and pointed to three tall standing lights in two corners and against one wall.

"For filming—filming models," Lawrence improvised as casually as he could. "You know, the pictures you've seen in magazines—women modeling new fashions."

"What a funny place to film them," Jonathan said. But he wasn't really interested. Oddly, he began to feel a little less tense.

Lawrence held his breath. He had been assured that the mild muscle relaxer he had put in the soda would not be detectable. What he would have liked most would be to have time to court the boy, and he had no doubt that he could successfully seduce him. But he wasn't going to be given that. So he felt he was justified in drugging him to make him more physically manageable. As Lawrence now went on talking in a slow, soothing, almost hypnotic way, he watched for the first sign that the drug had taken effect.

"All right," Mooney said, "let's take it from the beginning. Who could have gotten at your files?"

The studio apartment was so small that he and Patrick Tierney and Barry, all standing, occupied what room there was in the middle of the floor.

"I don't know," Barry said for the umpteenth time.

"Were any of your other pictures taken?"

Barry shook his head. "No, I haven't done that many. I think I'd notice."

"Well, look again. And look carefully."

Barry, almost sick with fright, went down on one knee again to look into the single file drawer. Quickly but thoroughly he examined every folder. "Nothing else is missing."

"Why would anyone want to steal them?" Patrick asked. The only answer that made any sense filled him with horror and fear on behalf of his son.

Mooney sat down on the cot. "You said you developed them. Where? You certainly don't have space for a darkroom here."

"I rent one at the photographic institute."

"Couldn't somebody have seen them there?"

"I suppose so."

"Look at me," Mooney said sharply.

Barry jumped and looked up to the taller man.

"I'm going to ask it all over again. Did you show them to anybody?"

Barry, terrified for Cheryl and now terrified for himself, did a fatal thing: he hesitated.

"Okay," Mooney said. "Who was it?"

8 1

"My—my girlfriend," Barry said. His own cowardice humiliated him. But he had been badly shaken by finding all the negatives of Jonathan's pictures gone. There was only one person who knew where he kept them—Cheryl. One dull afternoon they had come up here and made love on his lunch hour and he had shown her not only some of his other pictures, but also where he kept the spare set of file keys.

"Name," Mooney said.

"Cheryl."

"Cheryl what?"

"Cheryl Mason."

"Address?"

"I don't know . . . exactly. I mean, I've never been there."

"But you know her phone number."

"Sure. 555-4356."

"Is that office or home?"

"It's the only number I have. If she doesn't answer, somebody—or some service—picks it up."

"Where does she live?"

"In Queens."

"Where in Queens?"

"I dunno. She lives with her family."

"Yeah? And where do you have your loving get-togethers?"

"Here. Nobody's here during the day. Or maybe . . . well, sometimes they aren't here at night."

"Or you pay them to stay away? Right? Where does she work?"

"In an employment agency on West Forty-ninth."

"Have you been there?" Patrick asked.

"No."

"Why did you show them to her?" Patrick's questions were sharp, like a staccato beat.

82

"I always show her stuff I've done. She's interested."

"Was she more interested in the pictures of Jonathan than in the others?"

"Yes, yes, I guess so."

"What makes you think that?"

"Well . . . she said she wanted to show them to her boss. Something about . . . about kids appearing in commercials, about it being a great opportunity for them."

"And you believed that crap?" Patrick, his worst fears about the theft of the pictures realized, lashed out.

Barry winced. Those deep-seated unacknowledged doubts of the past hours were being dragged up to the light. "Look, Cheryl's not that kind of girl. I mean, there are kids on TV. You see them all the time."

"And reputable agencies handle them and won't have them anywhere near the studios without their mothers."

Mooney glanced at Patrick, but there was no point at this moment in pussyfooting around. He looked back at Barry. "Haven't you heard of child pornography?"

"She wouldn't do that," Barry said weakly. But he knew now that was what it was.

Patrick and Mooney stood on the pavement outside Barry's ratty building. Barry himself had fled on foot to the nearest subway to return to his office. He felt bitter and humiliated. Anger within him struggled with a stubborn remnant of loyalty to Cheryl. It was still possible she was innocent.

"Well," Patrick said impatiently, "what're we waiting for? Let's find her."

"What the hell else do you think I'm trying to do?"

"I mean let's go over to that address on West Forty-ninth Street."

"Okay."

They went to where Mooney's car was parked. Inside, he picked up a phone and dialed. Then he said, "Get me anything you have on one Cheryl Mason. Call me back."

The answer came before they reached the block between Eighth and Ninth avenues. The phone buzzed. Mooney picked it up, listened, then said, "Thanks." He put the receiver down. "Nothing," he said.

When the car pulled up in front of the address Barry had given them they both stared at the brownstone, which contained, on ground level, a grocery store. Before Mooney could say anything Patrick got out of the car and strode up the brownstone steps. Mooney followed.

Patrick examined the bells in the dirty outer lobby. Most of them had no names beside them. Impatiently, he pushed one marked SUPER.

"There's not going to be any super," Mooney said.

"What makes you so sure?"

"Places like this don't have resident supers. The guy who owns this isn't going to waste a perfectly good apartment on somebody he's going to have to pay—or even house rent-free."

"Doesn't he have to have somebody in charge of the property and maintenance?"

"Maintenance is a word owners of dumps like this have never heard of. He probably comes around and looks at it himself from time to time, or somebody does it for him. Let's try something else." Methodically he pushed each bell, waiting a second to see if anybody answered. Finally a female voice squawked through the box, "Whad'ya want?"

"Police," Mooney said laconically.

"The door's open anyway."

Patrick pushed the inner door and it flew open.

Mooney pushed the same bell again.

"Yeah?"

"Do you know anything about an employment agency in this building?"

"Here? Are you kidding?"

"Well," Mooney said to Patrick, "how do you feel about another five flights?"

They went straight up. By the time they got to the top, Mooney was puffing. Methodically, they started ringing bells. There were no signs announcing an employment agency. Most of the time the doorbells produced no answer. When it was apparent from listening that somebody was inside, Mooney kept on knocking until the door was finally opened. Several disgruntled citizens in various states of undress came to the door. No one had ever heard either of an employment agency or of a woman named Cheryl Mason until someone on the second floor, a thick-tongued man in undershorts and nothing else, said something that sounded like, "She used to live here," prior to passing out before their eyes and falling hard on the splintered wooden floor.

"Let's get him up," Mooney said.

They pushed their way in.

"Pew!" Patrick wrinkled his nose.

The stench—a combination of unwashed bodies and a broken toilet—was overwhelming. They walked back through the railroad apartment. In each room was a bed and nothing else. Needles were everywhere.

"We'll put him here for the time being," Mooney said, indicating the bed in the first room.

"Shouldn't we send for an ambulance?"

"That's what I'm intending. But I don't see a phone here, do you? I'll have to send for one from the car." They finished ringing bells on that floor, on the ground floor and in the basement. Nobody else who answered had heard of an employment agency or Cheryl Mason.

Finally they went down the stoop and over to the curb. Mooney slid into his car, reached for the phone and called for an ambulance. When he'd done that he dialed again and asked, "Any news of Jonathan Tierney? After a minute he looked out to where Patrick was standing. "No news," he said. Then he dialed the school and asked for Sarah Jennings. When he had spoken to her for half a minute, he again looked out at Patrick. "She hasn't heard anything either. Do you want to call Mrs. Tierney or shall I?"

"You call her. That'll upset her less."

After he'd hung up, Mooney said, "No news, but she sounds terrible."

"You mean drunk."

"No. Not drunk. Terrible."

Jonathan, Lawrence thought, was taking an unconscionably long time to show any effects of the pill in his soda. "Drink your soda, Jonathan," he said.

"I don't like it," Jonathan said. "How much longer are we going to wait before Dad gets here?"

"He must have been held up. Now, drink your soda. He'll be here in no time at all."

"I've got to go to the bathroom," Jonathan said. He turned and was out of the room before Lawrence knew it.

"Come back here!" Lawrence yelled.

The phone rang. Jonathan headed towards the front door of the apartment, but Lawrence cut him off. "You're not leaving here."

"You're not a friend of Dad's. He wouldn't have a friend like you." Memories of instruction by teachers at school, even by his mother on one of the occasions when she was sober, occurred to him. *If any man gets hold of you, or tries to*

*take you anywhere, scream, scream as loud as you can and as
long as you can. Somebody may hear you.*

So as he ran, Jonathan screamed and yelled as loud as he
could. "Help! Help!"

The phone was still ringing. Lawrence, who had run
straight for the apartment's front door to stop Jonathan, was
now trying to get hold of him. But Jonathan was as slippery
as an eel. He darted around furniture. Finally he flew into
another bedroom and locked the door from the inside with a
bolt under the knob.

Lawrence pounded on the door, then went to answer the
phone. Jonathan saw there was an extension on the night
table beside the bed.

Modeling his action on what he had seen in the movies
and on television, he lifted the receiver as quietly as he
could.

"What's that?" a man's voice said.

"Nothing," Lawrence replied.

Jonathan wondered why Lawrence didn't tell the man on
the phone the truth, that it was the click of the bedroom
telephone extension. But he was enlightened a moment later.

The man said, "Everything all right with the kid?"

"Fine. We're getting along fine."

"Okay. I want him bright and in good condition for the
filming tonight. I'm bringing up a new camera. I'll be there
around seven. Don't scare the kid too much. He's got to be
able to do his part. After that, you can scare him all you
want."

Jonathan replaced the phone and looked around him. This
was a far bigger bedroom than the other. In the corners were
more lights on stands. Cables trailed over the floor. What
looked like a television camera was in one corner.

Jonathan was neither stupid nor unimaginative. He knew
what they were for and why he was here. Cold fear ran

through him. He desperately wanted his father. But his father was somehow mixed up with this man. How else would he have known Jonathan was waiting in the doughnut shop for him? Unless, of course, he'd just seen him and pretended to be a friend of his father's.

Jonathan tried to calm his panic and remember everything Lawrence had said about his father. He knew his father was a writer, or was that from something he, Jonathan, had told him? His mind was in a whirl. Who could be trusted? Jonathan lay down on the bed, trying to shut out the sounds of Lawrence pounding on the door. After a while the pounding stopped.

Curious. Jonathan found himself then thinking about his mother. Not the blowsy woman who lately was so seldom sober, but the woman he remembered when the two of them had gone to a street fair and eaten knishes and hot dogs, the woman who used to read to him and play with him and would comfort him when he had nightmares, turning on the light, sitting on the bed and putting her arm around him, saying, "It's all right, Jonathan. It's only a dream, darling, just a bump in the night." Thinking about it brought a sense of safety. He knew that the safety wasn't real, that it didn't change anything about the man on the other side of the door. But it made him feel better just the same. "It's only a bump in the night," he said to himself quietly.

Then the pounding started again.

Jonathan sat up. His limbs felt a little heavy. Fear went through him once more. He remembered the soda. But he'd only sucked that one piece of ice. Maybe two. He had stood and stared out the window, holding the soda, the ice in his mouth, while the man talked and talked and talked. But he hadn't drunk from the soda. I didn't drink from it, he reassured himself.

"Jonathan," the man called, "let me in this minute. I

mean you no harm. You'll like some of the games I'll teach you. Let me in."

Jonathan stood there, saying nothing. Then abruptly the pounding stopped. Jonathan found that more frightening than the noise. That meant the man was probably going to get tools to force the door open, or to get someone to help him, someone who wouldn't believe Jonathan no matter what he said.

He looked around frantically. Curtains lined the windows, but heavy as they were, they wouldn't hide him. He went to the window and looked out. Maybe someone from another window would see him or, if he opened the window, would hear him. But the windows wouldn't budge. Jonathan didn't know whether they were simply stuck or were sealed.

There was a sound at the door. Jonathan whirled around. Whoever was on the other side was doing something to the doorknob. There was an odd clicking, scraping sound. Jonathan glanced quickly over the room. Besides the door to the hall, there were two other doors. One, which was open, led to the bathroom. The other was to a closet. Jonathan ran over to the closet and yanked open the door. There were all kinds of strange clothes inside—net things that stuck out, dresses, pants. But Jonathan didn't have time to examine them. He was about to plunge through the clothes to hide behind them, when he noticed how deep the shelves were above the clothing. Boxes of all sizes were on them. He'd do better up there behind the boxes, he decided.

Quickly he hung on to the bottom shelf, then pulled himself up. Getting from there to the top shelf was easy. Pushing the various boxes to the front of the shelf, he lay down behind them.

Lying there, he found himself staring up at the ceiling paper. The design of the paper seemed to consist of a dizzying pattern of squares. One large square near the corner seemed to have thicker lines than the others. He put his hand up and felt it with his fingers and realized the lines were cracks. His heart started to beat faster. Placing his hands against the square, he pushed up. It moved at one corner. He pushed harder. The whole trapdoor lifted, making a slight noise. He lay quiet, listening. But all he could hear was the same clicking, scratching sound at the bedroom door. Getting his sneakered feet under him, he stood up. His head and shoulders seemed to be in a small attic. Around him were more boxes and a big trunk. Gripping the sides of the square hole, he jumped, pulling himself up and hauling himself inside. Then, as quietly as he could, he fitted the door back and lay on it, his heart beating.

Cheryl, unaware of the man who had been following her at a safe distance since she left the restaurant, made her way back to her place of work, which was not the fictitious employment agency whose address she had made up on the spur of the moment, but the room above the film-developing studio between Seventh Avenue and Broadway.

"How's the boy wonder?" Ben asked when she stepped from the elevator into the second floor.

"From Nowheresville. I tried to get the idea across of his taking pictures of kids, in the park or on the street, you know, for commercials, but he didn't bite."

"Maybe he can be made to."

"Yeah? How?"

"Leak the fact that he took the pictures he gave you to the police and tell them that they're being used for porn movies. The cops aren't going to swallow that he didn't know. We'd tell him that if he did a few more pictures for us, then we'd tell the cops that we made a mistake, that he was innocent."

Cheryl thought about it. She had been working since she was sixteen, first as a hooker, then as a model for some of the seedier porn magazines and, later, in films. She had learned that what mattered was getting paid, and how and for what and through whom the money came mattered little. She worked for people who meant what they said and saw that those who got in their way or didn't cooperate were punished. None of this had she ever questioned. She had lied to Barry about living in Queens with her family. Her jobs had paid her way out of the home where, since she was twelve, her father had assaulted her physically and verbally. When he'd had more than three drinks he abused her sexually, and her mother was always too weak and too frightened to help. She now lived in a small apartment in Tribeca, the newly gentrified area below SoHo. She had let Barry pick her up in a disco. He was young and she found his small-town innocence oddly attractive. It was only when he showed her the photographs of Jonathan that she saw he might have other uses. But, having hesitated at little in her life when it promised profit, she found herself unwilling now to black-mail Barry. Unfortunately, in her enthusiasm over his pictures of Jonathan, she had shown them to her boss, and since then his interest in Barry and his photographs was greater than her own.

"Let me see what I can do," she said, and congratulated herself that she had had the foresight to steal Barry's negatives one afternoon when he and his roommates were at work and that she had not made the mistake of telling her boss Barry's full name or his address.

When she left the studio off Broadway she got on a subway to go downtown to her apartment. She got out at Canal and then started walking north and west. The man caught up with her when she was in an alley between Greene and West Broadway.

"Hello, Cheryl," he said.

She turned quickly. "Hi, Leo." Her heart started beating. "Long time no see."

Leo had been useful at one point in her life. He had, in fact, served as her pimp. Then he introduced her to Ben, who saw her further possibilities. Through Ben she found her way into porn films and decided there were better methods of making a living than on her back. Leo hadn't been happy with her decision. For one thing, it was a bad example for his other girls. He told her to come back or she might find herself unable to pursue any career at all. Cheryl, riding high, told him he was a loser and to get lost. Afterwards, she remembered various girls he had cut up and, belatedly, felt afraid. But her courage returned when a slight professional miscalculation on his part had landed him in jail. She figured that by the time he came out she'd be pursuing her career in California. He had indeed spent a few years behind bars, where his grievance against Cheryl had grown ugly. But he was showing up a little bit earlier than she had bargained for. He didn't say anything, but something about the silence and the way he stood filled her with terror for her life.

She moistened her lips. "Leo—"

The silencer muffled the shots that went into her, one in her heart, one in the middle of her forehead.

Leo stood looking down at her, making sure she was dead. Stooping, he took her bag, removed all identification from it, putting it in his pocket, and threw the bag back down again. Then he walked to the end of the alley and melted into the usual traffic on West Broadway.

6

At the end of her favorite soap opera, Katie Leonard was in a repentant mood. Vodka had eased her early morning grumpiness. On the other hand, the particular sequence she had been watching had been about the terrible destruction alcohol can cause in a home. Also, the face of the man who had been loitering had appeared again and again between her and the television screen, and at the end of the hour the face was less attractive than she had thought. Impulsively, she picked up the phone and dialed Martha.

It was picked up on the first ring. "Hello?"

Katie could tell that Martha had been poised, hoping and waiting for news about Jonathan. Quickly Katie said, "It's me, Katie. Listen, there's something I want to tell you, although it may mean nothing."

"Oh!" Martha's letdown was obvious, but Katie refused at

this point to be deflected. "I should have thought of it
sooner, but I only remembered, after we talked, that there
was a man standing around outside today and yesterday. I
noticed him because . . . well, I just did."

"What man?" Martha said sharply.

"I just told you. A man. I don't know who he was. He sort
of loitered across the street and strolled back and forth."

"Why didn't you tell me this sooner?"

"Look," Katie said, her minimal supply of understanding
depleted, "you want me to tell you about him or you want to
have a fight?"

Martha took hold of herself. "Sorry. Let's begin at the
beginning. When did you first notice this man?"

"I don't know. I'm not sure. It could have been a couple
of days ago, because when I saw him I had the odd feeling
that I'd seen him before. So I decided I must have seen him
at one of the street parties around here or something. Then I
saw him yesterday, off and on. And then this morning."

Martha put a shaking hand to her forehead and pushed
back her hair. Her headache was like a drum beating inside
her skull, and nausea gripped her stomach. "You're about
three doors down from me, Katie," she said. "Help me to
visualize this. Was he more in front of my house than yours?
Did he walk around? Did he just stand still?"

Katie started to enjoy herself. "He stood for a while more
or less on the sidewalk outside your building. Then he
strolled away for a while, I guess in the opposite direction
away from me. Then when I glanced out again he was coming back towards me again."

Martha fought back her physical misery and tried to summon recently unused faculties. You're a reporter, she told
herself silently. Once a reporter, always a reporter. No matter what.

"Katie," she said, as calmly as she could, "can you tell

me what it was about the man that made you notice him? I mean, I realize he was standing there and coming back and forth. But was there anything else?"

Katie was silent for a few minutes, then, "Just this vague feeling that I'd seen him somewhere."

"Can you describe him? Come on, you're an artist!" It was flattery but it was also true. Before she acquired her handsome alimony, Katie Leonard had done some interesting pencil sketches of notable people. Lately she hadn't done any. But anything was worth a try. "Do you think," Martha said, "you could draw his face for me?"

"Sure. It was a good-looking face. Well, maybe not good-looking, but interesting. Shall I come over there?"

"Please, Katie, do. I don't want to leave the phone."

For the first time in rather a long period, Katie felt wanted and important. "Of course. I'll get my stuff and come along."

A few minutes later she came up the front steps with a large sketch tablet under her arm and some charcoal pieces in her hand.

Martha, who had been watching for her, buzzed her in and waited for her at the apartment door.

It was the first time Katie had seen Martha in a few days and she found the other woman's appearance shocking. She was used to the bloated stomach and the perpetually flushed face. But Martha's skin now seemed a greasy white, with a film that appeared to come from sweat on the forehead and around the mouth. Martha was smoking, and the hand that held the cigarette shook and jerked as she raised the cigarette to her lips.

"You need a drink," Katie said, meaning the best.

"No!" Martha almost shouted. More quietly she said, "I don't want to talk about it. Draw the man's face, Katie. At least we'll have something to go to the police with."

Katie had a whole array of reasons stopping drinking so abruptly could do more harm than good. She decided to give voice to at least one of them. "You could have a convulsion, stopping cold turkey like that."

"Katie, please! I know what I have to do."

Katie shrugged. She'd done her part. "All right. Let me sit down."

Katie, whose talent had always been for the lightning sketch, drew a few lines. A rather distant likeness of Lawrence's face leaped onto the page. "Do you recognize him?" she asked Martha.

Martha stared at the face. She had seen that face before somewhere, but she couldn't remember where. The memory was neither clear nor strong. "I'm going to call Sergeant Mooney," she said, and went towards the phone.

But Mooney wasn't there. The officer who answered said he'd tell the sergeant next time he called in, and added, "Why don't you bring the drawing here. Maybe somebody here will recognize it."

Martha reported her conversation to Katie. "But I can't leave here," she finished. "Jonathan might try to reach me."

"Do you want me to go to the precinct?" Katie asked.

Martha didn't have too much faith that the police would take Katie seriously. She wasn't drunk, but to any trained eye she wasn't entirely sober. And men, workingmen, had, in Martha's opinion, a tendency to discount whatever was said by an overweight middle-aged woman. She'd once written an article on the subject, documenting the fact that middle-aged women in a man's world were inclined to be slighted; fat middle-aged women were especially slightable. And Katie, billowing around in her muumuu, was both. When you added a strong smell of liquor coming out of the mouth . . . But what else was there to do?

"Okay, Katie, I'll give you the money to take a cab."

"I can pay for it myself. It's my contribution."

"All right. Thanks. Call me from there if there's any news at all or if anybody there recognizes him. Okay?"

Stephen Morgan's father, Albion Morgan, decided to pick up his son from school that afternoon. His last class ended at two o'clock, which meant that he could take the subway at 116th Street and Broadway in Manhattan, change to the express at Ninety-sixth and be in Borough Hall in Brooklyn Heights by three.

Happily he locked his office door, walked rapidly across the Columbia campus and dived into the subway. His luck held, because a train came along shortly and there was an express waiting across the platform for him at Ninety-sixth. Once on that, he opened his morning paper and devoted himself to the news of the day. In his more radical days, reading the daily paper was a test of how to contain his indignation and rage at Establishment indifference to the crying needs of social justice. But in the past few years he was able to peruse the paper without exploding or wanting to join the most recent revolution.

"Middle-aged complacency," his wife, in one of her more acerbic moments, had called it.

Maybe, he thought now, turning the sheet. But deep in his heart he knew it had something to do with his son, Stephen. For a man who had been less than enthusiastic about the idea of marriage, and had stated flatly that he did not intend to become a parent, he had turned into a besotted father, going to the lengths of arranging his classes so that he could meet his son after school at least twice a week. Those walks home from school, punctuated by a stop at the pizza or ice cream parlor, had become for him what charging the barricades had once been: his greatest satisfaction in life.

When he got out of the train he bounded up the steps of the Borough Hall station, walked rapidly to the school and congratulated himself that he had reached there at exactly the right time.

He was a little annoyed to see Stephen come out with Marguerite Stanley, the two of them talking, or rather, Morgan observed morosely, Marguerite talking and Stephen listening. She was a pushy, unattractive child, he thought, and why Stephen chose her as his best friend, he didn't know. Then he amended that. It was probably not his doing, but Marguerite's. Whatever. The fact was that she and Stephen were close buddies and that meant that he had to invite her along.

"Hi, Stephen!" he said as the two approached.

Stephen's face lit up. "Hi, Dad!"

"Hi, Mr. Morgan," Marguerite said.

"Hello, Marguerite," Morgan said. He turned towards Stephen. "How about some ice cream or some pizza?"

Speaking at the same time, Stephen said, "Pizza," and Marguerite said, "Ice cream."

"Pizza it is. Let's go to the place on Montague."

As they turned towards Montague Street Stephen burst out, "Dad, Jonathan's not in school and everybody's looking for him and the teachers were asking Marguerite and me and we said Jonathan was with his father. I mean," Stephen went on desperately, "that's what you said the other night. When you were talking to Ma in the kitchen."

"I said he was at an animal shelter," Marguerite said.

Morgan stopped in the middle of the sidewalk. "Let me get this straight. Jonathan didn't show up in school today?"

"That's right," Stephen said. "And Miss Babson asked if anybody knew where he was." He paused.

"And you said?"

"Well, I forgot you told Ma not to say anything." Stephen adored his father, but he was also a little afraid of him.

"So what did you tell her?"

"It wasn't his fault, Mr. Morgan," Marguerite loyally joined in. "He sort of likes Miss Babson and—"

"I'm not asking you, Marguerite," Morgan snapped. Why couldn't the child shut up? "What did you say, Stephen?"

Stephen gathered his courage. "I said Jonathan was with Mr. Tierney."

"Oh Christ! Since you were listening to our conversation, you heard your mother and me agree how important it was that Jonathan's father not do anything foolish to louse up his chances of getting custody, didn't you?"

"Yes." Stephen stared at his toes.

Morgan's spurt of temper peaked. "All right. It's okay, but next time ask me before you get entangled in a custody suit."

"Yes," Stephen said.

Marguerite took his hand.

For a moment Stephen was grateful for the gesture of solidarity. Then he pushed her hand away. His father would consider that a weakness.

Morgan wished that he and Stephen were alone. But short of asking Marguerite to leave them, there was nothing he could do about it now. Besides, there was the matter of Jonathan.

"Did anyone get in touch with his mother?"

Stephen didn't answer for a moment. No one had actually said she'd called Martha Tierney. On the other hand, the fact that Jonathan's mother had come to the school was well broadcast over the school grapevine. And then there was the policeman who'd questioned them. "Well, they must have. I mean, even before they called the policeman."

"They called the police?"

"Yes."

"My God, he really is missing. Does his father know?"

"He's got to," Marguerite said. "He was at the school, but we didn't see him."

"Well, I hope to God your saying Jonathan might be with his father won't ruin his father's custody plans." Morgan saw his son's fallen face. "It's okay. You didn't realize the seriousness. Let's get to the pizza place. They may have a pay phone there."

Police Officer Claude Johnson looked at the charcoal sketch brought by Katie Leonard. "I don't recognize it," he said.

"Don't you have pictures of criminals, sex offenders, that you could maybe compare it to?"

"Did you show it to Mrs. Tierney?"

"Of course. She told me to bring it here. She's a close friend."

That figures, Johnson thought. According to community gossip they were both drunks. The alcohol fumes coming across from Katie, as she leaned forward and talked, were powerful. Johnson, a conscientious officer, tried not to be prejudiced. But he was an elder in his African Methodist Church and it was hard not to class a drunken woman with the other abominations mentioned in the Bible. If she had been black, he would have been even more intolerant, because added to drunkenness would be the charge of bringing disgrace on her already oppressed people. But Katie was white. He glanced at the heavy woman. Under her raincoat she had on some kind of shapeless garment. Her hair, he noted, was stove black with no highlights. Dyed, he thought.

His wife wore her hair natural, which was the way he liked and approved.

"You can look at some pictures," he said. "I'll get out one of the books."

"All right." Then she added, "I'm an artist, you know, so I have a good eye for resemblances."

And for the liquor label, Johnson thought as he went to get the book containing several years' worth of criminals. Irritated, he didn't check the front of the book he brought back, or he would have realized it was photographs of men booked for assault and armed robbery.

Jonathan, lying flat, could hear the voices underneath.

"I tell you, he was in the room. He'd locked himself in."

That was the voice of the man who had kidnapped him. Jonathan knew that as long as he lived he would recognize it. In some ways it was a voice, or an accent, that reminded him of some of the prissier teachers at school. Then there was another voice.

"Yeah? Well, where's he now?"

"I don't know. Perhaps—"

"Perhaps what?" The coarse-voiced man spoke in mincing tones, obviously mocking the other man.

"Perhaps he unlocked the door while I was in the kitchen looking for a screwdriver so I could break the lock. And then got out of the apartment."

"Was the door unlocked when you came back from the kitchen?"

"I'm—I'm not sure." He had spent some time looking for the heavy screwdriver, then came back, and, without trying the door again, jammed the tool into the lock between the door and the doorjamb and pushed and twisted until the door sprang open.

"You mean to tell me you think the kid unlocked the door to get out and then took the time to lock the door behind him?"

"He's very bright."

"If he's that bright, he'd run like hell! Look, you say you don't know whether the door was locked or unlocked when you came back with the screwdriver."

Lawrence hesitated. "I assumed it was locked. I didn't try it. I'm sure he's still here."

"Okay, where? The door's open, the room's empty. Did you look in the closet?"

"Of course. And he's not there."

"Then he's gone. And if he got out it's your tail that's gonna be in a meat grinder. He's never seen me. But he's sure as hell seen you, and if he gets to the cops, then they're going to have you, because they've got your picture from ten years ago."

Lawrence was sweating with fear. "I can't see how he did it, though."

"Oh, you can't! You wanna have another look around? We've only looked twice." The voice was elaborately sarcastic. "If I was you I'd be thinking about getting out of here. He's gone. You're not going to get him back."

"He's not gone." Lawrence's syllables got even more precise. "He couldn't have got out without my hearing. I'm going to have another look around."

"You do what you want. I'm going."

"I don't know why you're here anyway. You said the filming would be tonight."

"I just wanted to make sure everything was okay. You sounded funny, like there was trouble. And I was right. The kid's gone. And I'm not happy about the idea that he may bring the cops back here."

"He's not going to bring the cops back here because he hasn't escaped."

"Fine. Find him! I'll watch."

Patrick was back in his sublet flat again, checking the answering machine to see if he'd had any calls. He had altered the announcement on the tape to identify himself as the current occupant and to urge callers to leave names and phone numbers. But now there was no blinking light to warn of waiting messages.

He found he couldn't sit down. Nervously he turned on the television to an all-news program and realized he was half waiting to hear an announcement of his son's disappearance.

Quickly he glanced at his watch. Three-thirty. Was it only —he did some calculation—eight hours since Jonathan had left home? Home? He pulled his mind away from Martha, where it had a tendency to settle. But to stop himself from angrily blaming her was almost more than he could manage. He decided suddenly that he would write down everything he knew or had heard about where Jonathan had been or was believed to have been since he left home.

Sitting down at the desk, he pulled a yellow lined pad towards him and got out a felt-tip pen.

After a moment he wrote in the margin,

7:30—Left home
7:30–7:35—Went to Megan Stanley's to see kittens.
7:55—Left Stanley's to go to doughnut shop to meet "nice man."

At that point, sickened by all the implications in those last two words, Patrick set down his pen and put his head in his hands.

"How's Simpson?" Marguerite asked her aunt. Although Simpson had looked normal to her that morning, she knew her Aunt Megan was upset that Simpson had seemed indifferent to his breakfast and had had an attack of coughing.

"Fine, thank God, or at least mostly fine. Dr. Buckner said he had a slight cold, that's all."

"So you took him to the vet after all."

"Of course. Didn't I say I was going to?"

"You were making up your mind when I left."

"Jonathan came by after you'd gone." The discomfort that had underlain everything else that morning surfaced. "When he left he said he was going to meet a friend at the doughnut shop."

"What friend?"

"He said he was a nice man—a friend of his father's."

"Aunt Megan, Jonathan's missing. He's not at school and everybody's looking for him."

"Oh my God!" Then he never got to school. The guilt that had been nibbling at her consciousness now thrust aside every other feeling. "I knew I should have called from the vet's. Tell me what happened at school."

"Stephen and I got sent for by the headmistress and a policeman questioned us. People said Jonathan's father was there, though I didn't see him."

"What did they say happened?"

"Jonathan was supposed to meet his father at the doughnut shop on Court Street. But he never showed up."

"Then why did he say it was a friend of his father's? I don't understand that."

"Stephen said it was supposed to be a secret that he was going to be with his father."

"What a mess! But I told him the place on Court Street was closed, so he probably went around the corner to the new one on Atlantic Avenue. I wonder if it makes any difference."

"What do you mean, Aunt Megan?"

"Well, do you think it would, well, help in finding Jonathan if I told someone that?"

"I dunno. Maybe so."

"I've told you, Marguerite, not to be sloppy in your speech. It's 'I don't know.' Not 'I dunno.'"

Old cow, Marguerite thought.

"I don't see any face that looks anything like the man outside my house," Katie Leonard said to Officer Johnson.

One of the officers who had just walked in looked carelessly at the book in front of Katie. "You been in an armed robbery attack, Miss?"

"No. I'm trying to find a—a possible sex pervert who loitered in our neighborhood this morning. You know that Jonathan Tierney, a neighborhood boy, is missing. So I think anyone who was hanging around would be important."

Johnson walked over, looked at the book, glanced at the cover, and said, "Sorry. I guess I got out the wrong book." He went back and got another of the books and took it to Katie. "Here you are."

Katie felt deflated and angry. "I shouldn't think it'd be hard to discover the difference between armed robbery and sexual perversion."

. . .

Martha waited for Katie to
come back from the precinct. Her hope of anyone there rec-
ognizing the sketch was almost zero, yet it was something,
however small, that gave her the feeling that an effort of her
own to find Jonathan was being set in motion.

This reminded her of Sergeant Mooney. It had been about
an hour since he had called. Intellectually she knew that if
there were anything new at all he would phone her. But
intellectuality had little to do with how she felt. And then
there was her physical misery to deal with. Her headache
still beat inside her head like tomtoms, nausea kept her from
wanting to eat anything, and the fact that she hadn't eaten
much since the day before was making her giddy. As though
the word had produced the effect, she suddenly felt her head
spin and she clutched the kitchen counter. The room around
her seemed to turn, head over tail, like an airplane. Her
stomach obediently rose, and she wondered for a moment if
she were going to go through another period of retching, as
she had the previous night. Sweat sprang out on her face.

Straight across the dining room, well within her sight,
were the bottles of liquor. She could feel herself unscrewing
one of the tops, pouring some into a glass, and drinking,
drinking, drinking, with the blissful sense of reality being
deferred.

After all, her other self argued, you're not doing Jonathan
any good by not drinking, and you'll be better able to think
on his behalf. You'll— She didn't know at what point she
had let go the counter and was walking across the carpet to
the cabinet where the golden and white liquors were kept,
her own fruits of the Hesperides. . . .

She had her hand on the top of one of the bottles.

"No, no, no," she cried. "No!" She stood up and flung the

bottle across the dining area, across the counter to the kitchen in the general direction of the sink. It curved and arced, almost in slow motion. When it hit, it hit the side of the sink with an almighty crash.

She stood there and cried, smelling the liquor fumes as they wafted over to her.

Then she got the mop, a pan and a brush, and went to work cleaning it up.

The trouble was, when she finally stood up, the dizziness came back. She sat down beside the counter. The phone rang.

It was Patrick.

"Heard anything?" he asked.

"No."

"Mooney and I've been in Hell's Kitchen trying to track down some nonexistent employment agency where Barry Pinkus's girlfriend was supposed to have worked."

"Who's Barry Pinkus?"

"Barry's the kid who took those pictures for me, the ones of Jonathan." He waited for her to make some crack about the pictures again, but she didn't.

She was watching her shaking right hand as the blood flowed from it. In brushing up one of the glass shards of the bottle she had flipped it right onto her palm, point first. All she said was, "What's Barry's girlfriend got to do with it?"

At this point Patrick was sorry he had mentioned anything about Cheryl. If Martha suspected that Cheryl had been involved in some kiddie-porn ring, it would obliterate whatever control she had. Patrick could almost hear her screaming abuses over what he, in his stupid carelessness, had let their son in for.

"It was just a question of tracking down anyone who'd seen the photos. I don't suppose there's anything going on at your end," he finished, without much hope.

"Not much. Katie Leonard insists there was a man hanging around the street here for the last couple of days. She came over and drew a sketch of him."

"I'm surprised she was sober enough to do that." He held his breath, waiting for Martha to launch her attack on his nasty tongue. But she didn't.

"Yes, well, she can still draw. The funny thing is, I have a vague feeling I've seen that face before, but I can't track it down. Or maybe it's just her drawing. Anyway, she's over at the precinct showing it to the cops there. Perhaps they can recognize it."

Patrick paused. "I think I'll go over and look at it myself. I can ask the phone company to forward any calls about Jonathan. They'll do that, I think."

"They will?"

"Sure, if there's a good reason. Why?"

"Because I've been sure I had to stay here myself, in case Jonathan should call. Or anyone else."

"You don't have to go to the precinct. You've already seen the picture. You said you partly recognized it."

"It's just a vague feeling. I can't seem to pin it down."

"You sound funny. You okay?" His deep anger at her prevented him from feeling any concern. On the other hand, she did sound odd.

"Yes." She hesitated, then burst out, "I haven't had a drink today."

"I wonder how long that'll last." The words were out of Patrick's mouth before he was aware even of thinking of them. "I'm sorry," he said. "I didn't mean quite to say that."

"You don't have any scruples about kicking people when they're down, do you?"

"If you're down it's because you didn't look after your son properly. You can't pin that on somebody else."

She hung up.

He called her back right away, but she let her answering tape reply for her. After the beep he said stiffly, "I'm sorry."

Lying flat on the trapdoor above the closet, Jonathan heard Lawrence rummaging around the room immediately outside the closet. Then there was quiet, although a sound came up every now and then, indicating there were still people in the apartment.

Jonathan prayed, Please don't let them find me. Please. He took a breath. And started to sneeze.

7

Jonathan lay rigid, his hand over his face, his finger pressing under his nose to prevent the sneeze from bursting out.

In the biggest room of the apartment, Lawrence was busy flinging open the doors of a large sideboard.

"You're nuts," his companion said. "That bureau is where we store some of the films."

"He could have hidden in here. He's slight enough."

But there was nothing but boxes and boxes of tapes.

"Come on. We don't have any more time to bother about that kid. He's back home by now, trying to tell the cops where this place is. I'm going to get the hell out, and you'd better, too, if you have any brains, which I doubt."

"If the cops come here, is there anything to link us to this place?"

"No. They'll get some pretty good porn movies, but

there's nothing on them to link us. Come on. My car's on the Drive. I'll give you a lift." He was convinced by now that Lawrence was more hazard than asset. When he first encountered Lawrence he sounded as if he'd be a good customer, and further, he seemed to have a successful line to the kid in the pictures—a kid who had the looks to go far in the films the man planned. But now the kid was gone, there was some danger that he could remember enough to get the police back here, and this screwball wanted to stay and take the place apart when it was perfectly obvious that the boy—no dummy—had split.

Trapped by rage and frustration, Lawrence didn't say anything for a moment. He had been stalking Jonathan now for nearly a week. And for days before that he had the photographs of the exquisite boy to look at and touch while he worked out various plans to accost him and get him away from his neighborhood.

His companion, Ben Nicolaides, who was also the proprietor of the second-floor establishment off Broadway, had first shown him the pictures, the ones that Cheryl had brought back after a lunch with Barry Pinkus.

Ben had known that not much mileage could be derived from the photographs by themselves unless the boy could be got hold of and induced to act in films. By showing the prints to Lawrence and feeding him the details as to where Jonathan lived and went to school, Ben thought he might kill two birds with one stone. He could, of course, have dispatched one of the other men he knew whom he had used before in the acquisition and seduction of children. But this eager, intellectual-looking man was far better for the purpose. From everything Ben had been able to gather from Cheryl about the boy—his father's being a writer and so on—he'd be more likely to cotton to a man who talked in the same way. Or so Ben argued to himself.

So Lawrence had gone to Brooklyn Heights and strolled around the streets where Jonathan lived and went to school. He was convinced that no one had noticed anything odd in his behavior, but he had not found an opportunity to talk to Jonathan until the morning he had followed Jonathan to Megan Stanley's house and from there to the doughnut shop on Atlantic Avenue. He knew the boy's father was a writer and that he had a literary agent. That much Ben had got from Cheryl and had passed on to Lawrence. From there he winged it and had done it, he convinced himself, remarkably successfully—until he had managed to break the lock on the bedroom door and burst it open, only to find Jonathan gone.

"He could *not* have got out," he said. "Look, you go on. I'm going to wait. I know he's here somewhere."

"And I think you're crazy. What's more, you could blow the thing if the cops come."

"I won't blow anything."

"And don't expect any help."

"I won't."

He waited until the man had left. Then Lawrence raised his voice. "I know you're here somewhere, Jonathan. And I'm going to find you."

The old sense of power filled him. For so long he'd been good—obeying the stupid doctors, taking the medicine that slowed him down, stripped him of his visions, tied him to the earth.

Now, as he always knew when he was allowed to be himself, when a blind, stupid and inhibited society was not dictating the terms of his freedom, now he could see the truth: the truth was himself and the boy. Glorious images filled his mind. Together they would be invincible. "I'm going to find you," he cried again, a clarion call to the magic future. *" 'Be through my lips to unawakened earth the trumpet of a prophecy,' "* he exulted. "Jonathan, I'll find you!"

He stood there for a moment, gripped in the illusion of power. Then it receded. Reality pushed at him. Had the boy escaped, somehow, as Ben had said? No, he would have known.

Just for the hell of it he went over to the door he'd forced open to see if there were any way he could lock it from the hall side. To his pleasure there was an old-fashioned sliding bolt high above the original lock. Lawrence moved it across. "That'll keep the little bastard in," he said aloud. When the suspicion that it would be unlikely for Jonathan still to be in the bedroom crossed his consciousness, he pushed it away. The boy was there—somewhere. And he would find him.

Cheryl's body lay in the morgue while the police tried to find out who she was. With all identification removed, she was simply one of the thousands of young women who came annually to the Big Apple with dreams of glory and wealth and love and fame and took the wrong step or met the wrong man. The police knew what kind of gun had killed her, and the coroner's office told them that apart from being shot to death, she was a woman in her early twenties in excellent health. After that they waited for someone to show up who was missing a daughter or a sister or a girlfriend or a wife.

After Mooney and Patrick confirmed that either Barry had given them false information about where Cheryl lived and worked or he had passed on the false information given to him, Mooney dialed Fremantle literary agency and asked for Barry. When he came to the phone, Mooney said, "Either you lied to us about your girlfriend's place of employment or she lied to you. There's no employment agency at that number on West Forty-ninth Street."

"Oh."

"Have you talked to her since we were at your office?"

"No. I called her service and left my name a couple of times, but I haven't heard."

"What's the number of the service again?"

"555-4356."

"Okay. I'll be back in touch."

Mooney put the receiver down, then yelled, "Joe!"

Another detective came to the door.

"What's the word on the service this Cheryl Mason used? I called in the number."

"Seems kosher. Patronized a lot by actors and dancers. Nothing unusual."

"Okay." Mooney picked up the receiver and dialed again.

Somebody answered on the third ring. "Service," a male voice said.

"This is the New York police, Sergeant Mooney. I'm trying to locate Cheryl Mason. Can you give me her address?"

"Just a minute."

There was a silence, then a female voice came on. "Why do you want Cheryl's address?"

"Because we'd like to question her about something."

"We'll be happy to take the message and relay it to her when she calls in."

"When was the last time she called in?"

"Before I answer that question I want to make sure you are who you say you are. What precinct are you with? I'll call you back."

Mooney told her and hung up. After a few seconds his phone rang.

"Well," the woman said, "you seem to be who you say you are. In answer to your question, Cheryl hasn't phoned in for her calls since yesterday morning."

"Can you give me an address for her?"

The woman sighed. "It's a box number. We send her bills

there. She pays by check, but there's no address on her checks."

"Which bank?"

"The National. The one on West Forty-second Street."

"All right. Now I'd like to have a list of the calls that have come in for her."

"Okay, but you're going to have to come in in person, with all your credentials. We tell our clients that we give out information about them to no one, and we'd go out of business if we didn't seem to keep our word."

Mooney grunted. It would probably be a waste of time, but he'd have to do it. "If she calls in, let me know. And let me know without telling her that I'm interested."

"Okay."

Later that afternoon he went over and picked up her list of calls waiting. Two of the calls were immediately recognizable as Barry's. Mooney went back to the office and called the two others. One was a bar, and the other turned out to be a pay phone on the street.

"Great," Mooney said to himself. "We're really moving."

Megan disliked calling Martha because she did not enjoy talking with someone who seemed to be half or wholly drunk most of the time. But she was a conscientious woman and felt that the mistake she'd made in misleading Jonathan about the doughnut shop on Court Street might have had consequences and should be reported. So she telephoned.

Martha, who had cleaned up the debris from the shattered bottle and opened the windows to let some of the October air in to dissipate the liquor fumes, was walking back and forth across the living room carpet. In an effort to try to stop her shaking, she had drunk several cups of soup, had eaten some crackers, and had drunk some milk before everything she'd taken in had been vomited up violently and suddenly. Fortunately, there was a bathroom off the living room and she had managed to get there before her stomach projected up the whole mess. A lot of it had gone onto the bathroom floor, but at least it was tile and was easily cleaned. She now felt better, but weak, and decided to take in nothing but water. It was at that point that the phone rang.

"Martha, this is Megan Stanley. There's something I feel I must tell you." And she explained her error in saying to Jonathan that the doughnut place on Court Street was closed. "I suspect he might have gone then to the one on Atlantic Avenue. As I told you this morning, he said he was supposed to meet a friend of his father's, somebody he described as a nice man, there. I gather from Marguerite that he was actually supposed to meet his father. And his father would have gone to the place on Court Street, while Jonathan, because of what I told him, may have gone to the one on Atlantic Avenue."

It was all Martha could do to hold on to her screaming nerves and not yell at this meddlesome woman whose misinformation might very well have caused Jonathan's disappearance or, at least, caused him to be in a place where he might have encountered danger.

"I'm sorry," Megan finished stiffly.

"I am, too," Martha said. "I wish—" I wish the hell you'd minded your own business, her mind silently shrieked. She said, "Thanks for calling." And hung up the phone.

She dialed Mooney's number but was told he was out of his office. "Please have him call me," Martha said.

"Can I tell him anything?" the man on the other end of the phone said.

"No." And then, "Is Mrs. Leonard there now?"

"Mrs. Leonard? Oh, the lady with the drawing. No, she left a few minutes ago."

"Do you have the drawing?"

"Yes. Do you have any information about it?"

"No—not about that exactly, but about something else. That's what I want to talk to Sergeant Mooney about."

"You can tell me."

But Martha didn't trust the run of policemen in a precinct. This was important and needed Mooney's attention. She didn't want it ignored and then forgotten. "No, please tell him to call me."

Just as she hung up, the phone rang again. She picked it up.

"This is David Jennings," a male voice said.

Martha wracked her brain for a moment before inspiration struck. "Sarah's brother?"

"The same. Sarah told me you were having a hard time, what with this crisis concerning your son and at the same time trying to fight drinking."

"I don't see what concern it was of Sarah's to go around telling various people."

"She's trying to be helpful, because she knows my own long fight with alcohol."

"If you're telling me I should go into the hospital or a rehab I'll tell you right now I'm not going anywhere until Jonathan is found. When that happens, well, maybe."

"I'm not going to tell you that. I know you want to stay on hand and so would I. I just thought I'd pass on one or two ideas to help you over the hump. Do you have any herb teas?"

"I just drank two cups of consommé, ate some toast, and then some milk, and I've just finished being very, very sick."

"Milk wasn't such a good idea. Try an herb tea, if you have one, and some dry toast. If you have soda, like Coke or Pepsi, that would be a good idea. They have sugar and you need sugar right now. Honey's good. You could put it into the tea. You'll feel better. If you need any more thoughts my number is 555-8956. Hope you feel better." And he hung up.

"Lousy moralist," Martha said. She started walking back and forth again. Then she went to the phone and dialed the number Patrick had given her. The answering tape clicked into function on the third ring. The trouble was, there was no beep and the tape went off. It was impossible to leave a message.

"Goddammit!" Martha yelled, and started walking again. She didn't know how long she'd been doing that when she found herself in front of the storage cupboard in her kitchen. The first thing she saw after she opened the cupboard door was a box of peppermint tea bags. On a shelf above was some honey. She put the kettle on to boil again and rummaged on another shelf. The box of melba toast was there and still unopened.

Five minutes later she was sitting on the sofa sipping some peppermint tea heavily laced with honey and nibbling on some melba toast. After eating two pieces of the latter and finishing the cup, she waited to see if her stomach rose again. But everything rested peaceably.

She continued to sit there, feeling a little less physically uncomfortable than she had since early morning. Across the room the liquor bottles seemed to sparkle and blink in the sunlight. She wrenched her mind away from them and thought instead about Jonathan and everything that had happened. The thing to do, she thought, was to arrange what she knew or had learned in some kind of order:

Jonathan had got up that morning and at seven-thirty had gone to see Megan Stanley's kittens.

He had told Megan that he was going to the doughnut shop to meet a friend of his father's, a "nice man." Horror at the implications of all that washed over Martha. But she forced herself on.

His father, unknown to her, had arranged to meet Jonathan in the doughnut shop on Court Street at eight o'clock. He waited there nearly two hours before he looked in the doughnut shops on Montague and then called the school.

Megan Stanley had told Jonathan that the Court Street doughnut place was closed. It wasn't, because Patrick waited there. But Jonathan may have gone to the doughnut shop on Atlantic Avenue.

Patrick had hired Barry, an office boy at his agent's, to photograph Jonathan.

Sarah Jennings had notified the police and Sergeant Mooney, and Patrick had left the school and gone to find out if the office boy had shown his pictures to anybody. After that they went somewhere else to find something else.

Katie Leonard had called to say that a man had been loitering around the street near their houses and she had drawn a sketch of the man. She had gone to the precinct to show the sketch to the police to see if they recognized it. . . .

Martha paused as something flashed across her memory and was gone. She put her hands over her eyes and tried to get it back. It wouldn't come, but it had something to do with Katie's sketch.

She stood up, poised to snatch her raincoat and go to the precinct before she remembered that she couldn't leave the phone. Stymied, she stood there, then picked up the phone and dialed Katie's number. There was no answer.

As time passed and Jonathan heard nothing from below, he took the opportunity to look around. He was in a sort of low, very small attic or storage place. As his eyes got used to the dimness, he realized that there must be some sort of light getting in from outside, because it was not completely dark, or at least it hadn't been. It was not much darker than when he had first scrambled up there.

Moving as little as he could so as not to make any noise audible downstairs, he turned his head and examined all he could see from his posture of lying on his stomach on top of the small trapdoor through which he had come. There were boxes around and a large trunk, and behind the trunk there seemed to be a faintly different light from the rest of the room. Staring straight at it, he decided that behind the trunk there must be a window of some kind. He would have given almost anything to scramble to his feet and examine the room properly, but any sound at all might lead the man below to his hiding place.

Slowly, wriggling and sliding himself forward, he moved towards the trunk and the dim light behind it. When he got there, he peered around the trunk and saw that there was indeed a window, or rather half a window, the other half of which was on the opposite side of the separation wall of the storage space.

Jonathan hesitated to slide around the trunk to the window, because that would mean he'd leave his post and if the man below discovered the square in the closet ceiling, Jonathan would not be near enough to prevent him from opening it up by lying across it. But he decided to risk it. He paused and listened. There was no sound from below. Jonathan pulled his sneakered feet under him in a crouch and silently crept around the trunk to the window.

Outside, the sky was dusk, though not as dark as the

interior of the little room, and there were stars and a moon lighting up the roofs below.

Jonathan's heart leaped up. That was the outside world, and seeing it from the window seemed to make it easily at hand. But he looked down and knew that was a delusion. He was many floors above the street. Far below in the darkness was what looked like an alley. Even if he could open the window he would die if he jumped.

The enclosure of the window was about three inches deep, so the window itself was that far from the end of the wooden wall or divider. Standing, Jonathan tried to slide his narrow body around the rim of the divider. But, thin as he was, there wasn't enough room.

What about shouting?

He could shout, and perhaps someone in another building would hear him. It was certain that the man below would, and would recapture him before people in other buildings or on the street would know what was happening or what apartment to come to.

It was the following afternoon that Barry, having left his fifth message with Cheryl's service, called Mooney.

"I know something's happened to her. She's never left it this long before calling back."

Mooney was beginning to think that, too, but he felt impelled to say, "Maybe she heard that you told me about her involvement with kiddie porn and is lying low."

There was a funny sound on the other end of the phone. Then, "Maybe there's an explanation that we haven't thought of. I mean, perhaps she didn't know what her boss wanted."

"She lied to you, didn't she? She gave you a fake work

address. Somebody stole your pictures, and you said she was the only one who knew where you kept the spare key."

"Maybe one of my roommates . . ."

"Do you really believe that?"

Barry didn't. But he remained silent for a moment.

"Anyway," Mooney said, "we checked them out. It's not impossible one of them stole the pictures. But at this stage of the investigations, it doesn't seem likely."

"Couldn't you find out if anything's happened to any girl that's like Cheryl?"

Mooney had been on the point of doing that anyway. "All right."

He called the morgue and asked if a girl fitting the description that Barry had given him had been brought in.

"As a matter of fact," the coroner said, "yes."

"What'd she die of?"

"A bullet through the head. Otherwise she was in good shape, in every sense of the word. Pretty little thing."

"I'm coming down," Mooney said. "And I'm bringing somebody who can give you a definite answer if it's the person I'm interested in." Then he dialed Barry's number again.

Half an hour later he met Barry at the city morgue on First Avenue at Thirtieth Street. Seeing Barry's face he said, "You all right, kid?"

"Yes." Barry suddenly realized his teeth were beginning to chatter and clamped them together.

It was a horrifying experience. He took one look at the damaged face that was uncovered for him and gave something that sounded like a sob.

"That Cheryl?" Mooney asked gently.

Barry nodded, and then burst out, "Yes."

An hour later he was sitting in Mooney's office. Barry had a coffee cup in front of him and was staring at it miserably.

"Okay," Mooney said. "I want you to tell me everything you know about her. Don't leave anything out. Where you first met her, where you've met since, what food she prefers, where she likes to go, what she said of herself."

"Why?" Barry asked. "She's dead. What's the use of picking on her now?"

"I'm not picking on her," Mooney explained. "I'm looking for a kid who's disappeared. Remember? She wanted his pictures and it looks like she had connections with kiddie-porn rings. Do you know what they do to kids? Want me to tell you some details we've learned in trying to catch them and put them in jail? You want that to happen to Tierney's kid?"

"No," Barry cried, almost in tears. "It's just that—that, well, it's so hard to think of her doing that."

"Yeah, I know. But don't bother with that. You've seen Jonathan Tierney. Keep your mind on what might happen to him, and incidentally what might happen to you if anybody here got hold of the idea that you were sort of helping Cheryl along in her porn career."

"That's not true!" Barry blazed out, with more energy than he'd shown all day.

"I don't think it is either. But we need your cooperation."

The threat was decently veiled, but it was there.

"So," Mooney went on, "speak!" He switched on a tape recorder. "You don't mind this, do you?"

Barry shook his head.

It was a long, rambling narrative that seemed to go on forever, except when Barry would remember something and then stop, near tears. Mooney stopped him once when the tape had run out and told Barry to wait until he had turned it over. Finally, after forty-five minutes of talk, Barry ran down. They sat there in silence.

Mooney said, "Where's that bar, the Shamrock, you mentioned?"

"On Seventh Avenue near Thirty-sixth Street."

"You didn't actually say so but I had an idea you didn't much like it."

"No. I didn't."

"Why?"

Barry's dislike was built on half a dozen impressions, none of which he really wanted to examine because he didn't want to ask himself why Cheryl invariably chose it when she had a chance. "I don't know," he said now.

"Come on, Barry. You're a bright boy. You have a good eye. You're a photographer. What was it you didn't like there?"

"It was kind of dirty and crummy, I guess."

"So is the Golden Nut, which you go to a lot, and O'Banion's. You've even gone there without Cheryl, and they're not exactly Upper East Side eateries."

Barry didn't say anything, trying to pin down impressions he hadn't wanted to receive in the first place. Mooney stared at him. "So what was it you didn't like about the Shamrock?"

Finally Barry blurted out, "There were a lot of gays there. They'd eye me and I felt uncomfortable, like I should be gay, too, only I wasn't."

"You ever speak to one of them?"

Barry shook his head.

"Did you see Cheryl speak to them?"

This hit the nerve Barry had been tiptoeing around. For a minute he didn't say anything.

"I take it your silence means she did."

"She'd be talking to some of them when I came in." He paused, then went on, sounding acutely unhappy, "Like she'd been there for a while. Maybe gone specially to see them."

"Did you ever talk to her about this? Get mad or something?"

Barry had. His jealousy was always near the surface. "Yeah. She said they didn't mean anything to her. That they were just part of her business."

"She was truthful about that, I guess. But what business did you think she was talking about?"

"I thought they were clients of her employment office." Realizing how green and square he must have looked, Barry blushed red. "I guess I sound like the world's prize moron."

"There's nothing stupid in trusting people. The bad part is that in a city like New York, half the time—more than half—you get into trouble doing it. Where'd you come from, Barry?"

With shame Barry confessed to the name of his small hometown.

"I don't know why you act like it was the family skeleton. I've been up there. It's near a lake, isn't it? One of the Finger Lakes?"

"Yeah." Suddenly the freshness, the clean air, the rather dull but friendly people seemed less awful to Barry. He had worked so hard for his sophistication. For the first time he wondered if it were all to the good.

"I went there once," Mooney said. "On my honeymoon. Stayed in a motel and went boating and fishing on the lake."

"Are you married now?" Barry asked.

"Divorced. Like practically everybody else. Okay, Barry. I'll let you go, but stay in touch if you remember anything you've forgotten to tell me."

Barry got up. He stood there for a minute. "You think the men in the bar there were some of Cheryl's customers?"

Mooney cast a sharp glance at Barry. "You mean like she was a hooker?"

"Of course not. I mean, well, like she was selling pictures to them?"

"Or giving them addresses where they could get more or get a different but related type of service."

Barry shuddered, then said, "G'bye," and walked out.

When he'd gone, Officer Johnson brought over the sketch Katie Leonard had left.

"What's that?" Mooney asked.

"This woman, Katie Leonard, a friend of Mrs. Tierney's, brought it in. Mrs. T told her to. She—the Leonard woman —says this is a picture of a man who was hanging out the street near their houses. Apparently Mrs. Leonard and Mrs. Tierney live close together."

"Did you show her pictures?"

"Yeah. And Mrs. Tierney wants you to call her."

Patrick had spent a sleepless night beside the phone in his sublet. The light on the answering machine was not blinking, which the instructions said would happen when he had a message, so he assumed no one had called. It didn't occur to him that he might have failed to reconnect the tapes properly so that anyone trying to leave a message would just get a click.

He couldn't sleep, so he walked back and forth, fighting the temptation to call Martha or Mooney or the precinct to check up on the latest development. He knew that the news of Jonathan's disappearance would shortly hit the papers because he would by then have become officially missing. And while in some sense that might mean that more resources would be available in the numbers of police involved, Patrick also had a strong feeling that because of his own best-seller status the chances of Jonathan's being quietly returned would be severely diminished. An analytical, intellectual man, Patrick liked to back up his feelings with documented facts, and he couldn't on this. There were equal arguments that the kidnapper of a child of a well-known parent would, out of fright, kill the child.

Even to think such thoughts was so terrifying that he felt he had to move, go somewhere, commit himself to some action. But if by any chance someone called, someone who was holding Jonathan, or Jonathan himself, then he'd want to be here. It was a bind as rigid as a straitjacket.

The next day Martha again sat staring at the array of bottles on the counter between the kitchen and the living room. She had spent the day drinking peppermint tea with honey and nibbling melba toast and waiting for the phone to ring.

It had been a night of horror. She had lain in bed twisting back and forth, her legs thrashing with nervous tension. Every now and then she had dozed off, but she had finally discovered that when she was not sleeping she was better off up, drinking some of the sickeningly sweet tea and watching television. Reading, so much the escape hatch of her earlier life, the comforter and panacea as well as the informer and inspirer, was no good now. She had stared at the page, the words bouncing off her mind like tennis balls off a wall. They meant nothing. Television, however stupid, was better. In fact, the stupider the better. When her searching dial hit a serious documentary or news program she now knew to pass on to some oldie, a crime or detective show. Only that held her interest for even a few minutes.

With yet more tea inside her and another show finished,

she'd go back to bed and doze off, only to awake a short time later and go through the same procedure again.

The bottles had danced before her eyes all through the night during her visits to the living room and the television set. But, holding the image of Jonathan in front of her like a standard, she had managed not to go near them.

Now, in the low point of the afternoon, she found she couldn't drag her eyes away.

Oh God, she thought. And then, as though chanting a spell or a charm, she said aloud, "Jonathan. I must stay sober for Jonathan." She forced her eyes away from the bottles. On the floor, near them, lay Susan.

"Where is he, Susan? Where is he?" The pale Siamese, lying on the floor, nose on paws, seemed both relaxed and alert. Martha had never been an ailurophobe, shrinking from cats in some primitive reaction. On the other hand, Susan had never for her been a creature in her own right. She was a toy of Jonathan's who, in Martha's opinion, had received more of his attention and affection than she deserved.

Now Martha got up and went over to Susan and knelt, reaching out her hand to stroke her, to make some kind of contact. But Susan sprang away from her and fled, pigeon-toed, down the hall.

"Goddammit!" Martha yelled. She burst into tears. The phone rang.

"Yes?" she cried into the receiver. "Who is it?"

"David Jennings." Then, "what's the matter?"

"What's the matter? You really want to know? My son has disappeared, I can't leave the house because he might call or somebody who knows where he is might call, his cat won't even let me come near her, as though I had some awful plague, and I haven't had a drink." She was ashamed of the sobbing that shook her. "I'm sorry," she wept. "I'm sorry."

"I'll be over," he said, and hung up before she could answer.

She sat there, half angry, half pleased. I suppose he's going to preach at me, she grumbled to herself. But she couldn't help feeling that the terrible emptiness of the house would, at least for a while, be alleviated.

He was there in less than ten minutes, ringing the bell. She went to the door and found she'd forgotten what he looked like, or perhaps it was that he looked different. From the few times she had met him either at one of the school affairs when he had been a teacher or at some function they both attended, she remembered him as heavy and red-faced. Now, although tall, he looked lean and the flush had gone from his skin.

"Can I come in?"

"Don't lecture me, David," she said. "I'm in no mood for it. But your suggestion about the tea, honey and toast was good. Thanks."

She led the way back into the living room. "Didn't you once teach in the school?" she asked.

"Yes, that was one of my various jobs, which I lost along with the other jobs."

"Until you stopped drinking."

"Until I stopped drinking," he agreed. He had on a gray suit and dark red tie and there was now gray in the dark hair.

At least his gray eyes were no longer bloodshot, she thought. "Well, what good advice do you have for me this time?"

"I take it you haven't heard from or about Jonathan."

"No."

His eyes traveled over the room and stopped. Following

129

his gaze, Martha turned and saw the bottles arrayed in regimental order.

"You know," David said, "I take off my hat to you. If I hadn't had a drink for only one day I could no more bear to have those bottles there than to have a glass full of whisky at my elbow every time I moved."

"Are you suggesting I should throw them out?" It was an idea that had occurred to her and that she had instantly rejected.

"I would."

"What a waste!"

He looked at her for a moment. "Is there anything I can do? Right now I'm working in a bookstore on Montague, so I'm less than five minutes away. You probably have female friends to do this for you, but if you need to have an errand done and there's nobody else to do it, I'd be glad to help. I'll leave my number here." He scribbled on a piece of paper and put it on the counter under one corner of the phone.

"All right. Thanks."

"I'd better get back. Nice to see you."

He was gone before she fully took in that he was leaving. Martha felt a little let down. She'd expected him to preach at her and she was looking forward to the resentment she'd feel when he did. She could resent his suggestion about the bottles, of course. She was thinking about that when the phone rang.

"Yes?" She knew her reply must sound as frantic as she felt.

"Mooney," the sergeant said. "You left a message for me to call you. Anything happen?"

Martha told him about the pencil sketch that Katie Leonard had left at the precinct.

"Yeah, I saw it. Did you remember who it was?"

"No, not exactly. But I had this—this sort of flash of

memory. I've seen that face before. But when I try to pin it down I can't. It goes away. But that's not what I called about. Megan Stanley, a neighbor, called me this morning and told me that when Jonathan was with her yesterday morning he told her he was going to meet one of his father's friends, the nice man he talked about."

"Yeah, I know that. I was at the school. What about it?"

"She remembers now that she told Jonathan that the doughnut place on Court Street was closed for renovations, so he must have gone to the place on Atlantic Avenue. And I wondered if anybody in that place would recognize that drawing as somebody who'd been there with Jonathan."

"Thanks," Mooney said. "We'll give it a shot. You're going to be there for the next hour or two?"

"Sergeant, I'm going to be here until I hear something from or about Jonathan."

8

After having had copies of Katie Leonard's sketch made, Mooney left the precinct with an envelope containing six. He went first to the doughnut shop on Atlantic Avenue.

It was larger and more brilliantly lit than the one on Court Street. Plain wooden tables were spread around the square area, there were stacks of doughnuts and other pastries under the counter, and disposal bins dotted the corners and the exit.

"What'll it be?" the young man behind the counter said as Mooney walked up.

Mooney took out his shield, showed it to the man and put it back in his pocket. "Sergeant Mooney," he said. Then he opened the envelope and pulled out a photocopy of the drawing. "Ever seen this guy before?"

The man glanced at it and shook his head. "No."

"Please look again."

"I ain't seen him, I'm tellinya."

"Were you here yesterday morning around eight to nine?"

"No. Yesterday was my day off."

"Who was here then?"

"Well, Willie was supposed to be, but he was sick. I guess it was the boss."

"Is he here now?"

"Yeah." He raised his voice. "Nick! Somebody here to see you."

A tall, heavy man came out. He looked to be in his forties and had a harsh, intelligent face. "Yeah?"

Mooney showed the drawing. "Was this man in here yesterday around eight to nine in the morning?"

"Who wants to know?"

Mooney again took out his shield and introduced himself. "Did you see this man or one who looked like him?"

Nick wiped his hands on a paper towel, then took the paper. He stared at it for a moment, then said, "Could be."

"Was he with a boy? This boy?" This time Mooney drew out a copy of the picture Patrick carried with him.

Nick took it in his other hand. "Yeah. I remember this kid. Good-looking. He comes here sometimes, along with the other kids."

"But yesterday he was with this man?"

Nick raised his head and stared out the window. Mooney was almost tempted to turn around to see if he were watching something, but he knew the man was trying to recall the previous day.

"The kid was here first," Nick said. "He came in and sat down at a table. Looked like he was waiting for somebody. Then the man came in. They talked. Then they left. They didn't buy anything."

133

Mooney felt his heart beginning to thud as it always did when a case had a break. "Ever see the man before?"

"No. What's this about?"

Mooney debated with himself. He preferred to give as little information as possible. But the news would soon leak out. There wasn't any way they could keep it under wraps—not with a well-known writer for a father.

"This kid hasn't been seen since yesterday morning. He thought he was coming here to meet his father. But this guy is not his father and neighbors have reported seeing him around the house in the past few days. In fact, one of the neighbors drew this."

"That's too bad." Nick looked at the drawing again. "It's not exactly like him, you know. It's just that you think of him when you see it."

"Could you give me any other details? Height, hair coloring, eyes, weight, age?"

Nick shrugged and looked back at the drawing. "About my height, that is, about five eleven. Dark hair, gray around the sideburns, thin, kind of . . ." He struggled with some thought.

"Kind of?" Mooney said helpfully.

The man shook his head.

Mooney had an inspiration. "If you saw this guy, without knowing anything about him, and were just guessing what he did, what would you say?"

Nick said promptly, "Schoolteacher."

That was the last thing Mooney was expecting, but he filed it away. "Okay. I'm going to leave a copy of this with you. Show it to anybody you think might be helpful. If you have any inspiration, call me here." Mooney handed him a card. "And thanks."

. . .

Jonathan woke up with a pressing need to go to the bathroom. He had been conscious of it before he slept. Now it was urgent. He looked quickly around. Light was coming from behind the trunk. He got to his feet. The only things in this small space were the trunk, three or four packing cases one on top of another, and a big pile of newspapers. It would have to be the newspapers, he decided, and crawling over there, relieved himself. When the urine started to flow off the top, he hastily moved some papers from farther down the pile and placed them around on the floor. He was afraid that if the liquid poured over the floor it might leak through into the closet and betray his presence.

In pushing the pile of papers around he made more noise than he had intended, and he waited, holding his breath. There was no sound from below. He then became aware of something that had only sporadically presented itself the night before—hunger. When excited or frightened he had always lost his appetite, so the fact that he hadn't eaten since the morning before only bothered him from time to time. Now it was a raging demand, and far worse was thirst.

Crouched over the trapdoor, he listened. Then, as quietly as he could, he lay down so that his ear was over the crack in the floor where the trapdoor fit. There was no sound that he could hear. Slowly, slowly, he slid his fingers under the handle in the middle of the door, making it look like a lid to one of his mother's coffeepots.

Suddenly, thinking of that, he thought about Martha and then about Patrick. His longing was so great he didn't think he could move. For the first time since he had gone with Lawrence, he felt the tears forcing themselves out of his eyes. Putting his hands over his face, he muffled the sobs he couldn't stop. After a while the stifled sobs slowed, and he wiped the tears from his face.

Once again he slid his fingers under the handle and exerted a little pressure upward. The trapdoor came up easily and without a sound. Jonathan found himself staring down into the near black of an almost completely closed closet. But with a lift of the heart he saw that it was exactly the way he had left it in his frantic climb up and last desperate effort to pull the door to behind him.

It was a risk, but a risk he had to take, so he leaned out of the hole, supporting himself on one hand on the top of a box on the highest closet shelf, and pushed the closet door farther open.

With the door open and by leaning down from his hole he could see a large part of the room and saw that it was empty.

Slowly, careful not to make a sound, he climbed down the shelves, making sure that he pushed nothing that would drop or create a noise by sliding. Finally he was down.

Peering around the door, he saw that the room was indeed empty. Luckily, the carpet was thick so he could cross the floor to the bathroom without making any noise. Once there he closed the door, went over to the basin and filled a glass with water. He drank that and then another glass and half of a third. His thirst appeased, he turned off the water and stood there, listening for any sound. But there wasn't any. Then he noticed that there was a small window at the end of the room. Walking silently over, he looked outside, but there was no fire escape near, nothing but a long drop to the small garden below.

Leaving the bathroom, he went back into the bedroom and crept to the door leading to the hall. Gently he took hold of the doorknob. Gently he turned it. But when he pulled, the door didn't move. He tried again. It still didn't move. There was, of course, the bolt. He stood, afraid, before making any effort to turn it, sure that it would create far more noise flipping over suddenly and noisily. Finally he grasped the bolt and tried to turn it. It wouldn't move. He then took both hands and tried. Nothing happened. He tried again, one hand on the doorknob and one on the bolt, but the bolt wouldn't budge and the door remained firmly closed.

He stood there. The disappointment was so great he could hardly move. How could he get out? How could his mother or his father or anyone ever find him? He would be here forever and would die and no one would ever know. Panic seized him, but something, some instinct for survival, kept him from giving in to it. I've got to think of something, he told himself. What would his father do?

He continued to stand there, his hands up against the door, leaning on it. He tried to think of something. But nothing came. His resolve, so strong a few minutes before, vanished. Suddenly he sat down, not caring if anyone heard him or not. But the apartment seemed totally silent, and the silence that was so reassuring before he discovered the door was locked now appeared threatening. What if everyone had deserted the apartment? What if no one would ever come in again? With the door locked how could he find something to eat? Would he die here and his body just lie in the room?

"No, no," he sobbed. "Please, somebody help me."

But there was no reply, no sound.

Eventually he stopped crying. Again he thought of shouting and yelling. But remaining caution kept him from trying it. So he sat cross-legged on the floor, his back to the door, staring at the room.

After a while he realized he was staring at the little bureau beside the bed. The furniture was white, as was the bed and the bedspread. The bottom drawer was partly open. Jonathan continued staring at the space between the drawer and the frame it was supposed to fit into. It was several minutes later when he realized he was reading the word "biscuits" on the top of a box that was in the open drawer. He got up and went over to the drawer. Inside was a package that read, "English Tea Biscuits." Opening the top he found several layers of cookies in small piles.

Only just remembering not to shout, he started putting them in his mouth, eating one after the other as fast as he could. After about the fourth he slowed down, remembering hearing somewhere in some class that the slower you ate, the longer the food lasted. But he kept on eating.

He had finished half the box when he heard a slight sound coming from the other side of the door.

He moved quickly, closing the drawer as quietly as he could and tucking the half-finished box under his arm. Carefully he brushed away any crumbs that might have fallen on the floor, and then, moving silently in his sneakers, he went back to the closet, climbed up the shelves and into the hole. He pushed the boxes around to hide the hole, then slid the trapdoor down. The last thing he saw as he slipped it into place was the white telephone on the bedside bureau. I should have called Dad, he thought, furious at himself.

Mooney rang the doorbell and waited.

Martha flung the door open. "Have you found out anything?" Her fear was so great that it hit him in the chest like a thrown weight.

"A little. Not a lot," he said, walking into the living room. "The man in the doughnut place on Atlantic Avenue recognized the drawing Mrs. Leonard had made. He said that was the man who was there and who Jonathan walked out with."

"Why didn't he stop him? Didn't he know there was something fishy about it?"

"How could he? He took it that the man was a friend of the family's."

"Couldn't he see—" She stopped because she saw how it sounded. She hadn't even got up yesterday morning when her son left the house. With far more reason to keep a close eye on her child, she hadn't bothered to see him off to school. In shame she put her hands over her face.

Mooney had a fairly clear idea of how she was feeling but couldn't think of anything helpful to say, so he asked, "Can I sit down?"

She took her hands away from her face. "Yes. I'm sorry."

He pulled a copy of the pencil sketch out of his pocket and unfolded it. "You said this reminded you of something or somebody but you couldn't remember who it is. Look at it again." He handed it over.

Martha took the sketch and stared at it once more. She waited for that flash of recognition, but this time it didn't happen. She kept on looking, but the more she looked the less the man's face reminded her of anything. She shook her head. "Nothing," she said.

Mooney got up. "Keep it. It's a photocopy. Put it up somewhere you can see it. Maybe the memory will come back."

He was gone before she realized he was going. The sketch was lying on the coffee table. Martha picked it up and stared. Still nothing. She put it back on top of a small pile of books and took up her restless pacing. Every now and then she picked up the sketch and examined it in detail. She got so she could describe in detail the man's nose, eyes and chin, the way he wore his hair. Yet the whole lacked impact. She could not bring back that overwhelming conviction that she had seen him before.

Before he left to go over to look at the picture, Patrick called Mooney.

"I tried to get in touch with you," Mooney said. "There's a picture here I'd like you to look at."

"So I heard from Martha. Why didn't you leave a message on the tape?"

"Because it's not working. There never is a beep. It stopped before I could say anything."

"Hell and damnation! I thought I'd made sure that this time I got the reprogramming right. I wonder who else has been trying my phone."

"I'd fix it if I were you. If you can't figure it out, I'd call the place where you got it and ask them to walk you through the programming."

"I didn't get it. It went with the sublet. But I'll call the manufacturer. I haven't dealt with this kind before. Look, about the picture. Can't you come here with it, or send somebody with it? I don't like to leave here, especially with the answering machine not working."

"Okay. I'll send somebody. Even if you don't recognize it, see if you get a flash, like he reminds you of somebody."

"And you say Katie Leonard drew this? Wonders'll never cease. She was always one of my wife's drinking companions."

"By the way," Mooney said, "when I showed it to Mrs. Tierney she didn't recognize it, but she said there was a moment when it suddenly reminded her of somebody, but she couldn't remember who."

"Helpful," Patrick said caustically.

"You must be pretty mad at her," Mooney said. "She's going through a lot."

"Yes. I expect she is, but I have a hard time feeling sorry. If she hadn't spent the last eight months boozing round the clock this wouldn't have happened."

Mooney reflected it wasn't his role to counsel patience to Patrick Tierney, or to express sympathy for Martha Tierney.

But he said, anyway, "Kids have been abducted from parents who weren't drinking, you know."

"I take your point. But I repeat, if Martha had been minding the store—looking after the boy whose custody she raised hell to get—he might not be . . . lost." He couldn't bring himself to say "abducted."

Mooney, on the other hand, had just about abandoned any other theory, although he was too good a cop to allow himself to leave any possibility unexamined. "An officer will be around with the sketch soon," he said.

Lawrence was in the kind of blind rage that had become more common since he had been dismissed from his job five years previously. Through a combination of good luck, an excellent lawyer and a fumbling district attorney, he had managed to avoid prison, but he did not see the degeneration of his life as any fault of his own. Those responsible were his iron-fisted, puritanical previous employers, the fascist legal system and the family and friends who had deserted him. The anger that, along with the manic spells, had increased in both frequency and power was now gripping him again.

He had been convinced that the boy was still in the apartment, a conviction that was strengthened by his own revulsion towards Ben Nicolaides, who had insisted that Jonathan had escaped, and by his need to believe that he had not been so stupid as to let the boy get away. He had had experience with little boys and he was sure he was right.

But this conviction had weakened during the night. He had banked on the boy's having to relieve his physical wants —hunger and thirst and his need to use the bathroom. With those urges pressing on him, Lawrence argued to himself, surely no eight-year-old boy had the determination to remain locked in whatever bolt-hole he had discovered. Lawrence did not question himself as to where the bolt-hole might be. Nor did he allow himself to remember the care with which he had searched in that room, any more than he permitted himself to consider that the boy had successfully eluded him and run away. He also didn't let himself remember Ben's sarcasm and mockery when he had insisted that Jonathan had got out and that he, Lawrence, was crazy. Other people had said that to Lawrence, and it always produced in Lawrence a searing rage.

But the boy had not appeared anywhere. And when Lawrence, after a fitful night, had slid the bolt back on the door and peered into the bedroom in which he had previously locked Jonathan, there was no indication that the boy was there. Once again he had looked in every conceivable crevice and had pushed aside the clothes in the closet. Nothing.

Finally, leaving the room and refusing to see it as an empty gesture, he bolted the door again from the outside. Then he left the apartment.

Now he walked east, striding quickly, keeping his head down. He had waked up angry and frustrated and hungry and had gone to make himself some breakfast, only to find there was no coffee left in the apartment kitchen, nor any fresh milk. He had had a vague memory of some English tea biscuits that he had bought on another occasion, but a search throughout the kitchen cupboards and drawers produced nothing. One of Ben's rules was: no perishable food, not even bread. As Ben, a lifelong city resident, explained, you never knew what could go bad and smell and/or develop bugs or, worse still, roaches. These had a way of drifting from one apartment to another through the walls and along the pipes, and the last thing he needed was to have some pest-control inspectors banging on the door.

Lawrence crossed West End Avenue and continued on to

Broadway. After buying a newspaper at the corner, and because he did not want to be noticed too near the apartment, he got on a bus, rode as far as Seventy-ninth Street, then got off and went into a hamburger joint. Sitting at the counter, he ordered coffee, juice and a bagel with cream cheese and jelly. In the days when he had held an honored position in a highly regarded profession, he had pretended to scorn such food, and had managed to maintain a near-macrobiotic diet, concentrating on vegetables, brown rice, fruits and whole grains, and would periodically expatiate to his students on the subject of the destructive eating habits of the Western world. His wife and son of that long-ago past had gone along with him, though he was aware that Michael, their son, periodically stole out to have a hamburger with the other kids, or a bagel and cream cheese. . . .

The only feeling he had now for the woman who had been his wife was one of contempt. If she had understood him better, if she had not taken away his son, he would not now be forced to find his companions in back studios and grungy little storefronts.

He opened his paper, bought partly out of habit to see if his name had occurred anywhere for any reason—for there was a time when every paper, however respectable, had carried the account of his disgrace—and partly because it was physically the biggest paper obtainable and he could hide in its folds.

When his breakfast came, he put the paper in his lap for a moment, thirstily drinking his juice. Then, arranging his juice and coffee to fit inside the paper, he raised it again, and went on reading behind his makeshift fortress.

But in that moment when the paper was lowered a man walked in the side door and sat down at the counter running at right angles to Lawrence. For a half minute he caught Lawrence's profile, and, when Lawrence turned towards his coffee, his three-quarter face. The man was in plain clothes, but he was a cop, and something about that face hooked on to something in his mind. Where had he seen it before?

The news hit the afternoon papers and the evening television news:

BEST-SELLING WRITER'S SON MISSING was one headline. "FO-CUS" AUTHOR'S SON ABDUCTED was another.

"The police have confirmed that Jonathan Tierney, eight-year-old son of Patrick Tierney and his former wife, Martha Tierney, disappeared on his way to school yesterday morning," said one attractive newscaster. "Patrick Tierney, author of the best-selling *Focus,* and his former wife are divorced. Martha Tierney lives in Brooklyn Heights, where their son attended St. Andrew's School, an elite private school on Remsen Street. Patrick Tierney has only recently returned from abroad and is living somewhere in Manhattan. No further details have been released by the school and Mr. and Mrs. Tierney cannot be reached."

But that had not prevented the various branches of the media from trying to reach them.

"Please, please," Martha had said tearfully into the phone, as the fourth paper and third television station had called, "please leave the telephone free. If Jonathan, or the —the people who have him—are trying to reach me, they won't be able to get through. And please, please don't come around here. If anybody—if somebody who was trying to get in touch found the place surrounded by reporters, I don't have to tell you that it could completely ruin any hope I—his father and I—have for getting him back. I was once a reporter myself, so I know what I'm asking."

And the papers had for the most part complied. They had also—at least for the time being—refrained from printing what was common knowledge in the world of journalism: that two years before, Martha had been fired for unreliability due to alcoholism.

Patrick, too, had had his callers, though not as many, owing to the fact that he was living in a sublet and was harder to track down. But one industrious reporter with contacts in the publishing house that put out *Focus* had run him to ground and called.

"Listen," Patrick said, "this phone has to remain open in case my son, or whoever has my son, is trying to get in touch. Any delay could mean Jonathan's life. I'll let you know the moment I have any news that I can share, but don't risk Jonathan's life. Do you have kids of your own?"

"Yes," the reporter admitted. "Okay. But I'm going to hold you to that promise to call me—not just all the press, but me—if you get any news that doesn't involve his safety."

Stephen Morgan and Marguerite Stanley had left school together and without too much consultation, had headed for the house across from Marguerite's, a gloomy-looking, red brick structure the worse for many years' neglect. They went around the garden to the back door, and Marguerite beat a special rat-a-tat on the door, amounting to a code.

The door opened a small amount and a thin, pointed face framed in gingery gray hair appeared in the narrow opening. "All right. Come in, both of you," Belinda Beauchamps said. "Tessa is not eating for me. Maybe she'll eat for you."

The smell in the house was considerable, but as Jonathan had often pointed out, no worse than the smell in some houses that boasted no more than two cats. "It's not the cats' fault," he was fond of saying. "People should change the litter more often." He was meticulous about changing

Susan's pan, partly because Susan had a way of using the bathtub if the pan were less than spanking clean and partly because he didn't want to give his mother any excuse for complaining about Susan. To be fair, he occasionally admitted to himself, she had never made the slightest suggestion that he should get rid of her. But he knew that for some reason he didn't understand, Susan irritated her.

Once Marguerite, who sometimes came home with Jonathan, said flatly, "She's jealous."

Jonathan was about to deny that as absurd, when it suddenly struck him it might be true. After that, he was careful to show affection to Susan only when they were alone.

As Stephen and Marguerite now penetrated farther into the house, the smell grew. It seemed least in the kitchen, by which they entered, and most in the halls, where pans with litter lined the walls.

"I like to leave the sitting room free," Miss Beauchamps explained airily.

She was bent now over a large tiger-striped cat who sat hunched up on the carpet. "Come on, Tessa, you know you like fish." As Tessa continued to ignore her, she said enticingly, "Look at all the other kitties. They'd love to have this fish, wouldn't you, babies?" And she forked up a piece of the fish and waved it in the air.

Tessa didn't move or turn her head. But the dozen or so of the thirty-odd cats in residence that were poised nearby, ready to leap at the piece of fish, moved slightly nearer.

"You see?" Miss Beauchamps said.

When Tessa went on showing no interest Miss Beauchamps lowered her fork. "I do hope there's nothing wrong with her." Her voice shook a little.

"Maybe she just doesn't feel like eating," Stephen said, trying to be soothing.

"I know you mean to be helpful, Stephen," Miss Beauchamps said reproachfully, "but there's something wrong. I know it."

There was a silence, while all three humans present pondered, each in his and her own way, a variety of circumstances: that Miss Beauchamps lived on Social Security and a meager pension from her days as a clerk-typist at a large and stingy publishing company; that most of what little money she had went on vet's bills, even allowing for the fact that the vet, a kindly animal lover, only charged her half his usual fee when he charged her at all, so therefore she was honor-bound not to take advantage of his kindness; that Tessa was now seventeen and, with the aid of Alexander, a large and fertile tom, now deceased, had once produced at least part of the household at present sitting around and waiting for the fish.

Marguerite thought, She'll die if something happens to Tessa.

Stephen thought, The stink in here is terrible. They'll take all her cats away if anybody ever finds out.

Miss Beauchamps thought, The only thing that will keep me alive if Tessa goes is that the others have to have a home. I have no money. If she's in pain—

There was a knock on the front door.

All three people froze.

Miss Beauchamps's eyes darted around to see if there were anything—such as a light—that would indicate she was in.

After a short silence, there was another knock.

Finally there was the sound of footsteps going down the stoop.

Before anyone could stop him, Stephen ran to the window.

Miss Beauchamps uttered a stifled shriek. "Don't let them see you!"

"I won't!" Stephen whispered back.

The curtains hanging by the window were once—in the days of Miss Beauchamps's parents—expensive and luxurious. Now the brocade was filthy with dust, rot and the remains of various feline sprayings. Miss Beauchamps had tried to wash and wipe off the dirtier areas, but she had been only partly successful. When pulled, chunks of the curtains were inclined to come away in the hand, a fact Stephen discovered when he pushed one aside so he could peek between the curtain and the equally filthy net half-curtain covering the actual window. Outside he saw two uniformed men and a black-and-white police car.

"They're cops," he said.

In the dim light of the room Marguerite saw Miss Beauchamps's face become sallow. "I bet it's not about you or the cats," she said, frightened by the woman's distraught look. She hadn't the faintest idea of whether she believed what she said or not; she simply wanted to offer some reassurance.

"I bet it's about Jonathan," Stephen said from the window.

"What's the matter with Jonathan?" Miss Beauchamps asked sharply. Of the three children, Jonathan was her favorite. He was the one who actually helped out. He brought cans of food every now and then, when his pocket money allowed, often played with the cats, especially Tessa, attempted to comb and brush them, when he could find a comb and brush, and even cleaned out the litter pans. He was, in Miss Beauchamps's eyes, a boy whose price was above rubies.

"He's disappeared," Marguerite said. "Nobody's seen him since yesterday morning. The police have been at school and everything."

"Oh!" Distress filled Miss Beauchamps. "Oh, I hope nothing's happened to him!"

"Yeah," Stephen and Marguerite said together.

All three went back to staring at Tessa.

"I think maybe you ought to call the vet," Stephen said.

Miss Beauchamps looked down at her pet. Slowly tears came out of her eyes and ran down her cheeks. Getting up, she went to the phone, dialed a number and spoke into the receiver.

"Dr. Morse is going to drop by on his way home from the clinic," she said when she'd hung up. "You know," she said a while later to Marguerite and Stephen, "I once had a conversation with God."

"You did?" Marguerite didn't believe in God, largely because her aunt was a passionate churchgoer. But she was willing to have an open mind. "What did He say?"

"He asked me who I wanted to have with me when I die and cross over into the afterlife. I told him all my cats who had crossed over, too. 'No people?' God asked. 'No,' I said, 'just my cats.' Of course," Miss Beauchamps went on, "I'd like to have you two and Jonathan. And Dr. Morse. But nobody else."

When Stephen and Marguerite were ready to go home through the back door, they came out into the hall, and dim though the lighting was, they saw that a piece of paper had been thrust under the front door.

"Hey! Somebody's left you a message," Stephen said.

Miss Beauchamps clasped her hands. "Oh God! An official health notice?"

"No. It's a picture of somebody. They've written on top, 'If you recognize this man would you please call this number?'"

"I'm sure I won't," Miss Beauchamps said.

"Here," Stephen said, coming back down the hall and handing the paper to her.

Marguerite peered over Miss Beauchamps's arm as she took it and looked at the drawing. "I think that was the man who I saw walking down towards Sidney Place once. He was sort of spooky."

"What do you mean?" Miss Beauchamps said.

"I dunno. He just seemed weird."

"Do you think it's got anything to do with Jonathan?" Stephen asked.

"Why should it?" Miss Beauchamps asked sharply.

"Aunt Megan told me that Jonathan went to the doughnut place on Atlantic Avenue to meet somebody."

"Yeah, but Jonathan was going to meet, well, somebody else." Stephen reminded himself that he was not supposed to reveal what he knew.

"Who?" Miss Beauchamps said sharply.

Stephen shrugged.

"Stephen, that's not an answer!"

"You know what they're saying in school," Marguerite said. "I think Steve means Jonathan was supposed to be meeting his father."

"He didn't meet his father," Stephen said. "His father and mother both came to the school. At least, that's what Cynthia Dean says. She saw them when she passed the head's office."

Marguerite was watching Miss Beauchamps's face. "Do you know who it is, Miss Beauchamps?"

"No," the aging, frightened woman said.

When they got out Marguerite said, "I think she knew who it was."

"Then why didn't she say?"

"Because, silly, if the police ever got into her house, she's afraid they'd take away her cats and have them killed. She's said that lots of times."

"Why should they do that?"

"Something about a health risk. You know how it smells. They'd take them to the ASPCA, and if nobody adopted them in a couple of days they'd have to put them to sleep."

9

The second break came when neighbors in the Tribeca area of Manhattan reported an intruder in the apartment next to them. There had been several break-ins recently. The street on the far West Side was often deserted, and it was fright more than good citizenship that provoked the phone call.

"He's there now. I hear him."

"Okay. We'll be there. Don't try anything."

A police car happened to be not far from the street, and they caught Leo red-handed trying to get down the fire escape, a clutch of Cheryl's photographs and negatives in his grasp.

"So what are these?" the cop asked when they were back up in the apartment, taking the pictures from Leo's hand.

"Nothing. Just garbage."

"Then why're you bothering with them?"

Silence. Leo was crafty and violent, but not too quick mentally.

"Whose pad is this?" The cop looked around the small apartment. There were glossy photographs mounted on the walls, all featuring a dark-haired, thin girl, each time with a different man. The cop went over and took down one framed photograph. "Not bad," he said. "Not bad at all." He turned it over. " 'Cheryl with Sid Rodosky,' " he read. "So what did Cheryl do, or should I guess?" He turned to where Leo, handcuffed, was being held by the other policeman.

Leo shrugged.

The man holding him by the arm shook it. "Answer the man, buddy."

"How should I know?"

The first cop went over, picked up the photographs that had been taken from Leo and looked at them. They obviously were not what he was expecting to see, because he said in a puzzled voice, "Who's the kid?" Then, with rising excitement, "Isn't that the Tierney boy—the one that's missing?"

Leo stared straight ahead.

The cop walked up to him. "Why are they here? What's the dame here—Cheryl—got to do with him? That is, if this is her apartment. And where do you come in?"

Leo didn't answer.

"Where did you find them?"

Leo remained silent.

"Maybe in the drawer there," the officer holding him said, nodding towards an open drawer in the bureau. The drawer was half out. In it were pieces of underwear and various other articles, but there were no more pictures. The other policeman went systematically through the remaining drawers and the drawers of an unpainted chest that, with chintz drawn in two curtains around the top, served as a makeshift dressing table. There was some costume jewelry in one of the drawers and on top of the dressing table, all of which seemed undisturbed. But there was nothing else of interest.

The cop looked again at the pictures. "Half the NYPD is looking for this kid. We'd better phone this in and get him to the precinct."

It didn't take the police long to learn that Cheryl was now lying in the morgue. A call was put in to Mooney, who had brought the identifier to the morgue and was now working with a special task force assigned to the Tierney case and the pictures were taken to his precinct.

Mooney looked at the photographs. "That's the Tierney boy all right, and these are copies of the pictures Pinkus took for the kid's father."

The burglary immediately took on larger ramifications.

Mooney and the other policemen questioned Leo, who put on his expressionless stare and said nothing until Mooney accused him of killing Cheryl.

"You can't prove nothin'," Leo said.

Mooney was fairly aware that this was true. The gun that had killed Cheryl had never been located, and probably wouldn't be by now.

"Maybe not about Cheryl, but we can sure tie you to the kid that's missing. He's pretty well known, in case you hadn't heard." And Mooney tossed over a couple of the papers that were carrying headlines about Jonathan and his picture. "Kidnapping's a federal charge, Leo. You were caught holding the photographs that Jonathan Tierney's father had made of him. We know the negatives were stolen from the photographer's files. You have them. Like I said, kidnapping is a federal charge."

"I didn't take him out of the state," Leo blurted out.

"But you know where he is because you put him there, or

you helped put him there. Kidnapping a child for immoral purposes is one of the most serious crimes there is. You can get the death penalty for it. Now, why don't you tell us where the kid is. Maybe things'll go easier for you."

Leo licked a mouth that had gone suddenly dry. "I ain't had nothin' to do with kidnappin'. That's not my line."

"What is? Child pornography?"

"I don't know nothin'."

"Sure you do. You knew enough to steal these. Why?"

He'd stolen the negatives because Ben Nicolaides had told him to. "We don't want nothin' tyin' this kid to us" had been Ben's words. His eyes had slid to the glossies that Cheryl had brought him. "It's a pity, though. A kid like that could go far. But go to Cheryl's place and get the photos and negatives. You ain't heard from her, have you?"

"Nah. Not lately."

"She doesn't hook for you no more?"

"Nah." But Leo didn't like to leave it like that. It was obvious Ben hadn't heard that Cheryl was dead. But he would, sooner or later, and Leo didn't want Ben thinking he had anything to do with it. "She said she knew where she could make more money for us."

"Doin' what?"

Leo had shrugged. "Didn't say."

"Well, I don't want her makin' money by telling somebody about those photos. So go get them."

"Why?" Mooney persisted now. "Why did you steal these?" When Leo continued to play dumb, Mooney got up. "Okay, you'll find out what a federal charge of kidnapping can amount to. And take those papers back to your cell. That boy's father's famous. He can pay for a lot of pressure. If you don't mind having that on your back, then it's okay with us. Take him back!"

Back at his desk Mooney stared at the photographs. He wanted Leo to be as scared as possible, but he also knew he didn't have time to spend on letting him stew. Jonathan's life depended on how soon they could find him.

Mooney went to the district attorney's office and put his case. "Leo has something to do with this damn kiddie-porn ring. I'd bet he knows where they'd take a boy like that. We can't let him be in their hands one minute longer than we can help. Leo's sleaze and he probably murdered that girl. But she's dead. Maybe Jonathan isn't yet. What can I offer him to get him to talk about the people in the ring and find out—maybe—where Jonathan is?"

Later that day Mooney went back to question Leo, but nothing he hinted at or finally offered moved him. "I don't talk until I walk from here," Leo said. He wasn't educated, but he wasn't stupid, either.

"We can tie you to this kidnapping, and I told you that's a federal case."

"You ain't got no way to tie me. I don't have nothin' to do with those pictures. I ain't seen 'em before and you can't hang that on me."

Mooney had a sudden longing to kill the man himself. He had managed throughout his professional life to remain remarkably distant from the crimes and criminals he dealt with every day. Don't judge! he'd told himself a hundred times. Let the courts do that. But child pornography was something else. Whenever he thought what might be happening now to Jonathan, what kind of creature the boy could be turned into, his stomach rose, as did his primitive desire to kill any and all who had anything to do with it.

"Let him cool his heels," he said now to the sergeant.

But he couldn't put his usual toughness into the statement. Time meant so much.

.   .   .

Miss Beauchamps stared at the drawing, holding the paper under a sixty-watt bulb at the back of the living room. "Five years?" she said to herself in a conversational tone. "Or is it six? We must go to the basement, Tessa," she went on. "But not until after the vet has come."

Ben Nicolaides saw the afternoon papers when he went out to lunch and they gave him a bad fright. The identification of Jonathan as Patrick Tierney's son was the worst possible news. A boy whose parents nobody had ever heard of was one thing. The child of a celebrity was another. Then, no sooner had Ben returned to his grimy office above the film-developing store than he heard from one of his informers and henchmen that Leo had been picked up for breaking and entering. After sitting and thinking for a while, he turned on a radio he kept in his office and moved the needle to an all-news station. It was only five minutes from the hour, so he waited patiently through endless commercials and minor stories to the main news at the hour.

Fifteen minutes later he had learned that the body of a woman who had been in the morgue for a day and a half had been identified as Cheryl Mason, that a small-time hoodlum who had always been associated with prostitution had been caught breaking and entering the apartment of the said Cheryl Mason, and, when caught, was clutching negatives of pictures of Jonathan Tierney, the boy who had disappeared.

After listening a few more minutes to make sure nothing else was going to be relayed, Ben turned off the radio and dialed the number of the apartment on 102nd Street.

"Ya better get out of there," he said. "The kid's big news

now, and it turns out his father is some kind of a celebrity. Did ya know that?"

"I know his father is a writer."

"Writers are a dime a dozen. This guy's an author, a celeb. I'm tellin' ya, ya better get out of there. Better still, leave the city."

"I'm not leaving while Jonathan's here."

"Are you crazy? How many times do I have to tell ya? He's split! He's not there."

"If he's escaped, then why hasn't he gone to the nearest precinct—or home? He's not a stupid boy and his people are sophisticated and educated. I know he's in this apartment— or maybe I mean the building—somewhere. I don't know where, but I have an idea of how to find out."

"You wanna go to jail for the rest of your life?"

"I'll be careful." And Lawrence hung up. He was in an exalted mood. A sense of power gripped him. He knew the boy was in the building somewhere. Ben had simply joined all the others to thwart him, as indeed had society as a whole, dating back to the days when his wife turned on him. . . . He closed his eyes while the heady rage filled him like a tonic. He was right. He'd always been right. Then he thought of the boy and a scorching hunger replaced the exaltation. It was a relationship that he had been looking for all his life, even before he knew what it was he wanted: teacher and pupil, Socrates and Plato. The Greeks, the wisest of them all, knew the secret of love. Now he knew and no one, not Ben, not the police or the boy's parents were going to thwart him. He would teach that divine boy about love. . . .

In the meantime, seeing the super in the lobby when he came back from breakfast had given him an idea. Getting up suddenly, he left the apartment and went downstairs, hoping that the super would still be there. But he was no longer in the hall. Lawrence hesitated for a moment, then searched the small lobby and the even smaller vestibule outside the locked front door for a sign or notice saying where the super could be reached. Eventually he found it: SEE BASEMENT.

Lawrence got back in the elevator and punched the letter B. When the doors opened he found himself in a large underground room that contained various devices for repair and maintenance of the building. In the corner was an office. Lawrence walked over there and found the super. He had his story prepared.

"A friend of mine said he had stored his trunk somewhere in the eleventh-floor apartment—eleven-B, that is. I've looked everywhere"—Lawrence gave a mechanical-sounding laugh—"in the closets, under the bed, and I can't find it. Then I remembered his letter told me to ask you—that you knew everything about the apartments and would know if there were attics or holes where he could have put his things." Suddenly and obviously Lawrence was holding a twenty-dollar bill.

The super looked at it and counted the cost of what cooperating with this jerk might mean. He had replaced the original super, who had been induced to retire, and was now paid by Ben in addition to the salary he received from the remote and uninterested owner of the building. Ben paid him partly to find his living quarters outside the building, and partly to turn a blind eye and ear to anything—any disturbance of any kind—emanating from 11B. So far, his healthy salary had required very little. But twenty dollars was twenty dollars, he thought, still looking at the bill. It was important that he stay on the right side of the tenant of 11B, but this man must be a friend of the tenant's, so what would be the harm of earning the twenty dollars?

"It's the top apartment so there's a sort of attic, or crawl space above the ceiling," he said. "Maybe your friend's trunk is there." His hand moved towards the twenty dollars.

Lawrence pulled it back. "How do I get up there?" he asked.

"There's a trapdoor in the closet of the main bedroom. You can't see it very well because it's way in the corner and the ceiling paper was picked so it wouldn't show. But it's there."

"I was right!" Lawrence exulted, handing over the twenty dollars. "I was right!"

Jonathan lay across the attic floor, staring out the attic window, filled with despair. It had been almost two full days since he had come here and he was now desperately afraid that no one would ever find him. He didn't know what to do. He could go down into the bedroom, but he couldn't get out from there. He could also be caught by that terrible man, and Jonathan, a New York City child, had a pretty good idea of what the man would do once he got hold of him. There were other problems. The English tea biscuits had long since gone. He was hungry and thirsty again and he wanted to go to the bathroom.

"Dad," he whispered. "Dad! Where are you? Mom?" His rage at his alcoholic mother continued. The whole thing was somehow her fault. But despite himself, he kept remembering scenes from the good times, when she laughed with him and read him stories and made up things to tell him or recited poetry or funny jingles to him. He had waked up with one of them running in his head: *From ghoulies and ghosties and long-leggety beasties, And things that go bump in the night, Good Lord, deliver us!*

"Have you ever counted up the people the good Lord hasn't delivered?" his cynical father once said.

"Shush!" his mother had rebuked, jokingly, because those were the good days. And she sent Jonathan off to

Sunday school, which, on the whole, he rather liked because it consisted mostly of stories about heroic people like David, and he liked such stories.

Remembering those, he wept, lying on the floor, his head on his hands, because he tried to muffle his sobs. He thought about Susan, and her funny, stiff-legged walk and her nice smell and her crossed blue eyes, and he cried again. He was lying there, thinking of Susan when he heard, distantly, the sound that he now associated with the closing of the apartment front door. He held his breath. The man could be coming in or going out.

Earlier that morning Jonathan had drifted off to sleep and only waked up to hear the sound of the front door being closed. His heart had leaped up then, but this sound was followed by the ringing of the telephone, which was picked up on the second ring. By sliding over and putting his ear to the crack in the trapdoor, he had heard the faint noise of the man's voice talking, and he knew then that the man must have been out and had come back in. It made him sick to realize that his captor had been out while he was asleep.

But now he heard the door again. After that there was no sound at all, none of the distant noises he associated with the man's being in the other bedroom: water flowing, television voices, talking on the telephone, the toilet flushing.

Quietly, not making a sound, he slid over to the trapdoor and listened with his ear to the crack. There was total silence. Jonathan counted to fifty. Then, gently as he could, he lifted the trapdoor and put it to one side. He stopped and listened some more. After that he climbed down and tore to the bathroom. As soon as he finished there he went to the telephone and dialed the number his father had given him and he had memorized. He heard the phone at the other end ring three times. Then there was a click, and he gathered himself to leave a message, but there was no beep. The machine had just gone off.

Jonathan couldn't believe what had happened. But he knew he didn't have any time to bother about it. He dialed his home, and with a feeling of relief beyond anything he'd ever known he heard his mother's voice. "Hello? Hello?"

"Mom!" Jonathan sobbed into the phone. "It's me."

Within half an hour Sergeant Mooney had received two tentative identifications of the sketch that Katie Leonard had drawn and he had had photocopied and distributed to all the precincts.

The first was from an anonymous woman calling from a public phone.

"You don't know me," the rather high-pitched voice said. "But that sketch of a man the policeman was handing out looks like Lawrence Miller, you know, the college professor who was arrested for child molesting. It was six years ago—a well-known college in New England."

"Who is this?" Mooney demanded, his heart beating.

"I'm not going to give my name and I'm calling from a public phone, so it's no use trying to get it traced. Goodbye." And she hung up.

Miss Beauchamps hurried away from the phone on Court Street. It hadn't taken her long to search through the newspapers she kept in her basement, waiting for her to do the research on contemporary history that she had always planned to do but which had been postponed by the more important need of rescuing stray cats. And she had remembered that case particularly, because when disgrace overtook him the professor was teaching at the college her father had once attended.

She disliked the police, whom she looked upon as part of

The Enemy, ready to pounce on her and her beloved strays, but Jonathan was in danger, and for him she had to do her part.

The second call came as Mooney was distributing the information about Lawrence Miller to the various precincts and waiting for information about him and his most recent whereabouts to come up on the computer.

"This is Detective Kowalski. That guy in the sketch you were giving out, I think I've seen him."

"Where?"

"In a hamburger joint on Broadway near Eightieth Street."

"When?"

"Around nine this morning."

Mooney sighed. "I wish you'd called me sooner. It looks like this guy has abducted a kid, an eight-year-old boy, and another caller has just said he was once a college professor who got into trouble molesting a boy about six years ago."

"I'm sorry. Things are kind of hectic."

"You say Broadway near Eightieth. Have you seen him there before?"

"No."

"Did he look like he once could have been a teacher in a college?"

"Yeah. Yeah, he did."

Mooney remembered the man in the doughnut joint on Atlantic Avenue. He thought the guy looked like a schoolteacher, too.

"Thanks," he said, and hung up.

"Darling," Martha said. "Darling, are you all right? Have they, has he—"

"No, but I know he's going to find me, Mom. I'm stuck in a kind of attic. I can't get down when he's in the house."

"Where are you?"

"I don't know."

"Think, darling. How did you go there?"

"We went to the zoo first. Then he took a cab and we came here."

"Where's here?"

"Somewhere in Manhattan. West Side."

"Can you remember the street number?"

"No, he said we were going to meet Dad. I wasn't looking."

"Can you remember anything, darling, anything at all? You're good at remembering things. Do you remember when you recalled a house in the country we were looking for had a red barn beside it? Can you think of anything like that?" Please, God, please, she thought. Help him to remember something.

"The door's black. It's sort of an apartment building. There's a funny knocker on the door, a leopard's mouth with a ball in it. To the left I could see the river. Next door, in the window there was a cat and some yellow flowers like the ones you brought home that Susan knocked over. Do you remember, Mom?"

Suddenly Martha thought of something. "What's the number there, Jonathan? Look on the phone!"

Jonathan looked, but as he did so he heard the click of the apartment door lock. Quickly, as quietly as he could, he put the phone back and ran back to the closet, his sneakered feet flying up the shelves. He lifted himself into the attic and replaced the trapdoor. The whole operation hardly took half a minute. Then he lay on the door, his ear to the crack, listening. He heard the voice of the film man first.

"I want ya out of this place. The boy ain't here. But the

164

cops already have pictures of you. Some of my boys have got the word from the precincts. And I don't want nothin' that's gonna lead them here. There's a car downstairs. I'll take you anywhere you want. But I want you outa here."

"The boy's here, I know. I just asked the super if—"

"You did what, you stupid jerk? Do you want to send the cops an invitation? Why don't you call them up?"

"Don't worry. That dumbo didn't know what I was talking about. I just asked about a trunk that a friend left but I couldn't find. He said there was a sort of half-attic or crawl space with a trapdoor in the closet in that bedroom. That's where the boy's been. I'm going to get him now."

"Are you crazy? There are already cops around the area. I've seen them."

"I'll just get the boy now. Then we can take him with us. I've been planning everything."

"You moron! I had that crawl space sealed up a year ago. I wasn't going to have that there with all the work we do in that room. I tell you, he's not there." It was a lie, but anything was worth getting this maniac out of the house and out of the area. If the police stumbled on this apartment, a great deal of expensive equipment would be lost and they'd probably be able to trace it to him and his associates. "It's sealed," he said finally. "Now, let's go."

"Who's that?" Lawrence said, looking past his shoulder.

It was an old trick but it worked. The man turned and therefore didn't see the heavy bronze figure of a naked man coming crashing down on his bald head.

Martha finally got through to Mooney after four tries. Every line seemed to be busy.

"He called me," she burst out when she finally got him. "Jonathan called me. He's okay as of now."

"Tell me everything he said."

Martha went through it. "He said they went first to the zoo and then into Manhattan on the Upper West Side."

"Did he say where?"

"No. But he said there was a house next door with some yellow flowers and a cat in the window."

"We got a report from a detective who saw Miller at a hamburger joint at Eightieth and Broadway. By the way, we know now it's a guy named Lawrence Miller who was once a professor at a college up in New England."

"I was there for one summer school years ago. He taught English. My God, that's where I remember him from! Then he got in trouble."

"Yeah, there was some question about his molesting a kid. He managed to keep out of jail, but he lost his job and his family. He was hospitalized for a while, but you know how that is. They release them with medicine they're supposed to take. Anyway, he's been a drifter ever since. Tell me, what was he like? What d'you remember about him? I don't know whether this'll help, but anything we know is to the good."

Martha pondered. She was impatient because she was frantic for them to get away and start looking, but as he said, anything might help. "He was attractive, in a strange sort of way. Lots of the girls had crushes on him. He was like— well, one of the girls I knew said he was like a mystic."

"Is that what you thought?"

"Sometimes, I guess. But other times, he seemed . . . unstable. Not quite . . . balanced."

"Anything else?"

"I can't think now."

"Okay. Thanks. Listen, try not to worry. We've narrowed it down. There are police all over the West Side looking. Now I have to go. I'll keep in touch." And he was gone.

Suddenly Martha remembered about the black door and the leopard's-head doorknob. Quickly she dialed Mooney's number again. But it was busy. She kept trying, but when she finally got through he was gone.

"Damn, damn, damn, hell and shit!" she yelled. Then she dialed Patrick's number, but after three rings there was nothing but a click. Frantically she paced back and forth. And once again saw the bottles across the room. She wanted her son more than she had wanted anything in her life, but almost as much she wanted a drink. "I can't drink now," she cried. But it would make her head clearer. She'd stop being so nervous. She could think. . . . She found herself walking over towards them. Then on the slip of paper David Jennings had left on the counter she saw his number.

Lifting the phone she dialed, with no idea what she was going to say. She recognized his voice when he answered. "Bookshop," he said.

"I'm going to look for Jonathan and I want a drink."

"Don't pick it up. Whatever else you do, don't pick it up. It won't make anything better. It'll make it worse."

His voice had a curious soothing effect. "Okay," she said. "Thanks."

"Where are you going to look?"

She told him about the phone call and what Mooney had heard about its being on the Upper West Side.

"I can imagine how you feel, but wouldn't it be better to let the police do the looking? They know more about how to do it."

"But they don't know what Jonathan told me about the black door and the leopard's-head doorknob. I have to go."

"Why don't you call them and tell them?"

Suddenly her being part of the search was overwhelmingly important. "I'm going to go myself and look."

There was the faintest pause. Then, "I'll go with you. Shall I meet you at the subway?"

"I was thinking of taking a cab."

"The subway's faster."

"All right. I'll meet you at the subway."

10

Jonathan, lying flat on the door of the attic, his ear against the crack in the trapdoor, had heard the murmur of voices from the outer room followed by a strange muffled sound. Then there was a noise that could be the bedroom door opening. Lawrence's voice, nearer and clearer, rang out.

"I'm coming after you, Jonathan. I know where you are. You won't be sorry."

The voice came closer rapidly. There were noises immediately below the trapdoor. Then Jonathan felt the door lifting below his cheek.

Panic filled him. Frantically he slid till his chest was over the trapdoor and he tried with all his strength to keep the door down, but it was rising inexorably.

"There you are, Jonathan!" The voice rang with a note that made Jonathan's flesh creep. Then, despite all the

169

weight Jonathan could put on it, the door lifted more and somehow was pushed to one side. Jonathan saw the man's face, the dark eyes bright and wide open.

Jonathan lifted the square trapdoor, then brought it, corner down, on the face that was now above the floor level of the little attic.

Lawrence gave an angry cry and ducked back, one hand over his nose. "You little—" A stream of filth came from his mouth. Jonathan picked up one of the boxes on the attic floor and threw it down. By pure luck it landed on Lawrence's face just as he was taking his hand away. For a moment he seemed to float, then he lost his balance and fell back.

"I'll get you!" he yelled.

Jonathan didn't wait. Slamming the door down, he moved to the trunk and shoved it with all his might over the trapdoor. It was heavy, far heavier than he had imagined, but fear lent him strength.

Hands below were trying to raise the door as Jonathan pushed.

A final shove, and the trunk slid over the trapdoor.

Heaving, his face red, Jonathan watched as the trunk seemed to hiccup from time to time as the man below tried to move it off the door. To add all he could, Jonathan sat on the lid of the trunk. He could feel, shuddering through his thighs, the frantic efforts of the man to raise the trapdoor with the trunk on top.

"Please," he whispered, not really knowing whom he addressed. "Please make it hold." Somehow the picture of Alec Guinness in *Star Wars* crossed his mind. "The Force be with me," he said to himself. "Please, please don't let him push it away."

After a while the prods from below stopped. There was a

short silence. Then Lawrence's voice rang out. "You haven't anywhere to go, Jonathan. I'll have you yet. And it won't be as pleasant as it could have been—at least not for you. You'll pay for this." The word ended almost in a snarl.

With the trunk over the door Jonathan couldn't hear what was going on below as well as he had. He had no idea whether Lawrence had left the bedroom or left the apartment.

Then, suddenly, when Jonathan had convinced himself that Lawrence had left the apartment, his voice came, clear with rage, right below.

"I can do a lot of things to get you out. I can build a fire below here. Nobody will be able to get to you then. Fire goes up. You'll be dead with the smoke before it reaches you, but if you aren't, then you'll burn to death."

There was a silence. Then in a different voice Lawrence said, "All I want is to give you love, to show you how love is made. You'll like it. Not many boys get this opportunity." Another silence. Then, "What do you want, Jonathan, love or fire?"

Jonathan sat there, his legs shaking, as he smelled the first tinge of smoke coming through the cracks around the trapdoor and from under the trunk.

Having given up trying to find by phone a repair service that would send someone to mend his answering tape right away and frantic because until that was done he remained a prisoner in his apartment, Patrick bolted out onto the street and offered a generous bribe to a local repairman if he would just return with him and fix his tape. Almost dragging him back, Patrick said, "As I've explained, it's an emergency. Now, fix this goddam tape so that people can reach me even if I'm not here." He paused. "That doesn't make sense, but you know what I mean."

The man played with the little tapes and the buttons on the machine. "You've done the whole thing wrong, Mr. Tierney. A smart man like you! I've got kids who can do this."

"Being mechanically deft is not my forte, but it is yours. Please do it as quickly as you can."

Martha and David got out of the West Side subway at Eighty-sixth Street.

"I still think we should have gotten out at Seventy-ninth," David said. "It's a lot nearer to the Eighty-first area where the police say Miller was seen."

"I don't know why I keep thinking that it's north of here. I just do. Why don't we split up?"

David hesitated. As he knew all too well, he would, under similar circumstances when he was drinking, use splitting up as an excuse to make for the nearest bar. But Martha's son was at stake. She was almost rattling to pieces, but she swore she'd not had a drink since she heard of Jonathan's disappearance, and she was in bad enough shape for him to believe it.

"Okay," he said. "You go north and I'll go south. But supposing either one of us finds it?"

Martha hesitated. "What I'd rather you do," she burst out, "is to help me go east and west on the streets. I don't feel he's south of here, and if he could see the river I don't think he'd be east of Broadway. But he could be either side of West End. Anyway, as we finish each street we can check with each other on West End."

"All right."

"Remember, a black door, a leopard's head with a ball in

its mouth as a knocker and a yellow flower in the window next door. Also a cat, though the cat's probably moved a thousand times since he saw it."

"And the flower can have been moved, too. Okay, I'll take the streets east of West End, you take the west."

Martha walked rapidly along Eighty-sixth Street on the south side and then broke into a run. It became obvious that the kind of door she was looking for was not among the apartment buildings on Eighty-sixth Street west of West End. Nor were they along the north side. At the end of Eighty-sixth, she rounded the corner at Riverside Drive, ran a block north, then turned into Eighty-seventh Street. As she sped along, she checked the doors on both sides of the street. When she reached West End, she saw David emerging onto the other side of the avenue. He waved and turned north, too. She waved back, ran up West End to Eighty-eighth and turned in there.

On several streets she found there were no black doors and no knockers that could be described as leopards' heads. There were lions' heads, but Martha was fairly sure that Jonathan, cat lover, would not confuse a leopard with a lion. And furthermore, in each case, the doors were red, green and blue, but not black.

She went on, mostly walking as quickly as she could, occasionally running. But her breathing was not up to the task, and sometimes she had to bend double, holding her side, trying to get sufficient air in her lungs. What was it some doctor had said to her? "Aside from anything else, Mrs. Tierney, there's nothing that can break down the body as fast and as completely as liquor, not at the rate you're drinking." At one time, almost sick with her inability to draw her breath, she was afraid that she would vomit right there on the nice-looking sidewalk between West End and Riverside.

Once David had come over to her, running easily. "Are you all right?"

"Yes," she said, her breath heaving. "Have you found anything at all that sounds the way Jonathan described?"

"No. Wouldn't it be a good idea to call in the descriptions to the police?"

"They're always busy and Mooney wasn't there when I tried to call before. If you're tired," she heaved sarcastically, "you don't have to go on."

"I'll go on," David said somewhat grimly, and just managed to keep himself from pointing out that he was in far better shape at this moment than she.

One of the policemen used his walkie-talkie to get in touch with Mooney. "Didn't she give you any idea about what the door looked like?"

"No," Mooney said shortly. "But I'll check with her."

He telephoned and listened as the phone rang and rang. Finally Martha's voice came on tape, asking him to leave a message. Angry because he thought she should have stayed at home in case Jonathan or anyone tried to reach her, he left a message asking her to call him. Then, because he realized this would send her hope soaring, he added that if Jonathan had given any description of the house where he was being held, he wanted to have it.

As soon as Jonathan smelled the smoke, fear gripped him. For a moment he couldn't move. Then, "No!" he cried. "No! No!" Then he yelled, "I'll come down! I'll come down!" He could somehow fight for himself when he got down. It was a better bet than being burned to death.

Lawrence heard him, but the fire, catching on the tinselly clothes in the closet, was suddenly out of control. His exaltation collapsed. Frightened, he retreated into the bedroom and towards the door. As he hurried out of the room he heard Jonathan scream. "Serves him right," he muttered.

His tape now properly installed, Patrick called Mooney, only to discover he was out. Then he called Martha and got her tape. Not finding Martha sent up his anxiety. Would she leave the house unless she'd heard from Jonathan? His heart started beating. He called Mooney's office back and asked to speak to somebody there.

After he had announced who he was, he asked if there was any further news about his son.

"Sergeant Mooney is up on the Upper West Side now trying to find where the house is."

"What do you mean?" Patrick yelled. "Have you heard from Jonathan?"

"Mrs. Tierney heard. The boy called her. He said he was being held somewhere on the Upper West Side."

"Why the hell didn't she call me?"

"Maybe she did," the officer said. He'd been there when Mooney tried to leave a message. "But when the sergeant tried to leave a message, your answering machine didn't work. Maybe it didn't work if Mrs. Tierney tried."

"Probably," Patrick said bitterly. "Do you know where on the Upper West Side?"

"I'm sorry. That's all I know."

Patrick almost threw down the phone and bolted from the apartment.

Dripping and panting, Martha came to a brief rest on the corner of Ninety-ninth Street and West End Avenue. Unless she'd missed the black door and the leopard's head, there was nothing so far that remotely resembled Jonathan's description, and this was considerably north of Eightieth Street. Had she been wrong to insist that David patrol east of her, rather than south?

She stood, one hand gripping the top of one of the new pay telephones. After a minute she looked down at it. Since for the moment she couldn't move, she might as well check her own phone to see if Mooney had left any more information.

What she got was his angry query about any further descriptions. "But I told him," she said aloud, as David came running up.

"Who're you calling?" he asked.

She answered as she dialed Mooney's number.

"Just a minute," the man who answered the phone said when she identified herself. In a second Mooney picked up the phone. "Mrs. Tierney?"

"Yes. I didn't tell you about the black door and the knocker like a leopard's head, did I?"

"No. Why didn't you tell me this before?" Then, "Never mind. I guess you thought you did. You're at home now, aren't you?"

"No, I'm at the corner of Ninety-ninth and West End."

"I want you to go back home. I'm not sure what we're going to find and I need to have you to refer to."

"I'll call you at the street corners from time to time. He's my son and I'm going to look for him." Then, because she was tired and sweating and so nervous she felt sick, she started to cry.

David looked at the dripping face. It was a mild fall day, but it was far from hot. "Are you okay?" he asked.

"I'm fine," she all but shrieked. "Now, let's keep going!"

·   ·   ·

Ben came to with the smell of smoke in his nostrils. There was a terrible pain in his head and he felt nauseated. At that moment Lawrence flung open the bedroom door.

"What happened? Where's the fire?"

"It started in the closet," Lawrence said briefly.

Ben's head cleared a little. "You started it."

Lawrence shrugged. "He wouldn't come down." His eyes narrowed. "You lied to me. You told me the attic was sealed. It wasn't. That blasted kid was up there. Well, I showed him. Let him fry!"

Ben rose to his feet and gave a shout of pain. "You're destroying all the tapes. You crazy jerk! What do you think I kept up there? All the tapes!"

He pushed his way into the bedroom, then started back. A stream of obscenities poured out of his mouth. But loud as they were, they didn't cover the sound of the fire engines clanking and shrieking towards them.

Jonathan, half insane with terror, stood still, then tried to remember everything he'd heard in his school fire drills. Get some water to soak towels. There was no water and no towels. He started whimpering with fright, like a small animal, and then he began coughing. Smoke poured from around the edges of the big trunk. Jonathan put his hand on it, with half an idea of pushing it out of the way to enable him to get below, but he snatched away his hand with a cry. The metal trunk was red-hot. Turning desperately, he saw the window, or rather the half of the window on this side of the wooden divide.

If he could only wriggle past the end of the divide! But he had tried that and failed. Then he recalled more advice from the school drills: Get down near the floor. There's less smoke there. He crouched down, but because the smoke was coming up from the trapdoor, it wasn't much help. He took a deep breath and felt the burning down into his chest.

"Please," he whispered. "Please help me!"

He then went towards the window and stood up, pressing his body against the end of the divider. The space was only a few inches wide. He pushed and squeezed and held in his stomach and chest. He couldn't do it. He almost gave up hope then.

He heard the fire engines racing into the street. Turning aside, he kicked his foot through the window, kicking it again and again as he screamed, "Help! Help! Help! Help!"

His leg was bleeding from a shard of glass. But by kicking a hole in the window, he could shove past the divider. He gave a final push and found himself in the front half of the attic. A window there gave out onto the front.

Bleeding, coughing, he ran towards it and, taking up a box, threw it through the small window. The firemen, summoned by anxious neighbors, saw him then, and the huge ladder started pushing up and turning.

It was Mooney who saw the two men erupt through the front door and onto the street and he stopped them cold with his drawn pistol. "Professor Miller," he said, "and our old friend Ben Nicolaides." As the two men were cuffed, he said, "If the firemen don't get to that kid in time, you're going up for murder."

"I tried to get to him," Lawrence screamed.

"Like hell he did. He lit the fire!" Ben, up for God knew how many counts of pornography, wasn't about to take any rap for child murder.

"Okay, son," the fireman
said. "Now, take hold of my shoulders with both hands. I'm
going to put my arm around you and then slowly turn you
around so you come down the ladder. I'll be holding on to
you, so don't worry!"

"Jonathan!" He heard his
mother calling as she ran along the street. "Jonny darling!
Be careful, be careful!" And then, because it sounded so
ridiculous in view of what he had gone through, she started
to laugh, and then began crying.

Eventually Jonathan was down. She saw him reach the
ground and stand a little unsteady for a moment. He began
to run towards her. As she went to meet him he seemed
suddenly to have a light shimmering around his head. Then
she was thrashing around on the ground, her arms and legs
pumping spasmodically.

The gathered crowd murmured.

"Get back," Mooney roared, coming forward.

Jonathan stared. It was the final horror. He started to cry.
As he turned away, his father ran to him and held him close,
his face turned away from whatever hideous thing was happening to his mother.

David and one of the firemen were holding her so that she
wouldn't hurt herself or swallow her tongue. As Mooney
came up, David said, "It's a convulsion."

"Is she epileptic?" Mooney asked.

"No, at least I don't think so. This is very common in
withdrawal. She hasn't had anything to ease it for the last
two days, and she hasn't had anything to drink."

179

Martha came to to see Mooney and David bending over her and, a few feet away, Jonathan with his face against his father. Patrick, his arms around his son, was also watching her. Beyond him were more police, firemen, and a crowd. She wondered what they were doing there. Then she realized she was lying down, and tried, feebly, to sit up.

"Don't push yourself," David said.

"What happened?" she murmured.

"You had a convulsion," David answered.

"A convulsion?" A memory floated into her mind. "Katie said I could have one if I didn't have a drink." She paused, and then, as more memory flooded in, "Jonathan!"

"He's all right," David said quickly.

"Jonathan!" she cried again and this time managed to sit up. Memory was beginning to come back. "Oh God!"

Jonathan turned his face towards her. All he could think about was the way her body had been thrashing. He clung to his father.

Martha struggled to her feet. "Jonny darling." She tried to move, but a fatigue beyond anything she'd ever known seemed to hold her feet. "Did he hurt you, darling?"

Jonathan shook his head.

An officer walked up and said to Patrick, "There's an ambulance here. We sent for it when—when Mrs. Tierney had the convulsion. Maybe she and Jonathan could go together in it, because we think he ought to be looked at, too, to make sure he's okay."

"Can I go with them?"

"Sure."

The emergency section of the hospital was controlled pandemonium. Patrick and David sat in the waiting area. They had been there for what seemed like an eternity. No one had invited David along, but he had come anyway, and at one point, after murmuring something about talking to the doctors, had got up and pursued a couple of them down the hall. When he returned, Patrick, not too pleased, said pointedly, "I don't think I know you. And what's your interest in all this?"

David held out his hand. "David Jennings. I'm an alcoholic—a recovering alcoholic—myself. Sarah Jennings, the head of St. Andrew's, is my sister. Before I drank myself out of the job, I used to teach at the school and met Martha there. After that I picked up a drink again and finally landed in a rehab. Now I work in a bookstore in the Heights and go to a lot of AA. Sarah called me the other day to see if I could interest Martha in the meetings."

"And you couldn't, I'd bet my bottom dollar," Patrick said grimly.

"She said that as long as Jonathan was missing she wasn't going anywhere. And I can't fault her for that."

"I guess not." Patrick stared down at his hands for a moment. "According to Sergeant Mooney, it was my hiring my agent's mailboy and general gofer to take pictures of Jonathan that started the whole thing."

"How so?"

"He showed them to his girlfriend, who had a little business going on the side with a kiddie-porn merchant—he was the other guy the cops were leading away in handcuffs tonight. He sold Miller the pictures and told him where to find Jonathan, information Barry's girlfriend had gotten out of Barry and handed to her partner." He glanced up. "Speak of the devil!"

"Who? The porn merchant?" David said and turned.

"How are the patients?" Sergeant Mooney said as he strolled up.

"Well, here's one of them," Patrick said as Jonathan came down the hall with one of the doctors. He got up and walked towards them. "How are you, son?" His voice almost cracked.

"I'm okay. He—the man who took me to the apartment didn't do anything. I got away from him," he added proudly.

"You're a bright, resourceful boy," the doctor said.

Patrick looked at him. "Is that right? Everything's okay?"

"Absolutely—physically, that is. We may recommend a counselor, but I'll talk to you about that later." He nodded at them and left.

Jonathan took his father's hand. "How's Mother?"

"I'm pretty sure she's going to be all right," Patrick said.

"You know your mother was pretty near to finding you when the fire started and the fire engines came," Mooney said. "And she wasn't feeling too hot, either. That took a lot of courage."

"Yeah," Jonathan said. Then he blurted out, "She drinks a lot." The bald statement lay there. "Maybe if she didn't drink so much I wouldn't have got stolen."

"Don't pin that on her," Mooney said. "She does her best. And she wasn't responsible for Lawrence Miller, the guy who abducted you, hanging around where you lived."

Patrick sighed. "I'm afraid that's my doing, not your mother's."

"No," Jonathan said.

"Yes." Patrick took a breath, and as simply as he could described the link between the pictures he had had Barry take and the man who had kidnapped him. "So you see, you can't blame that on your mother. Okay?"

Jonathan nodded. "Okay." After a pause he added, "I'm glad."

Martha came down the hall. She looked white with fatigue.

"What is it Jonathan can't blame on me?" she said. "It must be one of the few things he can't." There was bitterness in her voice.

Patrick turned to her. "I was telling Jonathan about Barry's taking the photographs and showing them to Cheryl and her selling them to Ben. By the way," he said, turning back to Mooney, "whatever happened to Cheryl?"

"She came to a bad end, I'm afraid. A former, er, business associate did away with her, and then went to her apartment to steal her photographs and negatives. It seems that Ben himself suggested he get the pictures back after Jonathan's kidnapping hit the news. But Leo was a clumsy burglar. It wasn't really his line of work. Neighbors heard him and called the police. The boys in blue turned up and brought him in. That's when the pieces started coming together."

David was looking at Martha. "What's going to happen now?"

She gave a tired smile. "I guess you and Patrick and Jonathan will get what you want. The doctors in here painted some unpretty pictures. They want me to get properly detoxed here and then go to a rehab."

David looked at her. "Will you?"

"Yes. I can't—I can't kid myself any longer." She took a breath. "I'm going to need some things," she started, and then hesitated.

"We'll get them for you," Patrick said, looking down at Jonathan. "And we'll keep an eye on the apartment, won't we?"

"Sure." He was holding hard to his father's hand.

Martha looked at her former husband. "You'll be staying

home—not traveling, I mean—while I'm in the rehab, won't you?"

"I will. I promise." He glanced down at his son. "We have some catching up to do."

"Afterwards," Martha started, then lost heart. After tonight, did she have any rights left?

"We'll worry about afterwards afterwards," Patrick said.

"Will you stay in your apartment or in ours?" Martha asked.

"I think it'd be a good idea for Jonathan to be in a different environment for a while," Patrick said.

"What about school?" Jonathan asked.

"There're such things as subways, even cars," Patrick said. "We'll work it out."

"You look dead on your feet," David said. "Go back and get some sleep. I'll come by and see you tomorrow."

"Thank you, David." Later, when she felt less awful, she'd be properly grateful. She knew he had eased the way for the hospital to get her into a rehab two thirds across the country—the same one he had been in. And he and they and the doctors had said three months. . . . But when they had talked to her about this a few minutes ago he had also said, "Don't think about that now. Take it a day at a time." Then he had smiled. "You can take almost anything for a day."

"Anything" would include not seeing Jonathan for as long as she was away. After the past months, would he care?

"Jonathan," she said, and walked hesitantly over to him. She was desperately afraid he would back away.

But he didn't.

As Martha approached, Patrick moved from Jonathan's side, leaving him free. Still Jonathan didn't move. Martha came up and put her hands on his shoulders. "I'm sorry, darling," she said. "I'll get better. You'll see. I promise."

Despite her pallor and the fatigue that made wrinkles under her eyes, she looked more like the mother he remembered with love and pain.

He put his hands on her arms. "Mom, get well soon."

"I will, darling. I will." She couldn't stop the tears, but she wiped them away. Leaning forward, she hugged him and felt his boy's lips kiss her cheek. "I'll write," she said.

She turned and looked at Patrick for a minute.

"We'll be fine," he said. "And don't worry about anything —if you can manage it."

"If I can manage it, I won't," she replied gravely.

She turned to David. "Thanks. I—I haven't always been very grateful. But I am now. Or at least—I will be."

He smiled. "I'll be in touch."

Then Martha turned and walked away from them, down the hall to begin her own long journey back.